WAKING UP IN A DIFFERENT TIME

Lance J. Breckinridge

Copyright © 2013 by Lance J Breckinridge
First Edition – April 2013

ISBN
978-1-4602-1547-0 (Hardcover)
978-1-4602-1548-7 (Paperback)
978-1-4602-1549-4 (eBook)

All rights reserved.

No part of this publication may be reproduced in any form, or by any means, electronic or mechanical, including photocopying, recording, or any information browsing, storage, or retrieval system, without permission in writing from the publisher.

Produced by:

FriesenPress
Suite 300 – 852 Fort Street
Victoria, BC, Canada V8W 1H8

www.friesenpress.com

Distributed to the trade by The Ingram Book Company

TABLE OF CONTENTS

I	Dedication	
II	Prologue	
1	Chapter One	The Awakening 10/28/2011
12	Chapter Two	The Re-Awakening 10/29/2011
22	Chapter Three	The Meeting
29	Chapter Four	A leap in time 10/30/2011
32	Chapter Five	WHATS NEXT?
36	Chapter Six	Getting together yet again
45	Chapter Seven	Another Meeting
49	Chapter Eight	Second Thoughts
54	Chapter Nine	A Visit with George
58	Chapter Ten	A Car for Barb
65	Chapter Eleven	In the meantime!
70	Chapter Twelve	The Great Jelly Bean Myth
74	Chapter Thirteen	The next Morning 11/2/2011 Real Time
83	Chapter Fourteen	A Meeting with Dave 11/3/2011 Real Time
91	Chapter Fifteen	A desperate Call to Dave 11/4/2011 Real Time
102	Chapter Sixteen	A Break in The morning routine
109	Chapter Seventeen	A Mysterious Phone Call
117	Chapter Eighteen	Lunch at La Flambé
124	Chapter Nineteen	Confronting the Group
132	Chapter Twenty	Upset with Barbara
135	Chapter Twenty One	Discontentment in the Group
143	Chapter Twenty Two	Is it Time to see a Doctor?
147	Chapter Twenty Three	Another talk with Lenny

152	Chapter Twenty Four . . .	Considering another group meeting
163	Chapter Twenty Five . . .	Planning the final meeting
179	Chapter Twenty Six	Finally the meeting
195	Chapter twenty seven . . .	Examining the clues
210	Chapter Twenty Eight . .	Suspects
222	Chapter Twenty Nine . .	A Hunt for the Stranger
236	Chapter Thirty	The big surprise
254	Chapter Thirty One	The road to Solution
273	Chapter Thirty Two	A meeting with Jack
288	Chapter Thirty Three . . .	An elaborate plan
316	Chapter Thirty Four . . .	The promotion
330	Chapter Thirty Five	The Celebration
354	Chapter Thirty Six	Preparing the way
382	Chapter Thirty Seven . . .	Buying a House, Planning the Move & Moving
480	Chapter Thirty Eight . . .	Back to work
486	EPILOGUE	

DEDICATION

Firstly I dedicate this book to my wife, who from the very beginning put up with my many idiosyncrasies and extravagant ways, she deserves recognition!

This work is further dedicated to my lifelong friends and family members, the many still here and those gone, along with the friends I have met along the way. Many of you have found your way into this book and snuck away again while others lingered for the whole story, you'll know who you are. Thanks for the help!

This book is also dedicated to all of you mystery readers out there, you know who you are, and it's for your enjoyment also I told this story.

My enjoyment is three fold, firstly: I enjoyed writing it, secondly: I'll enjoy you buying it and thirdly: I'll appreciate your enjoyment and wanting to buy the next book in the series, there will be another.

I further dedicate this book to all those who encouraged me to continue to write after my first book was completed, thanks for your confidence.

PROLOGUE

This book is about a young couple, Bill and Barbara Kelly and a group of their closest friends who unbeknownst to any of them are cast into an adventure that none sought and all wanted out of; at least that's how it would appear!

This adventure involves the group experiencing time travel, but not in the conventional sense or way that we have come to think of time travel, this experience was quite different.

At first they were all anxious to solve this mystery, but as time went on many lost interest thinking the problems would solve themselves that is all but a few, and those few were intent on getting to the source of the problem, solving the mystery, and getting back to a normal life.

As the mystery evolved tensions grew between friends and even between husband and wife, mistrust develops between the principles and outsiders are asked to help and soon relied upon to find the answers, but the answers were slow to come and eventually came quite by accident in the form of a discovery leading to the solution to the mystery and the surprise it had cancelled for so long.

Now the mystery solved and the surprise revealed the story continues with the aftermath of what had transpired a story in itself.

CHAPTER ONE
THE AWAKENING 10 28 2011

October 28, 2011 Bill Kelly a young newly married engineer was just starting to stir in bed while his attractive young wife Barbara was already up and about getting ready for work, it took her longer then it took Bill, who was not really ready to get out of bed just yet, remember their newly married, about fifteen months now, and he's a sexually aggressive young guy. Some men are night time lovers, some morning guys, Bill, was an anytime anyplace guy, a character trait to which his wife Barb, had no objection.

Bill yelled, "Barb what are you doing, come here, I have something for you!" to which she replied;

"No! You come here, I have something for you."

So Bill reluctantly rolled out of bed in their 24th floor Lake Shore Drive Condominium and headed for the bathroom where he found his voluptuous naked young wife holding a tube of toothpaste, pointing it menacingly at him with one hand, while resting the other hand on her hip and asking;

"What have you done with this toothpaste?"

"What toothpaste?" he asked, she looked curiously at the tube she held in her hand and said.

"This toothpaste!" moving it closer to his nose;

"I'm sorry hon, I don't understand."

"I bought this tube two days ago and it's almost gone!"

Well, Bill dismissed his wife's concern for the tube of toothpaste, blaming it on the previous late night out with friends and probably too much to drink, not to mention that Barb, appearing in her current state of undress, excited him to the point of great distraction, so in order to resist temptation he headed to the kitchen for his morning coffee.

The mornings activities continued normally, until Bill was in the bedroom getting dressed, when he noticed the book on his nightstand that he had been reading the night before while waiting for Barb to come to bed, he had just started the book, but the book marker was three quarters the way thru the book and realizing that wasn't right he called his wife.

"Barb"

"Yes" she replied.

"Come here a minute." Barb entered the room and said.

"What's up?"

Bill, picking the book up off of the nightstand showing it to Barb and asking;

"Did you move this book marker?"

"No, why would I do that?"

"I don't know why, maybe to get even for my lack of concern over the toothpaste!" He replied.

"You know, maybe the same person moved the bookmarker that used all the toothpaste!" she said with a gotcha smile on her face as she left the room. So Bill scratched his head finally concluding that they both probably had too much to drink the previous night and that was probably not a good idea during the week, that's what weekends are for he thought. Bill finished dressing and quickly finished his coffee before leaving for work.

On his way out the door, Bill said goodbye to Barb, with a kiss, a huge hug and an "I love you"

"Me too you" she would follow shortly on her way to the Dental office where she was employed as a dental hygienists, while Bill was employed as an Engineer in the suburbs for a large manufacturing company, both had good jobs and the Lake Shore Drive condo was their reward though Bill's daily commute to the suburbs was a bit of an inconvenience, but tolerable, as he was always going in the opposite direction of the rush hour traffic, an advantage he had living in the city and working in the suburbs the opposite was a commuting nightmare.

Once Bill was settled in at work that morning he decided to call his best friend George, who they had been out with the night before. They were celebrating George's birthday along with Geo's Fiancée Nancy, they were soon to be married and Bill would be George's best man. George had his own business and was a very successful salesman, selling commercial copying machines to both business and personal clients.

Bill dialed George's cell and while waiting for Geo to answer Bill noticed the papers on his desk were not arranged as he had left them the day before. "Hello" answered Geo.

"Oh hi" said Bill. "Just thought I'd call to see if you've recovered from last night yet?"

"Yeah I bounce back pretty fast buddy, I'm not an old married man quite yet" "Ya thanks, thought Bill.

"Listen guy did you wake up to anything unusual or unexplained this morning?"

"What?" said Geo?

"You know anything out of place or not as it should be?"

"No" replied Geo.

"Well I guess it's not important" Bill said, while explaining his and Barb's experiences this morning at home and now again in his office.

"Don't worry pal, probably just the morning after DTs" George replied. I don't get DTs thought Bill;

"Yeah you're probably right, but I got to go well talk later George."

"Ok" said Geo hanging up while Bill went back to wondering about the papers on his desk.

It was a confusing morning, hopefully the rest of the day would return to normal and Bill could continue the project he was working on, a cost savings project that the engineering department was required to submit on an annual bases.

Barb on the other hand didn't run into any other abnormalities on her way to or at work, so she pretty much dismissed the mornings surprises at home as just one of those unexplained circumstances not to be concerned about, besides she was looking forward to getting home and making Bill's favorite dinner tonight, spaghetti with meat sauce, meatballs, sausage and garlic bread and always with a nice red wine.

Bill's day was coming to an end and a couple of his co-workers had asked him out after work for a drink. He thought it sounded like a good idea but wanted to check with Barb first, he was considerate that way, so he dialed Barb's office and Lisa the office manager answered

"Triple "A" dental Lisa speaking may I help you?"

"Hi Lisa its Bill is Barb busy?"

"Oh hi Bill, Ya, I'm afraid she's with a patient can I have her call you or take a message?"

"Ya Lisa tell her to call me on my cell."

"Ok Bill I'll do it."

"Thanks Lisa, buy" Bill thought he'd go out with the guys for a quick drink and then home.

As soon as Barb heard Bill called she called him back, worrying about her surprise dinner, she dialed his number.

"Hi hon" (caller ID you know)

"Hi you called?" she said.

"Ya, the guys asked me out for a drink after work and I thought I'd check if you had any plans?"

"As a matter of fact I thought we'd have dinner and relax this evening, besides we were out partying last night."

"You know you're right I don't want to go down that road again, not so soon anyway, besides relaxing with you sounds much better, I guess I'll pass and see you at home."

"Ok buy" said Barb as they both hung up and both returned to work.

Bill got back to the guys, saying he'd have to pass on the after work activities til another time but thanked them for the invite.

Bill's boss, Jack Trax, stopped by Bill's desk to check on his progress with the current cost savings project as Jack had to update the committee at a meeting in the AM. He seemed impressed with Bill's progress, thanking him for the good work.

A SURPRISE DINNER

Real spaghetti sauce takes forever to prepare but luckily for Barb, she had some of her pre-made sauce in the freezer that she made awhile back or she would never have been able to plan a meal like this on such short notice, Bill would be grateful, by the time he gets home the wine will be chilled, the sauce will be cooking, the meatballs and sausage in the frying pan and the cooking odors filling the apartment so Bill would catch a hint of what was cooking as he entered the door of their condo.

As Bill left work getting on the expressway and heading toward the Chicago skyline and home he couldn't help but revisiting the days unusual occurrences, trying to rationalize what was going on, Bill was an engineer and equipped with an inquisitive mind and rarely just let go of a problem without a plausible explanation.

Arriving home and pulling into the underground parking area he had yet one last surprise for a day full of surprises, the parking spaces were assigned and his spot was taken by a strange SUV. Bill also noticed that the numbering system identifying the individual parking spaces had also been changed. He recalled when leaving this morning everything was as it had always been and neither he nor his wife was ever notified of any planned changes. Bill had to park outside in the lot as there were no guest spots in the underground parking, though there were some unassigned spaces.

Well on his way upstairs to his apartment he got upset all over again; anxious to call the condo association to complain and find out what was going on.

Approaching his door he picked up a faint, yet familiar aroma, of something he truly loved, could it be he thought, opening the door, what he suspected was indeed confirmed, his favorite dinner was filling the air with a pleasant aroma stimulating his appetite and almost making him forget about his parking problems.

Closing the front door behind him he said, "Hon I'm home, what's that I smell?" Barb retorted;

"Hi dear, you sound like you already know what it is."

"Ya, well it is a bright spot in an otherwise dismal day" he said.

"You won't believe what happened in the parking garage!"

"You didn't have an accident did you?"

"No worse, when I left this morning I pulled out of my normal parking place where I parked last night and when I came home tonight my space was occupied by another car so I had to park outside!"

"Are you sure you're space was taken, did you check the number?"

"That's another thing, the numbering system was changed, but it was my normal spot!"

Bill went to the phone to call the association to complain and find out whose car was in his spot, the call was transferred to an answering service where Bill left a message.

Barb was putting the garlic bread in the preheated oven while waiting for the water to boil for the pasta and telling Bill that dinner would be ready in about fifteen minutes. Bill sat in the living room pondering the day's events, anxiously awaiting a return phone call from the condo association so he could vent his dissatisfaction with the garage situation and try to understand what is going on.

Well while waiting on the phone call and the dinner, Bill turned on the TV to catch up on the day's news and weather.

The dinner was rapidly coming together as Barb went to the refrigerator to get the wine and calling to Bill, "Bill would you open the wine hon?"

"Ya sure" answered Bill as he got up from his favorite chair and headed for the kitchen, taking the wine bottle from Barb with a forced smile, Barb smiled back saying, "Dinner will be on the table in two minutes so have a seat." Bill opened the wine and poured two glasses and sat down as Barb took the bread from the oven and started to cut it "looks great" said Bill, as Barb finished putting everything on the table and sat down to eat.

Barb also had two small dinner salads on the table though Bill was not much of a salad eater; Bill raised his glass to barb saying;

"To my delicious wife and what I'm sure will prove to be a delicious dinner, despite an unconventional day." Barb smiled, raised her glass acknowledging Bill's toast, they both sipped the wine and continued with dinner as the phone rang, the timing simply in keeping with the rest of the day. Bill reluctantly answered the phone as his dinner cooled, "hello" said Bill.

"Mr. Kelly?"

"Yes"

"This is Gloria from the condo association I understand you called, how can I help you?"

"Oh yes, listen Gloria can I call you back we just sat down to dinner and this may take a little time."

"Oh sure I'll talk to you later than."

"Thanks and bye for now Gloria."

"Bye" both hung up and Bill sat down to continue his dinner, hopefully, without further interruptions and that's the way it turned out.

Bill was looking forward to a relaxing evening with Barb and started to help her clean up in the kitchen, but she said;

"Make your call I'll take care of this."

"Are you sure?" asked Bill.

"Ya go ahead dear" she said, Bill, taking his leave headed for the living room and the phone.

Bill dialed the association's number "hello" a sexy voice answered.

"Yes, I'd like to speak to Gloria please."

"This is Gloria, may I help you?"

"Yes this is Bill Kelly hi Gloria, I'm finished with dinner this time so no more interruptions I promise, the reason I'm calling is to report a vehicle in my space in the parking garage."

"Oh, did you get a license plate number on the car?"

"I did it's 'PP1010' it's a SUV."

"Ok well let's see, oh my, Mr. Kelly are you sure that veh. Was in your spot?"

"Yes why? And please call me Bill."

"Ok Bill, well it seems that car belongs to a new resident who should be in the parking garage in spot 22."

"Well he was parked in 22 but that's my spot though you re-numbered the entire garage the spots didn't psychically move, did they?"

"That's true Bill I don't understand the confusion I'm going over to the garage and look for myself and I'll get back to you, will that be alright?"

"Of course" they both hung up and Bill settled down while waiting for Barb.

The weather was just coming on and though the Chicago area was well into the fall the forecast was for mid to high 60's tomorrow and sunny and the lower 40's overnight tonight and tomorrow.

Barb finally came into the room indicating she was done for the evening and ready to relax, at least for the moment asking if it was a good night for TV or not, thinking she might read for a while. Bill thought it was a good night for him, but Barb's favorite programs weren't on tonight. Barb was already curled up with her book and looked very happy, as was Bill after that spectacular meal she had prepared for him; he ate so much that desert was out of the question at least for the moment.

A bit latter the phone rang once again, this time Barb answered it and that same sexy voice asked for Bill once again and Barb said with a smirk on her face, "It's Gloria she asked for Bill."

"Hi" said Bill.

"Hi Bill, it's Gloria, you were right the new resident was given the wrong parking assignment, they should be in 26, he's moving right now so you can go back to your own spot number 22, ok?"

"Ya, I appreciate your help, but it's late I'll leave the car out tonight and start over tomorrow, but thanks again."

"Ok, glad I could help, if I can be of further assistance please don't hesitate to call."

"Ok, thanks again and I will, goodbye Gloria."

"Bye" said Gloria.

"Well on a first name basis with the help, that was fast!" said Barb sarcastically, which was totally unlike her Bill thought, but decided not to comment discouraging any further confrontation, as Barb also had a bad day. Barb wasn't quite ready to let it go just yet though!

"You have never met that woman have you?"

"No" said Bill.

"Why?"

"Well I have and she's gorgeous!"

"Should I be jealous" asked Bill.

"Well if I had those tendencies, you'd have good reason to be!" she said, smiling, as was Bill, that seemed to cool the moment and bed time was starting to look very good.

"I'm going to jump in the shower, want to join me?" asked Bill, with little thought Barb said;

"Ya sure that sounds good I'll be right there." putting her book down; knowing she wouldn't get much reading done tonight anyway.

By the time Barb got to the shower Bill was already in there waiting and looking lustful as ever, Barb recognized the look and as she got in Bill said;

"You wash me and I'll wash you and whatever happens we can blame on (he was going to say Gloria, but quickly had second thoughts saying instead) your fabulous dinner." she smiled and started to wash his back, at least that's where she started, Bill had ideas of his own and whatever started in the shower was sure to continue in the bedroom. Well Barb handed Bill the wash cloth and now it was his turn to wander over her entire body while both of their minds harbored thoughts of what was sure to follow. After the foreplay in the shower, they quickly headed for the bedroom to finish, all too rapidly I might add, what had started in the shower, but they both had been looking forward to all day, sexual satisfaction!

Once again, after their bout with sex, they both picked up their books and read a short time before going to sleep for the night which they did after only reading a short time.

CHAPTER TWO
THE RE-AWAKENING 10 29 2011

The next morning as Barbara started to stir, yawning and trying not to wake Bill just yet, but slowly getting out of bed and going to the window to open the blinds, suddenly letting out an involuntary scream, startling Bill who flew out of bed yelling, "what the hell!"

Barb yelled! "There's a foot of snow on the ground and it's still coming down!"

"What let me see!" said Bill as he joined her at the window.

"My God it's supposed to be almost 70 degrees out today, what's going on, oh hell my cars in the lot and now it's covered with snow, I just don't understand this!" Bill thought for a minute and said quickly;

"Quick check the toothpaste"

"What?"

"Don't ask just do it!"

"Ok, ok" said barb frustrated as hell as she went to the bathroom to check.

"Ha, hon you know that full tube of paste we couldn't find yesterday, well it showed up today, I'm scared, I don't understand what's going on!"

"**What** how can that be? Are you sure you didn't find it yesterday and put it on the shelf?"

"Of course I'm sure" Barb replied.

Bill gave Barb a long lingering look, as if to say, sure I bet you did but just forgot, though Bill was not sure that was the case now, given the snow and all.

Finally Bill asked, "Do we even have any winter cloths out and ready to wear?" Bill quickly checked his nightstand and noticed his book was gone, but Barb's was still on her nightstand. Bill called to Barb.

"My books gone did you take it?"

"Heavens no, not again." as she entered the room looking at her nightstand noticing her book was still there, but wait, it wasn't the same book, she quickly ran to the nightstand grabbing the book up and yelling once again!

"It's not my book, Bill it's not my book, oh my God it's not my book!"

"Calm down" Bill said while he held her tightly, as she sobbed uncontrollably, this was ridicules Bill thought, what was going on the last couple of days. Bill looked at his watch indicating the date was the 17th but that couldn't be right,

"Hon turn on the TV and check the date today." he thought if he got her involved she would calm down a bit.

"Ok" she said going to the living room to turn on the TV and check the date, well that didn't calm her down at all when she found out the date it was December 17, 2011, they had slept for about two months, she screamed again, this time at the top of her lungs.

"**Bill, come quick, it's almost Christmas and I haven't even started my shopping!**" Bill came to check it out for himself and sure enough it was Dec. 17 2011, how could this be he thought

"Bill what's happened, What's going on, Is this only happening to us, What is it that's happening, I don't understand?"

"Hon try to relax, there must be an explanation, and we'll figure it out!"

"Ya know what, call George and Nancy and see if their having a similar experience."

"No you call I'm afraid." Barb said.

"Ok" Bill said as he dialed Geo's number.

"Hello, who's this?"

"Well I can tell by the sound of your voice you're going thru what we are experiencing."

"Ya its nuts around here were sleeping for months at a time and who knows what else, same there?" George asked.

"Ya, Barb's in a real tizzy and I can't seem to calm her down."

"Same for Nancy" said George, not to calm himself.

"Ya got any ideas" asked Geo.

"Not really, it's almost like, well I'm just goanna say it, like were traveling through time"

"What, have you gone over the edge my friend?" asked George excitedly.

Bill knew it was far reaching, but it was one explanation, mass hysteria possibly another reason, but no other possibility comes to mind as Bill takes the time to remind Barb that they were not alone in this predicament, unfortunately that didn't help Barb's current state of mind.

They both continued to get ready for work as they felt they needed to get out to see how far reaching this phenomena was and they didn't pay attention to any other changes in the apartment as they were overwhelmed at this point and were trying to recuperate from the mornings shock and get ready for the rest of what the day may bring.

Bill was concerned about digging his car out from under all the snow or maybe when he walked outside there would be no snow, it would have been an illusion as seen from their condo window, at this point anything is possible. Barb on the other hand was not as open to other possibilities she believed what she saw, she just didn't understand it, not at all.

"Do you want me to take you to work today hon?" Bill asked.

"I don't know, I don't think so I'll be alright." said Barb.

"Ok well I am going to get going, I have to dig the car out." giving Barb a kiss and a hug and assuring her that everything would be ok, though Barb appeared less than convinced, she tried a smile and said;

"Goodbye"

As Bill exited the building he confirmed that the snow was real and still there, but wait, his car wasn't it was gone, it had been stolen, he should have put it away last night when he had the opportunity, dam he thought as he headed back inside to call the police.

On his way back inside though and on a hunch, he went to the parking garage and sure enough there it was in its own spot and nice and dry, but how did it get there he thought, well no matter, just another piece of the puzzle to figure out, he got in the car and was off in a minute not having to clean any snow, in spite of everything else, that brought a smile to his face.

Barbs commute to work was uneventful and she was the first to arrive today, she checked the flip calendar on the reception desk which was set to today's date December 17, 2011 she turned on the computers to check her schedule for today, but she was anxious to talk to the other's in the office to see their reactions to this morning's events.

Arriving in the parking lot at work brought no additional revelations to Bill and everything appeared normal as Bill walked into the building, but when arriving in his office the first thing he noticed was that the cost savings file folder on his desk was gone. This surprised Bill who knew it was an important project and was not finished yet.

Bill got his morning coffee and noticed Jack, his boss, sitting around in his office and decided it may be a good time to ask Jack, ever so cautiously, about the cost savings project. Bill walked into Jack's office "Good morning Jack, I just had a quick question." Jack looking a bit preoccupied turned to Bill and said.

"Morning Bill what's on your mind?"

"Well I was just curious about the cost savings project?" kind of an open ended question.

"Why we closed that project a month ago Bill." Jack said curiously. Well that settled that and now Bill new why the file was gone.

"No I know I was just wondering how it turned out?"

"Oh, well fine as a matter of fact the savings is projected by financial to be grater the our projections"

"Great!" said Bill as he left Jack's office, realizing that apparently not everyone had been affected by the current turn of events, but what does that mean and who's affected and why is it selective. There are many questions to answer thought Bill, who's affected and what they have in common is probably a good place to start. Bill needed to call George again as he and Nancy were affected the same as Bill and Barb.

Bill dialed George's phone and waited for him to answer but he didn't, Bill hit the redial and once again no answer so Bill hung up deciding to try again later in the meantime he started going thru his desk trying to figure out what he was working on, he had no clue whatsoever, but he knew he hadn't been sitting there doing nothing for any length of time when he saw a note on his computer referencing a project 211 so he pulled up the file in the computer and noted it was a new furnace project and he was the project engineer so he quickly started to catch up via the computer files.

Later that afternoon he tried Geo once again and this time Geo answered "Hello"

"Hi Geo it's me, thought I'd give you a call to see if anything new has developed since this morning?"

"New? No we can't handle much more, Nancy is a wreck!"

"Ya, I know what you mean, Barb's the same way, I thought I was going to have to take her to the doctor this morning, which reminds me, I better give her a call and see how she's doing. The reason I called is to ask you to check with your friends and family to see if anyone else is having similar experiences."

"Ok, I will but so far there's no indication at work I seem to be the only one."

"Ya, that's what we have to figure out, who's having these experiences and what they have in common with us,"

"Well I'll let you go for now and call Barb, hopefully she's ok, buy for now George."

"Ya, buy Bill."

Bill dialed Barb's office and Lisa answered in her usual manner "Triple a dental Lisa speaking may I help you?"

"Ya Lisa, its Bill Is Barb busy?"

"No she's available hang on Bill."

"Barb pickup line 2 its Bill."

"Thanks, hi hon"

"Hi hon, how's your day going at work?"

"Ok I guess"

"Is anyone else in your office having problems?"

"No Just me."

"Well I'm working on that very issue as we speak."

"What do you mean?" said Barb.

"Well if we can figure a commonality we may be able to figure out what's happening."

"Oh, I see." said Barb that makes sense she thought.

"Well I'll see you tonight at home, for now though I got to go." Bill said anxious to get back to his computer.

"Ok, love ya, see you later." both hung up.

Bill continued to familiarize himself with his project and the team members, the project was an extensive one and he was the project mngr. as well as the electrical engineer on the project and had no idea of what was going on or where the project was at this point in time, he had a lot of catching up to do. Thinking ahead though, he couldn't help but think that what if he came to work tomorrow only to find out that the project had been completed and he, the project manager, had no involvement or even any memory of the job, well that scenario given the last couple of days was certainly possible.

While sitting at his desk, trying to think thru the day's problems and catching up on his project Bill thought he might invite Geo and Nancy over tonight to discuss the past couple of days events and try to collectively figure it out or at least make an initial attempt at solving the mystery.

Bill made another quick call to Barb's office to bounce the idea off his wife this time Barb answered the phone "Triple 'A' dental Barb speaking, how May I help you?"

"I can think of many ways you could help me, did you want to hear a few?"

"No" she laughed "What do you want now, I'm busy!"

"You don't sound busy, how come you're answering the phone? I was looking forward to hearing Lisa's sexy voice."

"Well if you hang on I can get her for you!"

"No, that won't be necessary; I'll live with the disappointment. The real reason I called is to say I'd like to invite George and Nancy over to discuss the last couple of days as they were having similar experiences."

"Ya, well I wasn't really looking forward to company, but if it will help I guess its ok, you might as well ask them for dinner, we can send out for something, I'm not really in the mood or prepared to cook a big meal." With that Bill said a loving goodbye and hung up.

Bill dialed Geo's phone once again, "Hello Bill, what's up?"

"Ya hi guy just thought I'd call and see if you guy's wanted to come over tonight so we can talk about what's going on, we'll call out for a pizza or something while we mull this over, can you make it?"

"Ya that sounds good, what time?" asked George.

"About 6:30 if that works for you guys?"

"Ya see you then" Said George.

Well now that that's settled Bill went back to work trying to give a little to the company that paid his bills.

However, Bill couldn't keep his mind from drifting back to the problem at hand, he was a problem solver and the overwhelming problem in his life right now wasn't his assignment at work, but the phenomena effecting their lives at work, at home and everywhere in between and he was going to figure it out and it wouldn't be the last thing he ever did!

Meanwhile back at Barb's office, Lisa couldn't help noticing that Barb seemed preoccupied with something and not quite herself so she decided to inquire as to any problem she may be able to help with, she really liked Barb and was concerned.

"Ha Kid are you ok?" asked Lisa.

"Ya sure" said Barb.

"Why do you ask?"

"Well you seem out of sorts the last few days, I don't know preoccupied or something, if I can help just yell, ok?" Barb thought this a good opportunity to inquire as to any changes Lisa may have noticed.

"Ya, I will, but tell me have you noticed anything out of the ordinary lately?" asked Barb.

"Out of the ordinary, what do you mean?"

"You know, subtle changes, things someone else may or may not notice, but you do or even more obvious things that others have noticed also?"

"I don't think so" replied Lisa.

"Well it was just a thought, I don't even know why I asked." said Barb as she got ready for her next patient.

In the meantime, George called Nancy to tell her of the evening's plans, she really liked Bill and Barb and he was sure she wouldn't mind him making plans with them without consulting her first; well he may have been wrong this time! Nancy a catering consultant and food connoisseur and critic in her own right was well established in her business and while still working out of the house she was looking for a small office space as she was expanding and needed a more professional looking place to interview potential clients. Her phone rang, the caller ID indicated it was Geo.

"Hi Babe, what's up?" Nancy asked.

"Does something have to be up, other than that of course, for me to call? Well as a matter of fact Bill called and wants us to come by tonight for dinner and to try and figure out what's going on the last few days, I said we would, I hope that was ok."

"Well to tell you the truth I'd prefer you'd check with me in the future, I had plans to work tonight but as long as you've already committed us I guess I'll make other arrangements and follow your led my Liege."

"Noted, I'll call and cancel!"

"No it's ok really, I'm still a bit upset I guess, but I'll be fine." Nancy said, asking about the time and if they need to bring anything. They said their goodbye's and the evenings plans were made as Geo went back to preparing a Quote for a substantial order to a California company.

Well the stage was set for tonight's dinner meeting and no one really had any ideas for the intended discussions other than to talk about the odd things that had been happening the last few days, but of course Bill would delve deeper into the problem once he got started, it was what he did.

CHAPTER THREE
THE MEETING

Well 6:15PM and George and Nancy were on their way to Bill's thru the yet unplowed Chicago streets, making travel less than enjoyable, but hell Geo thought, it doesn't compare with the other recent problems and the snow would melt eventually of that he was certain!

Arriving in Bill and Barb's parking lot and looking skyward toward their friends 24th floor condo, which they really enjoyed visiting as the Lake View was breath taking and always impressive, summer or winter.

As they entered the building they rang the Kelly's buzzer and a female voice came on asking who's there? Nancy replied.

"Come on you guy's, you know who it is!" Both George and Nancy laughing, as the buzzer sounded, they opened the door and headed for the elevator pushing the up button and while waiting for the car, George decided a little kiss was in order, though a much longer kiss ensued only to be interrupted by the arrival of the elevator and the opening of the door allowing several folks to get out.

They entered, pushed the 24th floor button and as the door closed George asked "Ha have you ever done it in an elevator Nance?"

"Done what?" Nancy asked, (playing the game) by this time Geo had her in the corner and up against the wall pressing her hard as the car stopped, the door opened on the 12th floor and another couple entered carrying a bottle of wine and smiling at them knowingly while pushing the button for the 20th floor, obviously a party was in the making.

Geo and Nancy collected themselves, in anticipation of being alone again shortly. The car stopped once again on the 20th floor and the young couple exited saying;

"Bye, bye!" and smiling, alone again Geo thought, but he could see the disapproving look on Nancy's face as she said;

"No! Wait til we get home George." George smiled shaking his head, in a disappointed affirmative.

The car stopped once again, this time on the 24th floor as they exited and started down the hallway toward Bill and Barb's unit they herd the door open in anticipation of their arrival and Bill steeped into the hallway saying "Hi guys, your right on time, hope you're hungry though we haven't decided what we're having yet, but now that you're here, you can help with that."

"It really doesn't matter as long as it's hot and a lot" George replied jokingly.

"I think we can handle that." said Bill as they entered the apartment greeted by the all too lovely Barb with her adorning smile and greeting both of them with hugs and kisses as you do with good friends.

George immediately headed for the window to see the Lake View as he always did when first coming in, he was a bit envious of the Kelly's view, he and Nancy had talked many times about moving there but to get a LSD high rise with a Lake View was expensive, when one was available! Bill was lucky he got a good deal prior to the renovations being started and subletting the unit from a friend before he and Barb were married.

Well after taking in the view, while the others were deciding on dinner, George asked, "Have you guys decided about food? I'll buy."

"I think Chinese seems to be the popular choice." said Bill.

"I'm good with that." George replied. The girls went to the kitchen to place the order from a local take out that had an excellent reputation while the guy's adjourned to the recreation room to discuss the evenings chosen topic.

Bill started the discussion saying, "I've thought about it carefully and the only thing I can come up with is that we seem to be moving thru time, ever so slowly and everyone's moving with us, but they have no recollection/realization of any changes, only we do and that's the confusing part."

"Ya, that's about the way I see it, but what is the commonality that makes us stand apart from all the rest of the world?" questioned Geo.

"I don't know if we knew that we would be on our way to the answer." Said Bill as the girls came back into the room saying it will be here in about twenty minutes or so guys.

"Good, but while were waiting, nobody's found anyone else yet who's going thru the same thing as us, is that right?" Bill asked, they all said that's right while looking at each other questioningly.

"Well, I for one haven't talked to everyone I know yet, but I'm working on it." Nancy said.

"Nor I" replied Barb.

"Well I guess we should start with our closest friends first and our colleagues and associates at work next and continue from there." suggested Bill.

"But more important right now, tonight, what have our observations got in common?" asked George.

"A good point" said Barb. "We experienced missing toothpaste, book markers moved and then books missing altogether, un-forecasted snow, cars moving by themselves and other scary things." Barb would have kept going, but was becoming upset again, so she quit giving the others a chance, but before anyone else could chime in the buzzer rang, Bill answered and a voice said 'Your food order sir' Bill buzzed him in as Geo came to the door with the money.

Bill said "Don't be silly, I got this, we invited you, go sit down." George shrugged his shoulders and walked away as the girls set the table for a Chinese feast, all were hungry but the discussions were far from over.

Soon the table was loaded with several choices of authentic Chinese Cuisine; everyone could sample from everything which is the way the Chinese intended there many offerings be consumed according to Nancy our Epicurean expert. During dinner Nancy brought up the fact that anyone else close to us and being affected in the same way would certainly call, as we intend doing.

Bill said "Ok, other than the four of us who would you call next to see if they had been caught up in the current situation?" they all thought for a moment and finally Barb suggested, Larry and Karen.

"Ya, Larry and Karen, that's who I'd probably call myself." said George; they all agreed that Larry a Nascar executive and his wife Karen a secretary for an investment firm would be an excellent choice to call they were very close friends and would be offended if we didn't involve them in what was going on.

"Well, let's call um than, Barb go ahead and make the call."

"No Bill, you call I wouldn't know where to start."

"Ok, hand me the phone will ya hon?" she did, looking relieved.

Bill dialed the number and put the phone on speaker while waiting for an answer, soon a female voice answered "Hello"

"Hi Karen, it's Bill, how you doing?"

"Good Bill and you?"

"Just fine thanks"

"Are you looking for Larry?" asked Karen.

"Ya, if he's available."

"He is Bill, I'll get him."

"Thanks" said Bill, as he waited for Larry, deciding how to best approach the subject.

"Hi Bill, what's up? Have you recuperated from the party yet?"

"Well, it's odd you should ask that's actually the reason I'm calling, we're sitting here now with George and Nancy, by the way you're on speaker, kind of a conference call, but we were wondering if you or Karen have had any out of the ordinary experiences lately?"

"Have we, you bet, the snow this morning for one, that wasn't forecasted or expected it was supposed to be 70 degrees today and it can't snow with that kind of temperature."

"Ya the snow surprised us all."

"Not all" Larry was quick to interrupt.

"The folks at the office weren't surprised to see snow; it was just me which I didn't understand." Larry said.

"Well along with the snow, we have been experiencing several unexplained events and it sounds like you guys are in a similar situation is that about right?" Bill asked.

"Ya several little things some almost went unnoticed."

"Ha Larry it's George do us a favor start keeping track, write um down and we'll keep checking back for updates in an attempt to figure this out ok?"

"Ya, no problem, we'll do that and how are you doing by the way?" asked Larry.

"Ya were good thanks."

"Well listen, Bill's idea is that we are moving in time very slowly but faster than everyone around us, I'm still trying to comprehend that, but you know Bill always thinking out of the box." George said.

"Ya, well we are glad you guys called as we thought we were alone in this, is there any others yet?" asked Larry.

"No just the six of us so far but yesterday it was just us." said Bill, now there are six thought Barb when will it end?

"We're going to go and think about this from a different perspective now Bill and we'll talk to all you guys later." said Larry, everyone said goodbye and Bill hung up.

"Well, it seems it's only our group of friends, at least so far and I think we should pursue that avenue, at least until we get a contradiction to that." said Nancy, all agreed.

Bill started to write down the following while mumbling to his self; it all started the morning of 10/28/2011 for all six friends involved so far, with similar experiences at home and at work.

"That's it shouted Bill, it started on the 28th but what we haven't considered is what we were all doing on the 27th, come on guys, what were we doing on the 27th?" asked Bill.

"My birthday party" Geo said questioningly?

"Ya we all did that" said Nancy, adding "Who else was there?"

"Are you kidding the restaurant and bar were loaded there had to be 250 people in the joint." Geo said.

"Well I say we start over in the morning, it's Sunday and we can all sleep in and no one has to work so we'll be fresh."

"Ya I'm for that lets go Nance." said George, getting their coats and thanking their hosts for dinner and giving goodbye hugs and kisses as they left with Bill and Barb watching them walk down the hall toward the elevator.

CHAPTER FOUR
A LEAP IN TIME 10 30 2011

The first to awaken the next morning was Barb who immediately went to the window to check the weather, discovering the snow was still on the ground, but couldn't help but feel something was horribly wrong, unable to put her finger on it she went to the TV in hopes of ridding herself of this terrible feeling.

Suddenly, she flew back to the window, which overlooked a portion of the parking lot and noticed a major change which was not there the night before when they went to bed. A brick building alongside a huge swimming pool, how could this be she thought, unable to comprehend how this could have happened overnight as they couldn't have been asleep for the length of time necessary to build this complex. She ran to the bedroom to wake Bill in her excitement before it disappeared, thinking it might be her imagination, hopefully he could figure this out also.

In the bedroom, while shaking her husband and yelling desperately "Bill, wake up, we have a pool and it's a big one!" Bill stirred rubbing his eyes saying;

"What the hell are you yelling about?"

"Get up and look you can see for yourself we have a pool." she said, Bill rolled up and out of bed looking at her as she took him by the arm pulling him toward the window.

"Look down there" she said, pointing toward the lot.

"My God, that's, I want to say impossible, but I'm looking right at it and in light of recent developments, I guess it is possible."

"I already turned the TV on let's see what's going on" said Barb as they headed for the req. room where the TV was and as they sat down, on the news there was a discussion about the preparations for the upcoming Presidential Inauguration, Bill and Barb looked Inquiringly at each other in awe as they heard the news caster say;

"Ya Obama will be on his way back to Chicago immediately after the swearing in of the new President."

"Who is it? They didn't say who it is!" Bill said, obviously upset at the turn of events as he didn't even know who was running against Obama.

We've slept almost a year thought Bill or maybe more, we don't even know the date, it must be late November or December 2012 or even January 2013 as the inauguration was being discussed in the news.

Bill felt scared for the first time since this all started, over a year ago now, or is it? Bill continued to think of the possibilities, more confused than ever, yet determined to figure this thing out.

"Honey turn on the computer, that will give us the right date and time so we have a starting place, we don't even know if it's still the weekend, as it was when we went to bed or if it's a week day maybe we should be at work, it's crazy!"

"Bill, according to the computer it's Tues. January 8, 2013" said Barb, also seeming more confused, but not as emotional as Bill.

"Well that means were both more than a year late for work, we'll be lucky if we still have jobs." Bill said.

"Well believe it or not Bill, that's not my primary concern right now."

"Mine either Barb; I'm confused though, about what should be my main concern, what's happening and why or what to do next?"

CHAPTER FIVE
WHATS NEXT?

Well, Bill thought, "I guess we should get ready for work and go in to see if we both still have jobs and get that over with and then call everyone together once again to continue our discussions about how this all got started and considering the passing of a year since we last talked we should all have a good deal more input."

Barb replied, "Hon, I think your right we should go to work and see what's going on there and then regardless of what we find at work, we should arrange for another get together with everyone and kick this around some more. I'll get ready, were already late so maybe you can drop me off today Bill." Barb said, as she started to get ready for work.

"That's fine it's on the way, I'll be ready in about 20 minutes hon."

"Ok, 20 minutes, that'll work" said Barbara.

As they both got on the elevator pushing the button for the parking garage, wondering how they would handle walking into work a year late, give or take a month or so, that's probably an experience most folks, if not all, have never gone thru before, but than most folks have never gone thru what they are experiencing either, it should be interesting.

Dropping Barb off at her office Bill had a few last minute instructions, "Ha hon, I'll leave it up to you to set up another get together with everyone and don't forget to include Larry and Karen this time and please try and find out who the new President is we don't even know who ran."

"Ok sweetie got to go, love you." as she gave him a kiss and jumped out of the car running toward the office door, Bill stayed, making sure she got in ok and pulled away headed for the suburbs and whatever surprises were in store for him there.

As Barb walked into the dental office she noticed Lisa sitting at the reception desk and turning toward Barb with a smile saying in her normal voice.

"Good morning sweetie, running a little behind this morning I see?" You have no idea thought Barb.

"Well no matter you don't have any patients this morning, nothing til 1:30 this afternoon." Lisa said.

Lisa, talking as if nothing was wrong, nothing out of the ordinary, certainly nothing indicating Barb was a year late for work, Barb remained confused as ever maybe more so and said;

"Good morning Lisa, buy the way who's the president?" How stupid thought Barb, but now it was too late, she had already blurted it out, what now she thought as Lisa said;

"Hah, why Barak Obama you know that Barb!"

"Ya I mean who's he running against, I mean who do you think he'll be running against?" Barb asked.

"Oh, ya know, I just don't know yet." Lisa said, wondering where that question came from to start with. Barb realizing this said;

"Well, that's enough politics for this morning but based on the news I must admit I'm a bit confused thinking a viable candidate would have surfaced by now."

In the meantime, Bill carefully took in the skyline and the scenery on the way to work expecting, quite honestly, to see some obvious change, after all change happens every day and certainly over the year, but so far nothing, other than the swimming pool at home.

Arriving in the parking lot at work, Bill took a deep breath, as he headed into the building, not knowing what to expect, yet expecting some notable change. Walking into the office though his initial impression was that there were at least no obvious changes and no one seemed surprised to see him. He'd been away a year and yet everyone treated him as if he were here yesterday, his confusion continued!

As he sat down at his desk though, he noticed he was no longer working on the furnace project and once again had no idea what he was working on. This was becoming an unpleasant daily occurrence, every time he walked into the office his job had changed and yet no one else in the office was aware of any changes, how do you explain that he thought?

Jack came by Bill's desk, asking Bill to step into his office for a moment and he did, after all, when the boss calls you go, but having no idea what he wanted this time.

"Well Bill you've been here what? About four years now and been doing an outstanding job all that time and I expect you'll continue. Your performance recently on the furnace project as project manager and design engineer was beyond my expectations and I had high expectations for you! You've earned the recognition we've decided to bestow on you, you're being promoted to senior engineer and engineering group leader over all facilities projects.

"Jack I don't know what to say."

"Of course you do" interrupted Jack;

"By the way I believe there are a few extra bucks thrown in with that promotion also!"

"Once again Jack I really didn't expect this."

Jack, had no idea how truthful Bill was being, Bill had expected to get fired or something, but the odd thing was the fact that Bill didn't realize the furnace project was completed and Jack did! It's as if Bill was moving ahead thru time but leaving all his knowledge behind recalling only the present day and everyone not effected by the phenomena had total recall of everything and talking to Bill as if he were there, though he had to be somewhere far in everyone's future! It was becoming more confusing every minute, the more Bill tried to rationalize it the more misunderstood it became.

Meanwhile back at Barb's office, Barb was taking advantage of the fact she had no patients until 1:30PM and making calls to everyone in an attempt to set up another get together as Bill had asked her to do, but making little progress as finding a time when all were available was not easy, you'd think they'd be more concerned thought Barb, as she dialed the next number on the list realizing there were three more friends at George's party they hadn't even considered yet, she'd have to tell Bill.

She had no idea how Bill had intended to contact all the people in the restaurant that night, it seemed like an impossible task to her and really made no sense, maybe talk to a few as a random sample and let it go at that.

Well hopefully by the end of the day, Barb would have set up a meeting time that all parties could manage and that would be that. Barb had a great idea for the meeting place and she was sure Bill would approve, she would surprise him later if she could work it out.

CHAPTER SIX
GETTING TOGETHER YET AGAIN

Barb did have an ingenious idea, motivated by Bill's need to question the restaurant customer's at George's party. She scheduled the next meeting at the restaurant, it seems they have a couple of small banquet rooms that are seldom occupied and would be available for them to use as a meeting room, which would allow Bill to question any customer's that may have been there the night of the party. This was a good idea Barb thought, I have to call Bill and tell him the plan as she dialed his number.

Bill, hearing the plan, thought this was great thinking on Barb's part, he was proud of her and made it known, but wait, The meeting was arranged for Wednesday Jan. 9, 2013 that meant going to sleep tonight and waking up on Wednesday to a new day or maybe ten years in the future and missing the meeting by years that's no good thought Bill and said so to Barb.

"Hon, on second thought, that may not work, in fact it will not work, the meeting has to be tonight, tomorrow everything changes drastically as we wake up yet again."

"Well everyone wasn't available tonight hon." Barb said, not knowing what to do next.

"Does it matter?" asked Barb.

"We're trying to figure out why this happened or how it happened and the answer will be the same regardless of when, if ever, we figure it out or am I wrong?" Bill thought for a moment and realizing she was right laughed and said;

"What if we wake up and the restaurant has gone out of business? Or burnt down, where will we have our meeting?" Bill questioned Barb, joking of course, while Barb smiled knowingly, adding;

"Well we'll see in the morning won't we?" they said goodbye and went back to work.

Barb, appearing more level headed, at this point in time than Bill who was becoming more frustrated with the passing of time. Bill a pragmatist who solved problems for a living and he couldn't wrap his arms around this problem to start the process of problem solving.

Bill sat back again not knowing what he was working on and not really caring as he was now basking in the knowledge of his promotion and how he would handle the new responsibility. For the first time in his career he would have people reporting to him, he would be the boss, he knew he was a good engineer, but would he be a good competent leader he wondered, this was a whole new experience to look forward to, hoping to be able to handle it in light of the currant distractions.

Bill was now getting anxious to end the already short day and get home to Barb to give her the good news of his promotion on top of all the upsets over the last couple of days or months or even years whatever applies he was sure it would serve to relieve some of her tension also.

As he walked in the door that evening he said, "Hi hon, it's me, home at last to experience yet another evening of marital bliss with the one I truly miss, hurry here and bring a kiss!" Bill tended to become a poet on rare occasion or perhaps rhymer would be a better description.

As Barb approached she said, "Well you're in rare form this evening my dear, what's the occasion?" as she kissed him adding a little bump to put him in the mood for later or even now should the response she expected be there, but no, he was preparing to tell her something, she recognized the signs, she'd seen them before.

"Well, despite the shock we woke up to this morning, the day went pretty well for both of us. You went far beyond expectations arranging for the upcoming meeting and as for me, well, Jack thought I didn't have enough to do so he gave me another job with so much to do he gave me eight engineers, designers and draftsman to help me do it!"

"Are you saying what I think?" Barb asked.

"Did you get a promotion?"

"Ya, that's the word I was looking for, promotion!" said Bill.

"Honey I'm so proud of you, what's your new title or job or whatever you call it!?" asked Barb enthusiastically.

"Well I'm the new facilities engineering group leader" Bill replied.

"Wow! That's a mouth full!" said Barb.

"What does it all mean?" Barb inquired anxiously, Bill laughing said "More money and that should make you happy dear!"

"What's for dinner?" asked Bill, hungry as usual;

"Hamburger helpers" said Barb;

"Oh good I like that, what flavor?" Bill asked.

"Wash up, sit down and be surprised." said Barb. As Bill did what he was told.

Well after dinner and cleaning up the kitchen, catching up on the evening news and still not finding out who the newly elected President was, but seeing a big sale on BMW's Bill's dream car and looking at Barb with a questioning eye saying, "What do you think hon? Maybe this year a new BMW would be in order? I have been patient as you know!"

Well thought Barb a promotion and raise maybe we could swing it this year.

"Maybe so she said" with a smile while sitting on the couch with Bill who suggested a shower and early to bed to consummate the marriage once again!

10 31 2011 REAL TIME

Waking up to what he thought or what was supposed to be Wednesday January 9, 2013 and the first noticeable change the weather, the snow was gone replaced by a bright sunny day as Bill opened the patio door allowing what felt like 80 degrees to hit him in the face reminding him that once again time had jumped ahead, always ahead he thought why not back? How far ahead this time?

Suddenly he found himself in the bathroom looking for signs of psychical changes, wrinkles, gray or missing hair, even checking his teeth for dentures, but no noticeable changes; he guessed that, that at least was good. He thought he'd wake Barb, as she was sleeping in late for some reason, he proudly took credit remembering the night before and his wife's insatiable appetite for sex, thinking he is the one who should be sleeping in.

He gently shook Barb saying "Ha babe wake up, you'll be late for work, it's summer but I don't know what year, we'll figure it out later, the coffee is on and I'm cooking oatmeal, you know how you like that." actually she hated oatmeal, the thought of it made her sick and Bill couldn't understand how anyone could dislike it, he was raised on it and couldn't get enough, but to each his/her own he thought.

Barb finally rolled out of bed and headed for the bathroom while Bill ate his oatmeal in the kitchen and turned on his laptop to check the date and when the computer warmed up and booted up the first thing he noticed was 08/14/2018 six years ahead of when he went to bed,

"Barb, he yelled, were going to find out if the restaurant were having the meeting at went out of business or not!"

"What do you mean?" She yelled back.

"We've been sleeping for six years and counting its 2018!" yelled Bill, jokingly Barb said "Well if that's true my hair hasn't gotten any longer and I weigh the same as I did six years ago"

"Ya how much is that?" he asked.

"You'll have to take my word for It." said Barb as she wouldn't be telling him.

Then she thought, gee, six Christmases have come and gone and there's nothing to show for it, no presents and worse no babies, we agreed on having kids after five years of marriage, and were approaching seven years and were childless, we'll have to have a serious discussion before were too old and the way it's going that could be tomorrow.

On his way out the door, he stopped in the bedroom where Barb was getting dressed to say goodbye and give her a kiss. "Remind me we have to have a talk on another subject." Barb said.

"Ok I will" On his way down the hallway toward the elevator his mind started to spin once again, filled with questions and confusion, Barb was right he thought, had we been asleep for six years her hair would have grown and his to, that was a great point and something to bring up tonight at the meeting.

Getting off the elevator at the parking garage the first thing he noticed was once again a strange car was in his parking space a black BMW 700 series his dream car; curiosity prevailed, as he took his keys out of his pocket and noticing that the remote device had a big BMW on it so he pushed the unlock button and sure enough the car unlocked it was his he thought, once again he was a happy man as he proudly entered his car and drove it out of the garage headed for work, he was totally familiar with the car and the controls. Yet he couldn't remember buying it or even what year it was.

Arriving at work today would bring many more surprises, the first being an unfamiliar person sitting in his office, at his desk and greeting him with a smile saying;

"Good morning Bill, I emailed you those reports you had asked for this morning."

"Ah that's great (looking at the nameplate on his desk, Dave Kerney) Dave." said Bill.

"Oh they brought up your new chair this morning I opened your office and let them in I hope that was ok."

"Ah ya, that was fine Dave thanks"

Bill had no idea where his office was or who he was so he started to stroll slowly past the row of private offices noting at the end a fancy carpeted office with a wooden and glass door bearing the name Bill Kelly Engineering Manager, as Bill approached the door an attractive young girl said "Good morning Mr. Kelly, coffee?" she asked, Bill looking subtly at her nameplate and seeing the name Judy Channing.

"Um, Ya, Judy that will hit the spot this morning thanks." she got up and headed for the little kitchen area as Bill went into his unfamiliar office. This was Jack's job he thought where the hell is Jack and how did I get here?

Soon Judy came back with a mug of coffee just the way Bill liked it and asked "Will there be anything else sir?"

"No I think that will be all, on second thought will you get me a copy of the organization chart?"

"It's on your computer sir; do you want me to pull it up?"

"No I need a hard copy"

"Of course I'll bring it right in for you sir." well Bill thought if I were to fool around on my wife this would be the girl I'd be fooling with she was a beauty, I wonder who hired her, it must have been me, Human Resources/Personnel would never have been this kind to me, he thought, well no matter, I'm not fooling around on Barb or even considering it, but if I was!

Judy returned with the chart and placing it on his desk in front of him asked, "Will there be anything else sir?"

"No that's it for now, thanks Judy."

"Yes sir" as she turned and left the office with a smile.

Bill totally out of it now, after realizing Jack, his boss was no longer his boss and had been moved to the home office and promoted to a corporate VP and Bill was now reporting to a central engineering manager out of the home office in Richmond Va. Well Bill decided he would figure it all out tomorrow, depending on what year it was when he got up in the morning or maybe he would have retired by tomorrow, laughing to himself, while worrying at the same time.

Bill decided to call George to break the tension of the moment and discuss the current turn of events. He hit Geo's Number on the speed dial; Geo answered quickly "Hi Bill, are you still in this century?" George's voice was tense and Bill detected the fear, so in an attempt to calm him Bill answered.

"Ya but not for long at the rate were going, by the way do you know who the president is now?" asked Bill.

"No, and I don't really care, as long as you know who, isn't!"

"Well Obama has been gone awhile, I think" said Bill, thinking things are getting better, at least for him; he's had two promotions and a new BMW in the garage, he had no idea what he makes though, he hasn't seen a check in six or more years, he'll have to check with Barb she takes care of the money.

"Well Bill, I guess we'll still see you guy's tonight, assuming the meeting plans are unchanged, considering six years have passed since making the arrangements."

"Ya, nothing's changed, as long as the restaurant is still there and the food is still good and the drinks keep flowing, we may not figure out anything but we'll be fat and happy, which reminds me, I should probably call Barb and ask her to call everyone as a reminder, not everyone has a six year long memory, but I see you have George, I'll tell her I talked to you."

"Ok see you tonight goodbye Bill."

"Ya goodbye George, say hi to Nancy."

Well, Barb had a few surprises in store for her at work this morning also, as she walked in there was another girl sitting at Lisa's desk who she did not know though the girl knew her well enough, saying;

"Good morning Barb, I see you got to the hairdresser ok last night your cut is as cute as ever, I wish I could do that with mine!" Obviously she'd been there for some time, but what happened to Lisa and what was this girl's name she thought.

"Ya, I usually leave it up to Penny to do what she wants within limits of course." As she looked for some hint of the girl's name, there was no nameplate at the reception desk as there was when Lisa was there. I know she thought, the computer has the name of whoever made the appointment shell look there so she went into the computer and accessed her appointments and sure enough her first appointment this morning was logged in by Ruth, she thought she'd try it out and said, "Ruth" the girl answered.

"Yes"

"This is my only appointment today, is that right?"

"Ya that's it so far Barb."

"Oh for some reason I thought there was at least two more, I must be thinking of another day." Barb said.

"Thanks Ruth"

"Sure"

About then the phone rang and Ruth said "Barb it's your hubby."

"Ok thanks Ruth." trying to get used to using her name.

"Hi hon, what a day what's going on by you?"

"Don't ask, I'll save that for latter, in the meantime, will you have time to recall everyone and reconfirm tonight's meeting? I already talked to George."

"Ya I can do that as it turns out I have a light day and may leave early anyway."

"Ok well I think I'll go to the restaurant straight from work the timing will be close."

"Ok dear, I'll get a ride and meet you there."

"Love you Barb, talk to you latter."

"Bye, love you to!"

CHAPTER SEVEN
ANOTHER MEETING

The work day was coming to an end for everyone and they were all preparing for the evenings activities. Barbara had contacted everyone once again including Jerry and Emily Goldberg the forth couple at the party, but she was not able to contact the single guy at the party, Dave Thomas a government employee (who recently lost his wife to a stress induced heart attack) and a casual friend of Jerry and George.

Arriving at the restaurant, realizing he was the late arrival, Bill apologized to everyone saying, "Sorry I'm late folks, but duty calls you all realize what that means, however I hope that hasn't prevented you from ordering your meals so we can get started with the job at hand this evening."

Recognizing that Jerry and Emily were there, Bill said with a smile "Hi you guy's sorry you weren't at our first get together, but to tell you the truth we didn't realize the phenomena was limited to our small group of friends and I believe that still remains the case, unless anyone knows different?" Nobody offered anything to the contrary, but Jerry said something that put Bill at least, on alert, Jerry said.

"I didn't realize we were all having the same experiences Bill" than Bill noticed that Jerry and Emily were wearing coats and it was almost 90 degrees outside, but he decided to let it go for now.

Dinner came, Barb had ordered for Bill so he wouldn't go hungry, they all sat down and enjoyed their meals; the restaurant was still very good after six years.

Bill was the self-appointed moderator and quickly took charge of the meeting after dinner. Starting out by summarizing what had been experienced by everyone so far. Basically everyone has had similar experiences with the possible exception of Jerry and Emily who were wearing coats in 90 degree weather and not offering much in the way of additional information or contributing to the meeting other than shaking their heads in agreement with everyone.

Bill finally decided to take a stroll thru the restaurant to see if he recognized anyone from the night of the party, Barb and others thought that was a bit far reaching, but decided to go along and help, thinking the more eyes the better. As they toured the eating and lounge areas the only one anyone recognized was Lenny the Bartender who they knew as they frequented the lounge, so they decided to ask Lenny a few questions about the party assuming that in Lenny's world the party was only a couple of days ago.

As Bill and Barb sat down at the all but empty bar, Lenny, a good looking young Italian guy approached them with a smile asking "Hi folks what can I get for you this evening?"

"Hi Lenny, two Gin Rickey's and a little conversation would be nice." Bill replied.

"Two Gin Rickey's and a little conversation coming up."

"Here you go folks two Gin Rickey's and the conversation is free."

"Thanks Len, a, do you remember the birthday party we had here for George?"

"Do you mean the other night?"

"Ya that's the one do you remember much about it?"

"Oh sure you guys were wild that night, I hope you all had designated drivers, you all seem to have had a good time."

Bill replied. "Ya listen do you remember anything unusual that evening?"

"Well, yah know, bartender's try not to remember things folks do when their having a good time, sometimes they embarrass themselves and don't want to be reminded, that evening though I don't really recall anything out of the ordinary, except maybe, naw not really."

"Come on Len, except maybe, what?"

"Well its nothing, a guy came up to the bar and asked me to send a special drink to your table and as I was taking the order another fellow came up and said to me, 'Forget it' I looked at the first guy who shrugged his shoulders and they both walked away together." that's odd thought Bill and asked Len;

"That's it?"

"That's it" replied the bartender.

"Well thanks Len!" Putting an extra tip on the bar, this was gratefully acknowledged by Lenny, as he pocketed the bills.

The Kelly's went back to join the other's and continue the apparently fruitless meeting and with few results the meeting was quickly adjourned to the bar for a better time and to save the evening from a total loss.

Things broke up at about 11:00pm and on the way home Bill and Barb brought each other up to speed on the day's news. Arriving home they both agreed they needed a shower and a good night's sleep, refusing to think about what changes might be in store for them tomorrow morning. Getting off the elevator at their floor Barb asked "Hon do you want a snack or something before going to bed?"

"No after sleeping for six years I can't believe I'm this tired, I'm looking forward to sleeping in tomorrow, I already told them I wouldn't be in."

"Well I have to work in the morning I have three early appointments."

"Sorry hon!"

"I bet!" said Barb.

Entering their unit Bill thought he may be in the mood for a night cap and asked Barb if she wanted one too, but she said "No, unlike you I have to work in a few hours and I already had enough tonight, I'll make yours though."

"That's one of the many reasons I married you hon, you're so considerate." Bill took his shower, alone this time and finished the evening with the drink Barb had made for him as he headed for the bedroom, drink in hand. There was no book on Bill's nightstand, he quit reading books in bed as he never gets to finish one lately besides he does enough reading at work.

Barb was just coming into the bedroom from the shower, her sexy little nightie, still in the dresser drawer, never to get wore out from excessive use by the way, as she sleeps naked. As for me, I wouldn't have it any other way thought Bill, this was truly a beautiful woman!

As she slithered into bed and under the covers in her usual seductive manner she leaned over kissing Bill saying, "Goodnight sweetie, sleep well and dream of me." Bill replied;

"Love ya and dream of you I will!" they both rolled over and went to sleep.

CHAPTER EIGHT
SECOND THOUGHTS

---

1 | 2011 REAL TIME

The next morning, as Barb yawned and sat up on the edge of the bed, but suddenly as if startled, she jumped up and ran to the window, which was becoming a daily habit considering the current situation, she opened the blinds, staring curiously outside looking all around for some significant changes, but noticing nothing the weather remained bright sunny and appearing extremely warm, not unlike yesterday or six years ago or whatever it was, but this morning reviled nothing new leading Barb to believe that maybe, things were back to normal, not yet realizing how wrong she was.

Bill still sleeping and not likely to wake up, if she kept reasonably quit, as she was trying to do, not wanting to wake him, but that was not the way things would turn out.

While getting ready for work and deciding to catch up on things she turned on the TV news channel and immediately realized things were not as they seemed. It was now June 2025 and a new President was being questioned about his first six months in office. Well the weather outside was the same, but obviously that was the only thing that was unchanged, it looked like Bill was going to be awakened after all as Barb headed for the bedroom once again, though much calmer then the last time she woke him up.

"Honey, I hate to do this, but you have to wake up, Bill come on, wake up, Bill, come on you've been sleeping for seven years and that's enough for anyone!" Bill stirring a bit looked somewhat angrily at Barb, asking;

"What's up, why are you waking me up and what's this about seven years?"

"Hon, I'm sorry, but it's June 2025 and the newest President is on TV talking about his first six months in office."

"Who is it?" asked Bill as he once again rolled out of bed."

"I didn't catch his name, but I'm sure if you sit down and listen you'll catch it, I have to leave for work!"

"Ok, I'll just do that hon, love you, do you want me to pick you up tonight?"

"No I'll be fine, think about what you want for dinner though and when you figure it out you could start cooking It." said Barb, knowing Bill was a pretty good cook and he had the day off.

"Ok, how about a kiss?"

"Now would I leave without kissing you?" as she kissed him and left with a smile.

Bill sat down in front of the TV and listened intently to the interview with the new President who he did not recognize or even catch his name yet, but vowed not to move until he heard his name though everyone calls him Mr. President someone was sure to use his name before the interview was over.

Bill somewhat impatient though while watching started thinking about work and decided to take a ride to the suburbs and work to see what was going on seven years later, **he would be sorry he did that!**

Bill showered, dressed and headed down the hall to the elevator not realizing the adventure that was about to unfold before him. In his car now and bound for the suburbs Bill started to become aware of some changes in the skyline he saw every day, but was unable to nail down the specific things that have changed, or had they?

BIG CHANGES AT THE OFFICE

As he pulled into the parking lot it was immediately noticeable that the windows and doors had been replaced on all three floors trimmed in dark brown against the yellow brick, it was an improvement. Walking up the few steps leading to the main entrance he noticed some unusual activity inside the foyer and opening the door he was greeted by a uniformed guard siting at a desk saying "Good morning sir, how may I help you?"

"Good morning, I'm just going to my office."

"I see and your name please?" Bill, not understanding all the questions and a bit confused by the guards not recognizing him said;

"Bill Kelly"

"Kelly, I'm sorry sir you don't seem to be listed in the employee directory."

"Not on the list! I'm the director of engineering, how long have you guys been here?" asked Bill somewhat angrily!

"Three years and I don't recognize you, but Mr. Ballock is the director of engineering and I don't have a Kelly anywhere in the directory sir."

Bill was lost for lack of a better description; he didn't know if he was fired, quit, moved to another division of the company or to the central office, he just didn't know. Time was passing to quickly and now he was losing track of details not knowing where he worked or even who he worked for! He thought he'd call Jack his old boss to see if he could help.

He dialed Jack's cell number, but quickly found the number was no longer valid so he thought to dial the central engineering number, but as he looked in his cell phone the number was gone, that was certainly an indication that he had left the company. The next call would be to Barb or George if he had changed jobs they would be the ones who would know.

Bill dialed Barb's cell and she answered quickly saying "Hi hon, what's on your mind as you relax today?"

"Relax hell, I decided to go to work only to find out I had no job and didn't work there anymore and what's worse I don't know where I do work!"

"Hon calm down where did you go to work at?"

"I went to Bracken Metals, where else would I go?"

"Bill you haven't worked there in years!"

"Obviously, but am I unemployed?"

"Of course not, your much to talented to be unemployed, you're self-employed now as a consultant and doing very well I might add."

"You know I'm sure your right, but something has changed we usually woke up with the same memories and going down the same road so to speak, but now your memories are different than mine."

"Well hon we can talk about that when I get home, in the meantime go home and check your computer, everything you need to know about your business is in there and I'm sure once you get in there you'll be immediately refreshed."

"Well I hope so babe, love you and see you later bye!"

"Bye sweetie" both hung up, as Bill left Bracken Metals and the suburbs, maybe for the last time and headed for the Condo in the city, still not knowing the name of the new President!

The more Bill thought about what Barb had said the less he could understand how everyone could know about him running his own business and he didn't know it himself. Up to this point there hadn't been any loss of memory or disorientation, they were just traveling thru time and that was enough to try to rationalize and deal with, but now he was a small business entrepreneur and he didn't even know it, what's next he thought?

As Bill continued his drive toward the city and home he decided to take a detour and stop by George's office to feel him out and see how he remembered things, up til now with the possible exception of Jerry and Emily, everyone was pretty much on the same page and now that seemed to be changing a bit, Bill had to learn more and thought George might help!

CHAPTER NINE
A VISIT WITH GEORGE

Arriving at George's office, not even sure if Geo was in, he was a salesman after all, but not the door to door kind of a salesman; he conducted most of his business at the office, though he did go overseas from time to time. As Bill approached George's secretary Brenda, he asked, "Hi Brenda is he in this morning?"

"Good morning Mr. Kelly, yes I'll buzz him for you."

"Thanks hon, he didn't know I was coming so if he's busy I can call him later."

"Oh no sir I know he'll be happy to see you." she pushed the call button on the intercom saying, "Mr. Roberts, Mr. Kelly is here to see you."

"Oh great send him right in Brenda." with an alluring smile she said;

"Go right in Mr. Kelly." Bill who was very popular with the ladies and knew it said with a flirtatious smile.

"Thanks Brenda" as he walked into George's office.

"Good morning Bill what brings you by this morning?"

"I know it's a bit unusual, but it's an unusual day so far George, by the way how's Nancy?"

"Oh um, she's fine though after two years of marriage I am detecting some subtle changes in our relationship." Bill laughing only slightly and saying;

"You know that's part of the reason I'm here."

"What do you mean?"

"Well I don't remember your wedding and I know I was your best man, at least I think I was."

"You were indeed, though I don't know why you don't remember."

"Well that's the problem I'm here to talk about George, I don't remember your wedding and I woke up this morning not realizing I no longer worked for Bracken Metals or that I started my own business as a consultant and Barb seemed to know it all, how about you old buddy did you know that I was in business for myself?"

"I did Bill."

"Well there you go, up till now we all seemed to move in the same general direction and now it's as if we have come to a fork in the road and your all taking the right fork and I'm taking the left and if it goes unchecked we'll drift further and further apart!"

"Bill I don't know what's happened, or even why it seems to be isolated to our small group of close friends, it makes no sense, but it has happened and I guess if we can't figure it out we have to let it run its course and see how it all shakes out."

"Well George, do you agree that we have moved almost fourteen years into the future for lack of a better description of what is happening?"

"Ya I agree with that."

"Well how would you explain the fact that nobody outside our group has aged even one day since this started, I can justify the fact that our group has not been affected by the passing of time, but not everyone?"

"Your right Bill it makes no sense at all, I must confess I never thought about that."

"Don't feel bad George, I didn't either until Barb noted the fact that her hair had not grown and that started me thinking, you know I have to talk again with Jerry and Emily, if you recall at the last meeting we had, whenever that was, they came in coats and it was 90 degrees outside, I meant to follow up with them, but I missed the opportunity, I think I'll follow up now."

"Ya, the Goldberg's tend to be a bit eccentric from time to time, you never know what to expect from them, but we all love um." George said.

"Well I'll get out of your hair for now pal, I may be causing you to lose a big commission or worse, miss out on a martini lunch, call me."

"I will, see ya bud" Bill left saying goodbye to Brenda on the way out.

Back in the car and on the way home once again, Bill continued to think and now about Jerry and Emily, he was becoming obsessed with the fact they came to that meeting in their coats, they certainly would not be the first ones to do that, but coupled with the events of the day it just added to the mystery!

As Bill pulled into the parking lot at home headed for the underground parking garage he almost hit a parked car, as he noticed something that startled him, he had to stop and get out of the car and look, the swimming pool and pool house were gone, he walked to the spot where it was, but there was no sign of it or that it was ever there! He went back to his car and pulled into the garage, parked and got on the elevator pushing the button to the 24th floor thinking only that he needed a drink, a big one and that's number one on his agenda now, secondly he needed to get into his computer and figure out what he could about his business, which right now he knew nothing about. Changes were coming much to fast he thought!

Opening the door to his unit and walking in, going straight to the liquor cabinet and grabbing a bottle of Kentucky bourbon and pouring a healthy three fingers over a few ice cubes and drinking it down before the ice could possibly have had any effect on the temperature of the bourbon, but that was just for practice the next one would be the real thing.

CHAPTER TEN
A CAR FOR BARB

It was 6:10pm when Barb arrived home, her usual time, when Bill asked "Hon, you know you work a mile and a half from home you leave work at 5:00pm and get home at 6:10pm every night and the reverse travel time in the morning using public transportation."

"What's your point Bill, I don't have much choice, unless you want to chauffer me back and forth, that's the price you pay using public transportation, I don't really mind though."

"I guess my point is, I think it's time you had your own car, don't you?"

"Well that would be great, but two BMW's in the garage would double the cost, do you think we can afford it?"

"Whoa, who said anything about a BMW, we can afford it, but would you consider something other than a BMW?"

"Those little Mercedes are cute too." Bill thought he may have made a mistake even broaching the subject, but there would be no turning back now, he would have to see it thru to its conclusion now, regardless of where that may lead!"

"Let's freshen up and hit a few dealerships hon."

"Ok" On their way out Bill asked;

"Where should we go first Barb?"

"Dinner I'm starved!"

"Dinner, I thought we were going car shopping?"

"Ya I guess we can stop later." said Barb. Bill headed for the BMW dealer as a first stop thinking about a small electric or Hybrid which in his mind would be an excellent choice for its intended use.

As Bill pulled into the dealer's lot he noticed a steak house across the street and not remembering it thought it might be a good place for dinner latter and suggesting it to Barb, found her to be in total agreement with the look of a hungry Lion and being unable to take her eyes off the restaurant as Bill got out of the car saying, "Are you coming?" looking at Bill she got out and walked toward the showroom while looking back at the steakhouse.

Entering the showroom they were quickly greeted by a young notably aggressive salesman with a smile on his greedy little face asking "How may I help you folks this evening?"

"Does your pizza come with a thin crust?" the salesman looking perplexed, Bill's sense of humor escaping him, he said.

"Sir"

"I'm just kidding we'd like to see that gentleman over there." indicating the elderly man sitting at a desk at the other end of the showroom.

"Oh, you mean Brian; certainly, I'll just get him for you sir."

"Yes Brian, thank you." said Bill, as the younger salesman went over to Brian's desk to inform him of the customer's request for him. Brian stood, smiled and walked toward Bill and Barb extending his hand as he approached the couple saying;

"Good evening, I'm Brian, how may I help you?"

"Hi Brian I'm Bill Kelly and this is my wife Barb and were just starting to look for a car for Barb as public transportation is becoming a bit of an inconvenience for us."

"Well I see you're driving one of our older 700 series they seem to last forever, how are you enjoying it?" Bill thought for a moment, realizing the salesman was going to try to sell them a much bigger car than they were looking for saying;

"Ya well were looking for something much smaller I was thinking about an electric or hybrid vehicle to be honest."

Brian not wanting to be insulting, but knowing Bill was clearly behind the times said, "Well as you know Bill everyone got out of that business years ago, I believe back in 2015 or so as they simply couldn't make them work well and the public didn't want them and as the price of oil came down and down the manufactures simply dropped them from their product lines, no one was buying them anyway!"

"Why not?" asked Bill.

"Well for one, people didn't want to sacrifice safety, comfort, and limiting their travel distance for better fuel efficiency, it just turned them off and there seemed to be no other way to do it. The cars had to be made smaller and lighter to start, thus less safe, batteries alone couldn't promise unlimited travel distance, some folks wanted to drive 700 to a 1000 miles a day on a trip while others were satisfied with 300 miles per day an all-electric vehicle couldn't satisfy either need. Hybrids were still small and less safe and not as comfortable as large gas guzzlers so as the price of oil was brought under control and the journey to replace fossil fuels came to an end, the bigger more comfortable and better riding vehicles survived despite the governmental regulations and the all-electric and hybrids are nothing more than a fading memory now."

"Well Brian that's quite a story, but were still looking for a smaller car to meet our needs."

"Well Bill we have smaller cars, but with reliable internal combustion engines."

"Well show us what you have Brian." said Barb, anxious to drive her new car to the restaurant across the street and look out the window at the car while eating her huge steak dinner!

Brian started out with the Z series two seat sports car saying "Well you wanted small and this is as small as we get and you would look great in this car, but I don't think it's what you're looking for am I right?" Barb smiled saying;

"Your right Brian it's cute, small, beautiful and expensive, but it's not me, what else do you have?" Brian smiled, Bill exhaled in relief as Barb followed them to the 300 series room where she immediately fell in love all over again, this time with a car.

As they entered the room Brian explained that the 300 series had earned the right to its own showroom, as it was the most popular model sold in America. The room currently housed eight models of various colors and price levels, but it didn't matter as Barb's attention was immediately drawn to a metallic silver model and she knew instantly that the shopping spree was over, as she got in and began to embrace the car. Bill realizing what was going on had already started negotiating a price with Brian as Barb asked Bill if they would be able to get another parking space in the garage, maybe next to Bill's car.

Brian came up with a price, after the usual salesman manipulations, commonly used in the retail sales business, which most people were aware of, but let the salesman run his scripted gambit, finally resulting in a price Bill could live with, while Barb was busy looking for the keys and asking Brian if he had eaten at the steakhouse across the street?

"Yes I have had dinner there a few times and I must say they are excellent, I've only had the Porterhouse, but it melts in your mouth and they bake a potato like no one else, you never leave hungry, I guarantee that you'll enjoy it. About the car though, I couldn't possibly have it prepped tonight it's late and the guys who do that are gone for the day, the best I can do would be noon tomorrow if I push, will that work?"

Bill, noting a look of disappointment on Barb's face, donned his authoritative smile and said, "Look Brian how much prep is necessary? I'm sure most, if not all was done before putting the car on the showroom floor, I mean look at it it's spotless and to tell you the truth I'm married to that lady and I don't want to disappoint her or I'll pay the price if you know what I mean, so can you help me here or not?" Brian shaking his head in agreement said;

"Ya sure Bill let me get it out of the showroom, fill it with gas and have the night mechanic go over it while you go to dinner and you can pick it up when you're done, I'll finish the paper work in the meantime and I assume you'll be financing it how much did you want to put down? All I need is a thousand but you can do any amount you want."

"No financing, put it all on this." handing his credit card to Brian saying;

"We'll be back after dinner Brian." Barb smiled as they left knowing she got the car she wanted and do to her husband's power of persuasion, would be taking it home tonight and she was finally going to get to eat, her day was made, but not yet complete.

Pulling into the restaurant lot across the street while continuing to thank Bill in a way he truly enjoyed, but being reminded that they only had so much time to eat and get back to pick up her new BMW before the dealership closed, she reluctantly stopped, promising to finish what she had started later and Bill knew she would!

They went into the lavishly decorated restaurant greeted by the mai-tre d named Carl who immediately showed them to a pleasant table assuring the couple their waiter would be with them shortly while giving them their menu and asking if this was their first visit?

Bill said, "Yes, but you come highly recommended, at least by the sales people across the street, I hope you can live up to their enthusiasm."

"Oh yes the BMW folks, they are here often and keep coming back I might add, trying to sell me a car and enjoying the food as I'm sure you will sir." Carl left getting back to his station as more folks were arriving.

Shortly Mike our waiter came to the table and introduced himself, telling us about the evenings specials and asking if we would like to see the wine steward, but we decided not, as we were both driving and Barb would be getting used to a new car, Mike then asked if we had decided on dinner. We had, we ordered and had a ginger ale while waiting.

The dinner, as promised, was excellent and the couple would return again and again as it was a dining delight, but right now it was time to pick up Barb's new BMW and that was now her number one priority, her hunger satisfied, as they once again drove across the street to notice her new car sitting out front ready to be picked up and Brian standing in the showroom with a smile ready to deliver the car as they parked and walked in. "Well how was your dinner folks?" asked Brian.

"Everything you said it was and more." retorted Bill and confirmed by Barb.

"Well if you folks would just follow me we can sign a few papers and you can be on your way." After the signing and Bill getting his credit card back Brian escorted them outside to the new car to familiarize them with the operation of the vehicle, congratulated them on their purchase and left them to their own devices as Bill gave Barb instructions.

"Hon you follow me and when we get home just pull into the underground parking and take one of the empty spots that are never used, tomorrow we'll get you assigned a spot ok?"

"Lead the way babe I'll be right behind you and we still have something to finish at home or did you forget?"

"You know I never forget a promise like that!" he said as they got in their respective cars and headed home.

Arriving at their condo and pulling into the underground, Bill pulled into his designated parking space and Barb pulling in right behind him selected a spot she knew to be unassigned and as close to Bill as she could get. Both getting out of their cars and Barb standing there admiring her new BMW, as Bill walked over to enjoy the moment with her saying "Like it?"

"I love it I can't wait to show it to the gang at work tomorrow!"

"Well let's get upstairs we have a lot to do before morning." as Bill reminded Barb of her promise to finish some unfinished business! Barb smiled as they walked hand in hand to the elevator looking back at her car all the way.

As they lay in bed arm in arm, after Barb had finished what she had started earlier that evening and now thinking about what surprises the morning would bring, while slowly falling into a peaceful slumber.

CHAPTER ELEVEN
IN THE MEANTIME!

Well, let's see what George and Nancy are doing on this eve of yet another unpredictable day. It seems they're just arriving home from a casual early dinner with Larry and Karen and discussing Bill for most of the evening. George was becoming worried about Bill's obsession with the current turn of events, his unexpected visit this morning at George's office reinforced George's concern, worrying about going down different roads and other concerns, my God thought George we all travel different roads every day!

Larry and Karen on the other hand were hung up on the fact that the apparent time travel experience involved so many people, time travel as they knew it involved one person, in a time machine of the traveler's own design, able to travel back and forward in time, an old movie of course, I'm sure you all saw it! The reality though was that time travel didn't really exist, so the only basis for comparison was an age old Syfy movie almost forgotten about long since. Yet now the theory among the group is that a small select group of people, with nothing in common other than their friendship, are traveling thru time together in one direction to some unknown destination with no obvious purpose, was a bit hard for the couple to comprehend!

"Look George, Bill's an engineer and lives in a logical world and our current situation defies logic, that causes Bill a great deal of concern as he can't get his head around the problem, but I believe if anyone will figure it out, Bill eventually will, I truly believe that and I guess I'm patiently waiting for that to happen as is Karen."

"How about Jerry and Emily" asked George?

"Well, they're an odd piece of this puzzle, you saw how they were dressed at the meeting and they didn't have much to offer/add to the discussion." Nancy said, in an attempt to offer something and get into the discussion.

"Jerry was his usual jovial self though when from time to time we got off the intended discussion and drifted into a good time among friends, Jerry told his Jokes, while Emily sat back, smiled and tolerated the moment as was her way" added Karen.

"Ya when Jerry got on a roll we all pretty much followed Emily's lead and sat back and enjoyed the moment which usually lasted a good deal longer than a moment, but boring he certainly was not!" replied Larry.

Jerry and Emily on the other hand were spending the evening at home discussing everyone else's assessment of what was happening. Jerry was busy in the kitchen cooking Spaghetti sauce for their dinner as they were expecting their friend Dave for dinner and the evening as he was a bit, actually quite a bit down after recently losing his wife and they thought they might help.

Dave was a scientist working for the government and never talked much about his job, but was the only other one in the group who could compete with Bill on an intellectual level at least when speaking about scientific subjects. It was funny really how Bill was on guard when Dave was around and the conversation centered on science, but they both enjoyed each other's company and were good friends.

The doorbell rang, as Jerry was busy adding to the spaghetti sauce, Emily said "I'll get it dear" as she went to the door opening it with a smile and welcoming Dave with a hug and a kiss, as he returned the greeting and handed her a bottle of red wine to go with the meal asking with his arm full of Emily;

"Is your hubby home? I hope not I got what I want right here!" talking about Emily in a joking way, but she enjoyed the moment.

Jerry walking into the living room while wiping his hands on a towel said "Ha Goombah"

"Goombah" questioned Dave, "You're Jewish my friend or did you forget that?"

"Ya, but I'm cooking spaghetti, role playing, getting totally into the moment that's what makes my sauce so good!"

"Oh I see, well I'm glad about that you do make the best spaghetti, I think it's the sweet sauce."

"Ya folks like that" Jerry said proudly as he led Dave and Emily back to the kitchen to continue tending the sauce. Jerry made his sauce from scratch starting with whole tomatoes, he'd been simmering the sauce for two days now and after many tastes and adjustments it was ready to serve so the pasta was added to the already boiling water and the garlic bread was just going into the oven.

Dave offered one comment "Ha Goombah, why, if your role playing would you wear an apron with a picture of a huge Turkey on it while you're cooking an Italian dinner?"

"Why don't Italians eat Turkey? Just kidding! I don't have an Italian looking apron I do have a red and white checkered table cloth though."

"Well don't worry you will have an Italian apron by Christmas!"

Jerry smiled as he opened the wine Dave had brought directing everyone to sit as he poured the wine and put the dinner on the table. "Ya know Dave the only thing I do better than cooking spaghetti is eating it." Emily took the opportunity, the dutiful wife she was, to say;

"Honey that's not true you do many things well." Jerry, his ego swollen to the bursting point said;

"Ya, well I was talking about cooking hon."

As the dinner progressed the conversation turned to Bill and Barb and Bill's latest theory about a split in the road he and Barb and the rest of us were traveling, which Jerry learned about via a phone call from George earlier that day after an unexpected visit from Bill. Dave rubbed his chin in a thoughtful gesture after hearing Jerry's story of Bill's concerns.

Dave said, "Consider this for a moment if a couple or even a group of friends were traveling thru time together, together meaning being in the same place at the same time and suddenly for some reason they were separated while traveling, you could conceivably end up in a different place and time then the others, couldn't you?"

"No Dave, were all traveling thru time, but were not doing it from the same place, we're all in our own Homes and traveling when we sleep apparently, waking up years in the future and we've all jumped ahead the same amount of years each night but so far we all remember things the same, that is until today and Bill's isolated incident."

"Well, to tell you the truth I'm considering an experiment to find out what's happening, but I need a great deal more input from everyone to design the test and I believe we will all be further enlightened as to what's going on in our lives!" Jerry became immediately inquisitive asking;

"What is it Dave, what's your test?"

"I can't say just yet Jerry, I don't want anyone trying it on their own without considering all the parameters and taking the proper precautions."

"I see Dave, is it dangerous?"

"Well if I'm right it could be and if I'm wrong it most definitely would be!"

"We'll let me help you guy's clean up I'm pretty good at doing dishes and such."

"So is the dishwasher Dave, besides we have that new Syfy movie I bought and we need to get to it."

"Ok, are you joining us Emily?"

"No Dave I'm not into Syfy, but thanks for asking you guys go ahead, I'll make some popcorn."

After the movie, it was getting late and Dave said goodnight thanking the couple for a lovely evening, great dinner, good movie and interesting conversation as he left for home.

Jerry told Emily he thought the evening a success and that Dave seemed in good spirits, but now Jerry was curious about Dave's test, knowing Dave, Jerry knew it would be well thought out and meaningful!

CHAPTER TWELVE
THE GREAT JELLY BEAN MYTH

Well it's probably a good time to further introduce you to the principle characters in our story and to do this I'm going to use an age old myth it should be fun, sit back and enjoy it as we take a short break from our story.

Well it seems our characters all grew up together and thought it would be fun if when they married they all participated in the Jelly Bean Myth, you know the one where the first year you are married you put two jelly beans in a jar every time you have sex and after the first year you take out one jelly bean every time you have sex, the point being that you'll never empty the jar!

Well they all considered this a challenge worth taking on as they were all sure the myth was **WRONG!** So Jerry went out and purchased six identical glass jars of about a half-gallon capacity not knowing how many they would eventually need and at the wedding reception the newly married couple would be presented with a jar and most guests, but not all knew the significance of the jar.

The first couple married was Bill and Barbara and at their reception Jerry presented them with the Jar saying, "You guys know what this is for, my only question though, is the jar big enough?"

Barb was quick with an answer "I hope not!" she said as she looked at Bill with a lustful smile, the guests all clapped and yelled words of encouragement, the couple blushed a bit and the activities continued.

Similar presentations were conducted at the other weddings til all were married George and Nancy being the last. Now they all had their jars and were working feverishly to not only fill their jars but also outdo the other couples. For a long time Jerry, being the practical joker he was, brought his jar along to any social gathering the couples attended to proudly show it off much to Emily's embarrassment.

Now let me reveal the secrets of these couples and their jars, many the couples don't even know themselves, secrets I found out using extreme covert methods that I'm not at liberty to divulge, at least not now. Remember these are young sexually aggressive, competitive couples who had long planned to test the Jelly Bean Myth and had every intention to follow it to the end to prove or disprove it once and for all. So here's how it all turned out though the couples themselves may not admit to it.

Bill and Barb the first couple married starting on their wedding night as Barb came to bed with a big bag of unopened jelly beans with an even bigger smile on her face and finding ten beans in the jar the next morning waking up to her new husband vowing to add to the contents before getting up that morning and did.

Here's the secret though Barb being competitive, but more important wanting to make her husband look good and unknown to Bill, added one jelly bean to the count each time Bill put in two beans.

Larry on the other hand, somewhat disappointed with his inability to fill his jar in a more timely fashion as compared to the other couples but realizing that the scientific fact is that men reach sexual maturity between 18 and 22 years of age and he was just north of 23 so he felt he was performing at a normal level and became less concerned about the eventual outcome or results of the test.

Here's the secret though, it seems his wife Karen loves jelly beans and unknown to Larry, she was dipping into the jar from time to time to eat a few beans making Larry's efforts hopeless in his eyes, though Karen never realized this nor did she realize that psychologically Larry was a beaten man and all do to her voracious appetite for Jelly Beans!

Well Jerry on the other hand who always had an angle bought jelly beans slightly bigger than everyone else's beans, for instances Bill and Barb bought gourmet beans as they liked them better but they were much smaller than the average jelly beans while Jerry managed to find a brand slightly larger than the avg. bean. So Jerry felt he had a slight edge on the game and it wasn't cheating because there were no specific rules spelled out as to the brand or size or the color of the beans everyone just did their own thing as did Jerry, but he was a deviant.

Here's the secret though, it seems that Emily, aware of Jerry's tactic for achieving his goal figured out mathematically the advantage Jerry had gained with the larger beans and it gave him a 20% edge on the rest of the group so unbeknownst to Jerry every time ten beans were added Emily would secretly remove two beans from the jar.

The last couple married George and Nancy Roberts felt they had to catch up with the others, though that certainly wasn't the case, perhaps they were the most sexual of all the couples so much so that George carried a small bottle of jelly beans in his pocket just in case and Nancy not to be outdone on their way out to anywhere she would ask if he had his beans with him? And every time she went to the store she would buy another bag of beans and leave them lying around as a reminder, not that George needed any reminding.

As for Dave after losing his wife the rest of the group just left the jelly beans out of the conversation as they should have out of respect. So there you have it, back to the story.

CHAPTER THIRTEEN
THE NEXT MORNING 11 2 2011 REAL TIME

As the sun started to rise above the Chicago skyline and yet another day struggled to leave the dark of night behind and half of the world began to stir and welcome the dawning day, some early risers already at work, while others were just Picking up their first cup of coffee and yet others still in bed starting to stretch and greet the morning, Bill and Barb fell into this category and a bit apprehensive about what surprises the day would bring.

"Good morning hon" said Bill, with his arms wrapped around his wife, afraid to get up and look out the window, unsure of what he might see!

"Morning, I thought we might go out to breakfast in my new car today before I go to work, I just love that car hon."

"That sounds great, a big breakfast before I go to work on my computer on the kitchen table."

"Don't complain Bill, I don't know what you're doing, but our checking account is growing by leaps and bounds so keep up the good work."

Curiosity got the best of Bill as he moved to the living room window, standing there for a long moment before reaching for the drape cord and pulling it exposing his nakedness to the world, but not caring as there was nothing in front of him but about three blocks of pavement and the Lake and being on the 24th floor he felt pretty safe from curious eyes and binocular scans, Barb was also extremely comfortable in front of the window in various degrees of undress, high rise living I guess.

It was another beautiful sunny clear morning you could almost see the 90 miles across the lake as Bill carefully scanned the city looking for any changes as subtle as they may be, but once again with the single exception of the pool and pool house in their own parking lot now being gone there was nothing, so Bill went to the bedroom window giving him a much different perspective of the city as he now had a 180 degree view seeing only the city and oh yes he had to put his shorts on as he had another high rise right across the street and they could look in on each other and binoculars were not required he and Barb had several occasions to linger at the window while watching an exhibitionist couple on about the 25th floor, but that was not what Bill was interested in today.

"Hon are you seeing anything out of the ordinary or not?"

"Not really I think I'll turn the computer on and check the date." Bill went to his laptop turned it on and waited for it to boot up. After the computer turned on Bill looked at the date and called to Barb.

"Hon, you know that new car you wanted to go to breakfast in, well its ten years old now and probably ready to be traded in on another new one, I do hope you enjoyed that car."

"What! Let's think about this for a moment, on our travels thru time, one thing remains true our group while traveling thru time and everyone else remaining in the present show no signs of ageing,

I can understand why we wouldn't age, but I don't understand why everyone else is unaffected so why would my car be ten years older and worn out?"

"Hon your right psychical things seem not to be affected, I do not pretend to know the answer yet, but it does seem that only our state of mind is affected and that, I believe needs more consideration, I'm going to call Dave and run this by him and get his opinion."

"Well that's fine but for now let's get dressed and check out my car and go to breakfast as planned."

"Let's" said Bill as the couple continued to get ready.

As they left the condo Bill said, "I'm hungry I hope our favorite restaurant is still there after all its Aug. 2035 according to the computer and we haven't eaten in ten years!" Bill was trying to maintain his sense of humor and keep Barb from becoming upset, but wondering who was more upset Barb or himself as he thought about it.

Getting on the elevator and pushing the button for the parking garage both were anticipating how they would find Barb's car they purchased just last night or was it ten years earlier, they were about to find out as the elevator door opened in the parking garage and they stepped out of the elevator, Barb smiled immediately, seeing her new car as she remembered leaving it the night before saying;

"See hon I told you" Bill though, being a bit skeptical said;

"Get in and let's check the mileage" Barb started the car and sure enough Bill was right! The odometer showed almost 50,000 miles though the car looked and even smelled new and neither remembered putting any mileage on the car except the drive home from the dealership the night before.

Bill was now convinced that a sit down with Dave and just he and Dave, was in order to discuss the subject from a purely scientific point of view, he's tried it involving everyone, but that doesn't seem to be very productive, it was time to take a different approach, he'd call Dave after breakfast and arrange a meeting.

After an enjoyable breakfast at their restaurant of choice Barb dropped Bill off at home and continued on her way to work wondering if Ruth would still be there as the office Manager or for that matter would the Dentist still be there, he had talked about selling the business from time to time over the years, well she would find all the answers to her many questions shortly.

As Bill entered the condo he sat down at the computer and phone, got comfortable and prepared to call Dave and propose a meeting between the two of them. Bill dialed Dave's number and waited for an answer as he manipulated his computer to his business files "Hi Bill, what's up pal?"

"Morning Dave, what year did you wake up to this morning?"

"To tell you the truth Bill I haven't checked yet, I had one of Jerry's famous Spaghetti dinner's last night and was just recuperating if you know what I mean."

"Ya, his pasta is really great even better than Barb's though I would never tell her that."

"Ya you're much smarter than that Bill, but I really think it's that sweet sauce he makes, I don't know anyone else that does that, do you?"

"No, I believe your right thou, it's the main difference with his sauce, from anyone else's I've had, it's good." Replied Bill, getting back to the point of his phone call;

"Listen Dave, I thought you and I could get together, one on one, to discuss our mutual problem, looking at it from a scientific perspective, I'm thinking we may be able to gain a little more insight into what were all experiencing, what do you think?"

"Well Bill, it's certainly worth a try, when would you like to get together?"

"The sooner the better I'd think, I'm home all day and am pretty flexible your work schedule would be the determining factor, so well work around that."

"You forget I work for the government so I'm pretty flexible myself."

"In that case Dave, how about tomorrow morning at my house and we can get started?"

"Name a time Bill and I'll be there."

"How about 9:00 o'clock I'll make us breakfast."

"Now that's an enticement, I'll see you tomorrow."

"Look forward to it Dave, see you then, bye for now." said Bill as he hung up.

"Bye" Dave replied.

Well it was still early and George and Nancy were busy trying to fill the Jelly Bean Jar though they should have been taking Beans out, but not having any idea of how long they have really been married they decided to keep filling it until they were beyond the current difficulties.

Larry and Karen on the other hand were going about their business as if nothing had happened figuring out that whatever brought them to this point would eventually bring them back to reality, they may be right and have the best solution to the problem to date.

Jerry and Emily were busy getting ready for the work day Jerry owned a successful pick and delivery service for the airlines (though government regulations were making it more difficult to earn a living everyday) having about a dozen trucks on the street at any given time and operating two warehouses to store and distribute the freight. Emily managed a jewelry store and was a good person to know if you were shopping for a gift for your wife, girlfriend or even yourself.

Bill simply couldn't get motivated to work today, though he had nothing pressing on his calendar for the day, so he just sat back and pondered the problem and all of a sudden realizing that there was not one child born to anyone in the group, they were all childless and that was unusual to say the least. Bill thought for a moment trying to rationalize that single problem and understand what it meant.

Well let's see thought Bill, If we are truly traveling thru time we would age normally and would simply leave the present behind but anyone not traveling in our time capsule so to speak would also age normally, but when we met those folks 15/20 years in the future they would show signs of ageing, that's the simple reality, but that's not what's happening! If time travel is as I imagine it to be and I'm a time traveler when I jump ahead in time I still exist in the present, but occupy the same space in the future, I'm getting a headache Bill thought!

The next perplexing or bewildering point to consider, we don't have a time machine, time capsule or mechanical device of any kind so how are we, as an obviously select group, experiencing the same phenomena, it is very perplexing indeed, maybe mass hypnosis or something of that nature and not time travel at all, that would explain it, but how were we hypnotized to start with and why our group, was it random? To many questions and no answers Bill thought. Maybe tomorrow Dave and I can work thru it, or at least make some inroads into the problem.

Bill decided to get back to work opening his business bank account and noting a balance of 82,000.00 with a pending deposit of an additional 14,000.00 totaling 96,000.00 and he could not figure out what he had done for all that money. So going thru his files he found his clients were mostly Contractor's and large industrial customers and the Illinois DOT it seems he was a safety consultant and had six safety engineers on the payroll three of which spend the bulk of their time doing in house safety training with another in Las Vegas and two full time west coast engineers, so he had quite a small business going, while he spent his time, traveling thru time and apparently leaving the business on autopilot!

Bill continued his day sending inspirational email's to his employees knowing they seemed to be doing excellent work as evidenced by his bank account. He decided to call Barb and see how her day was going and see if she had any plans for dinner, thinking he could help as he was at home and could get things started, he dialed her office number thinking she may be with a patient and not able to answer her cell the phone rang and a sexy voice answered saying "Dental office Ruth may I help you?"

"Hi Ruth its Bill is my wife busy?"

"Ya Bill she's with a patient and should be about another half hour can I have her call you?"

"Would you please I'd appreciate it."

"Sure will."

"Thanks bye Ruth."

"Bye Bill" hanging up Bill realized things must be normal at Barb's office after ten years had passed since she last went to work.

While waiting for Barb to call, Bill went back to work in the computer checking requests from clients for training or visits from engineer's to solve problems or meet with compliance officers to decide the circumstances surrounding a specific accident that OSHA may be investigating and represent their client in the investigation. Bill had no memory of how he got involved in this business, but he was manipulating his business files as if he had been doing it for years and apparently he had. The phone rang, it was Barb;

"Hi hon, how you doing today?" questioned Bill.

"Good, how about you, are you ok?"

"Well I've been working, it's surprising how much is going on in the business, the bank account looks promising though, I talked to Dave this morning and were going to get together in the morning and discuss this mess were in."

"That sounds great hon, listen I have to go I have another patient in about fifteen minutes and have to get the chair ready."

"Ok the other reason I called though is did you have any ideas for dinner or should we just punt?"

"Pizza got to go."

"Pizza it is bye" as he hung up on the call thinking pizza sounded pretty good, that settles that, back to work.

In the meantime Jerry was preoccupied with Dave's suggestion of a solution or at least a test to find a solution, but keeping it to himself for the time being and that puzzled Jerry, for the moment at least, why on earth did Dave want him to keep it quit?

Sitting at his computer Bill decided to take a trip to their favorite bar and restaurant where they all felt this journey had begun, to speak to Lenny once again, Bill felt Lenny may have something more to offer based on their previous conversation so why not try again he thought it might better prepare him for tomorrow's meeting with Dave also.

As Bill arrived at the restaurant getting out of his car he noticed few cars in the lot, not a very busy time of day he thought as he walked in the front door and saw few guests in the dining area and no one at the bar as he entered the lounge. The bartender smiled as Bill approached saying "Good afternoon sir, what'll you have?"

"Hi, to tell you the truth I'm looking for Lenny, but it looks like he's off today ha?"

"Today and yesterday, I guess he took a vacation or something, he just never showed up I got a call to come in yesterday I'm Bill the backup bartender by the way!"

"Hi Bill, I'm Bill also and as long as I'm here, make it a gin and tonic."

"Cumin up" Bill sat there drinking his drink thinking just another piece of the puzzle I knew Lenny was involved somehow, but how, that's the question. Bill finished his drink and said goodbye to the bartender and left for home.

Arriving back at the condo he dug out all the pizza menus so he and Barb could decide on dinner later. He decided to take his shower before she got home and headed for the bathroom, thinking this working at home is not bad he could be as flexible as he wanted and no one was around to comment one way or another, it's a good deal!

The day was coming to an end for all our players, Bill and Barb had their pizza and had updated each other on the day's activities as did the other couples while Dave had dinner in his apartment with a friend. So the day was at an end and all hoped that some solutions might be in sight, as the day dawned tomorrow.

CHAPTER FOURTEEN
A MEETING WITH DAVE 11 3 2011 REAL TIME

Well a new dawn, but no one was jumping out of bed to greet the morning there were no changes expected of any significance. Bill did get up earlier than he had planned in preparation for Dave's arrival, Dave was always prompt and there was no reason to believe today would be an exception so he thought he'd get started on the breakfast and getting started meant start thinking what he would serve, to this point he had no ideas.

As Barb got out of bed and headed for the bathroom Bill asked "Good morning hon, what do you think I should make for breakfast for Dave and I as I have no ideas?"

"Morning babe, I don't know how about pancakes or waffles, I could whip up a batter for you real quick and maybe make some of those Brown "N" Serve sausages to go along with it."

"That's what I love about you, always ready with an answer, sounds good I'll dig out the sausage." which he did as Barb continued to get ready for work though she had plenty of time and asking Bill;

"Hon did you turn on the computer to check the date yet?"

"No, but I will" as he sat down at the kitchen table with his coffee in hand and opened his laptop to see how far into the future their sleep had brought them today.

While Bill sat there waiting for the computer to boot up, Barb came into the kitchen and asked "Well, pancakes or waffles?"

"I hadn't thought about it, why does it matter?"

"Different batters dummy!"

"Ya know, I didn't know that, make it waffles I guess!"

"Waffles it is" said Barb, as she took out the waffle iron and started whipping up the batter.

Bill said, "Well what do you know, we only moved ahead two years it's April 7, 2037"

"That's almost like real time." said Barb jokingly, though Bill failed to see the humor, he was not handling the situation well, totally unlike him, he was worried.

As Barb was leaving for work she gave Bill a kiss and said "Don't forget, whip that batter again before you start the waffles ok?"

"Got it hon, have a great day and don't tire out at work today if you get my drift."

"I do and I won't, love ya bye." as she closed the door behind her.

Bill looked at his watch thinking, well about 45 minutes before Dave arrives, maybe I'll make a quick list of talking points before he gets here, so he can look it over while I prepare the breakfast. As Bill was completing his list the buzzer buzzed and Bill got up to answer it asking, "Dave is that you?"

"Ya, it's me how did you know?" Dave said, with his usual humor listening as Bill buzzed him in and opened the front door on his way into the kitchen to start breakfast.

Dave walked in a few minutes later saying "Morning buddy what's cooking?"

"Waffles and sausages, I hope you like um a lot of planning went into this breakfast I'll tell you that!"

"I love waffles and sausage, though I don't get them as often as I would like anymore."

"Grab a cup of the coffee Dave while I do my best to change that!" said Bill, as Dave got a cup and poured the coffee asking;

"Is Barb gone already, I was looking forward to saying hi to her?"

"Ya, got to keep her working ya know in case I lose my job, take a look at the list of talking points on the table there, breakfast will be ready soon." as Dave looked over the list, he commented, saying;

"Boy if I could answer all these questions we'd have this thing solved." laughing about it and saying;

"You know you do have some good points though." Dave said.

As Bill put the breakfast on the table he said, "Get it while it's hot I have more waffles in the iron and another dozen sausages in the pan, do you need more coffee Dave?"

"Not right now this looks and smells great and after that big meal at Jerry's last night I can see I'm headed for a weight problem!"

"Well enjoy I don't do this often." said Bill, as he sat down to partake of the bounty after putting another stack of waffles on the table.

"Tell me Dave, just what the hell do you make of what's going on here?"

"I have some thoughts Bill, but to be honest, at some point in the thought process things fall apart and I start all over and get so far and run into a brick wall again."

"I'm having the same difficulty Dave! I can't seem to rationalize the problem."

"I'll tell you something Bill, but you have to keep it to yourself and don't try it for reasons you'll soon understand, do you agree?"

Bill thought for a moment and said "Sure"

"Well, here goes, I thought that all the time travelers in the movies had a vehicle to travel in, a time machine of some sort, but we have nothing to use as a conveyance, there must be something though, so sleep must be the media that's being used to propel us thru time, what do you think Bill?"

"That sounds reasonable Dave, how do we prove it?"

"Well that's the kicker Bill it could be dangerous, but I think that one of us has to stay awake all night one night, to see if we remain in the same time and those sleeping move ahead thru time, but it could be risky the one staying awake could lose the rest of the group for good."

"Ya I see what you mean Dave, no wait, Barb goes to work every day and she doesn't lose track of Ruth her coworker."

"No but Ruth is not in our group of travelers, but if someone in the group, doesn't go to sleep and sleep is the conveyance, they won't be sent thru time, they would remain behind and lose the rest of the group, possibly forever and that's the danger!"

"I see your point and though we don't know for sure, it makes a lot of sense. If we did lose one of the travelers could we reconnect by the rest of us staying awake the following night?"

"Not likely which is why I should be the one to stay awake all night, I'm the only lone traveler, leaving no one behind."

"You'd be leaving a lot of friend's behind good buddy and that's not good!"

"Well I'm sure a good deal more discussion is in order before we travel down that road and I sure understand why you didn't want to tell the others just yet." replied Bill while Dave continued to inhale the breakfast Bill had prepared, seemingly enjoying every bite.

After breakfast, the two problem solvers continued their discussion, trying to figure out how they would implement Dave's plan, while doing a risk assessment, finally deciding before doing anything, the others would have to have their collective input into the decision, they were right!

The morning passed quickly and Dave had to take his leave thinking he may go into work for the afternoon and take care of some pressing business there, saying goodbye to Bill and reminding him to keep their secret from the others thinking one of them would foolishly try it, without fully knowing the potential consequences/dangers involved, Bill assured him he would keep the others in the dark so to speak, at least for now.

After Dave left Bill spent the rest of the afternoon on his laptop working on his own business trying to make some money to leave his lovely wife were he to get lost somewhere in the future, just kidding of course!

Lenny being missing was still bothering Bill as he was sure Len had more knowledge of the situation than he was revealing, but didn't know why he would possibly conceal it from them, was there something criminal going on and why did Len disappear, was he scared or paid to get out of sight, was there some kind of a conspiracy to contend with too?

The phone rang, it was Barb, Bill answered saying, "Hi hon how's work?"

"It's good, how's your day going, did Dave enjoy your cooking?"

"You bet between us we finished it all, the waffles were golden brown and loaded with butter and syrup and we killed twenty sausages, dipping them into the syrup also."

"Well I'm surprised you had time to discuss what you had intended talking about."

"Oh ya we talked for hours and even had some new ideas to consider." Oh no, Bill thought I'm talking too much and Barb's natural curiosity will take over and she won't let me alone!

"Well I got to go, see you when I get home and we can talk more."

"Ok dear see ya."

"Bye hon" said Barb as they both hung up.

Bill, not looking forward to dancing around his discussions with Dave when Barb gets home today, knowing her inquires about any progress he and Dave had made would certainly be forthcoming, maybe he could change the subject, after all he did have sort of a commitment for this evening from Barb and he was sure he could manipulate the conversation in that direction and both would benefit, he had a plan.

Bill was lying on the couch when Barb arrived home from work, thinking about Dave's idea seriously and Barb could see the stress on Bill's face as she said;

"Hi babe, you look beat today, are you alright?"

"Ya I'm fine, just running some things through my mind."

"Something Dave had to say bothering you?" she asked.

"No, no just trying to figure out how long this may continue and why it's only affected our small group of friends, that has to be the key to figuring it out and reversing the phenomena we are now experiencing. Enough about that though, you didn't overtire yourself at work did you?" Barb sighing a bit, but suddenly realizing what Bill was referring to said.

"Oh no dear, I save my energy for these evenings don't worry about that."

"Honey, I never worry about you having enough energy to get through a night of love making, I was just reminding you."

Well after a modest dinner and a relaxing evening in front of the TV, Barb could detect Bill's preoccupation with something and suspecting it had to do with Dave's visit earlier today Barb asked "Hon, how about if I make us a drink?"

"Yes that sounds good to me, make it scotch rocks hon."

"You got it."

"No I didn't I'm still waiting!" as Barb walked away rolling her eyes and thinking at least he still retains his sense of humor and saying;

"Ha-ha, that's funny I'll be right back."

As Barb returned, now wearing only her panties and bra and carrying two drinks and an unopened bag of, you guessed it, jelly beans, Bill took his drink, smiled as he looked at the jelly beans and returned to watching TV.

Barb snuggled up even closer than before thinking the evening was still young as Bill seemed to settle back into his preoccupation with the day's events, Barb was sure it had to do with Dave's visit and was tempted to call Dave to inquire about their discussions, but she decided not to, at least for now.

The evening continued at about the same pace while Bill, still preoccupied and a bit distant from Barb obviously had other interest tonight than what was previously planned by both of them, sex! Barb realized she could put the jelly beans away when she asked Bill late in the evening to go to bed and he replied, "You go ahead hon, I'll be there in a little while." That was one of only a few times since they were married, that he responded that way to her invitation to go to bed, she knew the night was lost and went to bed.

Bill continued to ponder the day's events and lost track of the time as he had made yet another drink trying to look at Dave's stay awake all night theory, thinking that if indeed the person staying awake would not experience time travel that night, why not have the entire group stay up all night and break the cycle, possibly even reverse it, Bill had to bounce his theory off Dave and get his thoughts, it certainly would reduce the danger of losing one person from the group Bill thought.

It was getting late he'd call Dave in the morning, for right now he'd have to get to bed and to sleep before he accidently stayed up all night and became lost in time from the others in the group for good. As he entered the bedroom he noticed Barb had fallen fast asleep and he was quick to join her as he could not take a chance on losing her in a different time zone or whatever would separate them according to Dave's theory, soon Bill was fast asleep also.

CHAPTER FIFTEEN
A DESPERATE CALL TO DAVE 11 4 2011 REAL TIME

Waking up the next morning, Bill found he was alone in bed, and immediately resorted to panic, thinking he had lost Barb in time, because he had stayed up to late and Barb was already traveling thru time when he went to bed. He called out;

"Barb, Barb!" he yelled, but no response, she was gone for sure, but where and how, was it something he'd done, he'd call her office, as he dialed the number he became even more inpatient;

"Hello" Bill interrupted saying, "Ruth is Barb there?"

"No she" Ruth was unable to finish though as Bill hearing no, hung up in haste, though Ruth had more to say.

Bill, thinking the worst decided to call Dave, realizing that if anyone could help he could and so he dialed his number Dave picked up almost immediately.

"Hi Bill" Bill cut him off quickly to saying;

"Dave, Barb's gone, maybe forever I don't know!"

"What are you talking about Bill did you have a fight or something?"

"Of course not, we never fight, she went to bed earlier than I did last night and when I went to bed she was already sleeping, do you think she was already traveling thru time and left me behind?"

"Whoa!" said Dave, "that's a whole lot of supposition; let's think about this for a moment logic dictates that if my theory is correct and she was already traveling when you went to bed she would have disappeared last night right before your eyes and that didn't happen she was there when you went to sleep, is that right?"

"Ya that's right Dave, but what do you think could have happened?" Bill, while waiting for an answer from Dave, herd his phone ring, noticing it was Barb's cell he answered quickly, while Dave was still on the other phone.

"Hon, my God is that you, are you alright?"

"Of course I'm ok; Ruth said you called in a panic!"

"I did and she said you weren't there!"

"What were you panicked about hon?"

"Because when I woke up you weren't here, you left no note or any indication where you might be, that coupled with the fact that I had some complex ideas as to what might have happened to you, hang on a second I have Dave on the other phone."

"Dave it's me again as you probably heard Barb's on the other phone and everything is alright, I call you later."

"Ok bye Bill."

"I'm back hon, well I'm relieved to hear you're ok and I'll see you when you get home and explain my concern this morning ok?"

"Ok babe, I'm glad you're ok too, you had a bad night last night and were sleeping so soundly this morning that I didn't want to disturb you, thinking you could use your sleep, there was nothing pressing going on this morning, so I just didn't bother you, though I probably should have left a note. You know its Friday maybe well go out for dinner tonight, what do you think?"

"That sounds good, got any suggestions on where?"

Barb thought a moment and said "Ya, why not just go to the lounge they serve great food right at the bar and Lenny's always entertaining."

"Sounds like a plan hon though I'm not sure Lenny will be there, I do like that hand packed burger they serve on a hard roll its great and their steak fries are out of this world, Oops, I should be more careful what I say, it could come true!"

"Ok Bill I'll see you later, keep the home fires burning, if you get my drift, last night didn't go as well as planned."

"Ya I'm sorry about that I guess I was preoccupied, ok I'll see you later love you!"

"Bye hon I love you to." said Barb as they hung up, Bill's mind quickly went back to trying to analyze the situation after realizing that Barb was alright but still his theory about going to sleep at different times, in his mind still had some validity and should not be dismissed to quickly, of that he was sure.

If he could go to sleep several hours after Barb and not change the outcome of the time travel, why would Dave's theory of one of us staying up and not sleeping hold any water? He and Dave needed to have further discussions.

As Bill's mind wondered over the last few days or several years depending on how you look at it, his thoughts suddenly went back to the swimming pool and pool house, here today gone tomorrow, how did that happen? Was this his imagination, but no, Barb saw it also, again mass hypnosis, a mirage, what brought about this hallucination, was it planted in his and Barb's mind somehow? As he thought further he was sure the answer would be at the condo association office, Gloria would be able to help he thought, so he decided to walk over to the office and look her up.

Walking into the office he noticed a young girl sitting at the desk smiling at him and asking "Good afternoon sir may I help you?"

"Yes I'm looking for Gloria is she in today?"

"She is May I say whose calling?"

"You may indeed." Bill said jokingly, as the young girl looked at him inquisitively.

"Oh, I guess, I asked that wrong, didn't I?" said the girl.

"No dear, you did just fine; tell Gloria it's Bill Kelly." she went to the back room and told Gloria that Bill Kelly was out in the front office to see her and Gloria responded quickly and with obvious interest, even to the young girl. As she entered the office area with a smile and seductive stride saying;

"Oh, hi Bill what brings you to our humble little office, I hope you're not still having parking problems?"

"Hi Gloria, no I think we got past that problem, but I do have a question that I'm sure you can help me with."

"Anything I can do to help, I'm your girl!"

"Well that's good to here I was sure you could help solve my problem." (It was like they were both talking about something completely different)

"Well what's your question Bill?"

"I was wondering if there were any plans to build a swimming pool or any discussions about the subject at the condo association meetings."

"Yes as a matter of fact it has been discussed at length, in fact there's an artist rendering hanging on the wall over there." as she pointed out the painting to Bill.

"Oh" said Bill as he walked over to the wall, unexpectedly accompanied by Gloria who was more than willing to discuss the pool the rest of the afternoon if Bill had wanted to. As Bill looked over the picture realizing it was exactly as the completed project that he and Barb had seen, but not understanding how that could be as he had never seen this picture before and asking Gloria, "Tell me Gloria is this rendering hanging anywhere else in the complex or just here?"

"No this is the only place it is displayed, tell me something, I know you're an engineer and you're showing a lot of interest in this project, is there something we should be concerned about?"

"Not at all it's a beautiful pool and I'm sure all of the condo owners will enjoy it immensely, but you've never sent out flyers or anything else to the association members as a reminder that the pool was in the planning?"

"No nothing like that, but you obviously knew about it Bill, tell me how did you find out about the project?"

"If I told you Gloria, you wouldn't believe me, I'm not sure I believe it myself!"

"My goodness now you've stirred my curiosity by introducing an element of mystery into the conversation, I love it!" talking to Gloria he noticed she didn't wear a wedding ring he thought her to be in her mid-twenties and a stunning looking woman with auburn hair a perfect match for Dave who he felt had been alone long enough, so now how to find out about her personal interest, the hell with it he thought I'll just ask.

"Tell me Gloria do you mind if I get just a bit personal for a moment and ask a question?"

"Ahhhh no go right ahead, but if I don't answer, it may be a little too personal."

"I won't get that personal I promise, but I was just wondering if you were seeing anyone." Gloria obviously a little taken aback and getting the totally wrong idea from Bill's question smiled and said;

"Well no Bill I'm not seeing anyone special, just casual dating, why do you ask?" Bill realized immediately that perhaps he had asked the question the wrong way and now had to quickly repair the damage before it gets out of hand!

"Well I can tell you this if I wasn't married I'd be asking for myself, but I am married, so I'm asking for a friend of mine, he's a scientist and a very young widower, but a great guy and I thought I might give him a little push in the right direction as he's been a bit sheepish when it comes to the ladies and you're the first girl I've met that I thought he would be interested in so I thought I'd ask." there I got thru that ok he thought now to see if there was any interest generated, hopefully she would show some interest, we'll see.

"I see well Bill I'm honored that you considered me for your friend and yes, I'd love to meet him why don't you give him my number and ask him to call me by the way what's his name?"

"That's great Gloria his name is Dave and I'm sure he'll enjoy meeting you and you him I might add."

"Well I'm going to head back, I have a bunch of work to do before Barb gets home from work and thanks for the help Gloria."

"Bye Bill" she said perhaps with a bit of disappointment in her voice as she liked Bill, maybe a little too much though.

Back at home Bill was working feverishly on his computer when he realized he had a pretty sizeable client base and didn't know how it was developed, he must have done the initial work as he was sure he had no employees when he first started the business so he must have gotten the clients on his own, but has no memory of it, how can that be he thought once again drifting into his problem solving mode, he was determined to resolve this problem and get back to a normal life.

As Barb put her key in the door she too was thinking about recent developments and how everyone's lives have been turned upside down and what it would take to fix it. "Hi hon, I'm home and ready for anything." she added laughingly.

"Hi back I took some steaks out for the grill is that what you meant?" knowing better, although the steaks would hit the spot he thought.

"No that's not what I meant, but we need to eat also."

"What did you do all day after figuring out I was still alive and well?"

"Ya know that's not at all funny, I was really worried, along with Dave and my discussions yesterday and the fact that I stayed up late and waking up finding you gone, I lost my rational for the moment and my state of mind was simply not prepared to handle Ruth saying you weren't there and my response hanging up before hearing the rest of what she had to say, wasn't like me at all I guess, I'm feeling the pressure of the moment."

"Why don't I make us a drink, while you start the grill hon?" Barb said as she headed toward the kitchen to prepare the drinks and yelling back at Bill "Do you want a baked potato with your steak?"

"Sounds good, do we have sour cream?"

"I believe so" said Barb.

"I premade the salads, there in the fridge hon" Bill said, as he lite the grill on the patio realizing it was a perfect day as the 24th floor was often pretty windy, but today the air was calm and perfect for grilling.

While having their drinks and waiting on dinner, Bill told Barb about his conversation with Gloria about the swimming pool and Gloria's reaction to his questioning the pool that didn't even exist yet.

"What on earth made you think about that pool and why bring Gloria into our problems?"

"I don't know I was just sitting around trying to figure things out and the only real psychical changes we've experienced was the pool, you know here today gone tomorrow it made no sense to me so I went to the person I thought might help."

"You went to, you mean, you called Gloria!"

"No hon, I went to her office to speak with her and it's a good thing I did for two reasons, first she had an artist's rendering of what the pool looked like and it was exactly as we saw it and secondly I think I managed to fix Dave up with Gloria aren't you proud of me?"

"Well I guess that's better than fixing yourself up with Gloria, but what makes you think Dave wants to be fixed up with anyone?" Bill laughing at Barb's apparent jealously, she had nothing to worry about and she should know that, but never the less he would reassure her once again as she was probably expecting him to do so.

"Well hon, in the first place Gloria is not my type, you are, and secondly Dave's been alone long enough in my estimation, I don't believe he's mourning anymore, he's just not looking for any companionship because he's too busy, so I thought I'd help him through those times."

As Bill took the steaks off the grill and Barb took the potatoes out of the microwave along with an additional vegetable the wine was already on the table so they both sat down to enjoy their dinner.

After dinner they both went into the living room to watch a little TV and remembering they had not checked the date today, they turned on the news and were surprised to find out it was Wednesday

May 20, 2039, 28 years into the future and no psychical changes to anyone to speak of.

Bill was now of the opinion that quite possibly they were all back in 2011, maybe they had never left, though he could not explain what was going on with the dates in the news or on the computer, everything pointed to their mental state and he would continue to pursue that train of thought, until somehow he could be dissuaded, perhaps by Dave!

MAKING LITTLE PROGRESS

Things were becoming a bit redundant every morning you woke up several years into the future from when you went to sleep, but had no indication except the date on the TV news or on the computer and it was so predictable that it didn't bother anyone anymore and that revelation in itself was an annoyance at least to Bill, but never the less Bill seemed to be the only one to continue to be concerned with the possible exception of Dave, it seemed to be a problem without a solution.

There was little or no progress being made after who knows how long, but Bill was determined not to let go, he would work thru the problem until it was solved or know the reason why.

The apparent lack of concern on everyone's part could be explained because no one was adversely affected, their lives continued as if nothing had happened, with the single exception being Bill. His several recent promotions and job changes, including his move to self-employment, yet another puzzling development, were all a result of recent developments, at least that's the way he saw it and everyone else had no obvious changes to their lives, except possibly Lenny the bartender who for some unknown reason has disappeared and what's that all about Bill thought! Totally unexplained and still a significant part of the puzzle of that he was sure!

Dave may benefit from what's going on if he follows up with Gloria that certainly has promise for both of them; Dave is certainly ready for the dating scene, but only time will tell.

As for the rest of the group they remain in the Status Quo and totally losing interest in the whole mess believing the problem would eventually fix itself, it came on its own and would go away the same way they thought, but little did they know!

Bill was quickly growing fatigued, calling group meetings together to address everyone's concerns, only to find their concerns were dwindling, and they were becoming bored to the point of being ridicules! These people were traveling thru time against their will and they no longer seemed to care, that is all except Dave he remained totally engaged in the problem solving mode. Even George was treating it as a routine distraction from the norm and Bill was beginning to understand the reason for their complacency, their experience was isolated to them alone and other than a date on a calendar and a few subtle changes, their lives continued almost as normal, making it difficult to perceive any danger. What the Hell was going on with everyone thought Bill!

Bill and Dave though would continue to fight their complacency and solve the problem, if there was a solution, there must be a way of reversing what was happening and get back to their normal place in time and life he thought.

"Well hon I don't know about you, but I'm going to bed." said Barb, invitingly and Bill immediately picked up on the signal and agreed as he shut the TV off, they both headed for the bedroom and the promise of the things to come, both of them he hoped! This interaction having been planned for two days or maybe two years depending on how you looked at it, may not last long as the anticipation may be too much to overcome, we'll see he thought he'd do his best though!

CHAPTER SIXTEEN
A BREAK IN THE MORNING ROUTINE

11 5 2011 REAL TIME

Well a new morning was dawning after an interesting night fulfilling long awaited promises of pleasure, satisfaction guaranteed and fulfilled. Barb the first to stir from her slumber turning toward Bill noticing him still in a deep sleep and not wanting to disturb him just yet got up and went to the kitchen table and Bill's laptop, turning it on and waiting for it to boot up so she could check on the date.

Busy making the morning coffee she heard the chimes on the computer signaling the computer had finished booting up and was ready for the day's activities.

Barb immediately noticed the date on the screen was Thursday May 21, 2039 and they went to bed on Wednesday May 20, 2039 so it was a normal night, no time travel or any other phenomena popping up at least not yet. Barb thought this a good reason to wake Bill and tell him the good news, she wouldn't dare go to work again without waking him anyway, so she went to the bedroom and shook him gently at first and then more aggressively saying "Bill wake up, come on time to wake up and face the world, I have good news, get up!"

Bill stirred saying "Morning hon what's up?"

"Get up and I'll tell you!"

"It's too early can't you just tell me while I lay here and enjoy the moment?"

"Ok well I checked the computer this morning and it's May 21st 2039 and we went to bed on May 20th 2039, maybe it's over."

"Well that's good news alright, but it's not over by any means, if it were over we'd be back in 2011 not 2039, but not traveling last night is curious."

"Well I made the coffee, I have to be on my way shortly or I'll be late and I have an early patient this morning, Ruth is coming in late today too so I'll have to double up until she gets in at about 11:00a.m."

"Ok give me a kiss and be on your way my dear!" Barb did with a smile as she headed for the door asking on her way out;

"Hon what are you planning for dinner tonight?" Bill responded sarcastically!

"I plan on enjoying anything you prepare as always hon." She laughed shaking her head in the negative and saying;

"Good bye dear!"

Bill left once again to his own devices decided to make a few phone calls over breakfast, once he decided what he was going to have.

Opening the cabinet door containing the cereal and carefully scanning the two remaining choices (1) unopened box of Cheerios and (2) a half empty/full, depending on how you look at it, box of Cheerios, so of the two choices available Bill decided to have Cheerios, with a banana that was not in the fruit bowl, he prayed for milk, but was sure there would be sugar as Barb used it in her coffee which guaranteed its availability.

This caused Bill's thought processes to go into overdrive once again, realizing that Barb may not have been grocery shopping for as many as ten years and they needed to correct this oversight quickly, he'd talk to Barb when she got home tonight.

As Bill sat down to his bowl of Cheerios it caused him to consider whether or not the milk was still fresh it may have been in the refrigerator for many years now, just one more inconsistency in the time travel theory (if that much time had really passed the milk would be sour to say the least) and another topic for discussion with Dave, who would be his first phone call this morning after breakfast.

As Bill cleaned up the kitchen after breakfast he went over, in his mind, all the inconsistencies in the time travel theory and was slowly convincing himself that time travel was not really what was going on here, though originally he was the one in the group who came up with the theory and would lend any credence to it. The primary driver for the time travel theory was after all the computer and the dates observed each morning after waking up, though the swimming pool and pool house did put the frosting on the cake so to speak!

Well time to call Dave about a much more pleasant topic Bill thought as he dialed Dave's number "Hello Bill, I was just about to leave for work, what's up?"

"Hi Dave, I guess I'm luckier than you and others I walk out of the bedroom and I'm at work, but I didn't call to make you envious, quite the contrary, I called because I need your help (thinking that making it a favor to Bill would make it easier for Dave to agree) with something."

"Well you know me Bill I'm always ready to help a friend, what can I do for you?"

"If you're on your way out Dave we can talk later or even get together for coffee or something as it may take a little time to discuss the proposal I have in mind."

"Your choice Bill, but your probably right, though I have a few minutes now, it sounds like you need a little more time than that, is that the case?"

"Ya Dave I'd like to talk in a little more relaxed atmosphere and not under the pressure of the clock if you know what I mean, so later would be better I guess."

"That's fine Bill I guess I'll let you go for now than."

"Ok Dave, we'll talk soon, I also have some new ideas about our problem, bye for now though."

"Bye Bill" both hung up as Bill was deciding on his next call which he planned on making to Jerry.

Bill was having a hard time dealing with the fact that no one seemed as involved in the problem as he was and that included Barb, Dave was more involved than the rest, but still nowhere near as much as Bill, didn't they care he thought, this really bothered him!

Bill was right he was so totally involved that he was unknowingly letting other things slip a bit including his business. He was becoming distressed, not wanting to get up in the morning becoming less involved in his business and obsessed with solving the problem at hand, he would soon need professional help if he continued to let it wear on him as it did.

Bill dialed Jerry's cell phone assuming he would be working and he was right as Jerry answered the phone saying, "Hi pal what on earth are you calling about this early I hope no one has died!"

"No, no we haven't talked for a while so I thought I'd give you a call and see how you guys are doing and how you're getting through the current problem were all having right now."

"Well, you know Bill we're managing ok, other than the date changing every morning I really haven't noticed anything different."

"You know Jerry the date changes every morning for everyone so why does that bother you?" Bill said laughing loudly as Jerry joined in the levity laughing with him both understanding the joke.

"Ya know though I have noticed a few subtle changes at the Air Line freight terminals mainly with the security, those guys are nuts and should be replaced with a better managed company! Now when I pull in there you'd think I was pulling into Langley, sometimes delaying me and others 15-30 minutes and time is money in this business, its ridicules!" Jerry said, in utter frustration, not understanding that we were now living in a state of total paranoia, with no hope in sight.

"Well hang in there buddy things will get better, but I don't want to keep you on the phone while you're driving so I'll say bye for now and we'll get together soon ok?"

"Ya we will for sure Bill thanks for the call and bye for now." After hanging up Bill decided to call George and then Larry as he wanted to keep in touch with everyone and keep updated so no pertinent information, no matter how insignificant it may seem, would fall through the cracks hindering the ultimate solution to the problem.

As Bill was getting ready to call George his phone rang and it was George's office number, Bill answered "Hello George I was just going to call you we must have some kind of psychic connection working here."

"Well, we may have a psychic connection Mr. Kelly, but its Brenda, Mr. Robert's asked me to call."

"Well Brenda! I can assure you as much as I like my best friend George, I melt every time I hear your lovely voice, where did you get it?"

"I guess I was just born with it, but I'm glad it pleases you Mr. Kelly."

"One thing Brenda, call me Bill my father was Mr. Kelly and he passed away six years ago."

"Ok Bill, I am sorry about your father, but proper office etiquette dictates I use last names and that's what Mr. Robert's wants."

"Don't worry about George I'll let him know I insisted, at least in my case you call me Bill, it'll be fine."

"Ok Bill, I'll transfer you to Mr. Robert's." as she buzzed the bosses phone;

"I have Mr. Kelly on line two Mr. Roberts."

"Thanks Brenda, Hi Bill, I thought you might be available for lunch today, to be honest I think I can interest you in a slightly more commercial copier for your in house office, I have a great machine in mind and over time it'll save you money I just happen to have one in my car!"

"Lunch sounds good George, sounds like we'll have a lot to talk about, but tell me one thing if you will what date did you wake up to this morning?"

"You know I didn't even check the date until I got to the office this morning, but as I recall it was only one day later then yesterday"

"I see, by the way I told your secretary Brenda she should call me by my first name, I'm a friend not a client and I insisted though I found her a little reluctant."

"Well if you buy this copier you become a client, but that's fine I'll tell her its ok."

"Good where for lunch?"

"How about the Poseidon's that Greek place just down the street from my office its good!" suggested George, Bill agreed and they decided to meet at 11:30am deciding to continue their conversation at lunch.

Well one more call to make, but for now Bill decided to relax for a bit and get ready for lunch and call Larry later this afternoon.

CHAPTER SEVENTEEN
A MYSTERIOUS PHONE CALL

As if the caller knew Bill's state of mind and decided to call to save the moment, Bill's phone rang, only to find no one home (Bill was out to lunch with George) at the time. The caller decided not to leave a message, they would try again later, or not the caller ID indicated the number was blocked so the caller wanted to remain anonymous. Certainly in Bill's current state of mind this will weigh heavily on his curiosity and drive him nuts so to speak.

When Bill returned home from lunch with George and with the new copying machine brochures in hand the first thing he noticed was the message light flashing on his phone, he hit the button to retrieve the message, but to his surprise there was no message and the caller ID showed the caller's number was blocked, this concerned Bill as he never had that happen before, now he was too upset to call Larry as planned. He threw the brochures on the new copier he had just bought on the kitchen table, sat down and wondered who the mysterious caller was?

A CALL FROM LENNY

He punched up games on his computer to help him relax a while, though that may not be the best way to relax especially if you're losing the game, but Bill continued to play when the phone rang again!

"Hello" said Bill.

"Hello I'd like to speak with Mr. Kelly" said the caller, Bill recognizing Lenny's distinctive voice said.

"Lenny is that you?"

"Ya it is Bill, I understand you've been trying to reach me, I've been away for a time, but I'm back now Bill and my relief bartender said you were in several times asking for me, so I thought I'd call and see what's on your mind and how I can help, after all you're a good customer and we want to keep you guys happy!"

"Well Len I appreciate that, but to be honest, I was looking for you for an entirely different reason, kind of personal I guess and totally unrelated to business and I'm sure you can help." after a lengthy pause Lenny responded saying;

"Ya Bill, I thought it might be something like that and possibly, I'm not sure, but possibly I may be able to help, we should probably plan on getting together and talking about it."

"I agree Len, when would be a good time for us to meet and where?"

"Listen Bill, I work tomorrow at noon and I don't usually get any bar customers until about 2:00pm so that may be the perfect time to get together and talk uninterrupted how does that sound?"

"Sounds good Len I'll take the opportunity to get my mouth around one of those great burgers you guys serve while we talk, so I'll see you tomorrow at noon."

"I'll be looking forward to it Bill, but for now I have to go."

"Ok Len in that case I'll say goodbye for now too."

"Bye Bill" as they both hung up, Bill returned to his state of deep thought, now further inspired by Lenny's unexpected phone call and concern that Bill had been looking for him and what he could do to help Bill, though Bill had not until now indicated that he might need help.

Well, the afternoon went on with little or no more distractions as Bill continued to analyze everything and now adding Lenny's return and his interest in Bill's problems to the calculus, but a long and hopefully productive conversation with Lenny will go a long way toward a solution to the distress the group has been experiencing, though the truth be known the only one really feeling stressed was Bill, but it would be nice to get everyone's life back to normal thought Bill.

Well Bill thought, I'd better call Barb and see if she wants to go shopping for groceries after work so we can get some food in the house, this after his enlightenment this morning looking for some choices in his breakfast cereal and finding few to one which was unacceptable.

Dialing Barb's office and counting to ten while the phone rang so he didn't sound angry or upset as a voice he didn't expect to hear said "Triple A dental Barb speaking how may I help you?"

"Well you can help me by joining me at the grocery store after work as we seem to be short a few items!"

"Bill, honey, what's going on you hate grocery shopping, I wish I had a recording of this so I could play it back to make sure I heard you right!"

"Well I had a little difficulty this morning with breakfast, it seems I had only two choices and they were both cheerios! So you know me I want to get past this problem and move on to the next, I do believe we are exhausting our food supply though moving through time as we are losing track of details like shopping and paying bills etc."

"I see" replied Barb with some concern in her voice agreeing to do the shopping without Bill's help; sure he would rather be doing anything but grocery shopping.

"I'll stop on the way home and pick up the groceries and maybe one of those rotisserie chickens you like for dinner, ok?"

"I like the way you think hon and get an assortment of cereal, we have none!"

"I will, but I'll be late getting home, so dinner will be late."

"No problem, love you, good bye."

"Bye hon" said Barb as she hung up wondering why the cereal had become such an issue today when Bill had so many other things to be concerned about.

In the meantime Bill decided to call Larry to check in on their wellbeing as they didn't talk on a regular basis or as much as the others in the group, though they are good friends, Larry and Karen were not as close to the group as they once were, he dialed the number, but it went to voicemail so Bill left a message to call.

Bill's thoughts went back to his meeting with Lenny tomorrow and how that would go. In the interim while waiting for Larry to call, Bill got on the computer and into his business files and his bank accounts noting a good deal of money was now missing from the accounts, one day it's there and the next it's gone and all without

Bill's knowledge of how it happened, this concerned Bill greatly it was as if the business was on autopilot and overseen by someone else, he was showing signs of stress once again, but determination also, the question becomes which will win out?

Bill decided on a nap later that afternoon and laid down on the couch immediately falling asleep and the next thing he knew he was being wakened by Barb, who with a smile asked if he was interested in eating as it was getting late and the dinner was on the table.

Bill waking up said "Hi hon, I must have dosed off, what time is it?"

"7:00pm dear I hauled all the groceries up and got the chicken we talked about and it's on the table, I did good don't you think?"

"I do, but you should have buzzed me and I would have come down and helped you with the groceries." As Bill went to the bathroom to throw some water in his face to wake up, while Barb went back to the kitchen to finish preparing the salads for dinner.

As Bill walked into the kitchen he said "Hon guess who called today, totally unexpectedly and out of nowhere."

"I don't know!" Barb said.

"Lenny, you know, from the bar."

"Who?' said Barb, appearing somewhat startled by the revelation, why on earth would he call?"

"To tell you the truth I'm not exactly sure, he said he heard I had been looking for him when he was gone and was curious about the reasons for that anyway were going to meet tomorrow at the restaurant and discuss it further."

"Discuss what further?" asked Barb, who was now curious about the whole thing with Lenny calling and then planning a meeting to discuss what, she thought, she needed to pump Bill further to find out what was going on in his head.

"I'm not entirely sure, but he definitely had something on his mind and I detected it may be serious so I agreed to meet him besides you know how I like there burgers and fries."

"I know, but for right now enjoy your chicken and salad, it's the best I can do tonight." As they both started to eat a sudden silence fell over the table almost as if their minds had drifted into different worlds far apart from each other.

After a long and silent dinner both retired to the living room and the TV to catch up on the day's news and their favorite shows before retiring for the night, neither looking forward to anything other than a good night's sleep.

Tomorrow with Lenny's input hopefully, Bill will gain more insight into the problem and bring everyone closer to the ultimate solution and an end to the confusion and disruption to our lives.

Later, both went to bed kissed and saying their goodnights, rolled over and fell fast asleep.

NOVEMBER 8, 2011 REAL TIME

The new day dawned, much too soon, as they both woke up to greet the rising sun over the lake and start the new day, Bill with much exuberance, expecting a great deal out of his meeting with Lenny, Barb with her effervescent and sparkling smile, but for some unknown reason a bit apprehensive about the meeting, both bounding out of bed, Barb headed for the shower and Bill for the kitchen to put the coffee on and check out the cereal supply after his disappointment yesterday.

As Barb, freshly showered, appeared suddenly wearing only her seductive smile taking Bill's breath away and asking "Is the coffee done yet hon?" as Bill answered while trying to recover from Barb's appearance saying;

"Ya, it's done are you in a hurry this morning?" Barb instantly understood what he was really asking and teasingly said;

"No I just thought I'd stop at the store and pick up a few things so we didn't run low on anything, I think I'm going to pick up a few things every day it's easier than trying to carry up a big order every time I shop." She really knew how to handle Bill.

Bill got up and went toward the bedroom disappointed and scratching his head saying;

"Hon, would you turn the computer on so we can check the date?" Barb opened the laptop, hit the on button and walked away to the bedroom to get dressed.

"Barb I was in the business accounts yesterday and found a good deal of the money missing and I don't remember moving any money around did you?"

"No, but could it be the payroll, you should call the payroll company and of course you're always getting an invoice from the printer's for training materials, it's probably legitimate expenses."

"I'll look into it further." he said as Barb was ready to leave for work and he was ready for an early breakfast looking forward to lunch at La Flambé with Lenny.

On her way out the door, after saying goodbye she asked Bill to call her after his lunch with Lenny and let her know how it went, he assured her he would as she left.

Bill decided on a lite breakfast of toast and juice, saving his appetite for lunch, but wait he hadn't checked the date yet as he looked at the computer while waiting for the toast to pop up. Friday August 23, 2039 only a few months had passed overnight, the radical jumps ahead seemed to have slowed, but moving ahead in time none the less.

After eating he got back into his banking on the computer and called his payroll company and was told there was a dispersal for payroll of $11,758.56 two days ago and then he called his accountant to find out if any invoices had been paid and they were to the tune of $6,251.00 so that accounted for the missing funds, but wait he didn't even know he had an accountant, but Barb seemed to know, he was confused once again, but at least the money was accounted for.

After resolving the financial issues in the business Bill realized he had never heard back from Larry yesterday or yet today and thinking that odd he decided to place the call again and dialed Larry's number, once again the call went to voicemail and this concerned Bill who left a more urgent message to get their attention.

Bill headed to the shower to start getting ready for his trip to the restaurant and his meeting with Lenny, anxious to probe Lenny for the information Bill was sure Lenny could provide even if he (Lenny) didn't know it.

An hour later, Bill ready to leave and still no call from Larry, well he thought he'd have to pursue it later realizing he had been calling their home number and probably should try the cell phone, but that's for later, as Bill left his unit and walked slowly down the hall to the elevator checking his watch realizing he was early it was only 10:30am and he was only ten minutes away from the restaurant, but he did need gas and maybe a car wash while he was at it he'd play it by ear. He was obviously anxious to get there, possibly expecting more than he would get out of the meeting, but at least he knew he would get the burger and that brought a smile to his face.

CHAPTER EIGHTEEN
LUNCH AT LA FLAMBÉ

Arriving at the restaurant about 11:20am and using the valet Bill walked in noting the restaurant area with only a few tables occupied and greeted by the Hostess, but indicating to her he was going to the Lounge noticing Lenny working behind the bar as he walked into the lounge area, no one else was there.

As he approached the bar Len said "Hi Bill your right on time notice the privacy we have right now?"

"Hi Len you were right, but it's your place of business I had no doubt you'd be right about the bar trade, I do hope the waitresses are working though."

Len smiled signaling one of the girls standing at the other end of the lounge to come over and she did. "Hi Chris this gentleman would like to order something from the Kitchen."

"Certainly, hi I'm Chris what can I get for you today sir?"

"First of all let's start off on the right foot I'm Bill, not sir and I'll have one of those burgers medium rare on the hard roll with mozzarella cheese and a dill pickle steak fries, catsup and mustard"

"Well you certainly know what you want, by the way Bill, we call that our Sub burger and it comes two ways a half pound or three quarter pound version which would you prefer?"

"Let's go all out shall we and make it the ¾ pounder and please make sure it's med rare that's a must!"

She smiled saying "You got it" as she walked away toward the kitchen and Bill turned toward Lenny who asked "And what are you drinking Bill?"

"Gin Ricky I think Len."

"As the lady said, you got it."

Shortly Len put Bill's drink on the bar asking "How do we start this discussion Bill obviously we've both got things to say, the problem is I really don't know what's going on."

"Well Len to date no one outside our group has been let in on, what we refer to as the problem, so you'll be the first. It seems we are all, we meaning our group, are on an nightly basis moving ahead through time (time travel if you will) and every morning we wake up 1,5,10 years or more further into the future than when we went to bed."

"**What!** Time travel, what happens you wake up ahead in time and then you, I don't know bounce back?"

"No, no you don't understand we don't bounce back we remain ahead in time, like right now it's Friday August 23, 2039"

"**What**! Yelled Lenny, are you telling me that you believe you're in the year 2039 right now as we speak, am I understanding that right?"

"Yes that's exactly what I'm telling you Len why do you find that so hard to believe?"

"Well I find it hard to believe because you and I are standing here looking at each other and talking and I know it's Tuesday November 8, 2011 and if you're in the year 2039 that would be impossible!"

"Your absolutely right Len that would be impossible, but what you fail to understand is you are in the future with me, you're in the year 2039 also!" Lenny hearing this thought about it for a long time wondering for a moment what Bill was on at first, but then realized he wasn't on anything he really believed what he was saying, this all may be related to what he had to tell Bill, or not, he now had no idea at all. Wait he had an idea as Chris came to the bar with Bill's food.

"Here you go Bill is there anything else I can get for you?"

"Med rare?" Bill said questioningly with a smile.

"You bet I checked it myself enjoy!" said Chris in a flirting departure as Bill anxiously prepared his feast with the condiments provided. Len picked up the check Chris had set on the bar and went to the register and rang up Bill's tab, while Bill looked on a bit curious and upset at the same time feeling he was being given the bums rush so to speak, which Lenny detected and explained, no Bill I'm not cashing you out I just want to show you something as he walked back to where Bill was sitting with the register receipt in his hand.

As Bill prepared to take the first bite of the sandwich he had been looking forward to for two days now Lenny said;

"Bill let me see if I understand this right, you're saying that you and I are in the same place in time and the year is 2039 is that correct?"

Bill nodding his head in the affirmative and saying "Ya that's right Len 2039."

"Well how do you explain this than?" as he handed Bill the register receipt just printed and dated Tuesday November 8, 2011, as Bill looked at the receipt, putting his sandwich down and pausing a moment, but finally saying;

"Len I don't really appreciate the humor my friends and I are having great difficulty with this problem, that's why I came here today, thinking you may have been able to help, but I see you just want to play games!" reaching for his wallet to pay the bill, totally disappointed with Lenny and thinking he may never come back here again!

Lenny said "No-no Bill I'm not joking with you, I would never do that I'm trying to help you guys out with what I know, and what I know for sure is I'm not traveling thru time and now I don't believe you are either!"

"How do I know you didn't set the date on the register to convince me?"

"I don't have the code to do that, but I have an idea." reaching into his wallet he handed Bill a twenty dollar bill and said;

"Take this and go to any store anywhere and buy something and bring the receipt back because if you do that I'm sure we will have a great deal more to discuss."

Bill looked at Lenny turned and started to walk out, but stopped short, turned back toward the bar and said;

"Wait I stopped for gas and a car wash on the way here." as he searched his pockets for the receipts finding them in his shirt pocket and looked at them for a long time before raising his head to look at Len with a puzzled look on his face and reaching out to hand Lenny the receipts, Len looked at both pieces of paper noting they both showed todays date November 8, 2011 Bill was overwhelmed, Lenny smiled and said;

"You better eat that sandwich before it gets cold Bill." Bill sat back down, friends again, but totally confused, he was glad, he really liked Lenny and was now sure he was trying to help, but could he?

Bill sat there eating his lunch trying to rationalize what he had learned so far, Len was right they were both in the same place at the same time and Len proved that was November 8, 2011 so why did bill's computer tell him it was 2039? It was now obvious he hadn't moved ahead in time his computer had, but there were other unexplained circumstances to contend with and things were starting to come together now.

"Tell me Len let's go back to the night of the party, I felt you had more to say about that evening, but were hesitant for some reason to do so, am I right?"

"Well to tell you the truth Bill, I'm not really sure if it's important or not, but the man asking me to make the special drinks for your party, was one of the party, however the gentleman who put a stop to it was not known to me, I never saw him before, but I could tell he had some power over the other man ordering the drinks. I know this because he and I met again a few days later, he's the reason I disappeared for a few days and he paid handsomely for me to do so, but it wasn't until recently that I put two and two together and made the connection between your party and him asking me to get lost for a while, I only made the connection because I ran into another of your friends and as a result I figured out what was going on, but not why!"

"Wow, that's quite a story Len, I don't quite know what to make of it, except to ask what it was you figured out, as for myself I've been unable to figure anything out for sure, I have some ideas, but nothing definite. Help me out pal what do you know that I don't?"

"Bill, what I can tell you for sure, is that apparently, you all think you're traveling in time and someone has gone through a lot of trouble and expense to make you believe that, but the fact is you are not in a time machine or moving through time, but the reason for this is a well-kept secret and I have no ideas about that."

As Bill finished his lunch, he shook his head in awe and disbelief, not knowing whether to totally believe Len or not, he was convinced that Lenny was sincere in what he was saying, but could it all be true and if it was what was the motivation and who was behind it?

"Len, which member of the group initially asked you to prepare the drinks?"

"Let me see I don't know his name for sure, so that leaves out George who I know well, but there was something about the guy, I just can't put my figure on it!"

"Could you point him out if you saw him again Len?"

"Absolutely I didn't forget what he looked like, but I'm sure I'll think of his name, it just escapes me right now, he's been in here often." Well that's a clue Bill thought as he pondered who it could possibly be and why.

"Len what exactly was special about the drinks he was ordering, you keep referring to them as special and I'm wondering what they could have to do with anything?"

"The only thing I remember that could have been considered special was he insisted on the drinks being blue, which left only a couple of choices and when he was trying to decide is when the other gentleman came over and put the kibosh on everything with only a gesture of his hand."

As Bill sat there the bar trade started to come in and Lenny started to get busy so Bill decided to finish his drink, pay the check and be on his way, he put a twenty on the bar and called Len over to clear his bill and leave a tip for Chris and put a hundred dollar bill on the bar for Lenny in appreciation for his help, but as Len walked up to where Bill was sitting he pushed the money back at Bill saying he was glad he could help and took the food check saying;

"This is on the house today." Bill, grateful pushed the hundred back smiled and said;

"Thanks for the lunch, but really this is for you I can't tell you how helpful you've been and how much it's appreciated!"

Len reluctantly accepted the hundred saying;

"Thanks Bill and I'll take care of Chris out of this."

As Bill turned to walk away he waved and said;

"I'll keep you informed as to what's going on pal and thanks' again I'll be forever grateful"

Lenny waved back as Bill left, not realizing how helpful he had been, but wishing he could have been more informative.

CHAPTER NINETEEN
CONFRONTING THE GROUP

All the way home Bill considered the enormous amount of information Lenny had given him and totally contrary to what he believed to this point, but now, Bill was being told that they were not traveling through time, who was trying to convince the group they were, more importantly why, what was their motivation and why was one of the party ordering blue drinks and who was the stranger, not part of the group who put a stop the blue drinks, the mystery was not unfolding it was evolving and becoming more complex to say the least.

Bill needed to talk to everyone once again, but first needed to dwell on this for a while and sort it out in his own mind. Should he talk to them as a group or one at a time? All these questions needed to be answered before he could talk to anyone; he had a lot to do before he was ready to proceed.

Arriving home, he immediately went to his computer to check the date and sure enough it was Friday August 23, 2039 not November 8, 2011 as he was now sure was the real date, or was it?

No he wouldn't allow himself to become confused again, but wait he needed to call Barb as he dialed her office really wanting to talk to Ruth hoping she would be the one to answer the phone and she was

"Hello triple 'A' dental may I help you?

"Yes you certainly can Ruth!"

"Bill is that you, hang on I'll get Barb for you."

"No! I want to talk to you, not Barb, just answer one question for me, what's today's date on your computer?" as Ruth continued to talk to Bill she motioned for Barb shrugging her shoulder's indicating she didn't understand what was going on as Barb took the phone saying;

"Hi hon what did you want?"

"Nothing really I was just wondering what date was on Ruth's computer?"

"You already know the date it's on your computer we checked this morning."

"I know Barb, but I didn't know the date on Ruth's computer and I would like to, humor me!"

"Ok its Friday August 23, 2039."

"Are you sure?"

"Of course I'm sure I'm looking at it as we speak why, by the way, how was your lunch with Lenny?"

"Very informative to say the least, but that's for discussion at home later dear, consider this for now we know were traveling thru time, but Ruth is not so why would her computer show the date as we believe it to be and not the date in real time that Ruth is in?"

"Well I, I guess I just don't know hon! I can't explain it, can you?" as a panicked look came over her, though Bill could not see it, he could detect it in her voice.

"Well don't concern yourself right now Barb we'll talk more when you get home bye for now, love you," as he hung up not waiting for her to say goodbye.

Barb, concerned about her husband and unbeknownst to him placed another call after Bill hung up, but who to, is unknown at this time.

Bill thought he would make one more carefully chosen phone call to confirm the date on his computer, but this time he had to be even more cautious as he dialed George's office number, "Sales Brenda speaking may I help you?"

"Hi Brenda its Bill Kelly, but don't buzz George it's you I want to speak with."

"Ohhhh ok Bill what can I do for you?"

"Well first of all have you been cautioned about talking to me about anything at all because what I want is really quite simple?"

"Ahhhh no Bill my conversations with you have not been censored so to speak, except to say I could go ahead and call you Bill, but that's a strange question, why do you ask?"

"Well suffice it to say that within our close group of friends something strange has been going on lately and I'm in the middle of trying to figure it out. So here's the question I talked about, look carefully at your computer and tell me today's date?"

"That's an easy one its November 8, 2011 is that it and why all the mystery surrounding that question?"

"That's difficult to explain right now, but in time I'll let you know, tell me is George in his office now?"

"No he's gone for the day, but I'm sure you can get him on his cell did you want me to put you thru?"

"No-no I don't want to talk to him I just wanted to know if he was in and if not I'd like you to check the date on his computer also, could you do that?"

"Sure but our computers are networked, the date will be the same on all our machines, I'll check though." she said as she walked into her bosses office and sat down at his computer to check the date and as she thought it was the same as her machine 11/8/2011.

"Bill it's me again and as I told you the date is the same as mine 11/8/2011."

"Thanks sweetie, you've been more help than you'll ever know, I'll be eternally grateful and someday I'll explain that, one last request don't tell George we talked, if he asks don't lie, but I'm sure he won't ask."

"Ok Bill I'm glad I could be of service, but I'm sure your computer could have given you the same info."

Bill laughing said "If you only knew, but for now I'll thank you once again and say goodbye, thanks Brenda!"

"My pleasure Bill goodbye." as she hung up totally confused, but grateful for the bit of mystery Bill had brought on what was otherwise turning into a boring afternoon.

Bill deciding to make a few notes along the way to the ultimate solution to the problem at hand, not realizing he was further from the truth then he had ever been before.

Bill wondered how George and the others, himself included, could be made to believe they were traveling thru time with so many contradictions right before them, but initially it was after all Bill's idea!

Suddenly Larry and Karen popped back into bill's mind and he realized again that Larry had still not returned his calls, this concerned him and Larry would now be the next call on his agenda, so he guessed he would talk to everyone in the group on an individual basis and that seemed to be the way it was going and would prove to be more beneficial in the end.

Dialing Larry's number, Bill's mind remained cluttered and confused with all the contradictory details, starting with his meeting with Lenny and followed up by the conversations with Ruth, Brenda and Barb, "Hello Bill is that you?"

"Ya Larry, man it's been hard getting hold of you, I thought there might be something wrong considering all that's been going on, but it sounds like you're ok, is that right?"

"Were good Bill we've been out of touch for a couple of days a little get away at one of those escape weekends, you know?"

"Ahhhh yes, been there and done that, those are great, where did you guys go?"

"We went to a little Hacienda up in Wisconsin good food, theme rooms if you know what I mean and the weather was great to boot."

"Sounds like you came home to rest up, but listen the reason I called initially was to ask how you've been tracking the date that our nightly travels have taken us to?"

"Well to be truthful Bill at first on the computer, but we've kind of taken a back seat as so many of you were following it so closely and regardless of what the date was it didn't seem to affect our daily life, so we just decided to put it out of our minds and let you guys figure it out!"

"Well that's certainly honest and to the point Larry, did you want us to let you know when we figure it out, or not?" Bill said as sarcastically as he could, upset by Larry's obvious lack of concern and contemptuous attitude!

"Ha Bill we don't mean to be dismissive, but it's hard to show concern when there is no apparent impact on our lives, I mean none at all so please don't get upset, if there is anything I can do to further your investigation I'd be more than happy to help, just ask ok?"

"Ya sorry Larry, we'll call if needed and we should get together soon ok?"

"Sounds good Bill Bye for now, see you soon ok." Larry said as he ended the call.

"Ok bye Larry" Bill said hanging up a bit upset with himself for losing his temper, but with his possibly being overly concerned, it was difficult, to understand Larry's lack of concern! Well the next call should probably go to Dave who along with Bill has been close to the problem and has had more suggestions to solving it than anyone else, but thought Bill, I still need to exhibit some caution when talking with Dave as he didn't want to lay all of his cards on the table just yet either.

Before calling Dave though Bill decided to look around the freezer to see what he could start for dinner to help Barb out and finding a package of ground beef which he took out to thaw deciding on hamburger helpers, always a good idea for a quick meal, that done he sat down at his computer to clear his mind a bit before calling Dave when the phone rang, the caller ID indicating Jerry and Emily's number as he answered saying "Hello" not indicating he had looked at the caller ID or even had one.

"Ha Bill its Jerry how are you?"

"I'm good Jerry to what do I owe the pleasure of this call, believe it or not I was just thinking about calling you later today and the next thing you know you're calling me."

"You know what they say Bill, great minds think alike and I guess it's true, today proves it, I just called to say hi and see how you guys are doing on sorting out our problem, I know you and Dave got together and if you guys can't figure it out no one can."

"The truth is Jerry we have a lot of theories we're working on, but as of this moment there just theories and not much more, but were working on it as a matter of fact I'm also due for another call to Dave as a follow up."

"Wow you have a busy calling schedule don't you Bill?" Jerry said laughing out loud so Bill was sure to hear him and then saying;

"I heard Lenny's back in town Bill, you know, your favorite bartender, maybe we should stop for a drink, any excuse you know!"

"Ya, we could do that Jerry, tell me though, how did you hear about Lenny?"

"I'm not sure really, my neighbor practically lives in there, he may have said something and I just don't recall right now."

"I see by the way how's Emily doing?" asked Bill, as he pondered Jerry's answer and humor laughing about Bill's calling habits, but for now he'd have to let it go and figure it all out later.

"She's well Bill thanks for asking and how about Barb?"

"Also well, but busy at work I guess, everyone's getting their teeth cleaned, I think she's busier than the doctor to hear her tell it."

"Well Bill, I just called to catch up and kind of pass the time of day as I'm off today, so I guess I'll let you go so you can catch up on your calling, we'll have to get together soon and maybe go for that drink, but for now I'll say goodbye and it's been good talking with you!"

"Ya bye Jerry, we'll do that drink real soon see ya." as he hung up and after talking to everyone but George, though Brenda had given him all the info he required and at least for now he was done, no he still had to contact Dave and then all he had to do was sort it all out, but to what end, he had no idea.

Deciding the only real progress he had made today was at his lunch with Lenny and afterword's, talking to folk's and picking up a few indicators' that could be interpreted several different ways, so interpret he would!

He thought he'd take a break before calling Dave as he was sure that would be a lengthy call and he was a little tired now as he went to the couch to rest.

CHAPTER TWENTY
UPSET WITH BARBARA

Bill was resting nicely as Barb came in the door, surprised once again, seeing him lying on the couch, it wasn't like him, though it was becoming more common to find him that way, and she was starting to worry.

In the kitchen she saw the thawed ground beef and the can of Manwich on the counter, realizing what he had planned for dinner she started to brown the meat, and put some frozen French Fries in the toaster oven and get out the hamburger buns for the sloppy Joes, letting him sleep a while longer as she prepared the dinner.

As the dinner neared completion she went to wake Bill, but found him already stirring and said "Hi honey dinner is almost done if you want to wash up, you were sure sawing logs."

"Hi Babe ya I guess I got kind of burned out today, it was busy did you say you made dinner, how did you know what I had in mind?"

"It was pretty obvious everything was laid out I just cooked it."

"Well lets enjoy it shall we?" Bill said, as they both sat down at the table to eat while Barb thought how she would approach the question of why Bill had tried to get info from Ruth and not her, but she felt that for some reason, she had to tread lightly.

"Bill, tell me something, why did you want to talk to Ruth when you called? You know you can get me anytime."

"I didn't want to bother you hon, besides the info I wanted was on Ruth's computer so I didn't really need you for that!"

"Well Ruth's or my computer the date is the same there networked!"

CONFRONTING BARB!

"Really, well how do you explain the fact that Ruth is not a time traveler as you and I are, so she's working in the real time and her computer has to reflect that and if there networked so does yours so please explain the contradiction to me and please don't Lie Barb!" A somber look come over Barb's face and putting her utensils down, pushing her dinner away she said with a tear in her eye;

"Bill you have never accused me of lying before and I'm very hurt, it's difficult to go to work every day and mingle with people who are not going thru what you and I are and try and keep your perspective, so I'm juggling two dates every day while at the office and when you call I tell you what you and I know to be true, regardless of what our office computers may indicate, I guess technically that's lying, but I'm just trying to protect my sanity!" as she left the table sobbing and headed for the bedroom closing the door behind her.

Bill feeling like an Ogre, sat there a while longer, contemplating what Barb had said and feeling it was a credible reason or excuse and being more than willing to give her the benefit of the doubt he went back to the bedroom to seek her forgiveness as he knocked on the door, respecting her privacy and allowing her the time she needed to compose herself, soon he herd, still sobbing "Yes"

"Can I come in so we can talk about this further?"

"You can come in, but I'm not sure I want to talk right now, it's devastating to be called a liar and especially by someone you love!" as the door opened and Bill walked in saying;

"Hon in the first place I didn't say you were a liar, I believe I said don't lie I cautioned you and that's not the same as calling you a liar, but in any case I'm sorry I upset you it certainly was not my intention to do so."

"Well I think that's a play on words and I may have taken it the wrong way, but I guess I love you so much it's easy for you to hurt me and up to now you never have."

"Well on the same note I have been trying to solve this and it seems that I'm the only one of the group that has any interest in what's going on and then when I believe my own wife is trying to deceive me I to get a bit angry!"

"I know this is taking its toll on you hon, but I sure don't want it to tear our marriage apart, I just don't know what to do about it though, other than rely on you and possibly Dave to figure it out, or just wait for it to fix itself."

"Hon you rest up for a while and just relax, I still have a few phone calls to make and I'm sure I'll be a while, if you need anything just yell ok?"

"Ok I will."

CHAPTER TWENTY ONE
DISCONTENTMENT IN THE GROUP

Folks were becoming more discontented with Bill's continued probing and suspicious questions, though everyone understood he was in his problem solving mode and was relentless in his quest for a solution, the truth, or at least an understanding of what has happened.

Bill's suspicions have recently turned toward his group of friends who were initially affected along with Bill and his wife Barb, but now even Barb's involvement was questionable though Bill was fighting the tendency to suspect Barb of any wrong doing, if he couldn't trust her, he couldn't trust anyone!

Lenny's explanation made sense and fell into line with what Bill was starting to believe himself, making it easy for Lenny to convince Bill his explanation was credible and Lenny's explanation made everyone else suspect, resulting in Bill's turning his investigations toward his friends and away from the time travel theory which was quickly losing credibility though there were some things that had escaped explanation, at least for now, like the swimming pool incident.

As Bill left Barb in the bedroom and remembering a call to Dave was still on his agenda, hoping he would not turn Dave against him too, realizing he still had to move cautiously when talking with Dave, Bill placed the call and waited, somewhat anxiously, for Dave to answer.

"Hello Bill I was just thinking about you, I just talked to Larry who was concerned about your degree of involvement thinking you may be overly involved and making yourself sick over it, I assured him that was not the case."

"Ya I talked to Larry myself and I guess I did get a little upset with him, but I apologized and I think we're good now."

"Well I understand Lenny's back and I thought maybe you and I could go by for a drink I know you were concerned about him being missing."

"As a matter of fact Dave I had lunch with Lenny today and I was glad to see him back to work he's a great Bartender and always fun."

"Oh I see said Dave, did Lenny say where he had been?" Bill thought Dave awful curious about Lenny's whereabouts; he didn't really know Lenny that well so Bill would continue this conversation with caution.

"No not really, but then we didn't really talk about it, we talked about many other things though."

"Oh did Lenny have anything further to offer about the night of the party or was that still a mystery to him?"

"Pretty much a mystery I guess Dave, though I did get the idea that he may be holding back something." Bill thinking that may get Dave off the subject for a while and protect Lenny's interest at the same time and as it turned out he was right.

Bill new it would be necessary to talk to Lenny again and try to get more detail on who ordered the drinks and especially who put a stop to the order, that may well be the guy who's in charge of the overall effort, whatever that effort may be and that is the real question why is this all happening? If we knew that the mystery would be over and we'd all get back to our normal lives.

"Well Dave I guess the reason for my call is to find out if you've had any further thoughts on the subject because I have and I wanted to pass them on to you and see what you think about them?"

"To be honest Bill, I still think one of us staying up all night is a viable idea, but beyond that I don't have a lot more to offer."

"Ahhhh ha, well to tell you the truth Dave, my thoughts have made that idea a bit out dated, because, I no longer think were traveling thru time, I do believe though someone is trying to make us believe that's the case and I don't know who or why, but time travel is no longer even a consideration, for me at least and I'm not going to waste any more time on it."

"Well Bill that's pretty positive, I guess I'm wasting my time following my theory, I should be following yours and I must say yours is easier to believe though the motivation somewhat escapes me, but let's further develop your theory shall we."

"Dave you seem to be a bit resentful and I certainly didn't mean to dismiss your theory without careful consideration, but the facts are before us, though we may interpret them differently, perhaps we need to defend our positions to each other and see who can make the best case for his theories and then move ahead."

"Well Bill" Dave laughing a bit;

"You win, I can't defend my/our position as I believe your new theory is in keeping with what I believed all along, but based on your theory at the time, that being time travel I went along and developed my solutions based on that so let's develop your new theory and solve the problem, I'm on your side!"

And that's the reason Bill was always a little intimidated when Dave was around, he was a formidable opponent, even when he was on your side, so now how would Bill bough out of this discussion gracefully without further fanning the fire?

"Well Dave, I'd like nothing better than having you and your expertise on our side in solving this mystery, forgive me if I made it sound like you weren't on our side all along, but my excitement in coming up with a more plausible explanation for the events we are experiencing may have made me less tolerant of other's ideas and I'm sorry."

MAKING A LIST

"Don't, apologize Bill what's our next move, why don't we sit down and make a list of all that's happened and systematically list the contradictions and eliminate the illogical theories and develop new ones?"

"That's a great idea Dave let's start now, first let's list what we know for sure, I'll start"
1. It all started the morning after the party, for Barb and I at least, with the following things happening:
   1.a Woke up finding a new tube of tooth paste almost gone.
   1.b Book markers were moved.
   1.c Parking garage problems, strange car in Bill's spot and the number system changed,
   1.d Nothing changed for George or Nancy so we did not follow up further.
   1.e The next morning brought more surprises an unexpected foot of snow on the ground and the computer showing a two month jump ahead in time and Bill finding his car in the garage when he left it outside all night!
   1.f There's also the fact that I lost track of what I was working on at work but gained two pro-

motions, supporting the time travel theory.
1.g   Don't forget the swimming pool and pool house, here today gone tomorrow phenomenon, that was and still is really confusing!
1.h   Then there's going to work one morning and finding the building façade totally renovated overnight and guards that were never there before, refusing to let me in as they didn't recognize me, I no longer had a job there.
1.i   Then finding out I owned my own business and in a totally different area, safety, where I had never traveled before, but my wife new all about it.
1.j   And don't forget, most important is the date changing on select computers indicating, to me at least time travel!

"That's how it all started Dave and it goes on from there, I don't know of your minute to minute experiences, but apparently not as drastic as ours, it seems Barb and I are more affected then the rest of you for some reason and I'm sure if I knew why we'd be a lot closer to an answer."

"Well Bill you've laid it out pretty well and I think that if we'd consider all the possibilities for each circumstance you've listed we may start to see things unravel and answers start to surface."

"Ya Dave, for instance the toothpaste, Barb may not have even put it out yet, it could still be in the cabinet as we hadn't finished the old one and she just forgot."

"Ya that's an easy one Bill and I'm sure there's a similar logical answer to the book marker moving ¾ of the way thru a book, you just started reading, you may have fallen asleep while reading and the book fell on the floor, startling you and you picked it up half asleep along with the book marker and slipped it in the book randomly and that's how you found it the next morning and considering your state of mind you drew the wrong conclusions."

"Dave you're absolutely right, but there some things that are not so easily explained and those are what we need to work on"

"Your right Bill why don't you pick one of those things and we'll wrestle with it for a while and see what we can come up with, you might be surprised, what do you think?"

"Ok Dave, let's see, Ummmm how about the office building façade at work completely changing overnight, that would be a three or four month project and would support the time travel scenario, which we have now discounted as being inaccurate, how do we explain that one?"

"Wow you picked one of the more difficult ones to explain, but let's give it a try shall we, now you said that you had forgotten totally the projects you were working on, the cost savings and the furnace project and those were big jobs and if you lost track of those activities isn't it possible you also forgot a project upgrading the building façade with new windows, doors and tuck pointing?"

"Wow is right, you sure got the answers Dave, I never put two and two together to come up with that, but sure if I forgot everything else why not that project and you came up with a logical answer without even thinking about it, I'm impressed!"

"Don't be too impressed Bill you and I both know that sometimes looking at things thru a second set of eyes or from a different perspective is very enlightening and in our jobs we do it all the time, you would have put it together on your own I'm sure."

"I don't know Dave sounds like you have more faith in my abilities at this point then I do and I believe your right, Barb and I seem to be more affected than the rest of you though I don't know why, maybe I did, but I forgot!" as Bill tried to inject a little humor into the conversation and Dave chuckling a bit seemed receptive to the subtle humor.

"You know Bill we've been on the phone almost two hours and solved a lot of problems or at least made significant headway, but my battery is running low so I think we had better cut it short for now and start fresh tomorrow, giving it a maximum effort once again for a few more hours, what do you think?"

"I can't argue with a dead battery Dave, so I agree as an option though we could meet and not have to worry about batteries."

"Whatever your pleasure Bill, just call and we'll decide then."

"Ok Dave I will, but I'll let you go for now bye."

"Bye Bill" as they hung up Bill thought he had a lot more to think about now, not expecting the quick solutions Dave had offered and Bill thought further, if Dave was right about the building façade and Bill had simply forgotten than there was a whole new problem added to the list, all of a sudden Bill is developing a history of forgetfulness associated with the problem and no one else seems to be experiencing the same memory loss symptoms. Let's list the memory issues Bill thought;

1. First day, Bill didn't remember leaving the papers on his desk the way he found them.
2. Though he left his car out all night, he found it back in the garage the next morning and didn't remember moving it.
3. Forgetting the cost savings had been finished a month ago.
4. Bill forgot what he was working on after the cost savings project, it was project 211 a new furnace project and he was the project Engineer.
5. Bill gets a promotion after his success on the furnace project and its completion, but forgetting it was completed or even started.
6. Bill walks into his office finding another employee sitting at his desk, not remembering where his office had been moved to or why and not remembering he had another promotion to Engineering Manager.

So there you have some of the evidence of his memory problems or could they be evidence of something else Bill thought! If it was memory related was it short term or permanent, but what to do about it, perhaps a visit to a Doctor would be in order, certainly a subject for discussion with Barb was indicated he would have to think about it and what kind of Doctor would he need to see?

CHAPTER TWENTY TWO
IS IT TIME TO SEE A DOCTOR?

Well time to discuss this with Barb he thought as he walked back into the bedroom, but found her fast asleep and decided not to bother her at this time thinking he'd call his best friend George instead as he was sure he could trust George's advice knowing he would have Bill's best interest at heart so he dialed George's number.

"Hello pal what's up? Are you calling to say you guys have figured this thing out and everything is back to normal or are you calling to say there is no solution and we have to live in the future forever?"

"No, no George I'm calling to say I've had some memory issues since this all started and I'm seriously considering seeing some kind of professional about it and was wondering what you'd thought about a move of that nature?"

"Gee Bill, professional help, do you think your nuts or something?" Bill laughing slightly, but only slightly said.

"Well I wouldn't exactly put it that way George, but I do think there is some kind of a clinical problem and I may need a Doctor to get to the bottom of it."

"Ah ha well what kind of a Doctor do you think you need to see for the problem you think you have Bill? I mean, you haven't had an accident or anything that might have caused amnesia or any similar memory loss condition, have you?"

"I don't have Amnesia George I know who I am and who you are for that matter, but I have lost the memory of certain select things that have happened since this all started and that's the problem."

"Well Bill if you believe the things you may have forgotten are related to the phenomena we are all experiencing then maybe just maybe you haven't forgotten anything at all, what you think you forgot never really happened!"

"Exactly George, but even if that were true I'd still need a Doctor wouldn't I?"

"Ya Bill I guess you would, but that takes us back to what kind of Doctor?"

"I guess our family Doctor would be the place to start, but once I tell him I'm traveling thru time, well you know where that will lead; the doctor will simply refer me right then and there to a psychiatrist so why not start there?"

"Bill if you have made your mind up that that's the kind of help you need than I support you all the way, but you may want to seek further advise certainly from Barb and Dave may have some ideas on a choice of doctors as he works for the government and they have extensive list of where they send their employees so consider that at least."

"Your absolutely right George and that's why I called you for both your advice and support and that's what I got so I'll say goodbye for now and follow your advice and talk to Barb, thanks again and Bye for now, say hi to Nancy!"

"Bye Bill" hanging up Bill headed for the bedroom once again meeting Barb coming toward him in the hallway, "Hi hon I was just coming to get you I have something to discuss with you and it is of great importance to both of us!"

"Well sure hon, what is it?"

"I've had some memory issues recently and they've developed to the point that I think it's time I seek professional help and I just wanted to get your input and suggestions so I can make a decision one way or the other."

"I see well I don't believe you need help of a professional nature I think the entire group is being affected to different degrees, but all are affected and when the problem is resolved the effects will go away also."

"That's an interesting perspective hon and I'm sure it is a correct one, but maybe if we can solve my memory problems that will solve everything and it will all go away."

"Hon whatever you decide is fine with me, but maybe you should talk to someone else for advice, Dave comes to mind as I'm sure he could be objective."

"That's a coincidence you're the second one to suggest I talk to Dave, so I guess it might be a worthy endeavor, I'll make my next call to Dave and see how that goes!"

"Oh who else suggested that Bill?"

"I called George while you were asleep and he was the one."

"I see, well it seems to be unanimous so far, maybe as you say it might be a good idea."

"Well that settles that, but that aside, I hope you're feeling a bit better after your short rest, maybe a good night's sleep will do us both good what do you think?"

"I'm sure your right at least I hope so, why don't you call Dave and then we will turn in early tonight."

"Sounds good I'll make the call now." Bill said as he dialed Dave's cell once again, but no answer, the call went to voicemail, oh Bill thought, Dave's phone must still be on charge, I'll try his home phone Bill thought as he dialed the number, but again straight to voicemail, he left a message, but was sure he would not be able to talk to Dave now until tomorrow and that was ok he was getting all talked out for the day anyway.

Bill let Barb know he could not get hold of Dave until the morning and they both went to bed for the night, the jelly beans though, would have to wait for a better time.

CHAPTER TWENTY THREE
ANOTHER TALK WITH LENNY

WEDNESDAY NOVEMBER 9, 2011 REAL TIME

After a somewhat restless night, Barb got up and started her morning routine, leaving Bill sleep as he had not yet stirred.

Without further thought, her morning routine now included turning the computer on to find the surprise date hidden in the electronic files somewhere which would further support the time travel theory they and their friends were experiencing on a daily basis now.

Well after the computer booted up the date showing was Tuesday August 27, 2039 indicating little change since they went to sleep the night before. As Barb continued to get ready for work she decided to wake Bill, once again she didn't want to leave without letting him know after her previous experience doing that, so walking into the bedroom and calling his name "Bill honey time to get up!" Bill slowly rolled over toward her and said.

"Good morning, off to work are you, did you check the date yet?"

"I did it only jumped ahead a couple of days and yes I'm off to work I made the coffee and don't forget to call Dave today Ok?"

"Ya hon I've got a few things to do today and that's one of them." as he got out of bed and walked Barb to the door and on her way out kissing her and patting her on the butt as she left, once again with a smile on her face.

Once Barb got to work and into the office the first thing she did was to make a phone call of her own, but to whom we do not know, these calls of hers were becoming a habit though.

Bill on the other hand poured his coffee and once again prowled thru the cereal cabinet to select his breakfast as he considered how to organize his day deciding along with a call to Dave he needed to see Lenny yet again, but which would he do first? He thought he would see Lenny before calling Dave as he might have additional info when he talked to Dave that would help the process.

After breakfast he checked his caller ID for Lenny's number as he didn't have it in his cell yet and finding it he dialed and waited for an answer hoping he hadn't disappeared again "Hello"

"Hi Len its Bill I was just calling to see if we could get together again I still, as it turns out have a few more questions that need to be answered and you're the one that has the answers."

"Sure Bill, whatever your pleasure, but truthfully, I don't know how much more help I can be?"

"You can do two more things Len and that would be identifying who it was that ordered the drinks and even more important helping me identify the stranger who put a kibosh on the drinks and why, but listen are you working today and if so how about I stop by and spend a few minutes gathering enough info to work on this on my own?"

"Ya I'm working stop in and let's see if we can figure it out Bill."

"Ok about the same time?"

"Ya that'll work Bill;"

"See you then Len bye for now."

"Bye Bill" well Bill thought nothing to do till lunch time, should I call Dave now or wait until I see Lenny and if we solve this thing, will the memory problems just go away, he didn't think so, it was a pretty complex situation and as for Dave he'd call after his visit with Lenny.

The morning passed quickly and it was time to leave for the restaurant as Bill finished dressing in preparation for his visit with Lenny and not even considering a burger today as the way he's been eating lately he would certainly be adding a weight problem to his growing list of problems.

As he started to leave he took one more look at the date on his computer and shook his head in wonderment, trying to understand, how a select number of computers with different IP addresses could be programmed to update nightly to a random date and ahead to some date in the future and all done without anyone, to his knowledge, getting near the machines. This added to his list of things to think about as he left for the La Flambé and a meeting with Len.

Arriving at the restaurant at 12:15pm leaving his car at the valet and walking straight into the lounge seeing Lenny behind the bar and once again waving and saying, "Hi Len, it seems like I was just here and here I am again, I guess I'm drawn to the atmosphere or maybe the great conversation in here."

Smiling and extending his hand to Bill, Lenny said, "Hi back Bill, I'm glad you enjoy the conversation and I hope you enjoy the service and drinks also and speaking of drinks what'll you have?"

Bill smiling also said, "Gin Ricky I guess heavy ice."

"You got it do you need a waitress also?"

"No not yet anyway, I'm kina watching the waistline if you know what I mean."

"Ya I know, but you know after you left yesterday I had one of those burgers you had and it was great I never had one before, but I'll have it again."

"Well your right Len and when you're ready I'll even buy it for you, but for now let's move ahead shall we, I really need two things, first we need to figure out who ordered the blue drinks and more important can you describe the stranger we've talked about?"

"Bill you know if you could get the group together again I'm sure I could point out the gentleman who ordered those drinks, but not knowing totaling what's going on I'm not sure why that's important on the other hand though I can give you a pretty good description of the other guy."

"Well Len the fact that the stranger stopped the drink order makes the drinks important, I have no idea why someone would do that unless the drinks were spiked with something and you were making them so you'd know why the color would be important, but apparently you don't so I'm not sure either, but the description of the stranger is important, agreed?"

"I agree and he was about 5'10" 175# about in his early 40's and a full head of short tight gray hair a bit wavy and neatly trimmed and he looked psychically fit wearing an expensive gray suit, Cary Grant looking."

"That's a great description Len, it sure sounds like someone I'm familiar with, but I can't quite put my finger on it, but I will I'm sure, has he ever been in here before or since?"

"Never before that night and the only time I saw him since was when he confronted me a few days later as I told you the other day."

"We'll see Len maybe I can arrange another meeting in one of your rooms with the group and get you another look at everyone to identify who were looking for, we'll see, I guess I've got a lot of work to do and I better get busy." Bill finished his drink said his goodbye to Lenny thanking him once again for the help as he left.

Handing his valet ticket to the valet and while waiting for his car he couldn't help but think about Lenny's description of the now infamous stranger and realizing he was somewhat familiar with that description, but also knowing that everyone must know someone answering that description making his familiarity less significant moving his efforts in a different direction, at least for now.

On his drive home he concentrated on what his next move would be and decided to make that a significant part of his discussions with Dave when he called.

Arriving home his first order of business was to call Dave, still wondering why everyone seemed to push him in that direction, but never the less it made sense, as Dave seemed at least to everyone else to be a significant part of the solution and Bill tended to agree. He placed the call and waited for Dave to answer, but the call went to voicemail, Bill left a message and hung up a bit disappointed.

CHAPTER TWENTY FOUR
CONSIDERING ANOTHER GROUP MEETING

Once again a meeting of the group needs to be organized Bill thought and the brutal facts brought to bear and considered by the group, in order to move forward with reaching a solution, at least that's how Bill saw it.

Still waiting to hear from Dave though Bill didn't want to move further ahead without discussing the options with Dave and the two of them deciding on the path to the solution together.

Finally the phone rang and the caller ID indicated it was Dave and Bill answered "Hi Dave I've been waiting for your call as we have several things to discuss, how you doing by the way?"

"Doing well Bill you seem to have things to discuss and are anxious to get started so what's up?"

"Well first of all I've had issues about my memory as we have discussed before, but it really started to bother me more, to the degree that I've almost decided to seek professional help a doctor and I've discussed this with others and wanted to see what you thought and if you could recommend a good doctor to see?"

"I suppose I could dig up the name of a good one, but more important I don't believe you need a doctor, I think once this problem goes away so will your memory concerns, were all having some degree of problems all resulting from what were involved in right now and I think our efforts should be concentrated on solutions and not on self-pity! I'm sorry Bill, but that's how I feel."

"Wow I didn't expect that Dave and I'm not sure I know how to take it, I've considered you a friend and now I have to figure out if a friend would be that blunt at this point though it might become appropriate at some point, you threw me for a loop buddy."

"Bill, please understand! I am your friend and as your friend, I believe that you have the ability to put your personal feelings aside and solve the problem, maybe I was put here to give you a little push in that direction if you falter, but never doubt our friendship ok?"

"I want to believe you Dave and for now I will and reconsider my thoughts about seeing a doctor, but I can't rule it out completely."

"Bill, I know you won't be sorry, after we solve this thing and you realize you know longer have a memory issue, but for now what were the other things you wanted to discuss?"

"I think we need to get everyone together once again, as I believe we have a lot more to report then in the past, we need to sort out the facts from the fiction so to speak and the only way to do that is as a group, get all the liar's into one room if you know what I mean."

"That's a pretty good idea Bill and would significantly reduce the time you've been spending on the phone; face to face is always a better way to converse, how were you going to set this up?"

"With your help I hope Dave and probably at the restaurant again, that seems to be an agreeable place to gather and the food and drinks are good, what do you think?"

"Ohhhh well I think we're a small group and could probably get together at one of our homes pretty comfortably because your right the food and drinks are great at La Flambé, but the temptation to break up the meeting and move to the bar is counterproductive that would be my objection to the restaurant." Bill thought that interesting or even suspicious that Dave didn't like the restaurant idea especially when he wanted to get the group there for Lenny to observe the folks and identify the one who ordered the drinks, strange indeed thought Bill.

"Ahhhh yes Dave you certainly have a point well maybe we can get together at my house and I can get the restaurant to send over some appetizers, I can even ask Lenny over to tend bar so we can concentrate on the subject at hand."

"Well it was only a suggestion Bill, but if you're going to go to all that trouble we might as well just go to the restaurant and be done with it." Dave sounding a little upset with Bill's idea, but restraining his objections a bit so as not to be obvious about his objections, could it be Dave had some alternative reasons for his reluctance?

DESIGNING A QUESTIONNAIRE

"Well it is something we can come back to Dave, but I think we should design a questionnaire for the meeting that everyone could fill out along with our discussions and we could evaluate it later, I'm sure if we design the questions properly we will see commonalities as well as contradictions, what do you think?"

"Wow Bill you're really into this thing, I guess I didn't realize you were as dedicated as you are to solving this, I should have been though, I've seen how tenacious you can be before, but this is going beyond reasonable you are becoming relentless in your endeavors, I have no doubt that you'll solve this on your own if need be, but I'm sticking by you pal to the end and if you want a questionnaire we'll make a questionnaire!"

Bill laughing loudly at Dave's analyses of Bill's efforts and saying, "Dave I didn't realize I was that involved in this thing until you mentioned it, but I guess I am and I think though that if the others were more involved, I could be less involved, with the single exception of your involvement which has been a significant help to me, continually putting me back on the track after I get derailed, so to speak, from time to time."

"Let's get to work on that questions Bill, I think we should limit them to a manageable number and let's consider multiple choice rather than essay type answers."

"Once again Dave your logic is impressive, multiple choice answers, I would never have thought of that, but it sure would be easier and make their cooperation in the questioner less objectionable, but it'll make our job, designing the questions, a little more creative."

"Well Bill let's try one, I'll start!" said Dave as he designed the first question and multiple choice answers, all while Bill wrote them down.

1. When did you first realize something in your life had changed?
    a. The morning after the party.
    b. After someone brought it to your attention.
    c. Subtle, unexplained changes at home or at work.
    d. All of the above

"Ya Dave that's a great example, why don't we try a few more, together this time and at least initially limiting the questions to ten, if you agree, I think we can collectively handle that."

"Sounds good Bill, let's go, you start this time and I'll jump in as we progress." Bill continued writing as both their inputs were recorded.

2. When did you first realize the changes in your life were possibly related to time travel?

   a. The date was brought to your attention thru the media.

   b. You noticed the inconsistent date on your home or work computer.

   c. The date was brought to your attention by a friend or co-worker.

   d. You noticed the date on your own.

3. Do you believe you are actually traveling thru time?

   a. Yes

   b. No

   c. I did, but not any longer

   d. Still Unsure

4. What do you intend doing to figure it out?

   a. Report it to the authorizes

   b. Work aggressively to find out what has happened.

   c. Leave it up to others to figure it out.

   d. All of the above.

5. What do you think caused this phenomenon?

   a. Unknown

   b. Mass hypnosis

   c. Chemically induced

   d. Occurred naturally

   e. A practical joke.

   f. None of the above.

6. If you believe an individual caused this, who could it be?

   a. One of the group

   b. An outsider

   c. A co-worker

   d. None of the above.

7. Who do you believe will eventually solve this?
    a. One or more of the group.
    b. The authorities.
    c. Solved by whoever started it.
    d. Unsolvable
    e. No idea.

8. How has this event affected your life?
    a. Little or not at all.
    b. Somewhat
    c. Totally upset
    d. Driving me nuts.

9. Have you experienced any psychical or psychological problems related to this experience?
    a. Yes
    b. No
    c. Some medical problems
    d. Some psychological problems
    e. Some of both

10. Do you believe this action for any reason is justified, from what you know at this time?
    a. Yes
    b. No
    c. Maybe

"Well there you go Dave we did it, we can go thru the questions and tune them up a bit, but I think we did good. I'm sure analyzing the results will be a greater challenge, but I think were up to it what do you think?"

"Bill, we can handle it now all we have to do is to organize the meeting and that brings us back to where to have it?"

"Well Dave considering all the help you've given me I think you earned the right to decide on the when and where so I'll leave it up to you."

"I don't know Bill now that we have a questioner to fill out we may need the additional room a meeting room offers and I think the req. area in my building has such rooms to use and they are free to the best of my knowledge, I can check, but we'd have to supply our own refreshments though that shouldn't be a problem."

"Ha Dave you're in charge and whatever you decide we'll make work, if you think that's the way to go then let's go and set it up."

"Why don't we canvas the group Bill and see what they think, hopefully we can generate enough interest to put it together, we need the entire group of player's or it won't work and we might as well forget it, in the meantime I'll check with the association as to the availability of the recreation center and then we can decide on a date."

"Ok Dave you go ahead and do that in the meantime I'll call George and Nancy and Larry and Karen if you'll call Jerry and Emily and we'll get this thing going and once we finalize the questioner I'll go ahead and print them up on the new printer I got from George."

"Sounds like once again we have a plan Bill, so I guess I'll let you go for now and go to work on my part of this and once I know the availability of the recreation center we can decide on a date for the meeting I'll call you, but bye for now."

"Bye Dave" as Bill hung up to return to his thinking once again and still not sure how to take Dave, he's helpful and accommodating sometimes he's testy keeping Bill on his guard, but once motivated he throws his whole self into the activity and does a remarkable job i.e. the Questionnaire.

Bill worked on typing the Questionnaire on his computer, with a few minor modifications, intending to call George afterwards and still thinking about Dave's objections to the meeting being held at the restaurant as before, could it be that Dave didn't want to confront Lenny making him the one ordering the drinks? Before completing the typing Bill decided to take a break and call George, he sat back, dialed the number and waited for an answer and he didn't have to wait long as George said "Hello Bill, boy I don't think we've talked this often since we've known one and other, at least some good has come of this confusion"

"Your right, but the more we talk the closer we get to a solution and Dave and I are getting ever closer now, but we need an additional group meeting to bring you all up to date and try an exercise that hopefully will help us bring this to a conclusion once and for all."

"When and where for the meeting Bill? I want to get my drink orders ready and diet a few days ahead of time."

"No, no George were trying to arrange to have the meeting at Dave's rec center for a couple of reasons, we'll let you know, we just wanted to give you advance warning."

"Ahhhh well I appreciate that, but to tell the truth I was looking forward to reading the menu while sipping those delicious drinks Lenny makes at La Flambé."

"Ya George I know I was looking forward to it myself for some different reasons, but Dave's planning this one so I got to go along."

"Oh ya, I know and that's fine, you guy's set it up and we'll be there with bells on I'm sure and full of nothing but cooperation to effect a solution to the problem, but I'll still be hungry and thirsty and longing for the delicious cuisine at La Flambé, but I and everyone else will suffer through the moment!"

"Come on George if it means that much to you I'll take you out to dinner myself afterword if that will make you happy!" Bill said laughing almost uncontrollably knowing George's sense of humor as well as he did and George joining in adding to the moment saying;

"Listen Bill, we'll just stop at Burger King on the way, can I bring you anything?"

"I'll let you know, Bye for now George!"

Bill, sitting there shaking his head knowing Dave's place was a mistake at least where George was concerned, he liked his food and drink, as did most of the group including Dave, but Bill thought we'll make the best of it.

Time to call Larry and Karen, making that the last call, for now at least assuming Dave will call Jerry and Emily. As Bill dialed he hopped he would not have to go thru what he did with George and with Larry he was sure he would not, Larry was a lot more laid back than George. Soon a voice said "Hello"

"Larry is that you?"

"Ya Bill what's up?"

"Well Dave and I just finished yet another conversation and are planning one last group get together with an interesting twist and hoping you and Karen can join us, we don't have a date or time yet were still trying to get an ok to use the recreation center at Dave's and once we get the go ahead we'll let you know, but for now we just wanted to give you a heads up and let you know it's being planned."

"Appreciate it Bill, but tell me are you guys any closer to figuring this thing out, or are we still hanging there and wondering what happened?"

"Were closer, but were still hanging there ourselves and that's one of the reasons for the meeting to bring everyone up to date, I think you'll be surprised at what we've learned."

"Sounds promising Bill you set it up and we'll be there!"

"Good Larry we'll look forward to seeing you, but I'll say goodbye for now and get back to work I may even call you back today."

"Ok bye Bill"

As they hung up, Bill once again became upset with Larry's apparent disconnect from what was going on unable to believe that anyone traveling thru time could be so oblivious to things unless he knew something no one else knew like they were in fact not traveling thru time and he has known it all along!

Well thought Bill it was getting close to the time Barb would be getting home and she'd want to be brought up to date on the day's events and there were many to talk about not the least of which were the many additional suspicions that had arisen after the many hours of talking today.

Siting in the kitchen Bill could hear Barb's key in the door as she arrived home from work saying as she entered "Hi hon I'm home where are you at?"

"I'm in the kitchen do you need help with something?"

"No just wondering where you were, I wasn't sure you were home or if you were out with Dave or something!" as she walked into the kitchen giving Bill a kiss and a hug and asking;

"Was your day productive dear?"

After relating the day's events to Barb and explaining all his new found suspicions he suggested some soothing therapy to unwind with later and of course Barb agreed with a knowing smile, while still wondering about Bill's uncertainty about Dave's involvement and commitment to solving the issues at hand.

They both decided to take a shower and relax watching TV for a while before going to bed, making love and waking up to a new day tomorrow or possibly years in the future neither knew nor cared right now.

CHAPTER TWENTY FIVE
PLANNING THE FINAL MEETING

(THURSDAY NOVEMBER 10, 2011 REAL TIME)

Well once again the morning sun was starting to push the darkness of the night to the west and rise over the lake telling the people of Chicago it was time to get up and greet the new day.

Again and in keeping with recent tradition Barb was the first to rise. It was Thursday in real time, but in traveling time, as it had become known by the group, the date had not yet been determined, but soon would be as Barb turned the computer on and waited for it to boot up.

Bill, getting up shortly after Barb was still waiting on Dave to call and let him know about the Recreation center and its availability for the get together, he had expected the call last night, but it never came and once again Bill grew impatient with Dave and the group suggesting to Barb that he was sure he was the only one trying to aggressively solve this thing! However, Barb to, seemed a bit indifferent this morning after a night of lengthy and totally satisfying love making, so to avoid a lengthy discussion she agreed with Bill and let it go at that.

Bill was in the kitchen pouring his first cup of coffee of the day and checking the computer for the date when the phone rang, it was Dave and Bill answered anxious to hear what Dave had to say, "Hello Dave, good news I hope, are we set up?"

"Well not exactly Bill we may have a problem there going to get back to me it seems that all of a sudden everyone wants to use the recreation facility, it goes for months without any interest and now you can't get in on a bet!"

Bill smiling on the other end of the phone without Dave knowing said;

"Well what do we do now Dave do we have any other options that you'd like to exercise, I guess we should wait for your people to get back to you and go from there though, did they indicate how long that would take?" though Dave couldn't see Bill, he sensed his being grateful for Dave's problem with the req. center, knowing Bill's restaurant plan may indeed come to pass.

"She indicated there would be an answer shortly, so I guess we'll wait Bill and then go with a different plan if need be."

"Ok Dave any further thoughts on anything we discussed yesterday or on the questionnaire we designed?"

"No, listen Bill let me get back to you my other line is ringing maybe it's the call were waiting for!"

"Ok Dave, go ahead and answer, get back to me when you are able." after Dave hung up Bill tried to figure Dave's next move to block Bill's attempt at the restaurant idea as he was sure he would. While waiting for Dave to call Bill checked today's date on the computer and to his surprise the date had not changed from yesterday's date it was still Tuesday August 27, 2039 what was wrong he thought is the computer broken or are we going to do yesterday all over again and get it right this time? Bill decided he would not add this to his already long list of things to be concerned about.

The phone rang it was Dave again "Hello Dave, how did we make out?"

"I have news, good or bad I'm not sure, but the center is not available until next month and I don't think we should put the meeting off that long, what do you think?"

"I agree Dave so what do you propose it's on you as we agreed?"

"Well as an alternative I guess the restaurant is the next best idea, but you as always are the MC and if you think you can control the meeting there we'll go with it."

"Ok Dave, go ahead and make the reservation and we'll notify the others and go from there."

"To be honest Bill you're more familiar with the folks there, so why don't you go ahead and take care of it?"

"Are you sure Dave?"

"Ya go ahead Bill it was your idea anyway and I know George and the others will enjoy it, as for me and to tell you the truth I enjoy the food there also, I'm only concerned about holding everyone's attention during the meeting."

"I'll give them a call right now Dave and get one of the rooms scheduled for us do you have any preference as to the day or time?"

"Well I think earlier in the day, late morning or early afternoon and possibly on a Saturday/Sunday would be better than after a long day at work and continuing into the late evening."

"I agree it will be easier to hold the groups attention, I'll try for this Saturday late morning, I'll say goodbye for now Dave and get to it, and I'll get back to you as soon as I know something positive!"

"Ok Bye Bill"

After hanging up Bill dialed the restaurant to make the reservation, but wanting to talk to Lenny first to check his schedule and plan accordingly.

"La Flambé may I help you?"

"Yes is Lenny there?"

"Yes sir, I'll ring the bar."

"Hello Lenny speaking."

"Lenny its Bill Kelly, how's your day going, the reason I'm calling you is to check your work schedule for this coming Saturday I'm trying to arrange a meeting there late Saturday morning with the group, a perfect time for you to identify the one ordering the drinks, so I hope you're working?"

"I'm working Bill, but as you already know I don't come in until 11:30am or so how early are you intending on coming in we don't open until 11:00am if that meets your needs."

"Ya that's good I'll figure on getting there at noon and go from there can you transfer me to whoever I need to speak with to make the arrangements?"

"Sure I'll transfer you to the front desk and anyone answering can help you and I'll look forward to seeing you Saturday morning Bill, Bye for now."

"Bye Len" Bill said as the phone call was sent to the front desk and answered by Anna who was extremely helpful with the room scheduling the room which was available and would be set up for Bill's group as requested.

Everything being arrange Bill called Dave back to let him know, "Hi Bill how did you make out, let me guess it's all arranged, so when and what time?"

"Saturday at noon Dave if that's ok and we get a lunch discount also, if you don't mind you can call Jerry again and I'll let the other's know on second thought you can call George or Jerry will think I'm trying to avoid him."

"Ok Bill sounds like a plan, oh by the way will Lenny be there for us?"

"To tell you the truth I don't know Dave I can call back though and I'll call you and let you know, but I'm sure they'll have a bartender." being as clever as he could, to answer Dave's question and avoid suspicion.

"No, not necessary Bill I was just curious if we were going to get the excellent bar service we've become used to at that restaurant and yes I'll call George."

"Ok Dave I'll say goodbye for now and get started with the calls."

"Bye Bill I'll do the same."

Hanging up Bill thought he'd better call Barb first or she will be upset and after her upset the other night he wasn't looking forward to going thru that again so he dialed her office "Triple A Dental Ruth speaking how may I help you?"

"I don't know Ruth I forgot oh I know is Barb there?"

Ruth laughing said "Of course she's here where else would she be I'll get her!"

"Thanks Ruth and by the way if I ever divorce Barb you'll be my first call."

"If you divorce Barb don't bother she's a great girl and we all love her here."

Obviously there were no patients in the office as Ruth yelled across the office Barb pick up two it's your hubby! "Hi hon to what do I owe the pleasure of your call today?"

"Hi I just wanted to tell you were having another group get together at the restaurant Saturday at noon, I hope you didn't have any other plans, did you?"

"No dear I'm at your beckon call, but I don't know how much enthusiasm you'll generate among our friends."

"Ya I know what you mean I hope it goes better than the last time we tried this, I think it will Dave and I have a few new things to throw at you guys and the new info will I'm sure generate more interest."

"Do I get a preview of your presentation or do I have to wait?"

"I have no secrets from you dear, but a preview may cause your lack of attention at the meeting causing others to do the same."

"You know I think that's certainly possible and I can wait!"

"Ok Barb, I knew you'd understand, but I got to go for now and call the others or we won't have anyone else there so I'll say bye for now, love you!"

"Bye hon love you to."

Bill's next call would be to Jerry and Emily, but first he wanted to take a moment to gather his thoughts, have a cup of coffee maybe a sandwich check his computer for any business appointments/opportunities he may have missed because of his involvement in what he was currently doing and then make his call.

In the meantime Dave was placing his call to George and Nancy to inform them of the upcoming meeting and confirm their attendance. Dave dialed their number and waited as it rang soon a female voice answered saying "Hi there Dave this is certainly a surprise are you looking for George?"

"Not necessarily, I'd rather talk to you, how have you been Nancy?"

"Well actually I've been fine, still trying to find office space somewhere though as the business expands working out of the house gets more difficult, but that aside were doing well."

"Oh well maybe I can help you with that office problem, the government gets a list of available properties every month by category and office space is one of the categories, I'll be sure to get you a copy."

"Wow that'll be great Dave thank you, well I'm sure glad I answered the phone, even though George isn't home I'm sure glad I was, your call gives me hope, thanks Dave!"

"Well hopefully it'll be helpful it can't hurt, but the reason I called is to let you guys know Bill has set up another meeting to bring everyone up to date on what we've discovered so far it's this Saturday at noon at La Flambé, can you guys make that?"

"We'll certainly be there Dave I know George will be glad he loves the food there."

"That seems to be the popular opinion and I agree so I'll say goodbye for now and look forward to seeing both of you at the get together."

Ok Dave goodbye we'll see you Saturday and thanks again for the help." Dave hanging up on Nancy happy he could possibly help her with her search for office space, but a little disappointed he didn't talk directly with George as he had a couple of additional things to discuss with him, perhaps another time.

After lunch and relaxing for a while Bill was ready to make his calls starting with Jerry and Emily and then on to Larry and Karen. Dialing Jerry's number Bill couldn't help thinking that if they were nearing an end to what had become such a disruption in their lives, how would they get back to normal, would they return to October 28, 2011 the start of this whole thing, probably not as real time had passed beyond then, maybe some date close to that though and how about his job and promotions or would he continue in his own business? who knows how far ahead they had actually come by now, but someone outside the group would know for sure so he was not going to worry about it considering all the other things he had to worry about right now!

"Hello Bill or is it Barb or maybe both it's the Kelly's on the caller ID and I'm sure glad to hear from one or the other or both of you, what's up?"

"Wow that's a great way to answer the phone Jerry I totally forgot why I called, let's see oh ya, when are we going to get invited to one of those famous spaghetti dinners of yours?"

"Ha Bill, you guys are welcome anytime, but you already knew that so what's really on your mind, not that I don't enjoy talking with you, but I know you're a man on a mission and not given to idle conversation or just passing the time of the day, so what's up?"

"Well Jerry, Dave may have already told you, but were putting together another meeting at the restaurant Saturday at noon to bring everyone up to speed on what's been going on and what we've found out so far, I'm sure you'll be surprised at what we've learned and how close we are to a solution and an end to this thing."

"That certainly sounds promising Bill you and Dave have been working tirelessly on this I know and we all appreciate it, we'll be at the meeting for sure Bill."

"Thanks Jerry, buy the way, how's Emily doing with all this, is she handling it well?"

"Bill she's so busy at the store I'm not even sure she knows what's going on or has time to care, her world starts and ends at the jewelry store, sometimes it seems like she's home for hours before she really gets home if you know what I mean, but I'm not sure she's not better off, not even thinking about it and letting somebody else worry about it for her, knowing it will eventually go away all together!"

"Well we will talk more Saturday Jerry for now though I have more calls to make so I have to cut this short, but it's been good talking with you and say hi to Emily."

"Ok bye Bill, see you on the weekend, thanks for the call."

After hanging up Bill had one last call to make, to Larry and nothing else to do until Saturday at the meeting so he thought he'd get right to it and get the info out a.s.a.p. so folks had time to plan, rather than their having to change plans at the last minute.

Placing the call he was thinking about Lenny picking out the individual who ordered the drinks bringing that mystery to an end and that hopefully brings them that much closer to the overall solution to the problem!

"Hi Bill, wow two days in a row were talking, that's a record I'm sure. I take it you guys settled on a date and time for the meeting, or am I wrong?"

"No you're right on Larry, it's this coming Saturday at noon at La Flambé and we have a lunch discount if you're so inclined."

"You guys are throwing the party you mean you're not buying the lunch, just kidding, ya we'll be there and take advantage of the lunch discount to!"

"Great were looking forward to getting together again and hopefully you'll be impressed with the progress we've made thus far, it's been a struggle, but were moving in the right direction and the ends in sight."

"Great Bill, well I guess Karen and I will see you then!"

"Looking forward to it Larry, say Hi to Karen and I'll say goodbye for now."

"Bye Bill" as they hung up Bill breathes a sigh of relief knowing he could relax for a while and prepare for Saturdays meeting that's Saturday November 12, 2011.

Bill sat back and reflected on the past 13 days or so since this all started realizing all that has happened;

He was an engineer in the facilities group at Bracken Metals and doing such a great job apparently that he had just received two consecutive promotions, completing two major projects that he had no recollection of, buying his wife a new BMW and losing his job, why he had no idea, starting his own business with a half dozen employees and didn't even remember doing it, but realizing he and others close to him who were in fact time travelers and were currently living almost 30 years in the future, but showing no physiological changes and all while seeing swimming pools and pool houses built overnight right under his nose and disappearing almost as fast and ten inch snowfalls followed the next day by 90 degree weather and that is just a start! How, was that all accomplished and why he thought?

The fact that while others in the group were affected to some degree, none were affected as drastically as Bill that is the real mystery he thought!

Well Barb will be home soon, maybe a dinner out tonight would be a good idea and a good way to wind down, that new steak house by the BMW dealer would be a treat Bill thought he would suggest it when she got home.

But wait Bill thought when everything goes back to normal does that mean the steak house created in the future would no longer exist in the present and Barb would no longer have her BMW and Bill's seemingly profitable business would be gone, it was sure difficult to just sit back and relax when his mind refused to relax and constantly conjured up new problems and things to think about! Maybe he had better call and see if the steakhouses still exist or if it ever really did?

On second thought maybe he should call Barb and see if she was in the mood for a night out or if she would spend the evening at home and relax as Bill was trying (Unsuccessfully) to do, he placed the call "Triple A dentistry Ruth speaking how may I help you?"

"Hi Ruth, may I speak to Barb please?"

"Sure Bill let me check she was assisting the doctor a few minutes ago."

"Hi hon what's up?"

"I won't keep you; I thought I'd call and see if you're in the mood for dinner out tonight, I thought that new steakhouse might be nice?"

"Sure that's a great idea you know me I'm always in the mood for a good steak and there great there, let's do it."

"Ok I'll see you when you get home."

"Ok gota go bye!" well that made up Bill's mind, now he too was looking forward to a great steak and trimmings and that was the place to get it.

When Barb arrived home Bill was ready to go and said, "Hi hon I'm sure looking forward to dinner tonight how about you?"

"Me too I'll just freshen up a bit and we'll be on our way."

On their way out Barb picked up a sheet of paper in the kitchen and then headed for the elevator, Bill not paying much attention to what she did and in the car on their way she started to read the paper and asked, "Bill what's this?"

"What he asked?"

"This questionnaire I picked up in the kitchen, what's that all about, is this for the meeting?"

"Hon put that down, you're not supposed to see that yet it wouldn't be fair to the others, we talked about that!"

"Ok but you're the one that left this laying around and my natural feminine curiosity took over." And the conversation continued as they pulled into the steakhouse parking lot which was almost empty so Bill parked his car rather than using the valet and they walked in greeted once again by Carl the MAI-TER D who seemed to recognize them or at least give that impression as Bill said;

"Good evening Carl good to see you again." letting Carl know they'd been there before, lessoning the tension there may have been, both professional and considerate of Bill, exactly the right way to handle the situation and you would expect no less from Bill.

"Yes sir I have a wonderful and private table for you this evening right this way." As they followed and were shown a table in a secluded area of the restaurant, but noting Brian their BMW salesman at a table with friends in another part of the dining room acknowledging them with a wave and a smile as they were seated.

Brian decided to walk over and say hi, as he approached extending his hand to Bill and acknowledging Barb saying, "The Kelly's, good to see you again, how's the car Barb? And Bill as I recall; I see you've come to like this place and that's good it keeps you coming back and keeps you close to us also when you're in the market for that new 700 series Bill."

"Good to see you Brian, Ya your recommendation for this place was sure right on it's really great, have a seat."

"No, no, but thanks I'm with a party and should get back, I just wanted to say hi, good seeing you again and enjoy the car."

Both of them said goodbye to Brian as he walked away and their waiter approached with the menus and introducing himself said

"Good evening folks I'm James and I'll be your waiter this evening will you need the wine steward?"

"Ya James, you can send the steward over and I think we'll have the stuffed mushrooms for an appetizer."

"Of course sir an excellent choice as he left them to look over the menu and send the wine steward to their table." In the meantime Barb wanted to continue her inquiry about the questionnaire she found in the house that Bill wanted to avoid talking about, but she was not going to settle for that and pursued her line of questioning asking Bill.

"Hon I was just wondering about this piece of paper and its purpose?"

"Well Dave and I thought it would be a good way to find out everyone's experiences and how they were affected by what was going on, not collectively but individually and we thought it would help us find out some answers, it's been very difficult as you know."

"I see and you don't think I should look at it when I'm going to see it anyway?"

"No your answers have to be spontaneous and if you know the questions and have time to think about them you'll have an unfair advantage over the others and the data won't be pure."

"I see, I guess you're right, well here you go." handing Bill the list and picking up the menu to decide on dinner.

"Hum ya know I think I'm going to have Steak Diane, how about you?"

"Ya I think I'll go for that monster Twin Porterhouse and double baked potato with asparagus and cream sauce." As the wine steward approached the table in all his regalia, presenting the wine list offering some suggestions as was his job and impressing the customers with his knowledge. Bill however played the game well saying;

"Good evening Steward you know we've decided on steak this evening and I believe we'd like a nice Cabernet Sauvignon or Syrah and served in a Bordeaux Glass please."

"Sir we wouldn't serve it any other way, but of course your correct, well the Cabernet than?"

"Yes thank you Steward." Bill said, as the steward left probably unimpressed by Bill, but Barb surely was impressed with her husband. The waiter soon returned with the appetizer and asking if they were ready to order and they indicated they were and their choices were written down and James left to place the order.

Bill tried one of the mushrooms stuffed with sausage and cheese of some kind and was so impressed he thought he attempt to get the recipe though he was sure that would be difficult, but try he would, Barb described them as scrumptious when she was able to blurt out the words as her mouth was busy enjoying the cuisine.

Well dinner as expected went well and was well worth the drive though Bill was unable to get the mushroom recipe, but he was not done trying as he told Barb of his plan to succeed with that Quest.

On the way home they talked more about their dinner and the upcoming group meeting, Barb concerned there may not be enough new info to justify the meeting or to hold the groups interest causing both Bill and Dave to lose their credibility with their friends, but Bill assured her that would not be the case unless the group already knew what they were about to be told and if that were the case then there was certainly some kind of a conspiracy in the works and that would open a whole new mystery to solve and Bill would be on his own!

As they arrived home Bill suggested a night cap, Barb passed, but Bill decided to have one and turned his computer on once again to check on the date before going to bed.

The date on the computer was Thursday August 29, 2039 and that was impossible Bill thought this morning it was Tuesday August 27, 2039 and now the evening of the same day it updated two days ahead, Bill started to call Barb but hesitated a moment siting down at the table to think for a second before calling his wife. The obvious conclusion was that someone either from the house or remotely was adjusting the date on Bill's computer, but who, why and how was that being done and if it was they had to have inside help and who could that be?

Bill has suspected this for a while now and maybe that's why he decided at the last moment to check the computer, but not suspecting what he found, that was a complete surprise; he decided not to bother Barb about it right now, at least until seeing what date was on the computer in the morning. Bill finished his drink shutdown the computer and went to the bedroom to find Barb already fast asleep after preparing for bed he carefully slipped in so as not to wake his wife and went to sleep himself.

FRIDAY NOVEMBER 11, 2011 REAL TIME

The next morning Bill was the first out of bed headed for the kitchen to turn the computer on and make the coffee while waiting, Barb followed quickly behind saying, "Good morning hon you're up already what's that about?"

"I just had a mission this morning hon and I wanted to make coffee so you wouldn't have to, so you didn't have to rush getting ready for work!"

"Your mission was making coffee?"

"No I did that as I was up already and I thought I could help you out."

"Well what was your mission to help me out!" she yelled, while Bill laughed and to Barb's dismay, as she threw her hands up in the air running from the room yelling in some foreign language I'm sure no one would understand!

When Bill finally stopped laughing and got control of himself he checked the computer and found yet another unexpected development the date jumped ahead yet another day to Friday August 30, 2039, why he thought at this point it simply made no sense.

When Barb was ready she went to work in a huff and Bill still not understanding why said goodbye and threw her a kiss as she bolted out the door.

The rest of the day was uneventful as Bill prepared for the group meeting tomorrow while wondering why Barb was so upset this morning right out of bed, but finally writing it off to a female thing and letting it go at that.

Once at work and realizing she was a bit short with Bill this morning she decided to call him and apologize for her uncalled for behavior, which she did and of course he was receptive and accepted her apology, promising to give her the opportunity to make amends later this evening, she agreed!

CHAPTER TWENTY SIX
FINALLY THE MEETING

SATURDAY NOVEMBER 12, 2011 REAL TIME

Well Saturday morning the day they've all been waiting for has finally arrived and the Kelly's are still fast asleep, while others are up and about and yet others just starting to stir, but all are prepared for today's activities and I might add a great lunch and an early start on the weekends drinking activities.

As Barb woke and stretched her arms in bed finding Bill quite awake himself putting his arm around her and pulling her toward him and finding her quite willing to make the short trip to his side and whatever followed, but asking if he wanted breakfast in bed or if she should fix something in the kitchen and he could stay in bed until it was ready, the answer, "By the time were done there won't be time for breakfast we'll have to wait until lunch at the restaurant." said Bill, as he pulled her closer to him asking where the Jelly Beans were and how many she had left in the bag?

Her reply "Hon I can always get more Beans right now let's figure out how many were going to need?"

After spending a couple more hours in bed and after Barb's apology last night, they continued doing what came natural to both of them a while longer, suddenly realizing they were going to have to get going or they would be late for the meeting they both headed for the shower (one at a time this time) Barb getting there first and Bill shaving while he waited his turn and realizing he was right, there was no longer time for breakfast only coffee, but he thought it was worth it.

As Barb stepped out of the shower, beads of water glistening on her freshly showered naked young body and saying to Bill, "Your turn hon" Bill turning to look at her, his thoughts on something quite different than the shower, but resisting temptation and slapping her gently on her butt as he stepped into the stall and telling her;

"If your still standing there like that when I get out of here, we will definitely be late for the meeting, not to mention the need for more jelly Beans!"

Barb knowing he meant it grabbed a towel and went to the bedroom to dry off and get dressed before he had the opportunity to make good on his promise, there simply was no more time for that!

Bill exited the shower and started toward the bedroom hoping to find Barb in a receptive mood, but knowing that was probably too much to expect given their earlier activities and their plans for the day, so he too, finding Barb almost completely dressed in the bedroom decided to get ready himself and follow his dreams later that evening. Looking at Barb he told her;

"You're lucky you know, but be forewarned the day is young there's always this evening and we have no plans for that, but I do!" Barb not to be outdone and always having a comeback said;

"I don't consider myself lucky and I look forward to your idle threats for this evening, let's see what tonight brings."

Dave along with George and Nancy were the first to arrive at the restaurant at about 11:45am greeting each other and George quickly grabbing a menu on his way to the meeting room after being directed by Linda the Hostess working at the front of the dining room.

Dave on the other hand went to the bar to find Lenny who happened to be in the basement getting some liquor for the bar and was not available at the moment. Soon Dave was joined at the bar by Jerry and Emily, asking Dave what they had to do to get a drink around here and no sooner did Jerry ask then a waitress came behind the bar and asked if she could help them as the bartender was tied up for the moment restocking the bar. Dave ordered a 7up and Margareta's for the Goldberg's and they all took their drink to the meeting room to join the Roberts finding George with his head buried in the lunch menu as Larry and Karen walked in followed by the Kelly's, Bill with his briefcase in hand and ready to go.

"Well I see were all here and on time, indicating were all interested in what Dave and I have to say today, that is all but George, who's obviously interested in something quite different!" looking at George and laughing, pointing out once again George's apparent interest in the lunch menu.

"So those of you who are interested in lunch they are offering a discount to us on anything on the lunch menu of 20% I've been told and half off all drinks so the trip was worth it if we accomplish absolutely nothing today."

"Well let's get the waitress in here and get our orders in so we can get to the meeting Bill." said George as Bill waived for the waitress to come in and take the lunch and drink orders, the group placed their orders and visited together as friends do while waiting for their food and enjoying their drinks including the BLUE drink that was delivered to Nancy, Bill catching it immediately headed for the bar and seeing Lenny said;

"Hi Len, what was that blue drink you sent over and who ordered it?"

Lenny looking confused said, "What blue drink Bill, are you trying to be amusing or are you just setting the theme for today's meeting?" Lenny said smiling.

"The waitress brought in our drink order from the bar and it was delivered with one blue drink of some sort for one of the ladies!"

"Bill, I made the drinks for your party and I made no Blue drinks, for you guys or for anyone else this morning, I thought you were kidding!"

"No Len I'm not kidding! A blue drink in a Martini glass was delivered with our drink order to George's wife Nancy, wait a minute and I'll be right back." As Bill walked back toward the meeting room Len watched him curiously, Bill walked up to Nancy asking her to come with him and bring her drink, but holding up an empty glass she said;

"What drink Bill, I think I need another." following Bill, to the bar, where Lenny was busy making another batch of drinks for the waitress standing at the end of the bar.

As Lenny approached them Bill said "Ok Nance, tell Bill what kind of drink you ordered."

"A Martini" she said as Bill looked at her in wonderment.

"No, no Nance the blue drink!"

"A Martini Bill I didn't have a blue drink!" with that Bill immediately went into his defensive mode and accepted her answer for now unable to explain what was going on as Lenny handed Nancy another Martini and she headed back to the room seeing the waitress bringing the lunch. Bill followed after asking Lenny to take a moment to wonder into the meeting room during lunch to identify the guy who had previously ordered the blue drinks, Len indicated he would.

During lunch all were making conversation, telling jokes and enjoying the moment, all that is but Bill, who was relatively quit as his mind raced barely touching his sub burger which he loved and should be hungry as he had no breakfast this morning. Barb noticed and asked, "Hon are you alright, you haven't touched your food and you've gotten quiet, what's going on?"

"No I'm fine just trying to gather my thoughts on how I'm going to make this presentation to you guys as I now have some new info I didn't have before which changes things a bit, but it'll be fine."

As they continued with their lunch, Lenny discreetly walked in, smiled at everyone asking "How are the drinks folks is everything ok?" Jerry responded saying exactly what was on his mind.

"The drinks are good, but the price is great!" referring to the half price deal Bill had arranged for.

Lenny responded saying, "Well I'm glad you're enjoying them I had hopped you would after they told me to cut half the booze from the recipe I was afraid you'd be disappointed, noticing the difference!" Jerry holding his drink up to look at it a bit befuddled, a disappointed frown or pout coming over his face as the rest of the group started laughing loudly and enjoying the moment knowing Lenny was kidding responding to Jerry's sense of humor and as Len waved and left heading back to the bar, Jerry also caught on and joined in on the laughter the good sport he is.

That was enough humor to get Bill to at least try his burger and enjoy his lunch so they could get on with the meeting. As everyone finished their lunch the desert was served and another round of drinks ordered, Bill decided to pay another visit to the bar to see Lenny once more before starting the meeting, he excused himself and walked to the bar.

As he approached the bar Len walked to meet him knowing the question Bill would ask next and he was right Bill asked "Well Len who is it?"

Lenny shrugged his shoulders opened his hands in a gesture Bill recognized and said "Is that everyone Bill?"

"He's not there is he Len?"

"No, no one in there is the guy." Len said, seeing the disappointment and confusion on Bills face saying;

"I'm sorry Bill are you sure that's everyone that was at the party that night?"

"Ya that's everyone Len." as he turned and walked away a somber and disappointed look on his face while Lenny looked a bit upset himself with how things had developed, shaking his head negatively, he too turned and went back to work.

As Bill walked back into the meeting room noticing everyone had finished their lunch he called for everyone's attention and as the room quieted, Bill stood, looking at his friends and after a short pause said;

"I hope you're not too disappointed today, but recent developments and I do mean as recent as a few minutes ago, have changed things, making my presentation a little outdated however some of what we had to say is still valid. Dave and I have discovered that time travel is not what's going on here, though someone is trying to make us believe it is. Some of you, I believe, have already figured that out or at least suspect it. The someone I mentioned, is in the wind so to speak and I have no idea who he/she is, or why there involved, or responsible for this conspiracy and yes, I said conspiracy, it is quite evident because of things that have happened that no one person could have pulled it off by his or her self. So are there any questions to this point?"

Bill was being careful and not forthcoming with what he now believed to be true, he knew now that part of or the entire group was part of the conspiracy and yes that included Lenny and possibly even Barb though he didn't want to believe that.

George had a question saying "Bill what kind of things are there that the suspect stranger couldn't have done on his own?"

"Several come to mind George but the obvious one is the swimming pool and pool house that popped up in our parking lot one day and gone the next that took a lot of planning and engineering to accomplish, I'm still not sure how it was done."

Larry then asked "Dave do you agree with Bill on this conspiracy theory and if so to what end, I mean is it an elaborate joke or is it more than that?"

"Wow that's a whole lot wrapped up in one question Larry, but let's see if I can address at least part of it. The conspiracy issue first, I believe there is more than one individual, probably several people plotting to accomplish a goal not an unlawful one, but with a specific purpose in mind none the less so a conspiracy, yes, a joke, no, and the purpose, well I have my ideas, which I choose not to share right now for reasons you'll understand when I do, does that answer your question Larry?"

"For the most part, yes, thanks Dave."

Once again Bill took over the meeting, asking for any additional questions and Nancy asked, "Bill what was that trip you and I took to the bar asking Lenny about some kind of mysterious blue drink all about?"

"That was really nothing Nance, I recalled what you had ordered, a Martini and when the drinks were delivered yours looked blue and I was curious about a blue Martini I had never seen one anywhere, but I'm now sure that it was reflected light in the room that caused the problem." Bill, covering that one up as the expert he is, never hesitating or stumbling and totally convincing.

"Are there any other questions folks?" Bill asked, looking around the room as once again George asked "Bill, to the best of my recollection and I could be wrong, you were the one who suggested the time travel theory, how did you arrive at that conclusion, how did that theory evolve?"

"Well, as I look back George, I think your right, I guess I did surmise based on little hard evidence, that we were somehow moving ahead in time, that was a result of a number of minor things happening, that Barb can attest to reaching that conclusion after seeing the date on my computer being a date in the future and no other explanation for it and then if I recall I called you and you confirmed that you were also having the same experiences."

"Ya I guess your right Bill, I was just trying to see if I recalled everything the way it happened and I guess I do."

"Well if there are no other questions, Dave and I have put together a little exercise in the form of a questionnaire 10 questions to answer as accurately and honestly as you can or it will be of no use, no discussions among yourselves in answering the questions, they must be your own answers, so that being said Dave will pass out the questionnaire which by the way he and I will be filling it out also so let's get started I can't see it taking any longer than a half hour to complete, but take as long as you need it's not a timed test and by the way you don't have to put your name on it, but at least indicate if you're a male or female, that will help." As Dave passed out the questionnaire everyone got started.

Though Dave and Bill knew the contents of the questionnaire ahead of time Jerry was the first to finish with a smile on his face and a question in his mind waiting for everyone else to finish so he could ask. Nancy was the next to finish followed by Larry and quickly by the rest of the folks. When Bill saw that everyone was done he asked the papers all be passed to Dave who collected them to be analyzed later. Bill once again stood and addressed the group saying.

"Well folks Dave and I hope you all found this meeting more productive than the last one I know we did and now we have one additional assignment for you and we can adjourn to the bar. The stranger I referenced earlier today we would like all of you to try and put a name to him, you may or may not have seen him that day, I'm going to pass out a description of him and it may ring a bell now or in the near future and if it does please let us know, we believe this to be the one behind the mystery, so please help! Now Jerry, I see you have a question what is it?"

"No-No, I was just wondering if there was a prize for finishing the test first."

"You mean the questionnaire, ya I'll buy you a drink at the bar."

"Thanks Bill and I'll drink it."

"Ok Dave have you got anything else?" Dave shaking his head in the negative and Bill adding;

"Well than that's it gang you can pay your tabs at the bar or the front desk as for me I'm headed for the bar and the first drink is on me!" as the group adjourned to the bar, Bill and Dave picked up the papers and other things that they brought and Bill asked Dave how he thought it went and Dave answered by saying "You know Bill

I thought you did a great job, but I detected a little tension in the group though it's hard to define, did you notice?"

"Perhaps Larry was a bit testy, but that aside I didn't pick up on anything else Dave."

"Well let's join the others Bill I'm sure you and I can pick up on this later and right now I'm thirsty and you're buying!" Dave and Bill both laughing as they went to the bar were the others already had their drinks, as they approached Lenny who asked;

"What can I get for you guys?" Bill answered sarcastically;

"How about a Blue Moon Len" Len detecting Bill's sarcasm looked at Dave and said;

"And for you sir"

Dave said "I'll have the same that sounds interesting" after Lenny served their drinks Barb walked up and said;

"What on earth are you two drinking?" knowing Bill's taste in drinks, "Blue drinks what are those?" Barb asked.

Dave answered "It's a Blue Moon Barb pretty good actually."

"Maybe I'll try one" Barb said as she waved for Len to come over and cuddled up to her husband while waiting. As Len walked up to her She said;

"Len could you make me one of those Blue things?" Smiling Len said;

"Sure thing Barb, how about you fellas, you ok?" Bill looking noticeably upset with Lenny caused Len to shake his head and walk away and Barb who also noticed Bill's obvious anger with Lenny asked;

"Honey what's going on between you and Lenny you both seem put out with each other?"

Bill not wanting to show his hand just yet said, "No Hun, I'm just preoccupied with the whole thing and I guess I'm not my usual cheerful self!"

Well things continued until about 3:00pm when they started to break up and everyone headed for home or other places. Bill and Barb decided to leave and after paying their bill and bar tab said goodbye to those who remained and headed for the door followed by Lenny who called to Bill saying;

"Ha Bill wait a minute!" Bill stopped turned toward Lenny allowing him to catch up saying;

"Ya Len what's on your mind?"

"Look Bill, I know your upset with me over those drinks and because I couldn't point out the culprit that ordered the drinks the day of the party and as for the blue drink today, I really know nothing about it and I couldn't identify a guy that wasn't here. I came to you remember and I'm on your side, things didn't go well today and I'm sorry, but I'm not to blame here!"

"Ok Len we'll talk again soon I'm sure." as Bill turned to leave he noticed what he had not noticed before. Bill the substitute bartender was working at the service bar in the back of the main dining room as he caught up with Barb who was waiting at the door his mind started spinning once again when Barb asked,

"Well did you boy's make up?"

"Ya sure I guess we're good where did you want to go now hon?"

"Let's go home and relax, but stop on the way so we can pick up some milk were running low."

"You got it" Bill said as he drove home stopping first at a neighborhood grocery store his mind running in circles all the time, as Barb ran into the store to get the milk Bill thought about the second bartender working at the service bar and the more he thought about it the more he wished he had questioned the bartender right then and there to put the possibility of him making the blue drink for Nancy to rest, but it was too late now he thought, or was it?

When Barb came out with the milk Bill quickly turned the car around and started back to the restaurant Barb saying, "What are you doing, you're going the wrong way we just came from here?"

"Unfinished business hon, I have to do this or I'll be forever sorry, sometimes you only get one chance!" Barb more confused than ever said;

"Well can you at least tell me where you're going?"

"Back to the restaurant to talk to Bill;"

"Bill, Bill?" she said somewhat confused as she didn't know the substitute bartender or his name.

"Ya Bill is the name of the other bartender!"

"Other bartender, I didn't know there was another bartender." Barb said as Bill pulled into the restaurant parking lot asking Barb.

"Did you want to come in or wait here, I won't be long?"

"Are you kidding I'm coming in with you, I have no idea what's going on and I'd like to." as they both got out of the car and went into the restaurant greeted by the Hostess at the door asking;

"Didn't you folks just leave, you must like the food here and how can I help you?" she said with a smile knowing they had something on their minds. Bill said.

"We would like to talk to your bartender for a moment if that's ok?"

"Certainly she said Lenny is at the bar."

"Not Lenny Bill your other bartender." Bill said.

"Oh I see is everything ok?" she asked looking concerned.

"Oh yes I noticed Bill was working on our way out and I had something I wanted to ask him and I just forgot."

"Of course sir, he's at the service bar right over there go right in." Bill and Barb walked toward the service bar and noticed Lenny moving in the same direction finally noticing them, they all arrived at the bar about the same time and Bill said to the bartender "Hi Bill, remember me?"

"Of course Mr. Kelly what can I do for you?" as Lenny turned to leave saying;

"You know I'll be back and leave you two to talk" but Bill Kelly said.

"No, no Len stick around you may want to hear this!" as Bill turned once again toward Bill the bartender asking.

"Bill I need your help with something did you by any chance make a Blue Moon or any kind of Blue colored drink this morning?" the bartender thought for a long moment finally saying;

"Ya as a matter of fact I did, I only made one drink like that earlier a Blue Hawaii for a gentleman who gave me a ten dollar tip for the drink, I directed him to the lounge bar explaining this was a service bar for the waitresses, but he didn't want to go into the lounge for some reason so he handed me a ten dollar bill to do him a favor, I did and he walked away with the drink."

"I see, Len who was the waitress who brought our drinks in for us?"

"Bonnie worked your party today Bill."

"Is she still here Len?" Bill asked.

"Ya I think she's on break." Len said as he looked around.

"What's going on here?" asked Barb wondering why all the fuss about a blue drink.

"It's a long story hon I'll explain later bear with me a bit longer!"

"Len, I believe I owe you a lengthy apology, but for now could you see if you can find Bonnie for me?"

"Ya sure Bill and then I have to get back to my bar, I'll send her over."

"Send her out to your bar Len we'll wait there and Bill thanks you've been a big help we won't tie you up any longer."

"Ok Mr. Kelly anytime I can be of service." As Bill and Barb went to the lounge to wait for the waitress Bonnie, who walked up to the bar just as they got seated.

"Hi I'm Bonnie are you the Kelly's? Lenny said you'd like to talk to me I hope your service at the party was ok, you're the first large party I've served, I do hope it was ok!" she appeared nervous and Bill thought he needed to put her at ease so he said.

"Bonnie you were perfect, no one including me would ever know this was your first party we were impressed with your professionalism and the service was great. The reason we wanted to talk to you was to find out about the first round of drinks you brought in, one was blue do you remember that?"

"Oh yes I made an extra ten dollar tip over that one!" she said smiling, totally happy over the tip and the credit and recognition Bill had given her, once again the ladies' man as Barb had often observed.

"Bonnie, how pray tell did one drink earn you an extra ten bucks?"

"Well as I recall I had just picked up the tray from the bar and started for the party room when a man stopped me asking me to give this drink to whomever ordered the Martini on the tray and he took the Martini and put the blue drink on the tray explaining they were friends of his and it was a joke, that's when he gave me the ten dollars he was very nice." Lenny overhearing this account of what had happened and appearing upset said;

"**What!** Bonnie, I can't believe you took a drink from a total stranger, that you didn't see made at the bar and deliver it to another customer to consume, it could have been drugged or worse, the drinks you serve come from the bar only!" Bonnie eyes started to tear when Barb stepped in to say;

"Come on guys your beating this girl up and she's still learning the business she meant no harm and I'm sure she'll never do that again will you hon?"

"No! I'm sorry, I'm sorry, I didn't think, but your right I'm sorry Mr. Kelly I hope everyone's ok I'm sorry Len I didn't know!" she said, sobbing now, almost uncontrollably as Barb took over taking her to the ladies room to settle her down. Bill turned to Lenny saying.

"Well Len I was right I do owe you an apology, I had no idea another bar was in operation and there was another source for drinks, it never entered my mind I guess!"

"Bill, I completely understand, I work here and it never occurred to me either, I guess those things happen, but I'm glad you figured it out and came back, I didn't want our friendship to be at risk."

"Well had I not seen Bill at the service bar on our way out I wouldn't have figured it out and a great injustice would have been done and that would have been a shame, I to value our friendship. You could do me one more favor Len if you wouldn't mind, see if you can get Bill and Bonnie to give you a description of the guy who ordered the blue drink today and let me know."

"Sure Bill that's an easy one, I'll call you when I have it."

"Thanks Len that'll be a big help." Bill said as Barb returned and said Bonnie was alright and on her way to recovery. Lenny asked if she would like a drink, but she declined saying;

"We're going to have to get going Len we've been here all day now and have other things to do; I'll take a rain check though."

"You got it Barb anytime, leave your husband at home though." he said kiddingly as they left the lounge, got in the car and once again headed for home and this time they made it all the way. On the way though, Barb asked Bill.

"Hon you don't suppose Lenny meant that, leaving you at home I mean, do you?"

"Why you thinking about taking him up on it, he's a good looking guy?"

"Of course not I've always liked him, but I thought it a little inappropriate given our relationship."

"Hon, he was just kidding, he said it for my benefit he was letting me know I was a lucky guy with a catch like you, I think it had to do with you taking Bonnie's part and rescuing her from our badgering, he thought that was pretty maternal of you and he liked that."

"I see, now I like him all over again, even more now, and speaking about maternal we may still need to talk about that, we may or may not be traveling thru time, but my biological clock is still running of that there is no doubt!"

"Yes dear! And what are you planning for dinner tonight?"

Barb, rolling her eyes said "I put together a new receipt for a chicken casserole that one of the girls gave me saying it was really good if we liked casseroles and we do."

"Ok hon I have some work to do, so you do your thing and I'll do mine and we'll talk another time about your biological clock, right now! I find it hard to believe any clock, or anything having to do with time at all!" Barb laughed and let Bill go about his business, but intending to bring it up again another time.

CHAPTER TWENTY SEVEN
EXAMINING THE CLUES

While Barb was busy in the kitchen making dinner, Bill decided to examine all the questionnaires from the lunch meeting, documenting all the various clues that led him and Dave to their conclusions as well as the many clues he had not yet discussed with Dave and put everything in some kind of chronological order for the purpose of going over it all with Dave, but first he would start with a list of clues and assign responsibility.

In order to accomplish this Bill had to make some assumptions and the first assumption he would make is that it was a conspiracy and everyone in the group was a conspirator and for the purpose of this scenario that included Barb.

INCIDENT	RESPONSIBLE
1. Toothpaste	Barbara
2. Bookmarker	Barbara
3. Book disappearing	Barbara
4. The papers on Bill desk @ work were upset	Bill?

5. Bill's book disappears	Barbara
6. Barb's book replaced with a different book	Barbara
7. A foot of un-forecasted snow 70 degrees forecasted	Nature?
8. December 17th date on the TV	Remote access?
9. Bill's car was moved from the lot to the parking garage	Barbara?
10. Pool house and swimming pool appear in parking lot	?
11. Barb's office calendars set to 12/17/11	Lisa/Barb?
12. Bill gets promoted to Project Manager	Jack Trax
13. Bill's second promotion to Engineering group leader	Jack Trax
14. At Geo's party someone orders strange Blue drinks	one of the group?
15. A stranger at the party cancels the drinks, description?	?
16. Swimming pool and pool house disappears!	?
17. Bill gets promoted to Engineering Manager	Jack Trax?
18. Bill's office building gets new Façade	Memory problem?
19. Bill loses his Job unknowingly and is not known at work	Jack Trax?
20. Bill starts his own business and doesn't remember	Bill?
21. Bill suspects a conspiracy and the groups involvement	Bill
22. Bill's home computer indicates future dates every morning	Remote access?
23. Bill's memory problems	Bill?????

24. George's office computers set for real date and time	Normal
25. Bill's home computer goes back to normal aft. 11/13/11 Mtg.	Remote access?
26. Bill loses business information in his computer, big problem	Remote access?

Well there's an initial list to be considered and indicates a lot of unanswered questions Bill thought, replace the question marks with names and he'd have the solution to the mystery, he was sure of that and sure he would need Dave's help with it, once again!

In the meantime Barb called saying "Hon dinner is ready!"

"Ok I'm on my way hon." as he sat down at the table to enjoy his dinner, somewhat preoccupied though as observed by Barb who asked.

"What were you working so intently on in there?"

"Well I have to go thru those questionnaires you guys filled out and list the commonalities for evaluation purposes along with Dave."

"Is Dave really that much help to you hon?"

"Oh ya he's amazing at times the way he comes up with credible answers to impossible questions, you heard some of that at the meeting today when Larry tried to put him on the spot, Dave handled it quite successfully I might add."

"Ya your right, how's the casserole by the way it's a new receipt?"

"It's fine, quite good actually!"

"I'm glad you're enjoying it hon, but I can see you're anxious to get back to work on your project and come up with some answers is Dave coming by today?"

"No I don't think he'll be here today and that's ok it'll give me a chance to prepare some documents and charts for Dave and I to evaluate and avoid Dave and I having to do that together and losing a day." As Bill excused himself and headed back to the living room and his computer to go back to work when Barb said.

"I'll clean the table off and you can come out here, you're probably more comfortable working out here anyway and by the way don't work to late you know you made a threat this morning that I promised to take you up on tonight and I intend to keep that promise."

Bill snapping out of his preoccupation with the task at hand for a moment and laughing a bit said "Don't worry hon I always follow through on threats and tonight won't be any exception." As he sat down in the kitchen with his computer and went back to work.

As he carefully considered the list of clues he had put together and reading #20 he realized, all of a sudden, that he owned and operated a business and he had never meet the people working for him and didn't even know their names, how could this be? He called to Barb asking her if she recalled ever meeting his employees or even talking to them and she responded, somewhat reluctantly, saying "Hon other than that one engineer you interviewed here I never meet the others or even talked to them!" Bill said.

"You know I don't recall that interview or any others, I don't remember talking to any of these guys about the business or anything else other than by email, don't you find that odd?"

Barb thought for a moment and responded by saying "Honey the last ten days, ten weeks, ten years, or even ten hours have been anything but normal, everything is to say the least odd, and I guess your question would certainly be included!"

A very intuitive answer Bill thought and if she were a part of the conspiracy she didn't give it away, but no, she was just being honest and the answer was reasonable.

At the restaurant Dave had indicated he would call Bill in the next few days to arrange a time for the two of them to get together to work on the questionnaires, Bill was sure Dave would like the list of clues and responsibility Bill had developed as a tool for solving the mystery. Bill liked Dave and was grateful for his collaboration in solving the problem, but was considering telling Dave of his suspicions about the group's involvement in the conspiracy, which included Dave.

Well that's enough for today Bill thought as he shut off the computer and joined Barb in the living room to watch television for a while before going to bed and making good on his earlier threat to Barb. As he walked into the living room he asked "What are you watching hon, anything good?"

"One of those vampire movies this one's pretty good."

"Well if you like vampires, maybe I should bite you on the neck and see how you like it, though I think I know."

"Neck biting later, for now the movie dear, but you can sit here close to me in case I get scared, so I have something to cling to."

Well the movie ended, but the evening just began as they went to bed and Bill did make good on his earlier threat and they both fell asleep with a smile on their face, their problems set aside for the moment as sleep came over them quickly.

SUNDAY NOVEMBER 13, 2011 REAL TIME

The next morning Sunday, they were both awakened by the phone's offensive ringing at 8:30am though it seemed earlier then that as Barb answered and handed it to Bill saying "It's Dave for you hon!"

Bill still rubbing his eyes took the phone saying "Hi Dave"

"Hi Bill, I hope I didn't wake you, but I thought I'd call not knowing if you guys had planned anything special for today and if not I thought we'd get together and work on this thing."

"No nothing planned, as a matter of fact I was expecting your call and getting together with you so pick a time and place, maybe you'd like to join us for breakfast here and we can work afterwards."

"Well I don't want to keep putting you guys on the hook for breakfast, how about if I pick the two of you up and take you out to breakfast on me, then we can go back to your place and work?" Bill looked at Barb, as he had Dave on speaker, who smiled and shrugged her shoulders in agreement.

"That sounds good to us Dave what time did you want to pick us up, we'll need about an hour to get ready."

"That settles it than I'll pick you up in an hour ok?"

"See you then Dave Bye for now."

"Bye guys" said Dave as he hung up telling his visitor he'd be picking the Kelly's up in an hour for breakfast and then going to their place to work. Dave's company acknowledged the information with a smile. **Who was the stranger with Dave?**

Back at the Kelly's the activities were busy and somewhat rushed especially by Barb who always took longer to get ready, saying to Bill as she ran around "That was nice of Dave to take us out don't you think?"

"I do, but Dave's a good guy and would never take advantage, by the way hon did you check the computer for the date today?"

"No I didn't why don't you do that?"

"No! I've given up on that I don't really care what's on the computer its Purposely misleading anyway and no longer has any credibility, at least none with me!"

"I see, well I'm going to check anyway, out of curiosity if nothing else." As she went to the computer and turned it on and waited for it to boot up announcing to Bill, "Hon it's back to normal again the date on the computer is Sunday November 13, 2011"

"Really?" questioned Bill, I can't understand that after the meeting were we declared the time travel phenomenon a hoax the computer goes back to normal, I need to add that to the list of clues."

They were ready sitting in the kitchen talking when the buzzer buzzed telling them Dave had arrived as Bill answered saying "Hi Dave were on our way down."

"Ok I'll be down here waiting." said Dave, as the Kelly's left their unit and walked down the rather long hallway to the waiting elevator, which seldom happens and getting in pushing the button for the 1st floor feeling little sensation as the high speed car accelerated downward with what seemed to be the speed of light at times and at other times seemed to take forever.

As they reached the ground floor the door opened and they were greeted by Dave and the rather mild November weather about 50 degrees and bright outside a pleasant day so far and getting better as Barb said "Good morning Dave you didn't have to do this you know, I can cook as easily for three as I can for two, though I will admit I appreciate the break."

"It's my pleasure Barb I enjoy spending time with you guys and I've enjoyed working on this mystery, so to speak, with you Bill."

"Do you folks have a restaurant preference, I know a pretty good Greek place that I frequent and it's very good."

"You're driving Dave, I'm sure you won't disappoint us." As they headed down the road in Dave's SUV Barb detected a fragrance she thought she recognized, but said nothing for the time being and sat back to enjoy the ride as Bill and Dave made small talk. As they drove the area and direction became familiar and Bill started to smile as the big SUV pulled into the Poseidon's parking lot just down the street from George's office. Dave looked at Bill and said "You've been here before haven't you?"

Barb immediately said "No Dave we've never been here it looks nice though."

"No hon, you've never been here before, I have with George and Dave's right it's a great place and the foods excellent."

"Well Bill it looks like you and I had the same introduction to this place, George, it's his favorite place around the area and he brings everyone here, I thought I was introducing you to a new place that you would enjoy."

"I'm sure Barb will enjoy it as much as you and I Dave so all is not lost, let's eat!" Bill said as they walked in, they were seated in an extremely comfortable booth and though the place was fairly busy, we didn't have to wait long for service, almost immediately after being seated an attractive waitress brought our menus and a pleasant smile to the table asking if we'd like coffee to start.

After finishing a great breakfast with excellent service, a pleasant atmosphere, good company and enjoyable conversation they left returning to Bill and Barb's house to reward themselves with some hopefully enlightening results for the work they were about to do.

After Dave parked his SUV they went into the building, walked to the elevator and pushed the up button and once again waited for the car to arrive, taking the opportunity to thank Dave again for the pleasant breakfast.

Once in the unit Barb put on a pot of coffee, she had decided to go out and leave the boy's to work without any distractions the guys got settled in the kitchen with the computer and Bill's notes, Barb served the coffee and asked "Is there anything I can get you guys before I leave?"

They looked at each other and Bill said "No hon were fine if we get to comfortable, we won't get any work done!"

"Ok I'm out of here, I'll be back about 8:00pm, I'm going to meet Ruth at La Flambé Lounge and we'll eat there so you're on your own."

"Ok hon see you" Barb kissed Bill and as she turned to leave, Dave said;

"Ha, how about me?" she smiled turned back and gave Dave a peck on the cheek also and left.

BILLS BUSINESS DISAPPEARS

"Ha Dave while you were busy kissing and flirting with my wife, I found something of great concern to me in my computer, look at this."

"Look at what?" Dave said.

"Exactly there's nothing to see my business is gone along with the bank accounts the records with the appointments the payroll records everything, **it's all gone!**" as Bill worked feverishly on the computer pounding the keys and deciding to attempt to restore the data back to yesterday, but oddly enough Dave didn't seem to be surprised or even concerned which Bill failed to notice because of his involvement with the problem.

Dave asked though "Bill didn't you have the business data backed up on a flash drive or something?"

"No Dave and I don't know why, but to be honest I didn't even know I had started a business, I had to be told by Barb can you believe that?"

"Actually Bill I can't, but be that as it may, I don't think you could have deleted the data by accident there are built in safeguards to prevent that kind of accident." Both men were computer literate from an operating standpoint, but they weren't programmers or hackers or computer science majors, so if a system restore doesn't work Bill's in trouble and he knows it. There's a lot of money involved in these records also, Bill was definitely concerned!

"Well here goes Dave" as Bill presses the command to start the system restore and the computer started it's manipulations to bring back the computer data to where it was the previous day as selected by Bill while Dave supports Bill with encouraging words and a pat on the shoulder, but as the system restore was completed and Bill looked for the business icon which still didn't appear, Bill said with great despair and sounding like a beaten man.

"It's gone Dave and all my efforts now have to be trying to put all that data back together or my business will be lost, I'm sorry I can't work on the other thing right now although you may be able to I've made a list that may help you."

"You know I may be able to help with this new problem you're faced with Bill if you let me take your computer to work, we have a few computer specialists there that may be able to retrieve that data in our computer lab that's all they do and they're very good. Why don't we get on with what we wanted to do today and give the new challenge to folks better equipped to deal with it!"

"Ok Dave I'm at your mercy and I'm desperate for any help I can get with this one, take the dam computer it only gives me false info anyway and now it loses what I desperately need to run a business, this PC has become a real problem lately, I may need to buy a new one."

"Good Bill, now let's take a look at that list of yours and see if we can make it work for us, I see you have a few names assigned but mostly question marks, so let's get rid of the question marks and replace them with names, shall we?"

"That's the idea Dave, but it gets hard from here, under the assumptions I made I filled in all the blanks I could and I'm sure you'll add a few so let's give it a try, but tell me something first, would it be possible to get into my home computer remotely and manipulate the data even if the computer was off?"

"I don't know Bill that's a good question, I guess it could be networked, but it seems to me you would have some indication of that on your screen and I don't believe the data could be accessed when the machine is shutdown, we can ask those questions at the lab they'd know."

"Ok, back to the list does anything jump out at you Dave, ya you've done a good job given the assumptions you've made and I don't think I can add to your list, unless you change the parameters, what do you think?"

"Ya listen let's change the subject for just a minute and let me ask you a question, we've talked about this before, but let's assume for just a moment that everyone's involved what's the motive, you too Dave, you would be one of the group, I'm the only one left out I'm the target so to speak, Why?"

"I don't think you're the target Bill, I think it seems that way because you're the most active in trying to solve the mystery and that puts you in the foreground and makes you take it personally, therefore you're the target, at least that's the way I see it."

"Well Dave that's another perspective and certainly a valid consideration, but I'm not convinced, though you make a strong argument everything points in a different direction."

"Ya know Bill, I'm sitting here going over these questionnaires and nothing is really unexpected the answers are typical, I really thought we'd get more out of this."

"You know Dave let's just look at the first question, I found it interesting that no one picked 'C' but me, not even Barb, she picked 'D' that means that nobody found anything in their homes changed or out of place except Barb and I and if I assume that Barb is part of the conspiracy that means that I am the target do you agree or not?"

"It could be interpreted that way Bill it's hard to dispute, but there may be other scenarios."

"Ok Dave let's try question number two, everyone answered 'C' again and you and I both know that every one of these folks has a home and office computer and they didn't catch the date on a computer someone had to tell them, that means the date didn't change on their computers, only on mine and once again that tells me I'm the target so to speak or they're all lying."

"Well Bill, you're certainly making your case, I'll have to look at those questions again, but with a different perspective this time."

"The only thing is the motive escapes me Dave, you want to give me a hint?"

Dave smiles and says "You're assuming I'm part of the conspiracy Bill and that hasn't been proven and I'm sure at this point, I'd be wasting my time denying it, so I won't waste my time just yet, but tell me if you think I'm part of this why are you allowing me to be in on your reasoning as I would know how close you are to the solution and report to the others, now you've confused me?"

"Wow that's short, sweet and to the point Dave, I hope I haven't offended you in any way, it was not my intent and I don't have an answer to that question, I need to think about it a long while I'm afraid, I'll sort it out in my mind and I will give you an answer, I promise!" Bill said.

Dave said. "Well now that we've put all our cards on the table, why don't we get back to the job at hand and solve this thing."

"I agree Dave how do you think we should proceed, do you want to try and analyze some more of the questions or should we work on the clues list I put together?"

"Let's try a few more of the questions Bill and see where that leads us."

"Ok #3 most answered "C" and a few "B" and one answered "D" which leads me to believe that if my assumption that they are all a part of the conspiracy is correct, than all are lying with their answers as we know for sure we were never traveling thru time and if they were part of the plot they would have known that from the beginning and the truth would have been "B" and nothing else and just to let you know Dave you answered "B"!"

"So what we've surmised so far Bill is the following, we're all conspirators and liars and you are the intended victim of the conspiracy, but why Bill?"

"Let's try one more Dave #6 almost everyone answered "B" an outsider and I to believe that, so I think it's imperative we find the stranger from the party and I'm confident that will bring this adventure to a conclusion and we can all move on with our lives, that is what lives we have left!"

"I couldn't agree more Bill so how do we proceed with finding this guy?"

"I think the key, for me, resides with Lenny, obviously if the group is involved they know the answer, but they won't disclose it to me, I suppose some of them may be innocent of any wrong doing at least I hope so, I would like to believe that Barb is not involved, at this point though, I don't know who to trust, I too am confused." Bill said.

Dave followed saying. "Let's look at that list of clues again Bill and see if we can't resolve a few of those, were wearing out the questionnaire and not making a lot of progress beyond blaming everyone of collaborating to make you a victim, but a victim of what and for what purpose we don't know, so I suggest we move on and figure it out!"

"I agree Dave and the clue that gives me the most pose and presents the greatest mystery is the swimming pool and pool house appearance and disappearance, if that was and I'm convinced it was a part of the conspiracy, what on earth was the purpose and to what end did it serve?"

"Bill, though I had never seen this swimming pool, I know it existed because you and Barb have both confirmed its existence or appearance and therein resides the answer I believe and I'll explain. I've given this a lot of thought since I learned about it and the only conclusion that makes any sense whatsoever is that it didn't exist, it appeared! I'll explain further, I believe it was a hologram and a pretty sophisticated one at that, but the technology is there and that's the only thing that makes total sense, have you considered that Bill?"

"To be honest Dave, I haven't and now that you suggest it I can't believe I didn't even think about the possibility of a hologram, but if it was done, it wasn't cheap and who on earth could afford it for a practical joke?"

"Well Bill, after a good deal of work today and a bit of tension, I think we have assigned responsibility to most of the clues, at least initially and we should probably take a break and see where this all leads. I have to admit, I'm a bit worn out after all the well founded accusations that I completely understand, but I'm sure the truth will soon be known and your right, finding the mysterious stranger is absolutely essential to solving this mystery and we should all concentrate on that, we don't need any more meetings, or getting together any more, we can communicate by phone if need be and I'll help anyway I can, just ask, I know you want to pursue other avenues and that's fine I'll keep thinking on my own and let you know if I come up with anything new."

"Certainly your right Dave, I too believe we've done everything possible to date, but I also believe we have to keep going it won't resolve itself and to tell you the truth I believe it's on me now, everyone else has done all they can or will do, I do hope I can clear Barb of any wrong doing though, that weights heavy on my mind. Well maybe we can get together for lunch or a drink soon and I do appreciate your help, regardless of your motivation and once again thanks for the great breakfast, but right now I have to get back to solving this mystery Dave."

"Ok Bill, I guess I'll take off I have a few things to attend to myself before this day ends and it's quickly coming to an end, so I guess I'll see you Bill." As Bill walked Dave to the door he said.

"Thanks again Dave." as he patted him on the back and opened the door for Dave to leave. Dave waves as he walks down the hall toward the elevator and out of sight.

Now that Bill and Dave have examined all the questionnaires and assigned responsibility to all the clues, he would need time to digest all they had learned and sort out all the possibilities in order to move ahead in a logical progression, what's next he thought?

CHAPTER TWENTY EIGHT
SUSPECTS

Well this mystery has evolved to the point where there were so many suspects that Bill considered it a conspiracy and the many suspects included both his wife and his best friend, but again he thought what was the motive? Certainly no one was trying to hurt him and he couldn't believe it a practical joke so what was the motive? Bill was sure the answer was in finding the mysterious stranger; he needed to talk to Lenny once again.

He dialed Lenny's number and waited patiently for an answer, he didn't have long to wait "Hello Bill what's going on?"

"Hi Len, I need to get together with you once again to resolve this issue with the stranger who came in and shutdown the drink thing, but I don't want to do it at the bar and interrupt your work I was wondering if you could come by and we could discuss it without being interrupted?"

"Ya I could do that Bill, but I don't know how much more help I can be?"

"Well I think if we give it a try together we may be able to ring out a little more info and be that much closer to figuring out who this guy is, so when are you available for a get together Len?"

"I'm off today and tomorrow Bill and I have no plans for either day so you pick it."

"I'd like to canvas the others first so tomorrow would be best Len, you pick the time."

"10:00a.m will work for me Bill how about you?"

"Ya that's great, Barb will have left for work and we won't have any distractions." as Bill gave Lenny his address and directions.

Lenny wrote down the info and said, "I'll see you tomorrow Bill do you want me to bring anything?"

"No just bring yourself I have everything else we'll need, see you then, bye for now Len."

"Bye Bill I'll see ya."

Bill decided to place a call to George his best friend believing that if anyone was on his side it would be George and his wife Nancy, as he dialed the number he wondered why his lifelong friend would turn against him, if indeed he had, Bill had not proven it he only suspected it, but why would George do that? The phone continued to ring and then, "Hi Bill, hearing from you so soon after the meeting, is everything alright?"

"Ya I was just wondering if you had thought of any possible clues to the identity of the stranger we had talked about?"

"Ya listen Bill can I get back to you I'm a bit tied up right now!"

"Ok I know you hadn't thought yet and that's ok we'll talk later!"

"No, no I wrote down some things, but I can't get to them right now I'm really tied up, if you catch my meaning, I mean hand cuffs and all and I will call you back!"

"I'm sorry George, I got it now!" Bill said laughing out loud realizing he had interrupted them again, not the first or last time he was sure, all their spare time was spent trying to fill the Jelly Bean Jar.

"Call me at your convenience George and say hi to Nance!" Bill said, still laughing almost uncontrollably now as he hung up.

Well Barb had not returned home yet so Bill continued with his calls this time to Larry and Karen a call he wasn't looking forward to as Larry seemed a bit put out with Bill at the meeting and Bill didn't know why exactly, but he was sure it wasn't his imagination, Larry had been distant since this thing started, but he should be expecting a call as he knew Bill would not let go of his pursuits.

As he dialed Larry and Karen's number he wondered how he would break the ice as he was a bit intimidated for some odd reason, they were good friends and he certainly should not be on guard so to speak, but never the less he was "Hi Bill or is this Barb?" Larry said waiting on Bill's response giving Bill the perfect opportunity to break the ice with a cleaver response.

"Hi Larry you know it's a shame that caller ID isn't gender sensitive just yet but it's coming I'm sure and that'll avoid the confusions when answering the phone, even giving one the option of whether or not they want to answer, but now that I got you and thanks to the lack of sophistication of the caller ID system and the fact that your home to answer I was wondering if you had time to consider the hunt for the stranger we talked about, Dave and I could use any help you may be able to give us?" Bill thinking he would include Dave's name making it easier for Larry to cooperate if he truly was upset with Bill.

LARRY HAS A THOUGHT

"Well Bill to be honest and probably contrary to what you may believe, I have given a good deal of thought to this mystery and as you know, I didn't see the guy were talking about and would have no clue about who it could be, but the more I thought about it, finally a possibility surfaced and that is you've had a couple of quick promotions lately and I believe a jealous co-worker may be responsible though I don't know who, you'd know better about that then me, what do you think?"

"Wow Larry that's probably, no not probably, that is the best and most credible possibility I've heard, I can't believe I never considered it, but probably because I don't work for that company anymore, though that doesn't eliminate the possibility, I was still working there when it all started."

"I hope that helps you guys Bill and by the way, Karen and I enjoyed the get together yesterday it was great and much improved over the first meeting, you two obviously really worked to make it a success and we believe it was." Larry said leaving Bill totally deflated over Larry's attitude and cooperation far in excess of what Bill had expected, not to mention his assessment of who could be involved, Bill would give it his full consideration and maybe now he could put a name to the stranger at the bar.

"Larry I want you to know I'm grateful for your well thought out perspective and cooperation, far in excess of what I had expected, frankly I thought you might be a little disconnected from the problem, I guess, I thought that because of prior talks we had, but I can see I couldn't have been more wrong and I'm glad I was as you sure have good insight into the problem, I think you hit the nail on the head so to speak, thank you again!"

"Thanks Bill I'm pleased I could be of some small help and I guess I did leave you with the wrong impression, but I thought that you had taken the lead on this and then Dave joined in so I did believe I could sit back and you folks would figure it out and we would all benefit from your hard work, besides whatever had happened it didn't really affect Karen and I, but I would never refuse to help if called on to do so."

"Larry I have a few other calls to make and I hope others will be as helpful as you have been you have moved us a good deal closer to a solution and changed our direction, once again thank you and we'll be talking to you soon I'm sure, but I'll say goodbye for now."

"Ok bye Bill and say Hi to Barb."

"Absolutely, bye Larry" as they both hung up Bill went back to his thought processes, no longer believing that his reluctance to call Larry was justified, quite the opposite, Larry was happy to take Bill's call and offered a well thought out assessment of the situation.

Well it was time for Bill to make yet another call and this call would go to the Goldberg's while he continued to wait for George to return his call, Bill knowing that could take a while considering what was going on there, so he placed a call to Jerry and as the phone rang he was sure he would not be as surprised at Jerry's response as he was at Larry's, but he could hope for a concerned and helpful response. "Hello" said Emily my caller ID says the Kelly's, which one?

"Hi Emily its Bill your caller ID is right on, you wouldn't believe the discussion Larry and I just had about the caller ID system, but I don't want to bore you with the details. How are you today, you haven't left Jerry yet have you? Just kidding he's a pretty good guy and an excellent cook, though I happen to know your quit handy in the kitchen yourself and that from a credible resource I can assure you. By the way the reason I called today was to ask if you guys had talked about the mysterious stranger were looking for yet and if so, did you come up with anything that will help identify him?"

"Not really Bill, but I know he's talked about something with Dave, though I don't know what it was."

"I see, well is he there maybe he and I can clear it up?"

"Oh, of course, but no he's at the warehouse, you're probably aware there having a lot of problems with the security company at the Airports and it's costing a lot of additional money for the business because of late deliveries, overnight storage and delayed pickups at the terminals due to increased security, so now there working Sundays to offset the delays.

"I'm sorry to hear that Emily, Jerry had casually mentioned some problems, but I didn't realize they were that extensive, I hope their able to work around the problems without too much difficulty."

"Yes so do I Bill their eating up what little profits their making, but you know how government regulations can wreak havoc on a small business. Jerry and his partner are ready to turn the business over to the feds and let them run it under their own regulations, but then they realized it wouldn't matter, not being profit motivated, they'd just operate in the red and tell everyone what a great job they were doing!"

"Your exactly right Emily, well if you'd tell Jerry I called and I'll get back to him later I'll let you get back to what you were doing before I took up all your time."

"Don't be silly it's always nice to talk to you Bill and I'll tell Jerry you called ok, I'll say goodbye for now though and say hi to Barb for us!"

"Thanks Emily and I will, Bye-Bye." Hanging up Bill thought it odd that Jerry would be talking to Dave about it, Bill was sure he was becoming paranoid about this whole thing, but wasn't overly concerned as he could see the light at the end of the tunnel realizing the end was in sight, at least that's what he thought!"

Hearing a key in the door and realizing Barb was home, checking his watch and seeing she was right on time 8:05pm and he hadn't eaten dinner yet, but betting she had, he headed to the refrigerator to see what he could throw together quickly.

Barb saying as she came in. "Hi honey it's me I'm home and I have a surprise for you, I think you'll like it!"

"Oh what is it?"

"You'll see in a minute Bill, are you hungry?"

"You bet I was just trying to find something to eat in the fridge, but not having much luck, I'd suggest we go out, but I'm sure you've already eaten, am I right?"

"Well you can stop looking I brought you your favorite burger."

"A sub burger from La Flambé?" asked Bill, how did she know I liked them so much, probably because when we go there that's my usual order, sometimes I eat one there and take one to go. I should have known she always thinks of me, how she could possibly have conspired against me I'll never know!

"Well hon, Lenny is coming over in the morning we have more to discuss and then I may take him out to lunch as a thank you for helping me. By the way, I haven't had a chance to tell you yet, but all the data on the business has been deleted from the computer and I have no idea how it could possibly have happened and neither does

Dave, but he's going to take the computer to work and turn a couple of government hackers loose on it and see if they can fix it!"

"What will we do if they can't retrieve the lost data, how can you run the business?"

"Honestly! I don't know the bank accounts are of concern of course, but I can retrieve those at the bank, I think for now I'll rely on the hackers and worry about it when they can't fix it!"

The phone rings and Barb says it looks like its George hon "Hi George"

"Hi Barb is your hubby home he called earlier, but I was tied up!"

"I know you mean that literally George, what did Nancy use to restrain you with this time?"

Bill hearing how the conversation was going took the phone from Barb, who was smiling as she put George on the spot for more detail.

"Hi George it took you a little longer than I expected, I've forgotten why I called you maybe just to pass the time of day, but no I remember now, how are you doing trying to figure out who the stranger is were looking for?"

"About that Bill, I have no clue he could be anyone; we know it's no one in the group of our friends, the bartender has already confirmed that, though all our friends were not at the party, so I'm confused to say the least!"

"You know George everyone I talk to has a little to offer even though they may not know it for instance you said, all our friends were not at the party and your absolutely correct and I'm sure that never crossed my mind, you've been a big help and didn't even know it, thanks!"

"Well Bill if you need further help just call, I'm glad to be of service, perhaps the next time I help I'll know what I did!"

"Ya George go back to your Jelly Beans and we'll talk soon, Bye for now!"

"Bye Bill" as Bill hung up he couldn't believe he never thought of the fact that all their friends were not at the party, the group collectively had many friends and now he would have to consider all of them and eliminate them logically and once again he would need Dave's help as the list of suspects was growing rather than the shrinking, the light in the tunnel was disappearing again, Oh my Bill thought, would this never end?

Another list would be required a list of friends and acquaintances that were not at George's Birthday Party, how detailed would that have to be to serve the purpose and include all possible legitimate suspects, that is something for he and Dave to figure out.

Another get together with Lenny tomorrow may bring to light even more useful information, Bill wondered how the law enforcement agencies were ever able to solve crimes, his experience thus far has been, the more you dig the more you learn the more complex it becomes and in this case the more suspects you eliminate the more you gain and the light at the end of the proverbial tunnel gets even dimmer. Bill's an engineer and should realize how involved problem solving can be, it's what engineers do!

AN ODD PHONE CALL

As Bill was finally able to get to his burger and enjoy it and he was hungry, the phone rang once again and Barb being the dutiful wife and seeing Bill starting to eat answered it saying, "Operator how may I direct your call?" hearing an unfamiliar voice on the other end saying,

"Have I got the Kelly residence?"

"You have this is Mrs. Kelly"

"I see this is Mr. King from the human resources department at Bracken Metals, I was looking for Mr. William Kelly is he available?" she had the phone on speaker and looked at Bill for direction and he shook his head in the negative, not wanting to talk right now.

Barb followed by saying "I'm sorry he's not home right now, but I'd be happy to take a message and let him know you called."

"Are you expecting him this evening?"

"I am, but I don't know how late." still looking at Bill and shrugging her shoulders in a questioning manner.

"Well if you wouldn't mind I'll leave you my number and I can be reached anytime this evening until about noon tomorrow when I'll be leaving town again or I can try back if that would be better?"

"Well I don't think Bill will bother you if he gets in late so if you want you could call back in the morning at your convenience as I'm sure he'll be here and I'll tell him to expect your call."

"That'll be fine, why don't we figure on that, I'll call in the morning unless I hear from him tonight in which case I won't call in the am."

"Ok than Mr. King may I ask what this is all about or is it a secret?"

"Gee Mrs. Kelly I wish I could tell you, but I'm afraid it's against the law though I'm sure Mr. Kelly will let you know the minute he finds out himself."

"Well I'm sure your right Mr. King, we have no secrets from each other, but I thought I'd give it a try anyway, I know he'll be curious, once again I'll let him know you called."

"That'll be fine Mrs. Kelly I'll say goodbye for now and look forward to talking with Mr. Kelly."

"Ok than Bye Mr. King" as they hung up Barb turned to Bill who was busy devouring the last of his burger and enjoying every bite and asked;

"What do you suppose that was all about hon?"

"I'm sure I don't know, a call from HRM is unusual, I'll probably call him back tonight I have Lenny coming in the morning and I don't want to be bothered during that meeting. You know I don't remember the circumstances under which I left Bracken Metals, that memory issue again, but I don't know if I quit or if I was fired or the reason for either, but whatever the case I have no idea why HRM would be contacting me this long after the fact. Bye the way the burger sure hit the spot; I didn't realize how hungry I was!"

"That all aside for now, how did you and Dave make out with your investigations this afternoon?"

"Actually we did very well uncovering many plausible possibilities, but unfortunately we also created some friction between us I can only hope it's not lasting or irreparable damage as I believe the fault lies mostly with me! I did however get some surprisingly useful info from Larry and George, but leading me down two different roads, I'll have to sort it out with Dave if he's still talking to me?"

"Oh I'm sure he will still work with you he's a good friend and he enjoys a good mystery I think; at least that's how I read him."

"It seems like the phone calls never end which reminds me I talked to Emily this afternoon and she's a bit worried about Jerry and the business which is having its difficulties and it sounds like Jerry isn't handling it very well, maybe you should give her a call and lend a sympathetic ear so to speak."

"Absolutely I'll do that maybe we can go to lunch or something, I'll call tomorrow, maybe I can stop by the store and do a little shopping while I'm there!"

"Hon a jewelry store isn't where you go to do casual shopping; your first idea lunch was a better idea, you might pursue that avenue!" Barb laughing, as she heard her husband beg in his own way and deciding not to put his mind at ease quite yet said,

"Well hon Christmas is just around the corner so I may stop just to get some idea's, but it would depend on how hungry I am when I make the arrangements!" Bill adding a bit of humor replied by saying;

"Ok I'll put a lock on the refrigerator and give you my credit card for lunch to insure the outcome!"

"That's funny, but I will take the card!" Barb said.

As the day was coming to a rapid end, Bill decided not to call Mr. King leaving that until the morning, the day had not been without its tense moments, but a good deal of info had been exchanged and Bill was sure progress had won out in the end. Tomorrow was yet another day in the recent adventure, today leaving new problems to resolve like the business info being lost from Bill's computer and an unusual call from Mr. King another meeting with Lenny and another call to Dave for additional help. It was time to relax a bit before going to bed and hopefully getting a good night's sleep before waking to yet an even busier day tomorrow. Bill called to Barb saying.

"Hon what do you say let's call it a day and turn in?"

Barb peeking out from the bedroom said "Hon I'm already in bed and waiting for you to join me, I'm into my new book it's a love story!"

"Ok well keep your nose in the book as I'm going right to sleep, I have a busy day tomorrow and you have to work."

Bill took his shower and got into bed he and Barb were soon both fast asleep, the day was indeed over.

CHAPTER TWENTY NINE
A HUNT FOR THE STRANGER

(NOVEMBER 14, 2011 REAL TIME)

Monday morning, their sleep thru the night undisturbed, as they both started to give in to the rising Sun peeping thru the blinds in the bedroom. Barb getting up first as she had to go to work and didn't like to be rushed, followed soon by Bill who was actually looking forward to todays planned activities, hoping to make significant progress on his quest for the ultimate solution the mystery they were dealing with for several days now. But first the coffee, Bill thought as he went to the kitchen to start the day in the usual way and yelling to Barb, "Good morning dear, I put the coffee on, did you want some toast?"

"Hi honey, ya sounds good make it an English muffin though and buttered if you don't mind."

"Mind, why would I mind, you got it, ready in five minutes!"

As Bill prepared Barb's morning snack he thought about how he would set the time line for the day's activities, he knew Lenny would arrive at ten and King would probably call before that and he would need to call Dave before he left for work to give him time to plan if he was still talking to Bill and the results of all that would dictate the rest of the day's activities.

As Barb finally appeared in the kitchen fully dressed and ready to leave for work, smiling as she picked up her buttered muffin and poured her coffee saying "I'll likely stop at the store on the way home were out of cottage cheese and a few other odds and ends, it's easier to pick up a few things at a time, then to do a big shopping after work, I'd rather save that for Saturday's."

"Ok hon whatever you decide I'll be tied up well into the afternoon or later I'm sure, why don't we have a lite dinner tonight, salads I think before I start putting on weight or worse!"

"OK by the way call me and let me know what Mr. King wanted I think I'm more curious than you."

"I will, though I expect to be tied up on phone calls a good part of the day." As Bill was saying goodbye to Barb on her way out the door the phone rang, the first call of the day Bill thought as he answered "Hello" said Bill.

"Mr. Kelly?" an unfamiliar voice said.

"Yes, Mr. King I presume?"

"Please Bill call me Dennis I'm hoping to remain on a first name basis if we can, I'm sure your curious about the call and to be quite honest I decided to make this call myself because I don't often get the chance in my job to deliver the more pleasant news usually the opposite is required."

"I see, well Dennis you've certainly stimulated my interest though I can't imagine what you could be referring too, so tell me what's on your mind?"

"Very much to the point, as I've been led to expect Bill, so, let's cut to the chase shall we, I'm calling to offer you your old job back as Engineering Manager and I understand there'll be a salary increase to go along with the offer there are some cursory details to work out, but the offer is valid."

"You've taken me quite by surprise Dennis, I had no idea that would be the reason for your call, I guess I assumed that position was filled when I left and now your offering me the job back, with an increase in salary, that's curious, but you may or may not realize I've started a fairly successful consulting business and leaving that behind would be difficult to say the least." Bill still not realizing, how or why he left Bracken Metals, making this a curious offer indeed.

"Ah Ha well would it be possible to be an absentee owner so to speak, higher someone to run the business and come back to Bracken? The type of business you're in wouldn't present a conflict problem, I don't believe and you could benefit from two incomes, sounds like a win, win to me what do you say!"

"Tell me Dennis what happened to the Engineering Manager you had?"

"Well Bill you know I can't talk about that, suffice it to say, that employee has moved on, I'm sure there's office talk you'll hear, but certainly not from me!"

"I see and of course I understand, just curious, I don't recall who took that job after I left, but you can't tell me that either is that right?"

"Right again!"

"I see, well I'll need some time to think about it Dennis, there are extenuating circumstances here and a quick answer is just not possible, I hope you can understand that."

"Absolutely let's see its Monday why don't I call back on Friday the 18th and see if we can't finalize things then?"

"Ya I think I can make a decision by then after talking to friends and family and seeing if its workable, the business and all, so I'll expect to hear from you on Friday Dennis and I can assure you I'll be busy thinking until then."

"Ok Bill it's been great talking with you and by the way Jack Trax said to say hello, under other circumstances he would have been making this call himself, for now though I'll say goodbye and let you get back to your day."

"Bye Dennis well talk soon I'm sure" as Bill put down the phone he couldn't believe what he had just heard, he was caught totally off guard, he poured a fresh cup of coffee and sat down to contemplate the moment and the last couple of days.

Looking at his watch he realized Lenny was do in an hour and he had to prepare mentally for that meeting, how would he extract the knowledge he was sure Lenny had buried in the back of his mind?

While waiting for Lenny, Bill recounted the last day or two, realizing he had been given a lot of useful info from several sources, first his discussions with Dave and the tensions brought about there, secondly the thoughts brought about by his conversation with Larry and Larry's idea that a vindictive Bracken Metals employee could be responsible, then the talk with George, who talked about all the friends and family not at George's party and the possibility of one of them being the mysterious stranger we were all looking for and finally the coup de gras the totally unexpected phone call from the HRM representative Dennis King from Bracken Metals offering me my old job back with an increase in salary and benefits, Bill still not knowing how he left the company other than going to work one morning and being denied entry to the building, it was all a bit too much!

Bill's mind was spinning like a top and in no particular direction he was even starting to get a bit of a headache as the buzzer rang snapping him out of the stupor/daze he was in and answering the door saying "That you Len?"

"Ya Bill it's me!" as Bill pushed the buzzer to let Len in and leaving the door open made his way back to the kitchen to make a fresh pot of coffee, soon Lenny walked in saying;

"Morning Bill, I'm not too early am I?" noticing Bill being a little out of sorts and a bit worn out.

"No you're right on time Len, I've been going over a few things in my mind that have come up the last couple of days and I have to admit I'm a little confused, but I'll work it out, can I interest you in a cup of coffee?"

"That would hit the spot Bill, just cream thank you."

"Here you go pal, why don't we get started, shall we. I've come into new info since we last talked leading me to ask different questions of you. I must admit at the latest lunch get together we had I was a bit taken aback when you couldn't identify the member of the party that ordered the blue drinks to start with, up until then I believe you and I were both under the impression it was a member of the group at the party, isn't that correct?"

"Absolutely Bill I knew the person from previous visits and he was defiantly someone I associated with your party and you and I expected to see him at the luncheon the other day, I'm also very confused!"

"Well Len there are many confusing aspects to what's going on and it gets more confusing daily and the only way I know to sort it out is to keep talking like were doing now, I hope you don't mind."

"Not at all Bill, I'm getting a little frustrated myself, so I can start to understand your frustrations and I truly wish I could be more help!"

"Len you've once again helped, not with a name, but you have described the guy ordering the drinks as someone I've been in there with before, maybe a friend or even a relative and knowing everyone I have ever been in the bar with I should be able to narrow it down and figure out who it is and that's progress. Knowing who that person is may help identify the mysterious stranger were looking for, I'm convinced that will solve the mystery and that brings us back to the stranger who cancelled the drinks and the description you gave me, is there anything additional you can think of about him?"

"He clearly knew, quite well I think, the man who ordered the drinks and they left together Bill."

"I didn't realize they left together Len, but why would I, thinking the guy ordering the drinks was a member of the party, so you see the more questions you ask the more you learn; now I know why the Police are so nosy when they are investigating something!" said Bill, as he got up to get another cup of coffee and checking his watch realizing it was getting close to lunch time he thought it might be a good time to take a break and take Lenny to lunch.

"Ha Len are you getting hungry, I thought we'd go out and get a bite and come back to finish or we may even finish at lunch, what do you think?"

"Sure Bill I could eat something."

"Ok then I know a pretty good little restaurant let's go shall we!" as they both got up to leave, Bill shut off the coffee maker and they both headed for the elevator and Bill's car and once on their way Lenny asked to pass the time "How do you like your BMW Bill it's my first time in one?"

"There nice, but a bit over rated Len, there are a lot of nice cars out there and what one manufacture does this year they all do next year, my personal opinion though, is when it comes to the luxury models, the foreign imports do a better job and the cost be dammed. Domestic model cars have more appeal in a different market. I think we buy enough cars in this country that both foreign and domestic manufactures can exist quite comfortably and that's the end of the commercial." Bill said as they pulled into the Poseidon parking lot, a restaurant quickly becoming one of Bill's favorites.

"I guess your right Bill, but I like my pickup nowadays there like a luxury car inside and practical on the outside and I often use mine like a truck so I believe I'll stick with it. I don't think I've ever been to this place Bill it looks good."

"I've never been disappointed Len, I think you'll enjoy It." as they were seated and given their menus to browse the server took their drink orders and walked away leaving them to decide. Bill quickly got back to the topic of the stranger and his identity, but Lenny shaking his head negatively said;

"Bill I honestly don't know how much more help I can be other than the description I gave you there isn't much more I know except, wait a minute there is something else it was his ring, it was large one of those fraternal rings I believe, I've seen this kind of ring before, but I can't remember where!"

"Well Len there you go your remembering more and more as we speak, but about the ring, what do you remember about it, anything at all?"

"It was large with a colored stone, red I think and some kind of symbol, maybe a fraternity ring, but it was striking and that's about it."

"Do you remember any details about the symbol Len?"

"No it was a pretty quick glance, if it hadn't been so large I probably wouldn't have noticed it at all, but he was a pretty small guy and the ring looked a little out of place on his hand!"

Bill wondered off a little into his world of thought, as something Lenny was saying struck a familiar note, but he just couldn't put his finger on it, so to speak, but he was sure he was close to an answer, Lenny had finally given Bill what he needed to solve the mystery about the stranger, though he wasn't quite there yet!"

"Len I think you've given me what I needed to get to the bottom of this, I think the ring is the clue we needed and you didn't even know you had the answer in the back of your mind, this is a worthwhile lunch to say the least and it's with a friend making it that much more enjoyable. Continuous conversation Len I'll never forget that, if you keep after something eventually you'll get there. Let's order shall we!" they ordered their lunch and continued their talk, but this time about generalized topics passing the time of day while they enjoyed their food.

As they left the restaurant for home, Bill thanked Lenny once again for the help though Len still didn't think he'd been that much help, Bill assured him he had.

As they pulled into the parking garage Bill said "Listen Len your welcome to come back upstairs and we can discuss what else has been going on, maybe you can offer a different perspective on this mystery, but I think you've given me a lot to think about today and that's just what I'm going to do, think about things for a while and see if I can get closer to a solution to this mystery."

"No Bill I think I'll let you go thru your thought processes on your own, it's easier to think that way, you don't need someone sitting there watching you think, that would drive me crazy, but that's me, so I think I'll go and leave you to what has become your passion, solving mysteries, I guess you're getting quite good at it, you seem to enjoy it anyway!"

"I have always enjoyed a challenge Len, but I have to admit this one is getting to me, I think because it's personal and I believe someone is trying to hurt me and that I don't like, but in any case I appreciate what you've done today and Barb and I will be in to see you at the bar soon and if there is a solution you'll be the first one I call."

"Ok Bill, I'm going to take off I'll look forward to seeing you guys soon, bye for now and thanks for the lunch!" as Lenny walked to his pickup, Bill watched and waved goodbye, then going back inside his own head to continue working on solving the mystery with the new info Lenny had just provided, but he needed to call Dave with the latest developments also.

Turning the key in his unit's door and opening it he saw Barb sitting there in the kitchen with a rather somber look on her face "Hi honey" Bill said.

"To what do I owe the pleasure of your company this early in the day, is everything ok?"

"Oh ya, but I hadn't heard from you and you said you'd call after Mr. King called, I didn't have any more patients today, Ruth could see I was preoccupied and talked me into going home, so here I am." Bill gave her a kiss and a hug saying;

"Well if you had gotten here a little earlier you could have gone to lunch with Lenny and I we went to the Poseidon and he thought it was great also, he was very helpful today and yes Mr. King did call and offered me my old job back with an increase in salary and benefits! I'm confused."

"You said yes didn't you?"

"No I said I had to talk to you and others and would decide later, he's going to call back Friday for a decision and I'll tell him then what I've decided, I'm still not sure, we have the business to consider were making pretty good money with it and we have problems to resolve with it right now!" Barb looking real upset and even allowing a few tears to run down her face said.

"But honey you're a good engineer and I really believe you liked your job better than your business, have you considered that?" trying to discourage the business influencing his decision on going back to Bracken.

"I have a good deal to consider Barb that's exactly why I didn't give Dennis my answer right away, but it sure is curious, especially when I don't even know why I left there in the first place, curious indeed, don't you think?"

"I think once you left they realized how much they missed your expertise and they want it back, that's what I think!"

"In any case I'm glad your home and if you make us a drink, I can make a call to Dave and maybe we can take advantage of your afternoon off and do something relaxing, what do you say?"

"I'll make the drinks and while you're talking with Dave I'll think of some distraction for us to deal with."

Bill sat down by the phone and dialed Dave's work number as he knew he'd be there and he was "Hello this is Dave"

"Hi Dave its Bill I hope I'm not interrupting you if I am I can call back."

"No, no it's fine Bill what's on your mind?"

"To be honest I didn't know whether or not to even call or if you would be interested after yesterday, but there have been several new and interesting revelations since we talked and I thought you might be interested in helping me sort them out."

"Yesterday, what happened yesterday? I must have missed something, but yes absolutely I'd be interested in helping, let's get together!"

"I must say Dave you never disappoint me, in spite of our disagreements yesterday your willing to jump back in and continue to help, you don't find many like you and it's appreciated, but I don't want to keep you on the phone at work so why don't you call me when you get home tonight and we can figure out a plan to get together, I have a great deal to tell you and unbelievable news from this morning, I'll explain when I see you."

"Ok Bill that's a plan I'll call you from home tonight bye for now."

"Bye Dave" they both hung up and talking to Dave reminded Bill of his plans to fix Dave up with Gloria, what ever happened with that, he thought it worth investigating after all she was a good looking and pleasant woman and Bill was sure Dave would like the companionship she would offer, he had suggested it to Dave, but never heard any more about it, follow up was indicated.

Barb brought Bill his drink and asked "You said they were offering you your old job back which old job were they referring too?"

"Engineering Manager, the one I had when I left hon."

"What happened to whoever had that job Bill, did he/she get promoted?"

"I don't know they can't say, but I suspect he/she couldn't handle it, at least that's the way it sounded."

"I see, well how did your talk with Lenny go today, you said he was very helpful, what more could he possibly tell you that he didn't tell you before?"

"Details hon, details, he described a ring the guy was wearing that he didn't talk about before, it never came up in our discussions, but it sure was helpful there's something about it that's familiar, but I can't quite put my finger on it yet."

"What kind of ring was it hon?"

"It's a large gold ring with a red stone and some kind of fraternity symbol on it according to Len."

"Well hon, that's why it seems familiar to you, gold rings with red stones are quite common especially with Italians!"

"No its more than that, I'll figure it out eventually I'm sure, he also described it as a large ring on a little man adding to the description I already have, helping me even more, a big ring on a little man, I can almost see the mysterious man, but no longer a total stranger, a bit out of focus perhaps, but becoming clearer all the time. Barb I'm absolutely sure that if I knew who he was, I'd know everything, of that there is no doubt and that is where all my efforts should be concentrated!"

"It sounds like your closing in on this thing I can't believe it's come this far and with all the misdirection swimming pools, snowfalls, time travel and all the other things that have happened, I do wish it was over and we could get back to our normal life together!"

"Hon, this thing is like an infection, were like the antibiotics working to stop it and we will, but like a medicine it takes time to take effect, we will stop it though!"

Well after a lengthy discussion with Barb and his call to Dave to arrange yet another get together, Bill thought it a perfect time to relax awhile with Barb and maybe even add a few Jelly Beans to the jar, but wait, they were supposed to be taking them out of the jar at this point in time, they had been married quite a bit longer than a year, but maybe, now that he's thinking about it, that's why the jar isn't getting empty, Barb's still putting beans into the jar he'd have to ask her as he was sure the jar should have been empty by now.

"Hon why don't we take our drinks into the living room, turn on the TV and settle down for a while doing what comes natural?"

"Oh, and what is it that comes so natural dear?"

"I know I don't have to answer that hon, I'd much rather show you as he took her hand and headed for the bedroom Barb in one hand and his drink in the other and finishing both of them on his mind.

As they lay in bed together after finishing their drinks discussing further details of the last couple of days Barb wanted to pursue Bill's thoughts about the job offer he had and why he didn't jump at the opportunity, this concerned her greatly as it also affected her security and peace of mind.

Bill on the other hand wanted to play his hand to the end and was reasonably secure in the fact that he had a business that was fairly successful and he wanted to know more about how and why he left or was allowed to leave Bracken Metals in the first place and a few weeks later they come knocking on his door to give him his job back with additional incentives, it made little sense.

The phone rang and it was on Barb's side of the bed so she answered "Hello Dave hang on he's right here." Barb handing the phone to Bill saying;

"It's Dave hon for you."

"Hi Dave your home early aren't you?"

"No actually I'm still at work, but as it turns out I'm not going right home and I have some idle time now so I thought I'd call and set up a time to get together tomorrow as I am off and we can use my house if that's ok?"

"Ya that's fine Dave and your house, you set the time I'm open to anything!"

"How about 11:00a.m. Bill, will that work for you?"

"Ya, I'll bring the burgers Dave how do you like them and how many?"

"Medium rare and I can probably handle two if there not to big everything on them though and hold the fries."

"You got it looking forward to seeing you in the morning and I have a lot to discuss with you and as I said a surprise as well, so I'll say goodbye for now and let you get back to work, thanks for the call once again Dave."

"Ok Bill bye, see you tomorrow."

The day was over for the Kelly's as they said goodnight after a long tedious day of investigation and revelation for Bill and Barb's concern for Bill's decision about putting off his acceptance of the job offer from Bracken Metals because of his business and other considerations he wanted to think about.

They both rolled over went to sleep and put the day behind them.

CHAPTER THIRTY
THE BIG SURPRISE

(TUESDAY NOVEMBER 15, 2011 REAL TIME)

Once again the morning sun peeped thru the bedroom blinds announcing the arrival of a new dawn and encouraging the Kelly's participation in the new day's activities, some planned, some not, but all expected to be eventful. As they both rubbed their eyes, looked at each other and got out of bed racing to the bathroom, Barb winning as her side of the bed was nearest to the bathroom door, so once again Bill had to wait for his wife to reappear allowing his use of the facility.

Bill went to the kitchen to make the coffee while he waited his turn in the bathroom knowing Barb would only give it up for a short time, as she would spend a lot more time in there getting ready for work.

Bill, still unable to get the big red ring out of his head, knowing the key lies there, but unable to make the connection, not giving up for a moment though, hoping Dave will be able to help sort it out today when they get together later this morning.

Barb in a bit of a hurry this morning as she had some early patients didn't even have time for her toast and coffee so Bill fixed her a coffee to go knowing there was a Burger King across the street from her office where she could get a breakfast item which he understood her and Ruth did quite often.

As Barb grabbed her coffee gave Bill a kiss said goodbye and flew out the door as if she were about to miss her flight yelling;

"I love you!" as she ran down the hallway to the elevator, hoping it was waiting for her, fat chance Bill thought as he closed the door and poured himself a cup of coffee.

As Bill sat at the table reading the paper his mind racing once again the phone rang and Bill now recognized the number as Lenny's "Hello Len what's up this early?"

"I'm sorry Bill did I wake you?"

"Heavens no, I've been up I am just sitting here with my paper and coffee."

"Good I didn't want to call to early, but I thought it might be important and even helpful to tell you about the ring I remembered the symbol, was an "A", it is a signet ring and the guy's last name must start with an A, does that help?"

"You bet it does Len, that really narrows the search, I'm sure with a little thought we'll be able to identify this guy now, I'm getting together with Dave in a little while now and we will figure this out I'm confident and it's all thanks to you Lenny, Christmas is just around the corner and there'll be something extra under your tree!"

"You don't have to do anything like that Bill just keep doing your drinking at the lounge and I'll be happy. I'll let you get on with your day and say goodbye for now, if anything else comes up I'll call, good luck with Dave."

"Thanks again Len and goodbye!"

Well, Bill thought, an "A" who do we know with a last name beginning with an "A" none come to mind, of course that doesn't mean I'd know anyone with a last name beginning with an "A", but someone in the group will I bet. Let me call Dave in advance of our meeting to give him a chance to start thinking about it.

As he dialed Dave's number hoping he was up and about not wanting to disturb him to early, but sure that would not be the case as Dave worked and as he recalled started at 8:00AM, so he was surely an early riser. "Hello Bill I hope you're not changing your mind about lunch I'm looking forward to those burgers."

"No of course not the burger's will be there, the reason I'm calling is to ask if you know anyone in our group of friends or acquaintances whose last name begins with an "A" I'd like you to think about that before I get there as it might be important, I'll explain later I don't want to take up too much of your time right now."

"I'll think about it and see you in a little while Bill."

"Thanks Dave I'll let you go for now bye, keep your appetite up."

"Bye Bill and I will be hungry." Hanging up Bill thought more about the ring and the initial "A" and what it could stand for, could it stand for a first name, Anthony for instances Bill knew an Arthur at his old job, he would have no ax to grind with Bill though, but the "A" could be a first name as well as a last name, which was the more common usage on a signet ring he thought?

Well it was time to start getting ready to go to Dave's and take up the fight once again, it seems that every time he talks to someone he benefits some and gets a little closer to the answers he's looking for, he makes progress and that's the reason he keeps going and will continue to pursue the solution to the mystery and believes he will solve it in the end and of course the solution would be the end, or would it?

Bill left the condo and on his way to Dave's stopped at a Burger King to pick up some of Dave's favorite burger's as promised and continued to the house where he found Dave anxiously awaiting his arrival grabbing the bag of burgers at the door and saying "Hi Bill good to see you and I see you kept your word, I didn't eat breakfast waiting for these today, there a welcome treat, did you get any for yourself?"

"Ya I think there's a couple in there for me, but you go ahead I guess were going to eat first and I'm good with that, have you got a couple of beers to go along with those burgers?"

"You bet I have Bill, now I wish I had asked you to bring some fries along with the burgers!"

"Look in the bag Dave, I think you'll discover all you need is in there!" as he took the beer from Dave and sat down to enjoy the lunch.

Dave digging into the rather large bag found the fries on top keeping the many burgers warm and immediately a smile came over his face, obviously grateful that Bill had not listened to him when he turned down the fries. As they were both enjoying their lunch, Bill outlined what they would talk about today saying "Dave, I'd first like to go over what has happened since we last got together and talked."

- Talking with Larry, he was convinced the mysterious person were looking for is possibly a disturbed/agitated Bracken Metals employee jealous of my two rapid promotions.
- George makes the point that all our friends and relatives were not at the party and it could be one of those who were left out.
- Lenny recalls a ring the guy was wearing, a large gold ring with a red stone with a symbol later turning out to be the letter A and he described it as a big ring on a little guy along with the description he previously gave us.
- Then comes what I describe as the coup de gras I got a call from a represen-

tative from Bracken Metals offering me my old job back with an increase in salary and benefits. Of course I said I needed time to consider it.

"So there you have it, that's why I'm here today and willing to buy lunch." laughing as he held up his burger in a solute type gesture.

"Well, that indeed is a lot to chew on, so to speak." said Dave laughing as well, holding up his fries in a similar solute.

Well after finishing their lunch and a couple of beers each, Dave was ready to get down to business and take apart each opinion individually starting with Larry's thoughts on the discontented employee asking Bill, "Bill do you know anyone at work that might fit Larry's scenario and implement this elaborate and I might add expensive plan to get even with you?"

Once again Bill, a bit exasperated, with Dave's obvious grasp of the situation responds by saying, "Dave your simply unbelievable in your assessment of the situation, it's almost like you had insight into the question and were able to rehearse the answers in advance, I can't believe I didn't consider the same possibilities, in which case I wouldn't have needed to call you to help me sort them out let's move on, I can't wait to see how you destroy George's observations!"

Dave laughing yet again responded by saying "Bill, I believe, your simply too close to this thing, making the assessment of information difficult at times where I see it from a different perspective and look at it with less emotion I guess, now for George's take on things, him suggesting that all the friends and family were not there is correct, but that is where the correctness ends, to suggest that friends or family not being invited would alienate anyone is a bit outrageous I mean think about it how many times are relatives or even friends not invited to weddings or christenings or even graduations and don't hire hit men to get even, it's simply not a valid point Bill."

"Once again Dave I bough to superior assessment of things and of course thinking about it I agree with you, but I believe you'll have a more difficult time with the next one."

"You're talking of course about Lenny's input and your right he has no dog in this fight, that we know of I might add, but he keeps adding helpful info, he may even come up with a name eventually, let's give it time and see."

"No, no, Dave I finally get to disagree, the reason Lenny keeps adding info is because I believe he has more to give though he may not know it and I keep after him to think and pull from his subconscious what I know to be there."

"Ah ha, I see Bill so you're the culprit, just kidding, that's a great method of interrogation and commonly used by the law enforcement community I'm sure, hopefully it brings out the facts though, rather than beating the object of the interrogation into submission. Yes I'm sure Lenny has been helpful and just how much will come out when this thing is over. The harder I think about it though I can't put a name to the initial "A" at least no one I know who could possibly have anything to do with the current situation."

"Well Dave we'll get back to Lenny I'm sure and now comes the Coup De Gras Bracken Metals coming back to me with a job offer with incentives after I'm operating a successful business, never knowing for sure why I left Bracken, I don't know if I was fired or quit or was just laid off, maybe my job was done away with, but now there offering me the same job back, so what do you think about this one Dave this is where I really need your help and consider how I found out I was out of a job there, going to work one morning and being denied admittance to the plant or even my office, by guards that never worked there before that morning. What do you think?"

"Bill I don't know how to start with this one, I believe I'm even more confused than you are so let's see, you have no memory of what happened to your job at Bracken or why you may have been let go. All you know for sure is you had two quick promotions in a relatively short time and then you came to work one morning and were refused admittance to the property, is that about it?"

"That's it in a nutshell Dave and now they want me back, go figure, I don't know what to make of it, but I have a business to run and I can't do both, though they suggest and seem to think I can."

"Sounds to me Bill like you're going to have to do a little sole searching, I mean some serious thinking about what you want to do and you have a myriad of choices, your luckier than most, you can do one or the other or even both or something totally different so it's on you Bill, no one else, but you might consider letting someone else run the business for a while as was suggested by the HRM representative while you give Bracken Metals another try and this time try and get a contract, it's common now a days, other than that I'm afraid I can't offer much more."

Bill's alert system triggered immediately he never told Dave that Dennis had made that suggestion, so how did he know? He wasn't going to let on just yet that he had picked up on that slip as he was sure that's what it was, but for now he would keep quiet and let things develop further as they certainly would.

"Dave your advice is sound and I guess it's on me as you indicate I'll have to consider it carefully before making a quick decision based on my gut so to speak." As Dave started to respond Bill yelled out! **"No, no not an "A" not an "A" it's a compass a divider not an "A" it's Jack Trax my old boss it's a Masonic ring it's Jack, Christ its Jack, what the hell's going on?"** Dave couldn't believe what he was hearing and tried to clarify what Bill was saying while trying to calm him down!

"Bill I don't follow, what are you yelling about, are you ok?"

"Of course I'm ok Dave don't you see, the ring that Lenny described as having the letter "A" as a symbol is really a compass it's a masonic symbol and a Masonic Ring along with the psychical description we were given By Lenny, it fits Jack Trax my old boss perfectly, I don't know why I didn't put it all together before, but I still don't know why, I have to get hold of Jack! I know he'll let me know what's going on, at least I hope he will, one thing is for sure though, I'm sure Jack is behind my being offered my Job back. I'll have to confirm my suspicions with Lenny, about the possibility of the "A" being a compass, but I'm sure that's the case!"

"Well if your right Bill you've come a long way today toward solving the mystery, but you're not there yet I'm afraid, it couldn't be that simple, there has to be a whole lot more to it than just figuring out that Jack stopped the serving of a tray of drinks, do you agree?"

"Yes I do agree Dave and who was it that ordered the drinks in the first place, it wasn't Jack, or any of the group, according to Lenny, but I'm confident now that I'll find out eventually and you're right we've come a long way today, but we have yet a long way to go. My next priority is to get hold of Jack somehow and ask him to fill in the blanks so to speak, I've known Jack a long time and I'm sure he'll help."

Looking in his cell phone for Jack's number, but realizing he had deleted it after leaving his job convinced he wouldn't need it again, Bill was visibly upset with himself, how would he get hold of Jack now, of course he thought, he'd just ask Dennis from Bracken Metals who would certainly give him the info and why not after all Jack had said to say hi to Bill while Dennis was in town.

Once again Bill thanked Dave for his help and assured him he would not need him again as this mystery was almost solved, he believed the solution was within his reach if he was able to contact Jack Trax, though he remained confused about the motivation behind this ordeal. He decided to call Barb and bring her up to date on the latest developments, dialing her office, he waited a bit anxiously for an answer, but he didn't have long to wait "Triple A dental Ruth speaking how may I help you?"

"Good morning Ruth its Bill is Barb busy?"

"Good morning Bill, no she's not busy at all I'm sure she'll be happy to hear from you, hold on a moment, Barb pick up two its Bill."

"Ok thanks, hi hon what's on your mind I take it you're at Dave's or are you back home?"

"No I'm still at Dave's and you won't believe what we have figured out! Jack is the stranger we've been seeking, the ring is a Masonic ring, do you believe that?"

"Jack, do you mean Jack Trax?" asked Barb.

"Ya Jack Trax my old boss, I'm trying to get hold of him to find out what the hell is going on and who's behind this, I can't believe it's Jack, what could his motivation possibly be?"

"Hon I don't know, he still works for Bracken doesn't he, or has he moved on to?"

"No, of course not, he's still there, at least to the best of my knowledge he is I haven't heard differently and Mr. King is obviously still in touch with Jack, Barb are you saying Bracken Metals is behind this or do you think its Jack?"

"You know Bill I'm more confused than ever now, what does Dave think, or is he as befuddled as we are?"

"Honey I don't know either I just wanted to call and bring you up to date I have to get hold of Jack to learn more and that may be a bit difficult so I'll let you go for now and see you tonight and maybe I'll be able to tell you more by then."

"Ok hon I'll let you get back to what you're doing and I'll see you later, bye for now!"

"Bye Barb, see you later." as Bill hung up he hunted thru his phone for Dennis King's number to try and ascertain Jack's contact number, a talk with Jack now was absolutely necessary to unravel this mystery. Bill found Dennis King's number and dialed it "Hello this is Dennis."

"Hi Dennis its Bill Kelly how are you?"

"Just fine Bill I didn't expect to hear from you this soon, you've decided already I take it?"

"No Dennis, please don't jump to conclusions, I didn't mean to mislead you by calling, no I haven't decided yet, but you can help me along the way to making a decision by helping me get in touch with Jack Trax I really need to talk with him, something's come up making it essential for me to talk to Jack."

"Well Bill I can give you his office number if that will help, he's usually there or you can leave a message with his secretary."

"Of course Dennis that will help, but what I really had in mind was his cell phone number to expedite the contact, I really need to talk to him!"

"Bill, once again you put me in an awkward position, asking for info I'm not at liberty to divulge to you as its personal and I can't give it out, I know you understand."

"Tell me Dennis Jack is high enough up in the company that I'm sure his cell is a company phone anyway, mine was when I worked there and I was nowhere near as high up the food chain as he is, am I right about the phone?"

Dennis hesitated to answer, but finally admitted Bill was right, but was still reluctant to give out the number, considering though that they were trying to recruit Bill back into the corporation Dennis thought it prudent to make some concessions to Bill and gave him Jack's cell phone number had it been a personal phone though he would not have done that.

"Thanks Dennis I'll be talking to you soon, but I have to go right now and try to get hold of Jack!"

"Ok Bill good luck with whatever you're trying to do Bye for now." As Bill quickly hung up he dialed Jack's office number first using the backup only if needed Bill listened intently as the phone rang soon hearing a female answer saying;

"Mr. Trax's office Maxine speaking."

"Maxine its Bill Kelly is he in?"

"Bill my goodness it's been a while, no I'm sorry he's at an offsite seminar til Monday the 21st can I take a message? I'm sure Mr. Trax would enjoy talking with you, I'll need your number though."

"The only message would be to call me it's pretty important or I may just try his cell number."

"You have his cell number Bill?"

"Yes I have it Maxine I thought I'd try his office first though, I hope they're not secluded in the conference, he wouldn't have his cell."

"I'm not sure Bill I'll take your number though just in case you miss him he'll get your message."

"Yes of course Maxine and thanks we'll talk again I'm sure but I'll say goodbye for now and let you get back to work." Before hanging up he gave his number to Maxine, but hoping he would be able to contact Jack on his cell phone first.

"Bye Bill good talking with you." as she hung up and without Bill knowing, she immediately called Jack to let him know what had transpired, being a competent executive secretary she knew how to handle any situation that came up and she did! She dialed Trax's cell knowing that he had it with him and when he saw it was her he would most certainly answer it, and he did.

"Hello Maxine everything ok?"

"Yes Mr. Trax I just thought you'd want to know that Bill Kelly called trying to get you saying it was important and he has your cell number not knowing whether or not you were sequestered in your meetings and not able to answer your phone."

"Excellent Maxine, once again as always you've done exactly the right thing, I'll see you on Monday unless something else comes up Bye for now."

"Goodbye sir" as she hung up she was quite pleased with herself knowing her boss was quite happy and pleased with how she had handled the situation!

Bill, on the other hand was torn between calling or waiting for a while, but realizing he was pretty much stalled on any progress without talking with Jack he decided to call and timing was everything he didn't want to call when Jack was in a meeting, but when he was on break or at lunch and he didn't even know what time zone Jack was in so how would he get this right? Bill knew, without even trying that as an outsider he wouldn't be able to get Maxine to acknowledge Jack's whereabouts, had he been an employee it would be another story, but he wasn't, so he would just assume Jack was in the Richmond area and start there.

Before calling Jack though he decided to confirm his thoughts with Lenny, so once again he dialed Lenny's number and waited for an answer. "Hello Bill"

"Hi Len just a quickie this time, I know you described the ring as having the letter "A" on the red stone, but did you see it closely or could it have been a different symbol like a compass or a divider, you know a tool?"

"That's an interesting question Bill, I'd have to think about that I guess, I thought I saw it pretty clear, but now that you mention it he was never that close to me he approached the bar close enough to get the other guy's attention by putting his hand on his shoulder and shaking his head negatively canceling the drinks and the both of them turned and walked away. I think when he put his hand on the other man's shoulder, is when I noticed the ring, I guess at that point I would have been about five or six feet away so could I pick up that much detail that far away I guess is the question, so let's experiment shall we?"

"An experiment?" asked Bill.

"Ya, hang on Bill!" Bill could hear Lenny talking to someone named Frank asking him to stand up and position his hand and next he heard Lenny saying.

"Thanks Frank, Bill I'm back, I just had a customer hold up his hand with a similar ring on it and I have to admit it was difficult to make out the details of the ring. Though unlike my previous observation, I tried to make out the details on Frank's ring and I really couldn't, so I guess your theory is correct and the symbol on the ring in question may have been something other than the letter "A", I'm so sorry; I didn't mean to mislead you."

"Don't be silly Len, you have nothing to be sorry about, you were just trying to help out, which by the way you did and also just to bring you up to date, we have, thanks to you, figured out who the mysterious stranger is and were still trying to contact him, but we got him, so no apologies from you please and thanks again Len, we'll talk later ok?"

"Ya bye Bill I have to get back to work anyway, I'm happy your making progress!" as they both hung up, Bill knew the next move would be to call Jack and looking at his watch decided to wait about an hour or so before making the call trying to catch him at lunch, eliminating the possibility of him ignoring or not getting the call.

While he waited he called George's office to pass the time of day and maybe even get to talk with Brenda who was anything but boring. Dialing George's number Bill thought it would be nice if George was out "Sales Brenda speaking."

"Hi Brenda its Bill is George in or will I be lucky and just have to talk to you?"

"Oh no he's in Bill, but you can call anytime to talk to me I'm never too busy to talk, after all its part of my job, but hold on and I'll buzz Mr. Robert's for you!"

"Ok thanks Brenda and I will call again!"

"Hi Bill what's going on I haven't heard from you for a day or so are you making any progress on our mutual problem?"

"Hi Buddy, ya as a matter of fact we are making significant progress, we figured out who the elusive stranger is, it's Jack my old boss from Bracken Metals!"

"You're kidding, Jack, what's that all about?"

"That's not all George I've been offered my old job back at Bracken."

"I'll be dammed, you don't say what's going on, you mean you figured out it was Jack so their giving you your job back?"

"No I was offered my job back before we knew it was Jack they sent an HRM representative in from Richmond to sit down with me and make an offer!"

"Really what did you say?"

"I told him I'd have to think about it and I would let him know by Friday, but I really don't know, with the business and all, I'm not sure I want to start over."

"I'll tell you pal and you can ask Jerry also, but being in business is not always as easy, as it is appealing, to those who haven't done it, you wouldn't really be starting over you'd be back with a company you've already spent several years with and enjoyed advancement and the trust they've placed in you, but you're a smart guy and I know you'll do the right thing and in your case running your own business may/may not be the right thing, you'll figure it out, but if you want to sit down and talk about it I'm there for you anytime you know that!"

"Thanks George I know I can always count on you and I appreciate the input I still haven't made a decision nor am I leaning one way or the another, but now I'll have to talk with Jack before making any decision as I'm trying to figure out what motivated the offer and I believe Jack will clear that up as he's in a position to know."

"Ok Bill I know you know what you are doing, but how does Barb feel about the offer?"

"She'd have me back at Bracken tomorrow George it's a matter of security and peace of mind for her, but the business is doing very well and I believe it will continue there's little competition in the field and I've got guys all over the countries hot spots for construction and their bringing in the revenue, but she's still uncomfortable and would like to see me make the change."

"Bill when all is said and done you guys will decide together what's best for your particular circumstance and make your decision together and I'm sure it will be the right decision and we, your friends, will support that decision."

"Thanks George, but I'll have to cut this short as it's time to place that call to Jack or I'm going to miss him and won't be able to get him until tomorrow so I'll say bye for now and we'll talk again soon say hi to Nance."

"Ok bye Bill and good luck!" as they ended the call Bill decided it was a good time to place the call to Jack and did, waiting for an answer he thought about how he would handle the contact, but the call went to voice male "This is Jack Trax leave a message and I'll get back to you I look forward to our talking."

"Jack hi its Bill Kelly, we need to talk some things going on that I don't understand and I need your expertise as in the past, you have my number call day or night, thanks." all Bill could do now would be to wait for Jack's call there was not much left to do til he heard as he had talked to everyone that he thought could further clarify things, he would just have to be patient for a while. Bill didn't have to wait long though as his phone rang and the caller ID showed Trax "Hello Jack its Bill"

"Hi Bill, dam it's good to hear from you boy, how are you doing since you left Bracken I understand you've started your own business, how's that going for you?"

"Jack I'll tell you it's good to hear from you also and the business is doing well, but to tell you the truth I've had an inexplicable time the last several weeks a story you won't believe and I'd like to tell you if you have time?"

"To tell you the truth Bill I don't have a lot of time right now so why don't you give me the short version now and we'll continue later as I'm coming to Chicago next week and we'll arrange to get together."

"You got it Jack here's the short version, first I left Bracken and I don't know why or even when, but as it turns out that didn't seem to matter, once I realized my friends and I were traveling thru time in excess of twenty five years into the future, somewhere in my travels I started my own business, but don't remember doing it, then I got involved in trying to figure out what was going on suddenly finding that my friends and possibly even my wife were involved in a conspiracy, when suddenly I was being offered my old job back at Bracken and somehow you were involved in this whole thing maybe even behind it, but I didn't find out why, so that's the short version Jack, what do you think?"

"Wow Bill that's a lot you mentioned in the short version, I'd sure like to sit down and hear the complete story it looks like I'll have to take an extra day or so and put aside a block of time for you and I to talk and I'll do that, I'll be in town on Tuesday the 29th Bill and we'll set things up at that time and you can tell me the whole story, maybe I'll have a story of my own, how does that sound?"

"Certainly Jack I'd love to see you again and talk about any subject, but this weighs heavily on my mind right now and it turned out to be quite a mystery and impacted on the minds and lives of many not just me, so yes I'd appreciate getting together and discussing this at length."

"That's exactly what we'll do Bill, but for now I'll have to say goodbye as I have another meeting to get to, you know how these management seminars are, well talk soon I promise!"

"Ok bye Jack" Bill a bit disappointed, with Jack's putting this off til November 29, 2011 and not even admitting/acknowledging his involvement in the overall conspiracy or even admitting to a conspiracy obviously it was more important to Bill than it was to Jack.

CHAPTER THIRTY ONE
THE ROAD TO SOLUTION

Finally after talking to Jack and somewhat disappointed with Jack's responses to Bill's questions, even though Jack had promised to give Bill further insight into what was going on at a later time, Bill was not happy, he was anxious to put an end to this thing and no one, not even Jack seemed as motivated as Bill, he felt he was in this thing all alone! Bill knew now that Jack was still an employee, an executive, of Bracken Metals and a friend, but certain that Jack knew what was going on and he too refused to help Bill, at least at this time.

As the week went on and Bill knew nothing more could be resolved til he had his sit down with Jack the week after next and he had no clue about who he could trust and frankly didn't much care anymore. He decided to get back to a somewhat normal life and put the mystery on the back burner for a while.

Taking his wife out to dinner, finding out about Dave's pursuit of Gloria, talking to Jerry about his business difficulties, maybe even giving Brenda a call and finally calling Dennis King as he would be calling Bill on Friday for an answer, but until Bill talked with Jack he would be unable to make a decision on Bracken's job offer, so he'd start out calling Dennis and dialed his number.

"Human resources Dennis"

"Dennis It's Bill Kelly"

"Yes Bill, I'm not even going to ask if you've made a decision as I'm sure that would be premature so what is on your mind?"

"Your exactly right Dennis the reason I'm calling is to tell you that it would be impossible for me to make a decision by Friday as something has come up that has to be resolved first and the soonest I would be able to say would be the middle to the end of the week of the 27th and if that's not acceptable then I'll have to take a pass."

"No-no Bill I've been tasked with offering you a position and taking your answer back to management, not making a decision on whether or not to rescind the offer, that's not up to me, and I'm sure that no one else will rescind the offer either, at least not under these circumstances!"

"That's good to hear Dennis, I'm not trying to be difficult, but I'd hate to accept the offer and later have to reject it, I'd much rather get all the necessary input and then make an informed decision."

"Let's see Bill you're indicating the middle of the week of the 27th why don't we say I'll call you on Friday December 2, 2011 and if you make a decision before that you can call me, will that work for you?"

"Indeed, I believe that will do just fine and I appreciate your flexibility in this matter, but as I've explained I'm taking steps to insure that whatever I may decide it's the right decision for all concerned."

"Well I'm grateful for the heads up Bill and I'm convinced your decision will be well informed and the right one for you and Barb, but if you decide against Bracken's offer it certainly won't benefit us, so I'll say goodbye for now and let you get back to working this out adding my good luck also!"

"Goodbye Dennis and thank you!" Hanging up Bill thought he'd call Barb and see if she wanted to go out for dinner and relax a little tonight, but first he decided to call Dave and see how he was doing with Gloria, maybe they could even double date for dinner, he'd have to think about that for a moment though not being sure how Barb felt about Gloria she had made some jealous comments in the past, he dialed Dave's number and waited.

"Hi Bill I was just thinking about you and now I'm talking with you."

"Yes you are Dave, but I have a different agenda this time though I could bring you up to date I guess, I finally got hold of Jack and he and I are going to get together on Tuesday in Chicago and until that meeting takes place, I can't do another thing, so I thought I'd just relax a bit til then which brings me to the reason I'm calling. We've been so occupied with what's been going on that everything else has been put aside at least that's been true for Barb and I so I was wondering if you had ever gotten hold of Gloria and how that was going? I would have never been that presumptuous Dave to stick my noise into your personal business, but I thought she was a special lady and a perfect dinner companion for you."

"Well first let me say I'm glad you were able to get hold of Jack and arrange a meeting, as for Gloria, well as a matter of fact you are right, she is special and not only a good dinner companion, but a great lunch and breakfast guest also, the truth is we've been seeing each other for a while now and I've been waiting for the right opportunity to thank you for bringing us together, but the timing somehow was not quite right and now it's out and timing I guess is no longer a problem, so thanks Bill I owe you one for sure she's a great girl and were getting on just fine!"

"I'm happy to hear that Dave, maybe we can double sometime for dinner or something and by all means bring her to the next group get together, I'm sure everyone would enjoy meeting her."

"I'll do that very thing Bill and thanks, but I gota run!"

"I'll say goodbye for now Dave I'm sure we'll talk again soon." as Bill and Dave ended the call Bill decided to call Barb and see if she would be interested in dinner out or a quiet evening at home, he dialed the number at work and waited for Ruth to answer.

"Triple "A" dental Ruth speaking may I help you?"

"Guess who Ruth, is Barb busy?"

"I don't really know Bill she stepped out for a while can I have her call you?"

"Ya Ruth that would be fine, she can get me on my cell as I won't be home for a while myself."

"You got it Bill how are you doing by the way?"

"I'm fine thanks and how about you Ruth? By the way did Barb go out for lunch?"

"Heavens no she's young and still counts every calorie Bill wanting to keep her girlish figure forever and not accepting the fact that forever is til she starts having children or reaching forty years old or whatever age it is when the bloat first starts to take over!"

"I don't know Ruth; you don't look like it's caught up to you yet, you still look pretty good walking away."

"Well thanks Bill, truthfully though I must be one of the lucky ones, there are a few of us out there and others are on a lifelong diet, some suffer from anorexia or bulimia but it's a lot of pressure on a woman and often makes life difficult, but if you're lucky enough to have someone that loves you regardless of your waistline you're a happy women and I see Barb as a happy girl!"

"Well I hope and believe she is and I do my best to keep it that way and working with you will help I'm sure because your great! I'll let you get back to your crosswords or whatever it is you do when the doctor's with a patient or out of the office."

"Ok Bill and I don't have any crosswords; we, Barb and I, work hard around here and don't have time for games besides we have solitaire on our computers."

"I see Ruth, well I guess I'm under the wrong impression, I apologize for being presumptuous, I'm sure you ladies work very hard and deserve that recognition, but in any case I'll let you get back to your computer, bye for now."

"Bye Bill and I'll have Barb call you on your cell." Bill went back to his agenda, to relax so while he waited for Barb to return his call he thought he'd call Jerry, but wait he'd try Dave first to check on any progress with his computer, dialing Dave's number and waiting he quickly thought about the consequences if they were unable to retrieve the info on the computer.

"Hello again Bill, you must have forgotten something what is it pal?"

"You're very intuitive Dave, yes, I forgot to ask about any progress on the computer, do your guys think there's a chance to recover any or all of the data, or is it an exercise in futility?"

"To be honest Bill I haven't checked back with them yet, I thought I'd give them a little time before bugging them so let's give them til Monday, I'm sure if they are able to do anything before then they'll call me."

"Ok Dave and I didn't mean to bug you, but for obvious reasons I'm concerned!"

"No-no Bill you're not bugging me, you're a friend and you can call me anytime you already know that though and you do, but their doing it as a favor and I just thought I'd give them a little time they know the importance and I can assure you they'll act accordingly."

"Thanks Dave and I won't bug you again about it I promise, I do appreciate the effort thanks, I'll let you get back to what you're doing it was just a quick question that I forgot to ask earlier and knowing the fate of the business will help with the meeting I'm having with Jack on Tuesday."

"I understand Bill and I'm sure we'll have a definitive answer by then."

"Thanks again Dave and goodbye for now."

"Bye Bill"

Bill not meaning to bug Dave, was aware that he had been a bit pushy with folks since this all started even to the point of their annoyance, but it became necessary he believed, to come this far as others seemed to be indifferent at times and even unwilling to cooperate to the fullest, while others seemed part of the conspiracy so Bill's pushiness became a part of the process.

Bill continued with a call to Jerry on his cell phone and a quick answer indeed he must have been waiting for a call and ready to answer,

"Hello is this you Dave?"

"Dave? No its Bill, Jerry don't you have a caller ID? Why would you think it was Dave as a matter of fact I just got done talking with him myself!"

"Bill no-no I'm outside and the screen on this phone is useless in the bright sunlight, but I had left a message for Dave and I thought he was returning my call, so that being said to what do I owe the pleasure of this call, have you guys made further progress toward the solution to this mystery?"

"Well yes Jerry we have however that's not why I'm calling, I thought I'd call and see how you're doing with your difficulties with airport security?"

"Oh how did you know about that Bill? I don't remember mentioning it, but yes were having our problems and getting nowhere trying to work them out, not giving up though as day by day we come closer to getting out of this business and trying commercial trucking and forgetting the airline delivery business."

"I'm sorry Jer can't you get help from the Airlines as their business is also impacted or at least it appears that way?"

"Of course it's impacted the time it takes to get the freight from the airplane to its final destination is increased, sometimes considerably, from what it was advertised to be and what the customers have come to expect, but the fact is it's still faster than any other mode of transportation and that coupled with the fact that the government has hired over sixty thousand employees to perform this service, necessary or not, their simply not going to admit it was not professionally implemented so we'll have to live with the results of big government intervention, or they'll simply let us go out of business!"

"To answer your question I heard about it from Emily, I called to talk with you and you were working on Sunday, I questioned that, she gave me a short explanation, so I wanted to call and see if I could help in any way, I'm sorry to hear about the problem Jer, won't your customers listen to your explanation of the causes of the late deliveries and accept the fact that you're working to fix the problem?"

"You know customers Bill, there not interested in excuses, just results, once in a while a late delivery will be tolerated, but on a recurring basis forget it, they'll start looking for another delivery service never realizing were all having the same problems. We have three kinds of customers, the one time delivery, the occasional repeat customer and lastly the daily clients who receive deliveries daily and even several times a day. Those clients are on contracts and are there for a reason they are often suppliers and have to redeliver the product on a schedule and can't make their schedule if I don't make mine, so you can see the problem."

"Yes indeed I can Jer I hope you and your partner can make some headway in solving your difficulties unfortunately your problems start with the feds and they really don't care about your small business difficulties, only about further growing their already to big government, so you have your work ahead of you and the end is not insight, I know absolutely nothing about the trucking business, but like any other business I think you have to get your clients involved they may be the only means to an end!"

"Your right Bill maybe I should hire you as an advisor."

"You couldn't afford me Jer, but my advice would be to do it on your own and save the money, you can call me anytime and we'll talk I don't charge my friends for that accommodation, so call, right now though I do have to go, still working on that other problem as you know, well talk again soon Jerry, ok?"

"Ok Bill and thanks for calling and caring and good luck with the mystery you're working on, bye for now."

"Bye Jerry" hanging up Bill thought about Jerry's problems, realizing his were indeed more difficult than Bill's to solve, but certainly not unsolvable, Bill's phone rang he answered saying;

"Hi hon were you out for lunch when I called? I hope you didn't eat too much! I called to ask you out to dinner tonight, what do you say?"

"Hi hon, No I didn't overeat today and dinner sounds great, where did you have in mind?"

"I don't know it depends on how fancy you want to get I understand the Poseidon has a pretty extensive dinner menu and the food is great there also, but it's up to you dear."

"The Poseidon Ya that sounds good for a change, my lunch experience there was enjoyable, the atmosphere there is pleasing also, let's do that!"

"Ok, well that was easy how about the rest of your day, how's that going?"

"Just fine Ruth said you were interested in our idle times and how we spent it, but honestly some days we have an overabundance of idle time and others we have no idle time and yet others we don't have enough time, running further behind every hour so it all evens out I guess."

"Yes it does, well I'll see you when you get home and we'll plan on dinner and latter relaxing with the TV it's been a long day and I'll catch you up at dinner."

"Ok hon I'll let you go for now and get back to my game of solitaire as were not too busy right now, love you!"

"Bye Barb love you too" as they both ended the call neither bringing up what Barb had been doing while out of the office when Bill called, even though Bill questioned her, she just blew it off and neither ever got back to it so it to remains a mystery, at least for now, but not forever, soon all will be revealed, by the one person who knows the whole story.

As Bill arrived back home to relax for a bit while waiting for Barb to get home from work, looking forward to dinner and more relaxing afterword's looking ahead to the long wait for Jack's appearance next Tuesday and what he would have to say in response to Bill's yet untold story.

As Bill relaxed he heard Barb's key in the front door and heard "Hi hon I'm home and hungry as hell are we ready to go?"

"I am, are you dear?"

"Ya I need a minute to freshen up give me five ok?"

"If you need a minute, why would I give you five?"

"You've had all day to practice your humor and I haven't, so I don't have a suitable response to your humor, at least not one you'd like so I'll just let it go and freshen up as I indicated and we'll go ok?"

"Wow ok dear I'll just wait of course!"

Soon Barb was ready and with her usual smile said;

"Ok hon let's go" and both headed out the door for the elevator, the garage and the restaurant while they talked about their days, though once Barb got started it was hard for Bill to get a word in, so he patiently waited, til they were settled in the restaurant at which time he was expecting a break in Barb's otherwise enthusiastic revelations about her day in and out of the office, then, giving Bill a chance to reciprocate with lengthy tales of his days activities, but would it work out that way he thought?

Pulling into the Poseidon parking lot and seeing quite a few cars there, but hoping they were not over crowded as service tends to diminish in restaurants that were crowded, they would see as Bills experience here had been favorable under most conditions and as they entered the main door a hostess was there to greet them and show them to a booth or table their choice, Bill asked for a booth and they were shown to a great booth in a reasonably quit part of the dining room though the restaurant was pretty busy, the hostess gave them menus assuring them their server would be with them shortly they smiled and thanked her.

"Well dear I told you about my day in detail don't you have anything about your day I might be interested in, you seem preoccupied and unwilling to talk!" Bill looked at Barb with disbelieving eyes saying;

"Hon I've been looking for a break in the stories of your very interesting day, I just wanted to give you enough time to finish and I must admit you held my interest til you did finish. Let me start by telling you of the good news first, Dave and Gloria are seeing each other and quite successfully I might add. I've talked to most of our involved friends today and spent a good deal of time with Dave, but most important is the fact that I was able to get hold of Jack after talking to his secretary Maxine for a longtime and I talked to Jerry, who is having problems with his business, we talked for a good while also. I was quite disappointed with my conversation with Jack; I think he was putting me off for some reason, at least until Tuesday, when he'll be coming to town for a couple of days."

As Bill finished his initial thoughts he noticed the waitress approach and decided not to continue just now;

"Hi I'm Judy your server this evening have you folks been here before?"

"Yes we have Judy and how are you?"

"Just fine sir thank you for asking would you like a drink before ordering, perhaps a carafe of our table wine?"

Looking at Barb questioningly Bill said, "Yes that would be fine and an order of those stuffed mushrooms for an appetizer if that's ok?"

"An excellent choice sir they are good aren't they? I'll be back shortly to take your order."

As Judy walked away Bill returned to the conversation asking Barb;

"Well hon what do you think especially about Jack's avoiding my questions, he was not only my boss for years he was a friend and I don't understand his total disconnect, hopefully Tuesday will shed some light on things!"

"I think your right hon Jack is a friend and I'm sure he won't let you down, but right now he's tied up with his seminar and has that on his mind."

Bill immediately realized he had not mentioned that Jack was at a seminar so how did Barb know that? Indeed something was going on and the occasional slip of the tongue by folks was confirming Bill's suspicions about a conspiracy and he didn't like it! He couldn't let on just yet that he suspected anyone or knew anything it might ruin his chances of getting any more info from the unsuspecting conspirators, so he would remain quit, for now!

Judy was returning once again with the wine and the appetizer and setting the mushrooms on the table asked,

"May I pour sir?"

"Of course Judy please do" she poured the wine into a red wine glass offering the sample to Bill for his approval, Bill sniffed the wine and checked for clarity and signaled his approval as Judy finished pouring both glasses and finally asking;

"Well are we ready to order?"

Bill ordered for both he and his wife and once again Judy left to place the order in the kitchen.

Out of nowhere Bill asked Barb about her old office manager,

"Hon I was just wondering, do you guy's ever hear from Lisa your old office manager any more, usually past employees, who left on good terms keep in touch and you never mention her I thought that unusual?"

"I agree Bill, but no, we don't hear anything I'm not sure whatever happened to her as you know I went to work one day and she was gone and Ruth was there, the doctor said she just quit for no apparent reason so the doctor called a temp agency and got Ruth, who I might add, is quite good."

"I was just thinking that the phenomenon we've been experiencing was further reaching than we first thought, I wonder how many other folks, that we're not even aware of are involved in this thing." Thinking that Barb would get his drift, but somewhat disappointed, she did not, or at least she did not let on!

Soon their dinner was brought to the table and the couple lost themselves in a rather enjoyable meal afterword's leaving for home, but deciding on the way to stop for a drink and wouldn't you know ended up in La Flambés parking lot and their favorite lounge, it would be a long night.

As they entered the bar they saw that Lenny was working as well as Bill the other bartender and they were busy, Lenny saw them and signaled them to his end of the bar with a smile and a nod as they took two stools near the service end of the bar indicated by Len,

"Hi you guys to what do we owe the pleasure of your company this evening?"

"Were just stopping for a quick after dinner drink on our way home and ended up here, but then where else would we end up?"

"Great what are you drinking this evening?"

"Ya know Len make it a couple of Gin Ricky's at least to start with."

"Coming up, two Ricky's" as Lenny walked away to make the drinks Bill said to Barb,

"You know hon there's a guy that's been a great deal of help to me throughout this ordeal and I'm very grateful for his help!"

"Well, yes indeed, he certainly has been helpful it's odd though how he's able to keep coming up with additional details after only a brief encounter with the, what did we call him, the mysterious stranger, subsequently identified as Jack Trax, I still find that odd don't you?" asked Barb, obviously still upset with Lenny and Bill not understanding why, but feeling the need to defend Lenny as he felt Lenny went out of his way to help.

Bill gave Barb a strange look, as if to say, you find that odd, what about your peculiar behavior lately, but he chose not to say anything at least not at this time and simply said;

"No, not really dear, the mind is a funny thing as you dig into your subconscious you'll find things pop up that you didn't realize were even there and remembering small insignificant details from time to time is part of that process."

As Lenny set the drinks in front of the couple asking "There you go anything else I can do for you folks right now?"

Barb quickly answered saying "No-no Len you've been quite helpful, you've really done enough, thank you!" raising her glass with her usual smile in a toasting gesture, drawing a curious look from both Lenny and Bill, but both smiled saying nothing!"

As Len walked away to take care of his customers Bill was tempted to say something to Barb, but had second thoughts once again and decided to let it go, at least for now!

After several more drinks and a late night appetizer from the kitchen they decided to call it a night and go home as Barb still had to work tomorrow, they paid their tab said good night to Lenny and left hoping they wouldn't get stopped by the police on the way home and they didn't, they only lived a short distance from the bar and had been lucky time and time again.

Once in their unit Barb said "Dinner was great hon I would never have thought about the Poseidon as a place to go for dinner, but it was very good thanks' I was impressed and would like to go again!"

"Yes it was good and we'll do it again I'm sure, do you want a night cap?"

"No it's late and I do have to work in the morning, but thanks anyway."

"Well I'm going to have one, I don't have to get up in the morning and I'm going to take advantage of it."

"That's ok hon I'm going to take a quick shower, you can join me if you'd like, or not." as Bill didn't respond as expected, he was still upset over her behavior in the bar with Lenny and in the shower she was sure she could reconcile his anger, but it just wasn't in the cards tonight.

Bill had his drink and went to bed finding Barb already fast asleep and looking forward to a good night's sleep himself as he turned off his lamp closed his eyes and hoped for a sexy dream suddenly seeing himself in George's office talking with Brenda and George not being there, what next he thought!

The next morning Barb was up and about early while Bill still slept, Barb made the morning coffee and her toasted English muffin and because it was Friday she wore jeans and a modest blouse, but looked good as always after putting on her face using little makeup, she didn't need much, if any, and she was ready to leave, checking on Bill's progress toward waking up and finding him barely stirring, giving him a kiss saying goodbye, getting only a moderate response she left, after leaving a note on the kitchen table.

Bill slept til mid-morning and woke up refreshed and ready for another day. He brushed his teeth and poured a cup of the coffee that Barb had left and decided how to start his day, realizing he couldn't work on his business because he no longer had his computer or any other way to conduct his business, so his day was open to just about anything and he decided to call Brenda as a way to while away the hours, but first a bowl of cereal.

In the meantime Jack was planning his trip to Chicago and talking with Maxine to make the arrangements as travel arrangements were part of her duties, executives don't do those kinds of things on their own. Jack placed a call to Maxine from his seminar;

"Good morning Mr. Trax's phone Maxine speaking."

"Good morning Maxine it's Jack, I need you to get me into Chicago by about noon on Monday and leave the return open, I'll probably be back on Wednesday, but I'm not sure yet, I have some pending business on that recruiting project were working on and hoping to finalize things!"

"Ok Mr. Trax I'll make those arrangements and send the details to your cell and computer within the hour if that will be alright sir?"

"That's fine Maxine everything else ok around the office?"

"Yes sir everything else is fine, how's the seminar, tolerable?"

"Barely, we'll talk latter Maxine!"

"Yes sir, bye for now."

Bill finished his breakfast and placed the call to Brenda "Sales Brenda, how may I help you?"

"That's the wrong question to ask me Brenda, especially this morning as I'm totally vulnerable, hang up, I'll call right back and you can answer differently ok?" Brenda laughing said;

"That's not necessary Bill, I'll answer the same way, I kind of like the idea, catching you in a vulnerable moment I mean, what's going on?"

"This morning, I called to talk to you, is George in?"

"No, he's not expected til noon so I'm all yours, at least for now!"

Bill caught the drift of that answer and didn't know whether or not to just let it go or make the next move, he decided to make the next move and see where that would lead it didn't take long to find out.

"What do you suggest we do to pass the time Brenda?"

"I can't leave so I suggest you stop by here, it's much better to talk in person don't you think?"

"I do and I'm on my way could I bring you coffee or something?"

"I'm just fine Bill; just bring you and a topic for conversation will do nicely!"

"I can't imagine conversation being a problem Brenda, but if it is we'll work around it somehow, ok?"

"Ok Bill, I'm confident you can handle most situations that arise, I'll see you when you get here!"

"Bye Brenda put the coffee on I'll be there before it's done!" hanging up Bill had no idea what he might be in for and before giving it much thought he headed for George's office not really caring about consequences, time will tell.

Arriving at the office and walking in he was greeted by Brenda a tall well-built blond with long hair worn up in a very sophisticated style while wearing a gray business suit with a skirt just above the knee's exposing from the hem down the greatest looking pair of legs he could remember and asking "Hi Bill, how do you take your coffee? I've never fixed it for you before, but I'll know the next time?"

Bill with a smile said "Cream no sugar and served with a smile!"

"I hope the coffee is good Bill, the smile is easy." as Bill took the coffee he allowed his finger tips to glide across the back of her hand, a gesture she didn't shy away from and even encouraged, indeed Bill was feeling very frisky and single right now and even a bit risky, he was vulnerable and headed for trouble and Brenda seemed to be encouraging his participation in what was quickly becoming the inevitable!

"Tell me Brenda, are you available for lunch?"

"Oh no I'm sorry I'm not allowed to leave when the boss is out of the office, but I am available for an after work drink."

"I see that's interesting and what time do you finish for the day?"

"Five o'clock and there's a great lounge at the Poseidon just down the street, unless you have another idea or someplace else in mind that you might like to go?"

Before Bill could respond his phone rang and it was Barb temporarily bringing him back down to earth.

"Excuse me Brenda I have to take this." as he walked away to answer the call.

"Hi hon what's up?"

"Hi, you know I just wanted to call and say I'm sorry, I know you're a little upset with me over my attitude with Lenny last night and I realize it was uncalled for and I feel bad, I'll make up for it tonight I promise, I love you!"

Well if Bill had anything growing between him and Brenda, if you know what I mean, it just died, once again if you know what I mean, now he had to undo what he did, life is complicated he thought.

"I love you to hon and I'll see you at home I'm out and about right now trying to get ready for Jack's arrival."

"Ok hon bye!"

As he walked back into earshot of Brenda he said;

"Brenda you know what they say about the best-laid plans of mice and men often go awry, well that's just what happened to us, I was really looking forward to a drink with you and wherever else that might lead, but unfortunately I'm having out of town business associates next week and I have to prepare for them and something has come up that requires my attention tonight, so a rain check?" Bad move, he left the door open and missed an opportunity to close it for good, unless he didn't want to close it? Once again time will tell!

"I'm sorry to Bill, perhaps another time there's always an empty bar stool somewhere and if not, I have a well-stocked liquor supply at home so yes a rain check would be good and is certainly appropriate."

"That's good to hear Brenda, but right now I have to get going and take care of business, we'll talk soon!"

"I'll look forward to it Bill and call me!"

"You bet bye Brenda" as Bill left George's office still not realizing how close he came to disaster and only thinking about what he had missed, but in his shoes I may have done the same thing, I don't know, but I do know Bill still is not out of the woods on this one and with all his other problems he didn't need to add to list!

Barb and Bill later met at home and Barb did make good on her earlier promise, making for an enjoyable evening and looking forward to more of the same over the weekend and that's pretty much how the next few days went leading to Monday.

CHAPTER THIRTY TWO
A MEETING WITH JACK

Monday morning and the day the couple had been waiting for finally arrives, the day the mystery may be solved or not, only time will tell, but time is growing short and tensions are building and as Bill knows other difficulties are surfacing also, difficulties not previously considered have presented themselves, difficulties named Brenda and now that has to be resolved along with everything else!

The couple (Barb and Bill), were both up together this morning, looking forward to today's activities, after a long weekend of sex! Bill was still finding it impossible to get Brenda out of his mind, indeed trouble was in the air and with no resolution in sight, but if Bill didn't do something to discourage her advances he could lose everything! After all it was his fault to start with, though he probably wouldn't admit to that, he had made a few initial advances himself!

Bill was looking forward to meeting with Jack and Barb was interested in the outcome of that meeting. Barb finished her coffee and toasted English muffin and after kissing Bill goodbye headed out the door for work. Bill continued with his coffee and dwelling on not discouraging recent memories of Brenda, considering calling her once again, but placed a call to Dave instead.

"Hello Bill I was just about to call you."

"Good news I hope Dave!"

"I'm afraid not Bill there still working on it, it has become a real challenge for them now, but they say it was a real expert who removed the data from the hard drive in this computer and only someone who programed it in the first place could have done it, probably with a worm having a payload built in it!"

"A what, a worm, what the hell are you talking about Dave?" as they were talking Bill's other phone rang, it was Jack!

"Dave I have a call on the other line and I gota take it, I'll call you back!" Hanging up on Dave Bill answered the other line saying.

"Hello Jack how are you doing? I didn't expect to hear from you this soon, I figured you'd still be in the air."

"Hi Bill, Maxine made sure I got here in time for lunch, what are your plans for the day?"

"Other than getting together with you Jack I have no plans."

"Fine why don't we meet for lunch, have you any suggestions Bill I'm in the mood for Steak how about you?"

"I like steak to I'll pick you up Jack where are you staying?"

"I'm downtown at the Hilton Bill, is that convenient for you?"

"Maxine takes good care of you Jack, sure I'll be there at 12:30 is that ok?"

"Works for me, I'll see you than Bill, I'll be waiting in the lobby." they hung up and Bill thought about how he would approach the subject with Jack at lunch, not really knowing the degree of Jack's involvement, but suspecting he was involved at the highest level and of course knew all the answers to any questions Bill might have, whether or not he would answer the questions was yet undetermined.

Before leaving to meet with Jack Bill wanted to get back to Dave and dialed his number not understanding about the worm problem Dave had mentioned before Bill had ended the call.

"Hello Bill back so soon?"

"Ya I had to take that call it was Jack Trax he's in town and we're meeting for lunch, but I wanted to get back to you and finish discussing that worm you were talking about, what is it?"

"It's complicated Bill, but simply stated it is a self-replicating malware computer program that can be used several different ways for both good and evil, the IEEE did an article on the subject a while back, you may have read it, I know you subscribe to that publication, In any case it's a significant problem and in your case it may make your data unrecoverable, the crew is still not sure, but they did notice you didn't have malware protection in your computer, you had virus protection, but today you really need both, that's the end of the commercial though!"

"Thanks for the bad news Dave, I know you're doing your best, in the meantime I'll start putting things back together manually, that'll take some time I'm sure, gota go for now we'll talk soon."

"Ok bye Bill, see you soon I'm sure!" hanging up Bill was ready to head for the Hilton and pick up Jack for lunch and start the inquisition. Arriving at the hotel Bill valeted his car and entered the hotel lobby spotting Jack immediately and Jack him as the two approached each other hands extended and smiles on their faces they greeted each other as old friends with a handshake and even a slight hug, Bill taking the opportunity to notice the masonic ring that Jack was still wearing.

"Bill, good to see you it's been awhile you're looking well as always and how's Barbara? Well I hope!"

"She is thanks for asking Jack and you're looking well also, Richmond's been good to you, we'll have you brought your appetite with you I think you'll like the restaurant I've chosen it's called La Flambé and it's great!"

Jack gave Bill an inquisitive look saying "It sounds great as long as they serve steak I'll leave the choice of where up to you Bill, I'm sure I won't be disappointed, I still remember my time in Chicago and the lunches we had together and you never made a poor choice where we ate."

Bill was hoping Jack would give away his secret of previous visits to the restaurant by unconsciously showing his familiarity with details once inside, it was called entrapment and Bill thought he was being clever not realizing Jack was on to him and enjoying the moment himself. Bill also made sure that Lenny would be working and could confirm that Jack was indeed the mysterious stranger!

On their way to the restaurant they engaged in idle chit chat about any number of topics avoiding any discussions about Bill's so called mystery.

Arriving at La Flambé as Bill valeted the car and watched Jack carefully, looking for any indication of Jack's familiarity with the area or restaurant, but saw none, still though he believed that once inside, Jack giving himself away would be unavoidable.

Entering the front door they were greeted by the hostess who immediately recognized Bill and said;

"Good morning Mr. Kelly how are you gentleman today? Can I show you to your usual table sir?" Bill noticed her name tag Linda and said;

"That'll be fine Linda."

"Right this way gentleman" as she lead the way to their table, after seating them and giving them their menus she announced their server, Bonnie, would be with them shortly and said for them to enjoy their meal.

Jack looked around and said "Nice ambiance Bill I especially like the use of wood and the drapes instead of blinds don't you?"

"As a matter of fact I do Jack, to be honest though I never thought of it that way, but now that you mention it, I do like it and by the way they have a wonderful and comfortable lounge here also."

"I see maybe we'll have to check it out after were done with lunch Bill what say you?"

"Great Jack I think you'll enjoy it!"

As the waitress approached and introduced herself saying, "Good morning gentleman I'll be your server today, I'm Bonnie, can I get you something from the bar today or perhaps the wine steward?"

"Hello Bonnie how have you been?"

"Of course Mr. Kelly how are you? I'm well thank you!" Recognizing Bill and recalling their last meeting, she was a bit embarrassed, but did a good job hiding it and kept her smile.

Jack added "I think a drink from the bar would be fine Bonnie, I'll have a perfect martini with two olives and a lemon peel"

"Make that two Bonnie it sounds good." added Bill.

"Very good I'll be right back than for your order." as she left to get their drinks from the bar, anxious to tell Lenny they were here as she was sure Len would like to know.

Jack decided to get down to business and started out by saying "Well Bill you said you had a story to tell and I'd like to hear it, so why don't you go ahead with your story and I'll just listen!"

"Well Jack, it all started on the 28th of October, at my best friend George's birthday party right here at this restaurant as a matter of fact." the story continued from there thru the rather enjoyable meal and afterwards on into the lounge were they selected a table, avoiding the bar for privacy reasons, but still saying hi to Lenny. It took Bill about two hours to tell Jack the whole story leaving out the part about Jack's involvement and at the end saying, "Well Jack that's about it what do you think?"

Jack thought for a long moment, took a deep breath finally saying, "Are you sure that's everything Bill because that's a hell of a lot, but I can't help thinking there might be even more to tell, but let me say this, I would like to get together with your friends who were involved with you through this ordeal because I have some insight for both them and you that may answer many of your questions and concerns, but I only want to do that with your permission and I only want to do it once, what do you think?"

"Why the secrecy Jack, What's it all about and why can't you just tell me what's going on and why is it necessary to involve my friends in the explanation?"

"Bill-Bill, don't get yourself excited, it's not like you, I'll say this much about it no longer is it a secret, But there is a lengthy explanation and I only want to go through it once and I want your friends involved because they are involved and deserving of the whole truth, its complicated and all for a worthwhile cause as you'll soon learn, but not quite yet, though I can guarantee you'll understand once you hear the whole story!"

"Ok Jack I trust you I always have and if you want us all together I'll arrange something, we could have it right here in one of the banquet rooms I've used them several times these folks are quite accommodating and as you now know the food is quite good."

"Yes Bill, go ahead and make the arrangements and have it billed to Bracken Metals and I'll put it on my card, you can arrange it for lunch or dinner tomorrow, your choice, can you arrange it that quickly or not?"

"During the week dinner would be better and I can schedule it right now if that's ok?"

"Absolutely do it!"

Bill waved for the cocktail waitress to come over and she did asking "Something else to drink sir?"

"Not right now dear, I'd like to schedule one of the banquet rooms for tomorrow night can you do that for me?"

"No sir, I'll get Linda the hostess for you right away, she can help you with that, and I'll be right back ok?"

"That's fine thank you" waiting for Linda Jack still had not indicated that he had been here before as Bill excused himself.

"Jack will you excuse me for a moment I want to make sure that the bartender that's working will be here tomorrow its Lenny and he's real good!"

"Sure, go right ahead Bill I'm not going anywhere, you've got the keys." laughing along with Bill, as Bill walked away toward the bar."

As Bill approached the bar Lenny poised to greet him saying;

"Hi again Bill do you guy's need another drink?"

"Not right now Len, but tell me, is that gentleman I'm with familiar to you?" as Len cast a subtle glance toward Jack once again and catching Jack looking in his direction also, Lenny said.

"Ya Bill I believe that is him, how did you find him so quickly?"

"It's a long story Len and I'm not even sure of the ending myself yet, but by tomorrow I will be, I'll let you know."

As Bill walked back to the table he realized once again he'd have to make all the necessary phone calls to get everyone together for the dinner tomorrow night sure they would all be available for a free meal and the answers they had all been looking for.

"Jack were set with the bartender and I'll have to start making phone calls to notify everyone about tomorrow night, so how would you like to come to my house and spend some time while I do that and you'll get to see Barb when she gets home from work, I know she'll enjoy that also!"

"You know Bill I'll have to take a rain check; I'd like to take a ride out to the plant as long as I'm in town and see a few of the old crew that's still around, but I appreciate the offer and I'll see everyone tomorrow night."

"Of course I didn't even think about a visit to the plant, but I would probably do the same thing and you're welcome to take my car if you'd like, I won't need it."

"No-no, I'll just call the plant and have a car sent, one of the perks we get as a VP, might as well take advantage, but thank you!"

"Ok Jack I'll get you back to the hotel and start on those phone calls I guess." Bill indicated to the waitress he was ready for the check and she brought it to the table asking,

"Will there be anything else sir?" as she placed the check on the table in front of Bill though Jack tried unsuccessfully to grab it.

"No that will be it for today dear." giving her his card and indicating to Jack it was his treat. Everything taken care of they got up to leave and both men waved to Lenny on their way out, once in the car and on their way Jack called the plant and talked with the plant manager indicating he needed a ride from the Hilton downtown to the plant and while they were still on the line he told his secretary to send a car immediately and it happened, Jack thanked him and hung up.

"Well that's done Bill and I want to thank you for the great steak you were right about that restaurant and it was wonderful seeing you again, I'd like to get back to Chicago more often but things are busy in Richmond and it's hard to get away, so when I'm here I do a lot of running around catching up and not getting much sleep, but it's worth it seeing old friends!"

As they approached the Hilton Jack told Bill to just drop him off in front and call him with the time tomorrow night to be at the restaurant, Bill indicated he would as he stopped in front of the hotel and Jack got out and waved goodbye with a smile, as Bill pulled away and headed for home, but with all that had transpired today once Bill was alone again his thoughts immediately went back to Brenda, what was next?

Arriving home Bill made a pot of coffee and thought about clearing his head of Brenda at least for the moment and calling the group to ask them once again to meet tomorrow night for a free meal that may be the only incentive they would need, that would certainly work with George and he would be the first call and of course Brenda would answer the phone and Bill wanted to avoid that, he would call George on his cell, but he knew the first call should go to Barb as he dialed her office,

"Triple "A" dental Barb speaking how may I help you?"

"It's me hon, I just wanted to tell you were having dinner tomorrow night at the restaurant in the meeting room once again, but this time Jack Trax is buying this will be a revelation meeting also and Jack will be the MC."

"That sounds promising don't you think, I mean you always trusted Jack didn't you?"

"Ya I did and I guess I still do, but I'm not as quick to trust anyone these days and by the way we may have lost the data in our computer permanently, Dave's experts are having little luck, so I'll have to start, very soon, gathering data manually so we don't lose track of the business, but I guess I can hold off one more day til our get together tomorrow night."

"I think your absolutely right just wait, did you call everyone to notify them or do you want me to help?"

"You know that would help as every call turns into an hour or more lately, will you have the time?"

"Sure I'll call Larry and Dave and you can call George and Jerry, will that work?"

"That'll work I don't think you'll have any difficulties with anyone, but if you do call me ok?"

"Oh what time should I tell them to be there 6:30PM like the last time?"

"Yes I'll call and confirm with the restaurant, but I'm sure that'll be ok, I'll let you go for now so we can get busy with the calls and I'll see you later!"

"Ok hon love ya bye" as they ended the call Bill's first call was to the restaurant to confirm the time and he did and the time was fine. He would confirm with Jack after everyone's attendance was confirmed for 6:30pm, but for now a call to George as he dialed the number;

"Sales Brenda speaking may I help you?" dam he thought he dialed the wrong number a Freudian slip or truly a thoughtless moment, he had no idea which!

"Hi Brenda it's me again is George in?"

Oh hi Bill, you sound distant is everything ok?"

"Ya sure a bit preoccupied I guess about that out of town visitor I told you about I'd like to see that behind us other than that were having trouble with the business and the local gin mill is out of gin, but things are getting better, I think!"

"I'll put you through to the boss and by the way I know where you can get the gin!"

"Thanks hon I'll remember the offer!"

"I hope you do!" as she buzzed George's phone;

"Hi Bill, what's going on in Bill's world, are you calling about lunch because I'm getting hungry!"

"Hi George as a matter of fact I am calling about food, free food, but not today, tomorrow night free dinner at the restaurant on Bracken Metals Jack's in town and is going to buy dinner for all of us and hopefully answer all our questions about the big mystery plaguing us all!"

"Wow free dinner, we'll be there what time?"

"6:30pm pal we'll be counting on you to be on time as there is a program to sit thru to get feed, drinks to."

"Ok Bill listen I have another call I've gota take, see you tomorrow night!"

"Bye George" as they hung up leaving Bill with still two calls to make, Jerry and Jack, but deciding to take a break before continuing and pouring another cup of coffee he sat down to think further about Brenda and just how far he wanted this to go, he really needed time to decide and a clear head and was running out of both. His phone rang, it was Barb.

"Hi hon, how are you doing with the calls?"

"I'm good only one problem, Dave wanted to know if it was ok if he brought Gloria and I said I would check, but I thought it would be ok."

"You were absolutely right it's fine if she comes with Dave did he understand that or do you want me to call?"

"No that's not necessary I think he understood!"

"Ok well I gota go I have two more calls to make and then I'm going to get drunk!"

"Well wait for me and I'll join you!"

"Ok I won't go into high gear, but I'm going to start, BYE-BYE hon!"

"Bye dear, see you when I get home." Bill dialed Jerry and Emily's phone and waited for an answer hoping a free dinner and looking forward to some answers would get their minds off their problems, at least for the evening.

"Hi Bill its Emily did you want Jerry?"

"I'll talk to Jerry but it's you I want gal!" Bill said laughing and joined by Emily who said.

"Leave it up to you Bill to always raise my spirits, your sweet, Jerry is not home just now is there something I can help you with?"

"Yes indeed you guys can help us enjoy a free dinner at La Flambé tomorrow night at 6:30pm my old boss is in town and he's buying and is gona make sense of what's been going on for us, so hopefully you can make it"

"Of course we can 6:30 you say?"

"Yes 6:30 and bring your appetite I'll make sure there is no expense to great, we'll look forward to seeing you then."

"Ok Bill bye for now, Jerry needs a lift and this will help thanks."

Well that being done only one more call to take care of and the rest of the day would be his with nothing to do but think about ruining his marriage and possibly his life with a gal named Brenda, the girl has way to much appeal to a guy in a vulnerable position he thought, what should he do?

The answer, do nothing, so in his retirement years he could look back from time to time and say to himself.

"I really should have done that, I wonder what would have happened."

"I wonder if she was as good as she looked?"

"I wonder what she's doing now."

"Would I still be married to Barbara if I had gotten involved with Brenda?"

"Would I have what I have today had I gotten involved?"

All those questions would be for later years while reminiscing, which we all do, but for now that possibility certainly numbers among the entire list of PROBLEMS confronting Bill right now and would have to be resolved along with the others, he couldn't simply turn his back on them thinking they would eventually go away on their own, they wouldn't! Some problems you can out live while others out live you!

Time to call Jack and let him know about the arrangements for tomorrow night, hopefully he was enjoying his visit at the plant and seeing old friends Bill thought as he dialed Jack's phone.

"Hi Bill did you come up with a time for me?"

"6:30pm Jack how's your visit going?"

"I'm down in engineering right now and everyone here say's hi to you including Judy Channing."

"Oh yes say hi to all for me Jack especially to Judy who was a great help to me back then and I'll see you tomorrow night, did you need for me to pick you up?"

"A good idea Bill, if it wouldn't be a problem, but I'd like to arrive there a half hour or so early, if that's a problem I could call for a limo."

"No absolutely not we'll pick you up at 5:30pm and arrive at the restaurant by six, is that ok?"

"You bet Bill I'll see you at 5:30pm tomorrow night in the lobby as usual and bye for now!"

"Bye Jack" all was set for tomorrow evening and Jack had the program well in hand, he was always a great MC at company events and Bill was sure nothing had changed. Bill relaxed for a while and deciding on a simple dinner took some pot pies out of the freezer beef for him and chicken for Barb.

Barb arrived home at her usual time and seeing the pies on the kitchen counter told Bill of her relief at not having to cook a big dinner.

"Thanks for the thought Bill I really wasn't up to cooking tonight and I'm not hungry enough to go out, the pies are a great idea I'll put them in the oven and we should eat in about 45 minutes or so is that ok?"

"Oh ya, that's good were set for a big dinner tomorrow night anyway, so we can take it easy tonight and relax I guess, at least that's my intention, how about you?"

"Ya relaxing, at least for a while, would be good saving our energies for later in the evening!"

"Bill caught Barb's meaning, but not being in the mood dismissed it immediately and moved the conversation to other subjects, asking how did Larry and Karen receive the news about yet another get together?"

"They were fine with it especially the free meal part!" Barb seemed to notice Bill's indifference toward her subtle suggestion about sex as an end to the day, it was not the first time lately and totally unlike Bill, she was becoming concerned.

As the evening progressed they talked about the upcoming event and the business, a subject Barb didn't seem to be overly concerned about and they watched their shows on TV the late news and as she suggested it was bedtime, Bill said he would finish his drink and be right there, Barb recognized the rejection and went to bed. When

Bill finally decided to join her he found her to be fast asleep once again and went to bed himself.

A NEW DAY

The sun rising over the lake once again and peeping thru the blinds of the Kelly's bedroom, bringing the light of a new day and blocking out the mysterious darkness of confusion, which has been hanging over the group for a long time now and possibly bringing all that to an end this very day.

Barb was the first one up once again and went to the kitchen to put the coffee on and making her way to the bathroom she woke Bill saying.

"Ha hon, get up it's a new day and it promises to be a busy and late one at that!"

"Ok I'm up; I'll make the coffee while you start the breakfast!"

"I already did the coffee the breakfast is on you I'm just having toast this morning and no lunch, looking forward to dinner."

"That reminds me hon can you get out of there a little early we have to pick Jack up at 5:30 at the Hilton he wants to get to the restaurant a little early tonight to make sure everything is set up for us per his instructions!"

"Yes I have no patients this afternoon so I will be home early, I can freshen up before we go out tonight and relax for a while before we do."

"That'll work out perfect hon, so I'll expect to see you early this afternoon I expect it will be a long night and resting up first would be a great idea, I'll try it myself!"

CHAPTER THIRTY THREE
AN ELABORATE PLAN

Bill was sitting in the kitchen having a cup of coffee when Barb arrived home early from work to prepare for the evenings activities, but wanting to have a talk with her husband first, she had things on her mind.

"Hi hon" giving Bill a kiss and sitting down at the table alongside her husband who responded saying;

"Hi I see you're right on time, good you'll have a chance to relax do you want some coffee?"

"No thanks' but I would like to talk to you for a minute if that's ok?"

"Certainly what's on your mind?"

"I was just wondering, are we ok, I mean it seems that lately you've been distant you've avoided our love making and are very short when we talk, your sense of humor seems to have taken a back seat and it's all happened over the last month or so, I didn't say anything before because I thought it was just my imagination, but now I know better and I'm concerned."

"Ah first I think were fine, but I'd like to reserve further comments and explanations til after tonight's activities if you don't mind, you'll understand when I explain."

"Ok Bill, but I want to finish this conversation, I have concerns that need to be addressed, I can wait til after the festivities this evening to have this discussion, but we need to have it."

"We will hon, but for now let's just relax and get ready for tonight shall we?" Bill knew what the problems were and the reasons behind the problems, he had lost his trust In Barbara. Because of that loss of trust, he became vulnerable and had gravitated toward Brenda, who seemed an easy mark and who did nothing to discouraged his advances, in fact she encouraged them and though he was resisting her encouragement/advances and fighting his desires, knowing that if he didn't regain his trust in his wife he would succumb or give in to his desires and possibly destroy his otherwise happy marriage.

The rest of the afternoon was spent relaxing and Barb was making herself beautiful an easy job in her case. Soon it would be time to leave and pick-up Jack at 5:30 and he reminded Barb saying.

"Hon I'd like to leave at 5:00 to pick-up Jack if that's ok!"

"That's fine I'll be ready" she was and reminded Bill about the rush hour traffic at that time of the evening so he said;

"Ok let's get going then I don't want to be late I'm getting hungry already!"

As they headed down the hall toward the elevator Bill said;

"Well what do you expect tonight, do you think Jack will owe up to who it is that's behind this or will he just admit his involvement, I wish everyone involved would admit it, that would make solving this thing possible." Barb responded.

"I don't think Jack would come all this way, spend all that cooperate money, just to admit his involvement, so I would expect more from him, I don't know, but if others were involved maybe they couldn't admit it they may have been sworn to secrecy under penalty of death or something!" Barb laughing a bit, but Bill and his suspicions failed to see the humor; one of the concern's Barbara had and wanted to talk about!

"So tell me Bill what do you expect tonight?"

"The truth Barb, like you I can't believe Jack would come here just to admit his part in this, he may just be a hired hand so to speak, not knowing all the facts, just another cog in the wheel, but somehow I really doubt that!"

"The truth will surface soon hon and then all the supposition will be over and maybe we can get back to our lives, or not!" Barb said, in a desperate voice.

Finally in the car and headed for the Hilton things quieted down a bit and Bill concentrated on his rush hour driving, a challenge in itself.

Arriving at the hotel none the worse for wear from the rush hour driving experience and pulling up in front Barb said "I'll go in and get Jack hon while you wait so you don't have to park."

"Good idea hon you'll recognize him won't you?"

"Of course we'll be right out" as she exited the car and made her way inside the hotel while Bill waited in the car.

Barb, walking inside and seeing Jack sitting in one of the large overstuffed couches in the lobby walked over and said;

"Hi Jack you must be waiting for me, what can I do for you?" while a woman sitting close by looked curiously at Jack probably thinking she was a bit young for him and much to sophisticated looking to be a prostitute, as Jack stood up quickly, putting his arms around Barb and giving her a huge hug saying;

"Well this is indeed a welcome surprise Barb are you my escort, I hope!"

"Absolutely" as she took Jack by the arm smiling at the nosey woman as she walked away with Jack snuggled closely to her side.

"Barb" he said you are as always a surprise, I can't imagine the thoughts we left that woman with."

"I can" she said with a smile as they walked out the door, arm in arm to the waiting car with her husband inside smiling and saying as the door was opened by the valet;

"Hi Jack, where did you pick her up she's quite a looker?"

"Yes she is, one in a million I'd say and smart to!" Barb insisted Jack take the front seat with Bill and she got in back as Bill finished greeting Jack and drove off leaving the valet with a similar impression as the woman inside.

On the drive to the restaurant they made idle conversation with Jack asking one odd question "Tell me Bill you've lived in Chicago all your life if I remember correctly haven't you?"

"You remember correctly as usual Jack, ya I've been here a long time, but you were raised here also do you ever miss it?" as Barb sitting in the back seat listened intently.

"I do, but you know sometimes you have to make some sacrifices in order to further your career, I don't regret my choices and I may come back someday."

As they arrived at the restaurant and pulled up to the valet Jack and Bill got out as the valet opened the rear door for Barb, who also exited the vehicle and they all walked inside the restaurant.

Once inside Jack immediately latched onto Linda the Hostess and rushed her off to a solitary corner to talk, about what no one knew. Barb and Bill went to the bar inspecting the banquet room on the way and noticing (4) four what the restaurant people call (6) six top tables set up and Bill expecting something quite different, but thinking it not a big deal, continuing to the bar and seeing Bill, the substitute bartender working instead of Lenny after Bill was told by Lenny he would be here, as the bartender approached the couple Bill said,

"Hi Bill is Lenny off tonight, I was sure he'd be working?"

"Oh no he's around here somewhere; did you want me to hunt him up for you?"

"No-no that's fine, but we will have a couple of Gin Ricky's"

"Coming right up" waiting for their drinks they noticed Jack and Linda walking into the banquet room and Bill said.

"I wonder what that's all about."

"Hon I'm sure he's just following up on the arrangement's he's made."

"That's just it Barb, I'm the one who made the arrangements not Jack"

"I don't know, it looks like he may have made some arrangements also."

"Maybe" as Bill brought their drinks the first of the group, George and Nancy arrived, George is never late for a meal Bill thought and tonight is apparently no exception.

"Hi guys, I see you beat us here." as the couple sat down next to Bill and Barb to order their drinks."

"Good evening folks how can I help you this evening?"

"Two Rob Roy's Bill isn't it?"

"Bill's right sir and two double R's coming up." just about then Lenny made his way behind the bar and walking up to the couples said;

"Hi folks are you being taken good care of, I'm sure you are Bill's a great bartender and it's not very busy right now, I'm told you're having a big group today, I'm sure everyone will enjoy the food."

Before Bill had a chance to respond Dave and Gloria walked in along with Jerry and Emily close behind, while they were all greeting each other and meeting Gloria at the bar Larry and Karen came and joined the group. The socializing continued all the while drinks were being ordered and prepared; even Lenny was helping Bill out, though no one knew that Lenny wasn't working tonight he continued to help as Jack approached the bar and Bill Kelly said "Jack what would you like to drink?"

"You know Bill I think I'll settle for a ginger ale right now and save my thirst for later when I can really enjoy it, in the meantime why don't you get everyone into the room and we'll get started I believe everyone's here aren't they?"

"I believe so Jack, folks let's move to the banquet room shall we!" Bill said, as Lenny gave Jack his Ginger Ale and they all headed for the room finding a podium all set up for the speaker's this evening.

As the group filed into the banquet room Jack went straight to the podium sipping on his ginger ale finally saying, "Ladies and gentleman if I may have your attention for just a moment." As the room quieted with some seated and others still standing and once again Jack said;

"Thank you – thank you I'll try and make this as short as possible I'm sure your all hungry and we'll get to that part of the evening in a moment, but first I'd like to make sure everyone knows everyone else, so I'll start out by introducing myself, I'm Jack Trax an old colleague and friend of Bill Kelly's and I recognize some of you while other's I don't I'm sure I'll know you all soon though, but I was out at the Bracken Metal's plant yesterday afternoon and I took the liberty of asking a few of those folks to join us this evening, I hope you don't mind, I've also asked a few other folks that some of you do know and that should explain the additional seating."

Jack's revelations brought looks of dismay and confusion to the room as everyone looked questioningly at each other and at Bill for a response that never came. Once again after a long pause Jack continued with the introductions smiling he said;

"Well let's continue shall we starting with an old friend of Barb's, Lisa Vanway and by the way if there is any applause, please, hold it to the end and we'll get through this much faster I'm sure, thank you and as long as were on Barb's friends how about Ruth Manning." That was just too much for Barb, as she really had no idea of the appearance of these two ladies and she screamed out in joy as they both walked into the room!

As things settled down again Jack Continued, "And now one more familiar face to most of you, Lenny Domenico the man behind all those great drinks you've come to love while you're here enjoy them along with the ambiance and by the way, I understand Lenny is considering a career change, I checked with Lenny before making that announcement don't worry, so enjoy his bartending skills while you can!" As those people were finding their seating Jack took another breather before continuing. Bill was not saying much, but you could see the wheels turning in his head as Jack prepared to get started once again.

"Ok here we go again and as I introduce the Bracken folks I'd like you folks to keep at least one seat open at every table for them to mingle with you as things continue they'll be able to answer any questions you may have, Judy Channing Secretary to the director of engineering at Bracken and a big help to Bill when he had that position, Hi Judy and now the director of engineering John Ballock, John welcome, and the plant manager at McCook Jack Richardson and from Richmond, Va. HRM Dennis King down here on assignment, Hi Dennis and finally Doctor Luke who none of you know, but will find him quite amazing to talk with, more about the doctor later though. Ok now let's have that applause, but not just for the new comer's for everyone attending this evening hopefully you won't be disappointed in the program and I know you won't be disappointed In the food I was fortunate enough to experience the cuisine at lunch yesterday and it was great there are three choices this evening Beef, Chicken Or Seafood if you choose Beef it's anything on the menu the chicken is Florentine and the seafood is shrimp lobster or sea bass, did I say that right Linda?"

Linda smiling said "Yes Jack you did fine if you ever need a job just call."

"I'll do that thanks, so the server's will be in now to take your order's and I'll mingle myself for a while, until after dinner, when I'll be up here again to tell a rather long story that I'm sure you'll enjoy, but for now enjoy your dinner and the bar and mingle, please mingle!"

Jack joined the group as hands were shook hugs were given and a few kisses along the way, the questions were many, but answers few and that would soon be resolved. The drinks were flowing and everyone was smiling and having a good time even Bill who was busy trying to figure out the reason for the entire group of unexpected guest, but remained somewhat confused, while Barb tried to figure out why Lisa had left though she enjoyed every moment with Ruth. Jack had cornered Dave, Lenny and Jerry while Bill was occupied with George, Larry and John Ballock, while Nancy, Karen, and Emily talked and Gloria and Judy Channing got to know each other as Jack Richardson and Dennis King along with Dr. Luke moved thru the groups, all were engaged as the three waitresses took drink and dinner orders some folks continued siting while others stood and yet others went back to the bar. There were no wallflowers at this party. Jack Trax was an excellent host and social director.

As dinner was about to be served everyone was seated and the seating went like this, Table one, Bill, Barb, Lisa, Ruth, Jack, Lenny and the Doctor

Table two, Jerry, Emily, Dave, Gloria, Judy and Jack Richardson

Table three, George, Nancy, Larry, Karen, John Ballock and Dennis King

Things quieted down a bit as dinner was served and continued for a little over an hour at one time or another during the meal comments about the food were nothing but positive everyone was happy and the new comers were impressed and would return if they could. Casual small talk continued throughout the balance of the dinner and desert and as the coffee was served, Jack got up once again and made his way to the podium to continue the evening's program.

With a smile on his face and a Manhattan in his hand this time, the Ginger Ale long gone he turned to the audience and said, "I'm back, did you folks all enjoy your dinner?" as he scanned the group seeing no negatives he continued.

"I'm glad, but now you'll have to pay the price and the price of this meal is sitting there and listening to my story, some of you will be amazed, some overwhelmed, yet awed by the reality of the truth your being told, but I promise none of you will be bored and if you are, I'll buy you yet another drink, but be honest, here goes, aha but first anyone needing to visit the facilities please do as I'm long winded." Jack in his urging everyone to take a potty break decided to do the same and left the podium.

Jack, back at the podium and everyone else seated with fresh drinks, Jack started by saying;

"This is the story of an **Elaborate Plan!** A plan by an industrial giant, a corporation with many thousands of employees, a plan to promote one of those employees to a corporate Vice Presidency, golden parachute and all that goes along with it, a plan to promote Mr. Bill Kelly!" with that the audience went wild with cheers of congratulations, Barb throwing her arms around her husband and Bill being encircled by everyone including Jack, Bill sat in disbelief, he had no idea and almost came to tears, but managed to maintain his composure til Jack finished his story.

Once again at the podium saying, "Ladies and gentleman please be seated we haven't started the story yet, corporate dictates say the announcement of a promotion to this level be made by a corporate officer, I guess that's me and a senior member of the HRM department and that's Dennis King over there, so we did that right I guess, right Dennis? we don't want to jinx you Bill." as everyone laughed at Jack's winning humor Bill was busy trying to see around Barb who was sitting on his lap and hanging on his neck almost choking him.

Jack continued, "So let's get started with the story I promised shall we, it seems that all companies have policies, procedures and protocols to adhere to and a large corporation has a group of people employed to continually write these things and update them and so when a search was started to fill the position, Vice President of Planning and Design, Bill's name surfaced quickly and caught on at the highest levels and meetings were held and over time a decision was made to proceed, But these meetings were also attended by HRM to insure that everything was being done within corporate guidelines and the law if it applied and in this case it was brought to the attention of the promotions committee that if Bill were promoted at this time a violation of policy would exist." Jack stopped to take a drink and refresh himself and stretch a bit giving everyone else a chance to do the same.

As Jack returned to the podium to continue the story and all were seated once again Jack looked around making sure everyone was back and said after taking a deep breath.

"Well back to the problem that I haven't mentioned yet it seems that when considering all the policies, procedures and protocols, Bill had just had three recent promotions in a relatively short period of time and at his young age he could not be promoted to another position for at least a year, and that simply wouldn't do in this case because of an immediate need, so an alternative plan had to be developed, and it was.

After having the committees go thru all the policies, procedures and protocols a **loop hole** was discovered, Bill would have to leave the employee of Bracken Metals for at least 45 days and leave having no knowledge of the plan to promote him, but at the same time his resolve had to be tested as well as his problem solving abilities, again not being made aware of the plan, he would have to be rehired to the position he held prior to leaving the company and once accepting that position, he would be eligible for an immediate promotion to a higher level position!

The plan we developed is as follows, and believe me what you are about to hear is a lot easier said than done.

First we had to move Bill back in time two years, prior to his most recent promotions and then move him quickly forward in time over about a months' time. To accomplish this we needed to hire a Hypnotist, a great one! It was the only way and that would only work if Bill could be hypnotized, we had no idea, but as it turned out he could be (looking at Bill) that's right Bill hypnotized! Well that's a story in itself and I'm not going to get into it right now, but take my word for it we got a great Doctor, Doctor Luke over there and we got it done, thanks Doc.

After that the first thing was to get Bill out of Bracken's employee, he didn't have to know why or even how while at the same time design a scenario to test Bill's resolve and problem solving abilities and what better way than convincing Bill that he was moving quickly thru time, I won't tell you who came up with that idea, but it became the operative plan, how to proceed became the problem! We realized we'd need a lot of help to pull this off, specialized help, other than the technical help needed we'd have to recruit some of Bill's friends and family and it was preferable to recruit these people on an individual basis and not let anyone know of the others involvement, sound complicated, it was!

The first and most important would be Barbara she was absolutely necessary because Bill had to be kept on track around the clock. We also needed Dave a scientist and in a credible technical position to guide Bill and help convince Bill of whatever would be required to augment the plan as necessary on a day to day or hour to hour basis as Bill had a good deal of respect for Dave's abilities. Next we'd needed a married couple, Bill's friends, being careful to select someone who'd be convincing, but not caving and telling Bill the plot, someone who was not around Bill always, but often and one considered by Bill to be a good friend, we selected Jerry and Emily, and now not a friend, but an acquaintance an outsider someone Bill had no reason to distrust Lenny the bartender at Bill's favorite watering hole so to speak and a great choice as it turns out. Now we had to pad our choices, we had to keep a covert eye on Barb at her office so we pulled Lisa out of the office and gave her a temporary job at Bracken while we replaced Lisa with Ruth a Bracken employee, naturally the doctor was in bed with us on this move and lastly Gloria had a part in this she would provide Bill the picture of the pool and pool house that Bracken had provided to her. Finally the rest of Bill's close friends had to be told as it was recognized that Bill would be calling them to confirm what he had been led to believe, that he was traveling thru time so to speak, so George, Nancy, Larry and Karen had to be told what to expect and just to go along with Bill in a strictly passive roll.

Before we get into the tech. part of this story I think another break is in order what say you all?" everyone got up and started talking in disbelief especially Bill to his wife Barb while others went to the bar, the washrooms and some just sat there and considered what they were being told.

"Well here we are again did I mislead anyone into thinking this would be a quick story, if so I apologize, you all lived this along with Bill and Barb and by now realize the complexities of putting something like this together, it wasn't easy and technically it started out a nightmare considering the demands made by the committee to convince Bill that he had lost his job, started a business, was traveling thru time and use his pragmatism and problem solving abilities to solve this mystery.

We needed computer hackers to get into Bill's computer and not only change the date nightly, but set up an imaginary business to convince Bill he had successfully left Bracken and we had to set up a ghosted bank account, the funds provided by Bracken and the props we needed included security guards at the office, which the McCook plant needed anyway, a phony building façade and even a pool and pool house that didn't exist, that was a challenge we thought, but it was really quite easy, once we found someone who could generate a hologram that huge, we did and I understand not all of you got to see that one, you'd have enjoyed it. By the way we had nothing to do with the un-forecasted snowstorm, how could we have done that? But it sure was timely and aided greatly in making our case for strange happenings!

What was about to unfold was a full blown movie production along with actors, writers, movie sets, props, technical advisors, producers and director and we were finally ready to move ahead with production. Finally ready to put the plan into action and George's birthday party was to be the launch pad for the elaborate plan, the script was written, don't forget the now infamous blue drinks, Barb would kick off the plan with a tube of toothpaste and a book on the nightstand the following morning and we'd go from there and we certainly did it went better than we could have hoped for, everyone played their rolls perfectly and believably and most importantly Bill fell quite Naturally into his problem solving roll and he didn't even have a script to work from. True a few adjustments had to be made to the script along the way, but the overall plan worked well and the proof is that we are all here today."

"Now are there any questions that I can attempt to answer?"

George said "Ya Jack tell me is this a normal way to select a potential employee and what does an operation like this cost?"

"George it's anything but a normal way and it would only be used when hiring or promoting high level employees and then only on rare occasions as in Bill's case, the company wanted Bill and was willing to do whatever was required to get him, your friends a very talented engineer and the cost, whatever it is, will be quickly recovered I'm sure, I don't know the price George, it's not all tabulated yet, this dinner is part of it unless you want to pay your part." Jack said jokingly.

George responded "No-No Jack that's ok and thanks for dinner!"

Bill stood up and asked "Tell me Jack, what you would have done if I had said no to the offer?"

Jack taken aback a bit said "I don't know Bill I've known you for years and thought I knew you pretty well and never considered you turning us down, but if you did, after I got fired I'd have come to you for a job I guess, why, are you turning us down?"

As Barb grabbed his arm tighter and looked at Bill he said "Of course not Jack it was just my turn to ask a question and I wasn't prepared with one!" Bill laughing a little bit catching Jack looking at him with a bit of concern, but no one else picking up on it.

Dave asked, "Jack with this promotion will Bill continue here or at the home office in Richmond?"

"Well Dave, if you don't mind I'd like to hold off answering that until I've had a chance to talk to Bill after which time he'll be able to answer that himself."

"Of course how foolish of me." said Dave knowing the answer to the question, most VP's reside in the home office and he was sure that would be the case here.

Well if there are no more questions I'd like to turn the podium over to Bill who I'm sure would like to address his friends and guests, I can almost guarantee that what you are about to here is not a prepared response, so Bill it's all yours. As Jack stepped away he was given a hand followed by a roaring applause for Bill as he stepped to the podium with a smile.

"Thank you (as the applause continued) thanks folks, firstly I'd like to know if I am still hypnotized Doc? (The Doctor shook his head negatively) Thank you Jack and Bracken Metals for your excellent choice (Long Lingering Pause as the audience applauded once again) in restaurants, the food and service here is great! I for one will be back, how about a hand for the folks at La Flambé, once again the applause broke out and after it settled down again and one last round of applause for all of you who did such a great job keeping this a secret and helping to convince me that I was going out of my mind! It worked, so come on lets here it for you, once again the applause rang out. Lastly I'd like to thank my lovely wife Barb who I'm sure had the hardest job of all living a lie twenty four hours a day to help her husband achieve success, she's a special lady, lets here it for Barb as a resounding applause started and continued for a long time finally settling down allowing Bill the chance to continue.

Well Jack, you don't have to come looking for a job, I'm sure I couldn't afford you anyway, I'm accepting your offer, but I'm confused about what job I'm accepting we'll have to talk about that. I see a smile on John Ballock's face so I'm sure he's safe, at least I hope so John.

I have to admit that I've never heard of anyone going thru this to be promoted, but I'm sure it's been done before somewhere, I can only hope Bracken Metals won't be sorry they selected me for this position and I'll do my best to do my best and if I'm successful I'll be successful and if that all makes sense to you, your all crazier than I am. (The audience laughed as Bill continued) I have to admit, I was beginning to get a bit upset with some of you thinking you were against me and my efforts to solve this thing and today came just in time, **believe me!**

That's about all I have to say right now and I think I'll get out from behind this podium and take my place with you good folks and mingle along with all of you and keep in mind Jack hasn't shut down the bar yet so enjoy the rest of the evening and once again thank you all."

As Bill walked away from the podium he was greeted by many with continued congratulations and well wishes as Lenny shook Bill's hand indicating he had to get back to the bar to help Bill as it was getting busy. Slowly things started to wind down as more people left; tomorrow was still a work day. After the Bracken people left only Dave, Gloria, George, Nancy and Jack were left along with Bill and Barb and all were getting ready to leave as the evening came to an end and final good nights were said as the couples left the restaurant and Bill, Barb and Jack got in the car and headed to the Hilton to drop Jack at his hotel.

As they drove Jack asked "Well Bill what do you think did you ever suspect that this was all being done on your behalf?"

"To be honest Jack, I finally came to believe it was a conspiracy against me, by my friends, but I had no idea why or what the motivation could be and then when I figured out that you were involved it changed my thinking and when Dennis entered the picture I became somewhat confused again, but I never figured out the real reason behind the mystery, you guys did a remarkable job, but I still question the necessity of it all I'll have to read those policies and procedures when I get a chance."

"When you do Bill have a lawyer sit down with you because you'll need one, I know!"

As they pulled up to the hotel Jack said his goodbyes as he would be catching an early plane in the morning for Richmond, but reminding Bill that he was expected in Richmond also on Monday to meet the President and Executive Vice President for lunch and his official promotion announcement and of course Barb was welcome to attend as discussed earlier that evening.

Bill and Barb said their goodbyes and told Jack they'd see him on Monday as Jack exited the car and walked into the hotel waving as he left.

On their way home Barb asked Bill "Well hon was it all worth it, it's a huge promotion, are you happy, I'm sure we'll have to leave Chicago though won't we?"

"Was it worth it, I suppose that a promotion to VP of a mega corporation is worth anything short of criminal activity, but at times it was intense and to tell you the truth I almost failed the test. I am for the most part happy and though we haven't been told we have to leave Chicago, I'm sure that will be the case and I have mixed emotions about that were not just leaving the city were leaving all our friends and our beautiful home and there is no way I could be happy about that, it's a case of mixed emotions, how about you hon, do you have mixed emotions?"

"Certainly I do and I have to leave a job I love also, but this isn't just about you or me, it's about us and our life, well make new friends and we'll always have the old ones and we'll keep close tabs on each of them, but were making our way thru life and have to do what we collectively believe to be right for our future and if we believe this move is right, all things considered, then we go for it!"

"Well right now let's go home and go for it, what say you?"

Smiling Barb said "Well I thought you'd never ask, step on it baby I tremble with desire, maybe we should just pull over here!"

"There was a time when I would have done that very thing, I'm sure you remember, but today I can restrain myself, under most circumstances so I'm not going to pull over in a shopping center parking lot, but if we come across a forest preserve on the way I could still be persuaded!"

The drive home continued and though they were both looking, no forest preserves were spotted and they had to settle for their place, the parking garage was tempting and Barb got real aggressive in the elevator, but Bill managed to restrain her til they got in the unit and then there was no stopping them, no coffee, drinks or TV by the time they got to the bedroom Barb was totally naked and Bill was not far behind, they both had sex on their minds love making would have to wait for another time as they started in the kitchen went on to the living room and ended up in the bedroom and when they both got to the point where neither one could breathe any longer they both rolled over and went to sleep totally satisfied and exhausted.

For the most part the next day, for the first time in a long while, would be back to normal; Barb would wake to yet another work day, quite possibly one of her last while Bill had many things to take care of before their Monday trip to Richmond, VA. For their official welcoming to the Bracken Metals family once again and not having to worry any longer about his business or solving a mystery, that was only a mystery to him and no one else!

As the morning sun came up once again over the Lake Barb found herself standing in front of the bedroom window totally naked with the drapes wide open, not an unusual occurrence on the twenty fourth floor of a lake shore drive high rise and something Barb did with some regularity, she enjoyed the fact that no one but another High Rise dweller with a telescope or pair of binoculars could see her and they were probably standing there naked themselves and would never see her anywhere else, but in the window and would never recognize her in a public place if they did run into her, she enjoyed the mystique. Bill and Barb had on occasion had sex in front of the window hoping to draw a crowd, but never knowing for sure if they had. High Rise living was to say the least an adventure!

Bill woke and joined Barb at the window in the same state of undress and wrapping her up in his arms asking if she had to work today?

She responded saying "Ya I have to, Lisa is coming back today and her and Ruth have to make a transition and then were all going out to lunch to say goodbye to Ruth she's been great I really enjoyed her being there."

"Ok I just thought I'd ask, I'm sure I could have thought of some interesting way to spend the day, I'll put the coffee on do you want your usual toast?"

"Yes dear that'll be fine this morning, but I do have to start getting ready and I don't know if I should give my notice to the doctor or not yet?"

"You know we should wait til we get back from Richmond, I don't know when I'm expected to be on the job, and you may have to stay here for a while after I leave to make arrangements for housing and so on."

Shortly after Barb left for work the phone rang and Bill answered "Hello"

"Hello Bill?"

"Yes this is Bill who's calling?"

Bill its Maxine, I guess I'll have to start calling you Mr. Kelly, But Mr. Trax asked me to call and let you know we'll be sending one of the Jets for you and wanted to know if you preferred Midway or O'Hare I'll also be arranging lodging for you and Mrs. Kelly at one of the hotels that Bracken uses it's a lovely place you'll enjoy it I'm sure."

"Oh thanks Maxine Midway would be fine I was just about to call for flight reservations, but a corporate Jet would be an experience and I'm sure fun, I know your choice of accommodation's would be more then fine and by the way Maxine, Bill would be just fine."

"Well thank you Mr. Kelly, but we secretaries have our protocols that we must follow, the jet is only one of the many perks you'll be enjoying and talking about perks I know your secretary very well we have lunch together often and she is a wonder and one of the fastest typist I've ever seen, you'll learn quickly to appreciate her, well anyway Midway airport at the 63rd street corporate hanger at 1:00pm Sunday 12/11/2011 and if your early or late don't worry on corporate jets you set the schedule, is that ok?"

"It all sounds good Maxine I guess we'll see you on Monday."

"No problem Mr. Kelly and I'll text you the pilot's cell number when I find out who your pilot will be in case there's a need to call him, other than that I think your all set and of course you have my number here if anything comes up, but I'll say goodbye for now."

"Thanks for everything Maxine and we'll see you on Monday bye-bye."

As Bill hung up he dialed Barb immediately to tell her the exciting news about the private jet, he knew she'd be even more excited than he was, as he dialed her number his phone rang and it was George's office, he hastened to take the call before realizing it may not be George and it wasn't;

"Hello"

"Hi Bill it's Brenda, I just heard of your good fortune and promotion and I wanted to call and say congratulations, George said you'd probably be moving to Virginia and for me that's the only bad news as **we never got to have our moment,** but I am happy for you Bill and wish you well and all the success I'm sure you'll have."

"Thanks Brenda, I appreciate the sentiment and thought and I'm sure I'll be in town from time to time and maybe we'll be able to go for lunch or at least coffee, we'll see, but thanks again and as long as I got your office is George in?"

"No he's out and about and not expected back today, he's taking a client out for dinner and drinks tonight, one of his largest accounts and the purchasing agent is a very attractive blond."

Bill laughing aloud said, "Well Brenda I'm sure the only thing she'll get out of George tonight is a great meal and a perfect martini or two, but I'll try him on his cell later, you have a good day Brenda and we'll talk again I'm sure, bye for now!"

"Bye-Bye Bill call when you get settled in your new surroundings!"

As they hung up Bill's mind wondered back to a movie he had seen once with a similar plot, he knew he had not seen or heard the last of Brenda, hopefully she would find another guy to stalk and get out of Bill's life as quickly as she came in, only time will tell.

Bill tried again to place his call to Barb this time hearing a unfamiliar voice answer saying "Triple "A" dental Lisa may I help you?"

"Hi Lisa its Bill I hear you guys are going out to lunch today, does Ruth realize your celebrating her leaving?"

"No-No Bill, were celebrating my return a positive not a negative, but I know Ruth is as anxious to get back to her office as I was to get back to mine, though I did enjoy my time at Bracken and they treated me very well there, did you know they offered me a permanent position?"

"No I didn't, but obviously you didn't accept and that's our loss I'm afraid and triple "A" dentals gain!"

"Oh that's right you're a big wheel at Bracken Metals now, a Vice President, congratulations Bill or should I say Mr. Kelly, you're not going to make Barb leave us are you, she's the reason things work so well around here?"

"Lisa you've always called me Bill and I know of no reason to change and as for us leaving the area, were not aware of that yet and won't know much more until next week after our trip to Richmond, so I can't answer your question just yet, but even if we are relocated I'm sure I won't be able to keep Barb from coming back to visit often."

"Well will leave it there for now Bill, did you want to talk to her?" as she put Barb on the phone;

"Hi hon we're about to leave for lunch what's up?"

"You'll never guess, I just got a call from Maxine, Jack's secretary and they're going to send a private Jet for us Sunday, one of the corporate planes and that's way beyond first class!"

"Wow that's something, I have to tell everyone here about it at lunch, but were on our way out right now so see you later ok love ya?"

"Ya sure I knew you'd be excited enjoy your lunch and I'll see you later bye for now."

"Bye hon"

As Barb hung up Bill realized he had absolutely nothing more to do in preparation for the trip to Richmond and meeting the corporate big wigs, somebody, he suspected Jack, had laid the groundwork for him and he hoped he could live up to their expectations, he would be the youngest VP on the 14th floor of the Bracken building, the 14th floor being where all the corporate officers including the President and the CEO had their offices and that's where Bill would find his new home unless there was another plan in the works that he was not aware of, he would find out Monday.

Maxine was to send an itinerary sometime today and then he would know Monday's schedule and that reminded Bill that he no longer had a computer to receive the itinerary he'd have to call Maxine to let her know. As he dialed Maxine's number he thought he might sound scatterbrained or something with all these questions and clarifications, but he was intent on making sure nothing went wrong or delayed this very important meeting next week so he placed the call.

"Hello, Mr. Trax phone Maxine speaking may I help you?"

"Hi again Maxine, Bill Kelly, I just remembered I no longer have a computer to receive your itinerary, I guess I need to go buy a new one and I don't have a smart phone, but I do have a fax, I'll give you the number and we can do it that way if that's ok?"

"Yes that'll be fine Bill and don't buy a new computer the company will give you one, I'm sure you'll get one on Monday, there very nice laptops and preloaded with all the corporate data you'll need and your secretary will upload it with all the daily info you'll need meetings, appointments, lunch and dinner dates, birthdays and travel data you'll need, I'm sure she is gathering your data right now and imputing it into your computer, you'll also be getting a new smart phone and corporate credit card, but I'm giving away too much info I better keep quiet, but most of what I've told will be on your itinerary anyway, you'll be busy Monday."

"Thanks again Maxine, I don't know what I'd do without you you've been a big help and I'm grateful, I guess I'll get to meet you in person on Monday at least I hope so!"

"I'm sure we'll get to meet soon Bill and I'll be calling you Mr. Kelly when we do, I'll have this itinerary to you within the hour, will there be anything else I can do right now or have we covered it pretty well?"

"No, you've pretty well covered it once again, I guess I'll let you go and well talk again before Monday, I'm sure I'll have more questions bye for now Maxine."

"Goodbye Bill" hanging up Bill thought he'd go to La Flambé for one of those famous burgers that he loved and maybe sit at the bar and visit with Lenny if he was working, so he headed for the restaurant arriving just about lunch time and noticing a bit of a larger crowed than usual, but there was plenty of room in the lounge and Lenny was at the bar as Bill walked in he was greeted by Lenny with a smile saying.

"Hi Bill I didn't expect to see you today, what brings you out?"

"You know Len I was hungry and I got your burgers in my head and couldn't get them out, so here I am."

"Gin Ricky and I'll get you a waitress Bill!"

"Right both times Len this will probably be the last one of these I'll have for a while." as Len made Bill's drink and waved a waitress over to the bar he said.

"Ya, you are going to be heading to Richmond I guess is that permanent? If it is we'll sure miss you guys around here!"

As the waitress approached, someone Bill didn't recognize, but introducing herself "Hi I'm Jean what can I get for you today sir?" Len smiled knowing Bill's response to her question and saying.

"Oh' no Jean, he doesn't like to be called sir! This is Bill, one of our best customers and a dedicated sub-burger patron." Bill smiling at Lenny's interjecting his thoughts before Bill had a chance to and saying;

"Jean don't pay any attention to him, he knows me to well it seems, but please call me Bill and I will have the sub-burger med rare with mozzarella cheese, mustard, mayo, tomato on a grilled French roll, pickle on the side and steak fries."

"Wow I guess you do know what you want Bill I'll be back" As she walked away to place the order.

"By the way Len one thing I never figured out who the hell was it that originally placed the order for the blue drinks at the party that night?"

"Oh you never figured that out, the truth is nobody, it was something I threw in to add a little mystery kind of an ad-lib."

"You're kidding an ad-lib it became the focal point of the whole mystery and you threw it in on a whim, I'd never have figured that one out Len, I'll be dammed!"

Well after lunch and a pleasant visit with Len Bill headed for home hoping to find his itinerary in the fax so he could get an idea of what was planned for Monday morning so Bill could be somewhat prepared. Once home the first thing Bill did was to check the fax and as promised the itinerary was there waiting for him as he removed the document from the machine and started reading;

The following Itinerary is for Mr. William Kelly on Monday 12 December 2011 at the Bracken building in Richmond, VA.
1. 7:00a.m. Limousine to pick up Mr. & Mrs. Kelly at hotel for transport to Bracken building.
2. 7:30a.m. to 8:30a.m. Mr. & Mrs. Kelly arrive at Bracken building, sign in at reception and are then escorted to the Executive Vice Presidents office and conference room Mr. William Blair, for an early coffee and welcome reception.
3. 8:45a.m. to 9:45a.m. Meet with Mr. John Pasmore President and COO in his office with representatives from HRM Mr. Wm. Foster and Legal Ms. Joyce Carey for the official promotional announcement and signing of the required documents for all corporate Executives.
4. 10:00a.m. to 10:30a.m. Mr. Wm. Kelly, the new Vice President of planning and design to meet the CEO, Mr. James Gross who will welcome the new VP to the corporation and the 14th floor.
5. 10:30a.m. til 12:00p.m. Mr. Kelly to tour his new office, meets his secretary, set the combination on his office safe, get his new laptop computer and cell phone and most important select his new office chair from the three choices he will be given.
6. 12:00p.m. to 2:00p.m. Mr. and Mrs. Kelly to Executive dining room for a welcome lunch with the entire 14th floor Executives and their wives.
7. 2:00p.m. to 4:00p.m. Tour the Bracken Building and prepare to leave for the hotel.
8. 4:15p.m. Limousine to hotel and checkout.
9. 5:30p.m. Limousine to airport to board Bracken Jet to Chicago.
10. 7:45p.m. arrive back in Chicago.

After reading the itinerary Bill realized they would have a busy day and decided to make a few notes on questions he would need to ask the different people he would meet.

That's how the rest of the week and weekend went; Barb did some shopping for the trip as well as Bill who had some things to pick up himself. There were a few casual dinners and a lot of talk among themselves about the certainty of a move to Richmond and how that transition would take place, as well as their concerns about leaving their friends, this seemed to concern Barb more than it did Bill and Barb was also concerned about leaving her job, their 24th floor LSD condo and their future in general, would it be worth all those sacrifices, but of course it would be and Bill would remind Barb that on a carrier path you went where opportunity took you and when you became a corporate officer you truly achieved success or at least were well on your way!

CHAPTER THIRTY FOUR
THE PROMOTION

Sunday morning the overnight bags packed and the coffee was on as Barb looked perplexed and asked Bill "Hon what do I wear to travel in, I mean a private Jet and all I don't know what people will expect me to wear?"

"Honey it's casual travel, dress the same as you would if you were on a commercial flight and wear your smile, now how about some breakfast?"

"Ok do you want some ham and eggs or Pancakes or I see even waffles are on the menu this morning, do any of those sound tempting or did you just want your cereal, I have fresh bananas if you'd like?"

"You know now that you mention it ham and eggs does sound good if it's ham off the bone a English muffin and do we have any hash brown's?"

As Barb busied herself getting breakfast on the stove, Bill was getting his briefcase together with the papers and documents he thought he might need to get rehired, so to speak at Bracken, he also packed two suits in his garment bag as Barb had packed an evening dress and a business suit in her bag so both were ready for any occasion that may arise. It was approaching 9:00am as Barb called Bill to the table for his breakfast when the phone rang and Bill could see it was George calling and Bill's breakfast was hot, Murphy's Law he thought, as Barb, being the dutiful wife answered the phone saying, "Hi George we can't talk right now Bill's still home!"

"Hi sweetie, I guess my timing is off again I'll just have settle for talking to Bill this time, but I'd much rather talk with you!"

"I'll have him call you George he's in the shower is it real important you know were leaving for Richmond this afternoon and are going crazy getting ready?"

"No not important, just wanted to wish you guy's good luck and a safe trip, take some pictures of the Jet inside and out ok, are you coming back on Monday also?"

"Ya were back in Chicago at 8:00p.m. And I'll take pictures for all to see, thanks for the call and your thoughts, we love you guy's too."

"Ok honey if Bill gets a chance have him call if not I understand and we'll talk when you get back, in any case have a safe and fun trip bye for now."

"Bye George, I'm sure Bill will call love you!" hanging up Barb said.

"He's a good friend hon and we'll miss him and Nancy the most I guess, though I'm sure we'll miss all of our friends, it's hard to imagine starting all over again and in totally unfamiliar surroundings."

"Hon don't be too upset, I'm being promoted to a Corporate VP position in a fortune 500 company at an extremely young age, I'm sure everything will work out for the best, we'll make many new friends and never lose the ones we have and Richmond is not that far from Chicago so you can visit often."

"You say I can visit often don't you mean we, I wouldn't want to come back alone!"

"What I meant hon was that I'll be working and I suspect traveling from time to time and between those times if we are able to return together fine, but you may want to see your parents or visit friends and there is no reason why you couldn't do that on your own, if I was otherwise occupied."

The morning continued as Bill finished his breakfast, with discussions about many subjects as time passed, soon it was approaching the time to get ready and leave for the airport to catch their plane. Bill decided to call their pilot and confirm his arrival in Chicago; he dialed the number and waited, soon a voice answered saying "Hello Joe Janasek speaking."

"Yes Joe this is Bill Kelly I was just checking to make sure you weren't delayed getting into Chicago, have you arrived yet?"

"Yes Sir Mr. Kelly we landed about an hour ago and just finished refueling, just waiting for you and Mrs. Kelly to arrive and we'll be on our way to Richmond."

"That sounds good Joe, we plan on arriving about 12:30pm so I guess that gives you enough time to grab a sandwich or something, do you have to takeoff at a special time or do you have some latitude?"

"Yes sir there's a great little restaurant right across the street that we go to when were in town on layover and no we serve at your pleasure we can depart anytime we have a departure time of 1:00pm, but that can be changed without any difficulty so we'll see you when you get here."

"Thanks Joe we'll see you soon."

Hanging up Bill said "Ha hon the planes on the ground waiting for us, so were all set I guess I'll call George back he said as he dialed the number.

"Hello Bill, listen I thought I'd call and see if I could offer you guy's a ride to midway, I'd like to get a look at that plane anyway, I don't have many chances to see a private Jet up close and then we could pick you up Monday night."

"Hi George, ya know we already decided to drive, but I appreciate the offer the parking is inside the fenced in area so I'm sure the car will be ok for a day or so, but if you really want to see the plane meet us there and I'll arrange a quick tour!"

"What time do we need to be there Bill and we will be there to see you off."

"We plan on arriving at about 12:30p.m George at the corporate hanger on 63rd street so we'll see you and Nancy there."

"See you at 12:30 buddy bye for now."

"Hon George and Nancy are going to meet us at the airport and see us off; George really wants to see the Jet though I'm sure."

"That's great I'll be glad to see them both will they let them see the plane?"

"I'm sure they will the pilots probably show it off all the time I can't foresee any problem."

They gave the condo a once over to make sure everything was shut off and it would be secure for the next couple of days as they made their way down to the garage with their luggage to depart for the airport both dressed casually but warm and comfortable as they drove out of the parking garage Bill stopped right across the street at a fast food drive through to get both of them a coffee for the drive to the airport and they were off headed for a real adventure starting with a ride on a private Jet.

After about a 35 minute drive they arrived at the airport and pulling into the fenced in private parking area they noticed that George and Nancy were already there and talking to a couple of uniformed pilots, as Bill and Barb got out of the car they were approached by the group hearing George say there's your passengers now guys, as the two pilots held out there hands saying.

"Mr. and Mrs. Kelly welcome to Bracken Air I'm Joe and my first officer here is Mike we were just about to show your friends the plane if you have no objections."

"No-no of course not Joe, lead the way!"

"If you folks will just follow us the ships in the hanger where it's warm and comfortable, there very accommodating here, they treat us very good every time we come to Chicago."

As they entered the hanger they noted three Jets, Joe explained pointing first to the smallest "That's a Lear 45 there, a Cessna Citation and that's us a Gulfstream G5"

"Wow a Gulfstream that's the Cadillac of jets isn't it?" George asked and Joe responded saying.

"The Rolls Royce Sir, please climb aboard and have a look around."

"This is something Joe it's beautiful, how many of these does Bracken have in the fleet?"

"Just one Gulfstream a Falcon 900LX and two Citations in the fleet and we keep them all flying most of the time."

The seating was two couches and four swivel chairs all in leather; a hidden bar fully stocked with the Executives favorite selections, one of the pilot's jobs was to make sure the bar was properly stocked, depending on who was riding and he demonstrated this by showing Bill the bottle of their favorite gin, Bill and Barb were impressed as was George who was making his way to the flight deck to check out the toys up there. The cabin was also equipped with a TV with flight data information center available if selected and you can even get the pilot's view on takeoff and landing if you choose.

Joe told Mike to arrange for the tow out of the hanger to the tarmac and to prepare for departure which Mike did after excusing himself. Well folks, talking to George and Nancy, if you've seen enough, it's about time for us to depart, I hope you'll watch the takeoff from your car or you can stay right here we'll be using that runway right there, I've enjoyed showing you folks around maybe someday you'll be one of my passengers, I'd enjoy that.

As they all steeped off the plane the two couples said their goodbyes and gave each other hugs and kisses and the Robert's wishing Bill and Barb a safe flight and good luck tomorrow at Bracken. The Kelly's boarded the plane with the two pilots as the tow motor arrived to pull the plane outside onto the tarmac and the air stair was retracted and closed while George and Nancy watched with great interest waving to the Kelly's as the plane started to move out of the hanger once on the tarmac and the tow disconnected the Richard's heard the engines start and the lights came on and soon the ship started to move toward the departure runway only a short distance away from the tarmac George and Nancy watched intently as their friends left, only for a day or two this time, but they knew eventually it would be for good and they were sad about that eventuality.

The Gulfstream moved into takeoff position and almost immediately started to roll faster and faster until the nose came up and they left the ground pointed at what appeared to be almost straight up like a rocket seeming to climb much faster than a commercial airliner and soon disappearing into the clouds, leaving George and Nancy walking back to their car a tear in Nancy's eye.

In the meantime Bill and Barb looked out of the windows of the sleek and luxurious jet as it turned east toward Richmond VA.

Shortly after takeoff one of the pilots came on the speaker announcing they were just passing thru 10,000 feet on their way to

33,000 feet their assigned cruising altitude today. Gee Bill thought, just like the airlines, announcements and all, but better. Soon Mike the first officer came back to the cabin to offer the couple a drink and familiarize them with the bar, showing them the refrigerator where the food and assorted fresh sandwiches were kept telling them to help themselves while he flew the airplane in a joking way of course and with a reassuring smile as he went back to the flight deck inviting them to have a peek up front at their leisure if they so desired, a perk not offered on an airlines.

Bill made a couple of drinks and they engaged in idle chit chat while the jet clicked off about 10 miles a minute on the short 550 mile trip as Joe came back to visit once they got to 33,000 feet as seen on the flight data display In the cabin a gadget that interested Bill, but generated little interest for Barb who was more interested in going forward to the flight deck to have a look around and see out the front window as she put it.

"Just checking to see how you folks are enjoying the ride as you can see we've reached our cruising altitude of 33,000 feet, pointing to the display with a ground speed of just over 600 mph making this a relatively short flight of about 70 minutes gate to gate so to speak as he looked at his watch Joe said we should be starting down in about ten minutes so enjoy the flight and let us know if we can do anything to make it more enjoyable."

Barb asked "Joe can we come up and look around where you guys sit and see out the front window?"

Smiling Joe said "Follow me"

Once in the rather small cockpit Joe invited Barb, who seemed the most interested to sit in the left seat, his seat, which she did with no hesitation as Mike smiled at her, but watched over her cautiously as she took the seat while Joe talked to Bill, Mike explained the various displays to Barb who was ready to take flying lessons and turning to Bill saying.

"Hon I want to take flying lessons can I do that?"

Bill looking at the two pilots saying "Thanks guys, I thought she might have gotten interested in the PTA or Ladies Auxiliary, but now she wants to fly!" shrugging his shoulders and smiling he went back to the cabin and left Joe the task of getting his seat back so Barb didn't have to land the airplane!

As Barb returned to her seat of choice she said to Bill;

"Wow that's really neat up there hon, I could sit up there all day long and the view is simply breathtaking I've never seen anything like it!"

"Well if you'd really be interested in learning I'm sure it could be arranged hon."

"Really do you think I could, it might be expensive!"

"Well see" Bill said, as he noticed the flight display indicating the start of their decent now showing 31,600 feet and going down and pointing to the display, letting Barb know what was happening, who now had renewed interest in what was going on with the display and in the cockpit. When the altitude showed 8,000 feet the seatbelt sign came on and audible signal sounded as they both buckled up to prepare for the landing in Richmond.

Following an almost perfect landing and taxi to the parking area reserved for Bracken Air and hearing the engines shutdown and Joe exiting the cockpit saying;

"Well folks I see your limousine is pulling up to take you to your hotel, but before you leave we'd, Mike and I, would like to say it's been a pleasure having you onboard today and I mean that sincerely it's been a treat for us and we hope to see you again soon, that said, have a great stay in Richmond!"

As Joe opened the door for us to exit Bill shook his hand asking if they would be taking them back to Chicago tomorrow evening, but Joe didn't know as he had not seen the schedule yet. Barb thanked him profusely for her unbelievably pleasant and informative flight experience, for her it was a thrill a minute and she promised she was going to learn to fly thanks to the two of them. As they left the plane their luggage had already been loaded into the limo and they were greeted by a good-looking chauffer in a uniform introducing himself as Berry and welcoming them to Richmond as he opened the door for them to enter the limo, they both waved to the pilots who waved back as the door closed and they were off to the hotel.

On the way Berry pointed out the local points of interest and sights conducting an informal sightseeing tour as he drove even pointing out the Bracken building a mile or so away on their way to the hotel. As they arrived in front of the hotel, after about a half hours ride from the airport Berry exited the limo and hailed a hotel valet to take care of the luggage. As the couple exited the vehicle they thanked Berry and asked if he would be picking them up in the morning or would it be someone else, Berry assured them he would be picking them up bright and early at 7:00am per the schedule he had been given and with that said goodbye, unless they would require anything else, Bill assured him they were good and said thanks as Berry drove away.

The couple signed in at the front desk and was shown to a mini suite reserved by Bracken Metals for Bill and Barb. Bracken was one of the hotels best clients and Brackens guests were given the VIP treatment.

They arrived at the hotel about 4:30p.m. Local time, and decided to relax a while before having dinner at the hotel dining room which was highly recommended by Berry when dropping them off, tomorrow would be a busy day so they thought they'd turn in early and get a good night's sleep in preparation for the day's activities tomorrow and that's just what they did.

5:30a.m. arrived early as they both woke up and rushed to the shower, Barb winning once again, but decided to share with Bill after all it was his day and a little fooling around in the shower would be a nice way to start his promotion day and it may help him relax a bit. In any case after the community shower they dressed and went down to the dining room for a continental breakfast and afterword's waited in the lobby for their limo to arrive.

6:55a.m. when Berry arrived at the hotel to take the couple to Bracken Metals for the day's events, as Bill and Barb walked out the front door of the hotel Berry opened the limo door and greeted them with a smile saying "Good morning folks a bright sunny day today a good sign I think" (Knowing the reason for their visit, but saying nothing) Bill replied saying.

"I believe your right Berry, it's destined to be a very good day, so, let's get started shall we!"

"Yes sir!" As he shut the door behind Bill and Barb, walked around the car got in and headed for the Bracken building and the beginning of yet another new adventure for the couple.

Arriving at the Bracken building on schedule and entering the lobby greeted by a lovely young lady who introduced herself as Jeannie Henning and indicating she would be our escort for the scheduled events today.

The day went almost exactly as indicated on the Itinerary Maxine had sent and after signing in at reception they were escorted to the 14th floor and Mr. William Blair's office suite for the coffee and welcome reception.

Things progressed threw out the day as planned to the point where Bill was officially promoted and signed the legal documents, he was now the new Vice President of planning and design and not at all sure what that meant, he was an engineer and hoped it had something to do with his area of expertise, in any case he never suffered from a lack of confidence and was sure he could handle it, no matter what it entailed.

In the course of the day they met everyone on the 14th floor except for those on vacation or out of town on business, but the meeting that most impressed Bill was at 10:30a.m. when he met Ms. Corrina Borders his new secretary, she was a living dream, long blond hair that she wore up and curves that would challenge the imaginations of cartoonist around the world her skin smooth and flawless and perfectly toned, legs that were indescribable, a smile as sincere and beautiful as Barb's, her breasts pronounced (possibly implants) but not obtrusive or overly done (worth investigating Bill thought) and an MBA in business 33 years old and never married, Bill noticed Barb noticing and once again new this would be trouble if he didn't get control of his feelings right now!

Corrina gave Bill his new laptop and took time to show him how to get into the Bracken system and get his email, schedule and other info he may require, she also gave Bill his new cell phone being quick to show him that she was on his speed dial along with other 14th floor executives he may need to contact and after selecting his new office chair he bid Corrina goodbye for now saying he would keep in touch and would see her on his next trip to Richmond, expecting to make several of those trips til he was relocated to Richmond on a permanent basis.

The rest of the day wasn't worth further mention after meeting Corrina, except to say they had spared no expense on the luncheon,

Prime Rib and Swordfish with the finest red and white wines, it seemed every available executive on the 14th floor and their wives showed up to partake of the bounty. Their chef was talented enough to work anywhere he choose, the cuisine was delicious and the presentation exceeded expectations I'm sure! Beyond that it went pretty much per the itinerary and went well, but Bill was anxious to get back to Chicago and start getting involved in his new job.

On the limo ride to the airport that evening Bill went out of his way to engage in conversation with Barb so he didn't seem preoccupied though being promoted to a corporate VP would have been a reasonable explanation for the preoccupation, Bill didn't want to fan the fire so to speak though he didn't even know if a fire existed.

As they arrived at the airport and pulled up to the waiting jet Barb was happy to see Joe and Mike standing there waiting to greet them once again. As they exited the limo they thanked Berry as he put their luggage on the plane with Mike's help and supervision while Joe congratulated Bill on his promotion and once again welcomed us aboard.

The subsequent flight into Chicago was uneventful and smooth while Bill and Barb engaged in idle conversation about the day's events, Barb obviously proud of her young husband's success, but still concerned about the move to Richmond now that they officially knew that was to be his base of operations and the move was now inevitable, it was explained that the company would buy their condo in Chicago for the fair market value and find them a place in Richmond to live, their real-estate people had already started the search for them and had some leads.

Barb would stick her nose into the cockpit from time to time to say hi and look around, she loved looking out of their window and they tolerated her invasion of their space Bill thought they even liked it, she was attractive and had a pleasant smile and manner which most people liked about her.

Soon the flight data readout in the cabin indicated their initial decent into Chicago had begun and Barb took her seat once again telling Bill that the flight computer indicated 20 minutes to landing at Midway, she was totally into this flying idea and Bill was starting to believe she was serious about taking lessons, only time would tell, her interest had been peaked, thanks to the two pilots up front.

Soon the seatbelt sign and audible warning came on; they buckled up and prepared for their landing. After about five minutes they once again experienced an almost perfect touchdown, these guy's made it look easy Bill thought as they taxied to the corporate hanger and tarmac where the plane would be left for the night as Joe and Mike had a layover in Chicago tonight in order to collect some salesman tomorrow afternoon and take them to New York.

As the plane stopped on the tarmac and the engines shutdown Joe stepped out of the flight deck once again and with a smile and said "Well folks home again, hope you enjoyed the flight, I'll help you get your luggage to your car." Barb quickly responded saying.

"Joe, once again, that was a great landing, who did it you or Mike?"

"Well we work together up there, but that one was all Mike, though I'd like to say I did it, but don't tell him he's swell headed enough!"

Joined by Mike they unloaded the luggage and loaded it into the couple's car and the two pilots shook hands with Bill saying their goodbyes to the couple as Joe said.

"Well, Mr. and Mrs. Kelly it's been an interesting couple of days, Mike and I have enjoyed chauffeuring you around the sky's so to speak and hope to do it again soon, Mrs. Kelly I hope you follow up with your interest in what we do and take a few lessons yourself I'm sure you'll do well and with that we'll leave you folks to enjoy the rest of the evening as we head for our room after putting the plane to bed and arranging for fuel filling out the log books etc.

Bill and Barb said their last goodbyes got into their car and left for home, after a busy two days.

Bill asked in a joking way "Hon did you want to go out to dinner, I have the corporate credit card now you know?"

"No let's just go home we can grab a takeout on the way I really just want to take a shower, put my feet up and relax, I have to work tomorrow even though you don't you know!"

"What do you mean I have my laptop and I'll check my schedule in the morning and spend some time in the computer checking out Bracken Metals?"

"You worked for them for several years Bill what's to check out?"

"Ya but not in this capacity and not with this kind of corporate info at my fingertips, it will be informative I'm sure, I have many new things to learn and that's working my dear. You know I might take a ride out to the McCook plant for a visit, the last time I did that I was refused admittance I wonder if I would have the same problem this time or if they would even recognize me, indeed, I think that's how I'll spend my morning!"

On the way home they stopped at a Burger King drive-thru for takeout and went home to relax the rest of the evening.

Upon entering their condo Barb immediately went to the bathroom to run a bath and returned to the kitchen to eat her dinner with Bill and afterwards took a long soothing bath while Bill played with his new computer, after about an hour they both retired for the night.

CHAPTER THIRTY FIVE
THE CELEBRATION

Well waking up to a new day and the start of a new life for our couple as Bill looked to find Barb already up and standing naked once again in front of the bedroom window the drapes wide open, for everyone interested to see and maybe for one of the last times she would be able to do that, not enjoying the moment though as she usually did with that evil little smile, replaced now by a somewhat desperate frown and Bill not knowing exactly why, but starting to feel a little guilty as he walked up behind her, put his hands on her naked shoulders and said, "Hon don't worry we'll adjust just fine I'm leaving too, were young and this may not be our last relocation, you'll be fine after all we have each other and that's been a winning combination so far and I'm sure that will continue!"

As Barb moved her hands to his already on her shoulders she said, "I know hon and I'll be fine I'm just adjusting to the idea it's a big change for both of us, but men seem to handle this kind of thing better than women do, but I'll handle it don't worry, make the coffee!" she said with a forced smile as she turned away and walked into the bathroom to start getting ready for work.

Busy in the kitchen making the coffee and Barb's toast while searching for some cereal for his breakfast, Bill, out of nowhere, allowed his thoughts to wonder to the lovely Corrina, now his secretary and while totally aware of the corporation's rules on fraternization, but also realizing he was a bit of a womanizer and had no idea how he would remain professional in his daily activities with this woman wondering in and out of his office, she was simply to attractive he thought and he knew he was easily led astray! Well he'd have to deal with it knowing it would become a problem that would not simply go away.

While busy in the kitchen the phone rang, it was George, Bill answered happy to talk to his friend.

"Good morning George this is a bit early even for you what's going on?"

"Anxious to call and see how your day went yesterday and what you found out about where you'd be working from etc."

"Well George the day went well, we met all the corporate big wigs at a nice reception and lunch, toured the executive floor and offices including my new digs, signed a lot of documents and got a lot of gifts, laptop, cell phone and even a corporate credit card, but for Barb the plane ride was the big deal though she did meet the wives of most of the corporate officers, the details of the day were well planned I even had a time slot to pick out my office chair if you can believe that."

"Ya that all sounds great, but how about your move to Richmond, how soon does that need to happen, or does it?"

"Yes pal we'll be going to Richmond, in fact til we get there, I'll be commuting back and forth for a while they're going to buy our condo and look for another house for us in Richmond, they have a real-estate firm that does this for them all the time, so we don't have to do anything, but wait."

"Wow I guess that's what happens as you climb the corporate ladder of success, I wish you all the best and we'll miss the hell out of you guys, but listen were planning a little celebration get together for the two of you and I want to make sure you're going to be in town for the event, though that's not totally necessary (laughing loudly) it wouldn't be quite the same without you, so we decided not to do a surprise thing."

"You don't have to do this you know, but the more we see you guys before we leave for good the better it will be and Barb is having a bit of a hard time."

"Listen why don't you come by the office and we can talk about it, you know timing and all." as George paused for a reply Bill thought about Brenda and thought better about seeing her any more than absolutely necessary, so he said.

"You know George I'm going to be tied up today at the McCook plant, why don't we meet at the Poseidon restaurant tomorrow for lunch and we'll discuss it than."

"Ya that'll be great Bill and you can break-in that new credit card, I'll bring my appetite!"

Bill laughing said "That's fine George see you there at noon ok?"

"Ok buddy, I'll let you go for now, you have plans for the day and it sounds like work, see ya!"

"Bye George, see you tomorrow at noon, say hi to Nancy."

Barb grabbed her toast as she kissed Bill goodbye on her way out anxious to get to work and mingle with everyone, Bill decided not to talk to her about giving her notice, the time was not right and she may do it on her own without being prompted to do so, at least that's what he was hoping would happen.

Bill headed for the shower to get ready for his trip to the plant to see if a corporate VP could get in without a hassle.

After his shower he dressed in casual attire and headed for the parking garage and his car, thinking this might be a fun trip to McCook as he was turned away the last time he made it.

Though he had made the drive many times before, somehow it seemed different this time and pulling into the parking lot had a totally different feeling also as he parked the car and walked toward the entrances to the Administration building and up the concrete steps to the main entrance. Opening the large heavy glass door Bill was greeted by a uniformed guard who smiled and asked "Good morning sir may I help you?"

"Yes I'd like to see Mr. Richardson or Mr. John Ballock."

"I see do you have an appointment sir?"

"No I was in the area and thought I'd stop in and say hi to Jack and John, but there not expecting me I thought I'd surprise them!"

"I see, so I won't find you on the visitors list I guess."

"I'm sure you won't, but if you'd call Mr. Richardson I think everything would be fine or maybe I can just go into engineering and visit I know the way!"

"I'm sorry sir, but we don't allow unescorted visitors to walk around the plant, insurance and security reasons I'm sure you understand."

"I do, but if you would call Jack I'm sure an exception can be made in this case, I used to work here and I know my way around, but I appreciate you following your policies."

Ed the guard was getting a bit upset with Bill's insistence and about ready to call another security guard to eject Bill from the building, but first he thought he'd make one last effort to satisfy the intruder and call Jack Richardson's secretary.

He dialed the number and soon Mr. Richardson's secretory Rita answered saying "Mr. Richardson's office Rita speaking."

"Rita its Ed from security I have a guy here and he insists on seeing Mr. Richardson or Mr. Ballock, but he's not on the visitor's list today!"

"I see did you tell him that we do not receive visitors without appointments as the staff is too busy for walk-ins?"

"I told him that, but he is pretty insistent (Bill was enjoying the moment, but was about to end it before it got out of hand) asking that I call you."

"What's his name Ed?"

"I'm sorry sir I didn't get your name?"

"Bill Kelly, Mr. Richardson will know me I believe."

"His name is Bill Kelly Rita"

"WHAT!! DID YOU SAY BILL KELLY!"

"Yes Ma'am I did Bill Kelly hello-hello-hello!" he was talking to a dead phone and soon a whole entourage of people came running, Rita, Jack Richardson, John Ballock, Judy Channing and the Chief of security, what the hell was going on Ed thought he didn't need this much help, he could handle the problem!

The chief of security pulled Ed aside saying, "Don't you know who that is?"

"Ya he said he used to work here, what's going on?"

"Look in the corporate VIP book and see if you recognize anyone in there!"

In the meantime everyone was apologizing to Bill for the obvious misunderstanding and confusion, but Bill was taking it all in stride and once again enjoying the moment as he was carted off to the executive dining room for coffee while Ed stood there with his boss pointing to Bill's 81/2" x 11" picture in the corporate VIP manual an experience for all and a training exercise for Ed the security guard and soon for the rest of the security department.

Once in the dining room and being served coffee and Jack insisting Bill stay for lunch, it was meatloaf day and their chef made a great one, Bill agreed and the conversation and everyone's interest turned to Bill's experience in Richmond and the 14th floor as many of them had never been there, Bill talked freely as he was among old friends and acquaintances, they all enjoyed the airplane stories the most especially the part about Barb taking flying lessons.

During lunch Bill met a few new faces and afterwards had a short, but enjoyable meeting with Jack before leaving for home.

Bill considered the day a success and was sure he would not have any difficulty getting into the plant in the future. As he drove back to his Condo he felt good about himself and his life and thinking the challenge put before him was worth the difficulties it caused, yet he wouldn't want to go through it again.

Arriving home that afternoon he opened his laptop to check his mail and any messages he may have from Richmond finding a short message from Corrina which read as follows;

"Good morning Mr. Kelly, I thought I'd touch base with you to make sure your new computer was working well and to see if you had any other problems or concerns that I may be able to help with, if not, have a good day and I'll keep you informed of anything going on around here."

Bill answered the message saying "Good morning Corrina, thanks for checking on me, but I haven't run into any problems yet though I have been going through the computer and am impressed with data available especially the organization charts, I'm going to have to set up a meeting with the folks reporting directly to me and possibly one level of mgmt. under them, well discuss how to do that, I don't know if I want to bring them to us or if I want to go to them as their all over the country.

Well talk soon,

Bill Kelly

With that done and finding no other messages he closed the laptop deciding to call a few friends and pass the time of day exchanging pleasantries, other than business he really had nothing else to concern himself with, the condo sale would be handled by the company as well as finding them a house In Richmond, with the Kelly's approval of course, so his biggest job now would be to help Barb through the transition.

Bill's first call was to Dave anxious to find out how his relationship with Gloria was going as he dialed the number.

"Hello Bill I guess your back, how was the trip? I understand you had a ride on a corporate jet that must have been a thrilling experience to say the least!"

"Ya well I think Barb was more impressed then I was though it was a lot different than flying commercial and a lot more pleasant I can assure you, but the whole trip was an interesting experience, they sure know how to treat you at the home office."

"As you know Bill when you get to the corporate executive or corporate officer level the perks are notable the jet is a perfect example and I'm sure by now your aware of many more, those guys, which you've now become one of sure know how to live!"

"Moving on Dave, how are you and Gloria doing? She's a swell girl and I wish you both well!"

"Were doing really well Bill thank you and your right she's great and we have a good deal in common and complement each other, but time will tell I guess."

"That's great Dave I'm sure we'll talk soon, but listen I've got a few more calls to make before Barb gets home so I'll have to let you go for now and once again I want to thank you for all the help with that other thing you were an inspiration when I needed to be inspired, thanks!"

"I'll let you go for now Bill and thanks for the call, I'm sure we will talk soon, I do enjoy your take on many issues, Bracken and I both appreciate your intellect, but for quite different reasons, of that I'm certain!" hanging up Bill thought it would be nice if Dave and Gloria could make a go of it, maybe something permanent as they were both great people and needed a significant other in their lives.

Today's date was Wednesday December 14, 2011 and Bill wanted to get in a couple of trips to Richmond before Christmas to put in an appearance and start getting involved in his area of responsibility and he didn't know the protocols for scheduling the jet for a ride, but he knew who to call with this problem, Jack Trax and there would be no problem reaching him anymore, his number as well as all the corporate executives numbers were in Bill's phone. He dialed Jack, "Hi Bill how's the newest VP doing today?"

"Hello Jack, doing fine just trying to take care of some details in Chicago to get ready for the move, but I do have a question, I need to get back and forth to Richmond one or two times before Christmas and I didn't know how to get a ride on the jet or if I should fly commercial?"

"Well the quick answer to your question is for me to explain how that works, so here goes firstly, the planes are available by pecking order the CEO, PRESIDENT & COO, AND EXECUTIVE VP

AND CFO all have first choice and then the rest of the staff, the corporate VP's that's us, you and I and the other VP's and we have our own pecking order so to speak based first: on time in the VP position and secondly on the importance of the trip, so your right on the bottom of the list, but there are (4) airplanes and usually at least ones available, we also use the aircraft to move sales people around when available. Now we have a transportation division and one of their responsibilities is to schedule the planes their number is in your phone.

Here's the long and short of it, if you need a ride have your secretary arrange it for you, she'll know exactly what to do and she will handle it and if one of the planes isn't available she'll schedule a commercial flight for you, use her!"

"That's a lengthy explanation, leaving no stone unturned Jack, I knew I'd call you and you would have the answer, I appreciate it, none of that ever came up yesterday in Richmond, but I got it now, thank you and one way or the other I'll see you next week I'm sure."

"Ok Bill, remember use your secretary, there all very competent, we couldn't exist without them of that I have no doubt!"

"Thanks Jack and bye for now" hanging up Bill decided his next call would have to be to Corrina as he hit the speed dial on his phone "Mr. Kelly's phone Corrina speaking."

"Hi again Corrina, I understand you can help me get a ride to Richmond on Monday is that right?"

"Absolutely Sir, did you want to use one of our planes or fly commercial?"

"Our planes would be preferred, but whatever's available will work Corrina."

"I'll call you back shortly sir, will you be traveling alone?"

"Thanks Corrina, yes I'm alone and I would like to arrive as early as possible on Monday morning."

"I'll get right back to you sir." hanging up Bill thought he'd have to get used to the pampering he was experiencing, but he certainly was not going to discourage it.

It took about fifteen minutes and the phone rang, it was Corrina he answered "Bill Kelly"

"Yes Mr. Kelly your all set one of the Citations will be at midway airport at the corporate hanger at 6:00a.m. Ready to leave when you arrive, I hope that will be alright and accommodate your schedule, we were lucky they were deadheading home from Indianapolis and now they will take a short detour and pick you up."

"Your amazing Corrina, I'm not used to this kind of service, what time do I have to meet the plane?"

"It's what we do Sir so you'll have to get used to it, we take care of our VP's, you can meet the plane anytime you want they won't leave without you and I'll just give you the crews phone number if you need to contact them for any reason, you'll get a follow up email with details sir and I'll be looking forward to seeing you on Monday."

"Great bye for now Corrina." hanging up he thought he'd be looking forward to seeing her also, but he'd keep that to himself!

Bill's next call was to Barb to let her know he'd be going to Richmond on Monday and while he was making that call, George was busy planning a celebration for Saturday night and making all the calls necessary to arrange things at the La Flambé their favorite haunt. George wanted to limit the party to Bill and Barb's closest friends and family their parents, any siblings and the group of friends involved in the production of the mystery and Jack Trax if he could make it as well as Lenny.

George talked to Nancy a catering professional who decided on hot and cold appetizers rather than a big dinner, Nancy would contact the restaurant and tell them what she wanted which would allow more time for mingling and celebration rather than eating, so you could tell it wasn't George's idea! George decided to call Barb and have her invite her folks and Bill's mother as his father was deceased and George didn't have either of their numbers, George would handle the rest of the invites, he dialed Barb's cell and waited patiently as the phone rang knowing that if she was with a patient she wouldn't be able to answer, but shortly she answered.

"Hi George what can I do for you today?"

"Hi hon you probably know that were planning a celebratory get together for you guy's Saturday night and I need you to call your folks and Bill's mother and invite them along with the siblings and Jack Trax, I'm sure you have a better way to get in touch with him than I do no dinner just Hors d'oeuvre's hot and cold 6:30pm at La Flambé."

"Oh you guys are sweet; of course I'll call the family and Jack as a courtesy, I'm not sure he'll come, though he may surprise us, but it's a long way."

"Thanks sweetie and Nancy say's hi! By the way this is your invite so I won't have to call again ok?"

"I'll have to check with Bill and see if we have other plans George we may have to go to Richmond."

"No-no I already talked to Bill everything is being planned for Saturday night!" Barb laughing and having to put George's mind at ease said.

"I'm just kidding you George, but it was fun we'll be there of course and I'll make the calls."

"Thanks hon I'll be talking to you goodbye for now!" as Barb hung up her phone rang again and this time it was Bill.

"Hi hon my phone is busy today I just hung up on George who's planning the party for Saturday night."

"I see the reason I called is to tell you I'm going to Richmond Monday morning for a few days to kind of settle in and check on properties etc. also I'm trying to figure out how and when to meet the people reporting to me, you know just start getting involved in my job I can't just sit around idle it doesn't present a very good first impression."

"That'll be a first hon we've never been separated since we've been married, would you like me to come along with you?"

"To tell you the truth I thought you'd rather stay here with your job and friends as long as you can as that will end soon when we make our permanent move to Richmond, but if you really want to come and sit in a hotel room all day alone, as I'll be pretty busy, I'll make the arrangements."

"Ya know I think your right that would be pretty boring I guess I'll stay here and do some Christmas shopping while you're gone."

"Now that's an idea, to tell you the truth I haven't even thought about Christmas with all that's been going on."

"Are you flying commercial this time?"

"No there sending the jet for me at 6:00am Monday morning one of the planes was deadheading back to Richmond and there taking a short detour to collect me on the way, I'm meeting them at midway."

"Oh dam! I love that plane, you're sure lucky to be able to travel that way!"

"It's a different plane this time one of the smaller Citations, but I'm sure it's nice, I'll take a picture and email it to you, I do appreciate the convenience though, it sure beats the airlines!"

"I guess I'll take advantage of your being gone and ask Nancy and the girls to go out to dinner one evening and their always asking me to go to the boat gambling with them, that may be fun, I'm sure I'll keep occupied one way or another, when would you expect to be back?"

"I would guess by mid-week and no later than Thursday depending on when I can get a flight, unless I get tied up on something, but I'll call every day to keep you up to date!"

"Ok well listen I have to get back to work, I'll see you tonight I took some frozen sauce out well have spaghetti for dinner if that's ok?"

"One of my favorites you know that, I'll have a light lunch so I don't ruin my appetite for dinner!"

"Ok hon love you and bye for now." Barb said, as she hung up and went back to work leaving Bill to continue his phone calls; he really did enjoy that regardless of what he might tell you!

The week came and went Bill made all his calls contacting all his friends and prepared for his upcoming trip to Richmond looking forward to his first interaction with Corrina as her new boss though she had already helped him with several things, setting up his new laptop, cell phone, office furniture and arranging a flight to Richmond for him on one of the Jets, but he had yet to sit in his office all day relying on her to take care of his needs.

Tomorrow was Saturday and the get together at La Flambé was on the agenda for the evening, the party was to congratulate Bill on his promotion, but Bill and Barb knew it would also be an opportunity for them to say goodbye to their friends collectively, they would do it on an individual bases at a later date, but emotions would run high both in celebration and in sorrow.

Barb still had not given her notice at work and seemed reluctant to do so, Bill was sure she would do it in her own good time, but that time was rapidly approaching, she may need a push Bill thought, but he didn't want to push too hard, he knew it would be hard for her to do.

THE MORNING OF THE PARTY

Saturday morning and Barb was the first to wake up and knowing today would be a busy day she shook Bill telling him to get up and face the new day with a smile there was much to do. Bill on the other hand preferred staying right where he was and let the day continue on its own, it would do fine without his help and he could wait until it was time to get ready for the evenings activities before getting up, but Barb wasn't going to settle for that so he got up knowing if he didn't she'd keep insisting (another word for nagging) until he gave in and rolled out of bed.

In the kitchen Barb was busy making breakfast and coffee as Bill walked out saying;

"Good morning hon" giving her a kiss as he sat down to check his laptop for any info from the office and finding an email from the Citation pilot confirming his arrival in Chicago by 6:00 am and their being ready to leave at Bill's pleasure from the corporate hanger.

"Ha hon look at this" showing her the email emphasizing how well they take care of their VP's, once again Barb was impressed as she smiled saying;

"You're sure enjoying this aren't you hon? And well you should you worked hard to get here, but I hope you're not taking advantage,

I'm not sure how to handle all these perks you're getting and more important how will you're boss perceive you running all over the country on the corporate planes?"

Bill laughed saying, "Hon don't worry they have four planes for a reason and that's to use them, they could have bought one plane and kept it for the exclusive use of the CEO or COO or even the CFO but they increased the size of the fleet to accommodate the VP's as well and when there not busy even the sales staff uses them so I'm doing what they expect and even encourage me to do."

After breakfast Barb busied herself deciding what she would wear tonight at the party while Bill answered a few emails including the one to the pilots and spent a little time in the computer looking at the organization charts once again while trying to separate the commonalities between the engineering and the planning and design areas as there seemed to be some cross over between them, oh well he thought that may be one of the first things on the agenda for next week at the office along with Corrina's help.

The day progressed, the afternoon came and went and it was time for the couple to get ready for the evening's festivities. After their showers and getting dressed they were ready to leave for the scheduled event as Bill observed Barb's tension starting to grow once again, he hoped she would start to get used to the idea soon and appreciate the rewards that go along with the changes they both would have to make.

As they left for the restaurant Barb managed to put on her party face and prepare to enjoy the evening, after all, our friends have gone through some trouble to arrange the celebration for us and would be disappointed if we appeared to not enjoy ourselves and Barb knew that, but she was a trooper and wouldn't allow that to happen!

Arriving at the restaurant and pulling up to the valet parking both were ready to meet their friends and family in celebration of Bill's good fortune, his promotion and all that went along with it.

Walking in they were greeted by Linda and shown to the party room, on their way noting that Lenny was not behind the bar and continuing to where all the guest were waiting in anticipation of their arrival and though it wasn't a surprise party they all yelled "SURPRISE" anyway, Bill's mother was the first to greet him embracing him proudly and telling him his father would have been proud beyond belief, next Barb's parents approached, her father with words of encouragement and a handshake, her mother with a hug a kiss and a we'll miss you son. As Bill scanned the room he noticed everyone was there including Lenny and Dave was there with Gloria, behind everyone was a table full of a fabulous selection of Hors d'oeuver's as they made their way to the feast awaiting their scrutiny, friend's family and good food it was perfect they thought.

George took the time to read a few greetings from folks unable to attend, among them a note from Jack Trax, the man probably singly responsible for all that has happened to Bill, it read;

"Bill I'm truly sorry I am unable to attend the celebration your friends and family have arranged for you and Barb, but duty calls as I'm off to Seattle to settle some business, a demanding job, but you'll find that out. I hope George takes the time to read this to the folks in its entirety because I'd like everyone to know that over the years I've known you, observing your abilities and dedication to your work, I believe no one is more deserving then you for the recognition you're getting and though I'm sure all are proud, no one is more proud of you than I! Congratulations to you on a well-deserved promotion and to Bracken industries for their intuitive decision and selection.

We'll see you soon in Richmond I'm sure, call if you need anything and once again good luck.

After George read a few more notes from friends that could not attend, the party continued on a rather informal bases with everyone talking to Bill on an individual bases remembering old times and making known their regrets on loosing Bill and Barb from the area with Barb assuring them they would be back often to visit and keep up with current events and reminding everyone that the telephone still exists. Dave and Gloria took several opportunities to talk with the Kelly's and Bill feeling somewhat responsible for bringing them together encouraged them both to keep the relationship going.

As the evening continued the time finally came when everyone demanded Bill make a little speech so after several more coaxing's Bill finally conceded and stepped up to the podium.

"Well-well I didn't have anything prepared for this moment, so I'll have to punt; first I'd like to thank you all for being here with Barb and I, when you talk about mixed emotions, this is definitely what you're talking about, Barb and I absolutely have mixed emotions as we, hon come on up here with me I may need help (Barb joined Bill at the podium) as we look over this gathering of friends and family knowing that soon we would no longer be able to see you at the drop of a pin we would be six hundred miles away, but you'd never be that far from our thoughts or from our hearts, we will keep you close, we'll miss you all!

Now for those of you who are interested as I suspect most of you are judging by the questions we've been getting here tonight; Bracken industries is going to buy our condo, unless one of you want it, George? So that takes the burden of selling it off us, they are also locating some properties for us to look at in Richmond so I'm guessing we're going to be here at least another month or two though I'll be traveling back and forth to conduct business and at this point that's the best I can tell you, we'll let you know if anything changes. I see the ladies are bringing out more to eat so let's enjoy the rest of the evening shall we."

Once again the folks all gathered around Bill and Barb and even some of the restaurant staff and employees came by to congratulate Bill, Lenny finally made his way through the crowd extending his hand to Bill and saying.

"Bill I haven't known you and Barb as long as most of these folks, but in the short time I have known you guys I've come to like and respect you and I look forward to your visits to the lounge and our talks, I wish you both well and hope you will enjoy your many successes, I'll miss you at my bar and hope you will visit us when you're in town for a sub-burger so we can catch up from time to time, I'm glad I can call you a friend."

"Lenny, the pleasure is mine I can assure you and I certainly appreciate all the help you gave me thru this ordeal, I feel, I too have made a friend and I'm grateful for being given that opportunity, I will be back for that burger!"

The event continued, well wishes from all and as the evening's end drew near folks started to leave and soon only four couples remained and adjourned to the bar for some serious celebrating, Bill and Barb, Jerry and Emily, Larry and Karen and Dave and Gloria. George wanted to talk about the plane ride to Richmond and Barb was happy to accommodate him speaking as an expert and future pilot herself, Lenny wondered behind the bar to help Bill the relief bartender and take care of us, his friends. The evening soon ended with hugs, kisses, goodbyes and I'll call you tomorrow as they all headed for the door and their cars.

On the way home Barb seemed in better spirits than on the ride here both admitting the party was exceptional and did much toward raising Barb's spirits, Bill finally asked Barb if she had turned in her notice at work though he knew she hadn't and she said.

"Not yet hon I've thought about it and I think I've decided to do it Monday, I owe the doctor that much he's been good to me and it may take some time to find a replacement, I don't want to leave him in the lurch although I'm sure he already knows I'm leaving, I mean how could he not know?"

"I'm sure your right dear, but you probably should give him notice, making it official."

"Monday it is!" she said as she changed the subject a bit admitting she liked Gloria more than she thought she would, they had talked quite a while tonight and she found her quite pleasant and thought she would be good for Dave. Bill agreed as long as she was good in bed, but got slugged before he could say it.

"Just kidding"

Pulling into the garage Bill had plans for topping off the evening and was sure Barb would gladly go along, so he said on their way up in the elevator.

"I'll race you to the shower!" and Barb said!

"Why don't we both take a shower together?" Bill quickly agreed and said as they exited the elevator;

"Why don't we get it on in front of the open window, we might thrill a few distant neighbors?"

"I'm game for that!" she said as they opened the door to their unit and both rushed in uncontrollably tearing off their cloths as they headed for the shower, the window thing may never happen tonight the way things were going, but perhaps another time."

Both Bill and Barb woke up late the following morning, it was Sunday and they both laid in bed tossing and turning finally deciding to go out for breakfast, but first a little morning delight to work up an appetite, though breakfast may turn into lunch.

After both exhibited their passions and fell back to sleep, waking up for a second time several hours later, but this time it was past noon, they were both starved and nothing was going to stop them this time from their new priority, food! Their other desires now well satisfied, so both jumped out of bed headed for the bathroom to start getting ready for their trip to the restaurant and food, lots of food!

They enjoyed a great lunch at the Poseidon and returned home as Bill had to start packing for his trip to Richmond in the morning and for the first time since they were married Barb would be spending a few days alone with her job and her friends, there were a lot of firsts lately and hopefully things would normalize soon.

While packing Bill couldn't find his Dopp Kit and after looking for a while he asked Barb where she had hidden it and she replied hastily.

"Where you couldn't find it dear and it must have worked, you're obviously having difficulty!" Barb can be a bit of a smart ass having a repertoire of quick response sarcasm's available for most situations and is not bashful about using them when required and this was one of those times! Bill of course knew that and took her response lightly as Barb helped him look for the kit.

Packing took the better part of the afternoon and when he was done he was ready to relax for the rest of the day, but Barb had other plans. A romantic dinner with candles and wine was in order, followed by an evening of love making, the intent being to leave Bill with a lasting impression since he would be gone for several days and would be alone in Richmond, Barb wanted to keep it that way and possessed that ability in her repertoire of feminine wiles, using it generously when required!

Barb put her plans into the works asking Bill what he would like for dinner. His response,

"You know Chinese might be nice hon what do you think?"

"I'm good with that I'll run across the street and get it, what's your pleasure?"

"Pot stickers and Sesame chicken for me, maybe some sweet and sour shrimp which we can split."

"Ok and I'll get some teriyaki beef with peppers and tomatoes and maybe I'll just have it delivered, what time would you like to eat hon?"

"Whatever your schedule dictates hon, probably around our normal dinner time would be fine, I'll be right here on the couch when it arrives."

"I'll place the order, set the table, cool the wine and then I'll join you on the couch and let you occupy my time until it arrives, how does that sound?"

"I see where this is going hon and I can't say I mind so join me on the couch if you will and let nature take its course once again."

"As long as nature takes its course here babe and not in Richmond where you're working closely with that gorgeous secretary Corrina or any of those lovely women working on that 14th floor, if their half as smart as they are pretty, I'm sure they're the ones running the company!"

Ah-ha! Bill thought finally the truth was coming out, Barb was aware of the ladies I'll be working with and she was more than a little jealous realizing I was the youngest executive on the floor. He had to take this opportunity to reassure her there was nothing whatsoever to worry about or his life would quickly become unbearable.

This may be the whole reason for her continued reluctance to make the move to Richmond; he should have realized this as he noticed Barb's awareness of the ladies when they were in Richmond, but until now he never put 2 and 2 together.

Bill laughing a bit in order to put her at ease said; "Hon in the first place it's not worth me losing my job over an office romance that would be going nowhere, being married to the hottest, prettiest, sexiest and most loving girl in town and that is any town big or small. Secondly corporations have rules against fraternization between executives and their employee, so I guess what I'm saying is that there are no pluses in pursuing that kind of a relationship, especially in my case having you to come home to!" Bill thinking he had handled that well waited anxiously for Barb's response.

"Honey that's very reassuring and of course I trust you completely, but when a woman has a catch like you there's always room for doubt and caution should be the operative word!"

"Hon you'll be cautious and I'll be TRUE BLUE your favorite color!"

The buzzer buzzed and the food was here the candles were on the table as Barb took the wine from the refrigerator and called Bill to the table for dinner. The secret to eating Chinese is to try a little bit of everything on the table, rather than eating just one selection, that way you find out what you like and dislike for the next time you order as there are usually so many selections to choose from its easy to become confused.

After dinner Barb cleared the table loaded the dishwasher and settled down to continue with her plan and of course before you knew it they were both in bed saying their goodbyes and leaving their impressions with each other, both just a bit insecure in their upcoming separation, but for totally different reasons! After what seemed like hours of love making and in fact it was, they both rolled over and went to sleep as Bill was getting up at 4:00am in order to get to the airport early in the morning and meet his plane.

MONDAY MORNING

Indeed the morning came early as Bill responded to the offensive alarm calling him back to life once again to face the world, which he did reluctantly and with some protest, noticing his wife still sleeping soundly, but finally rolling out of bed stumbling to the bathroom and hoping the Pilots were more awake than he was as he headed for the kitchen putting on a pot of coffee to get him through the day. Still looking jealously at his sleeping wife and knowing he had to wake her to say goodbye or she would be unforgiving, but he would wait to the last possible moment to do this, allowing her to sleep as long as possible.

He had laid out his business suit last night to travel in today feeling the casual look was no longer appropriate as he was now officially a member of the elite group of corporate executives and should publically present that image. As he started dressing he shook Barb gently waking her and kissing her goodbye, telling her to go back to sleep, but she was awake now and decided to get up and see Bill off.

Barb poured a cup of coffee as she had no intention of going back to bed now that she was up and about as she asked Bill;

"Hon, as long as I'm up, do you want me to take you to the airport so you don't have to leave your car unattended for days?"

"No-no the car is safe there it's locked in at night I believe, I'm sure it will be fine, there's no sense you getting dressed and running out in the middle of the night, you should go back to bed!"

"No I'm up now I'll just take my time getting ready for work after you leave, you'll call when you land in Richmond won't you?"

"Oh sure right after I check in at the hotel I'll call on my way into the office, that sounds a little strange to say after not going into the office for a few months now, but I'm sure I'll get back into the routine quickly, that reminds me did I give you my office number in the event you need me in an emergency or something? I'm sure Corrina will be able to contact me in the event I have to turn my cell off and you can't get me."

"Yes dear I have the number."

Bill gave Barb a last hug and kiss as he grabbed his luggage on the way out the door detecting a slight tear in her eye as he left her standing in the doorway on his way to the elevator.

CHAPTER THIRTY SIX
PREPARING THE WAY

As Bill arrived at the airport he spotted his ride, Bracken had their name on the whole fleet of planes as well as their limos. The Citation was smaller than the Gulfstream, but a beauty none the less, as Bill got out of his car the two pilots approached him, but how did they know who he was as he had never met them before it wasn't Joe or Mike, so how did they know, coincidence he thought. The first man reaching Bill extended his hand and said "Mr. Kelly, Sir I'm Carey your pilot and this is Scott your first officer at your service may we take your luggage and get you settled in I understand you've already had a ride on our flagship the Gulfstream, but were partial to the Citation and think you'll enjoy it every bit as much sir."

"Well its good meeting you fellows also and I'm sure you're right about the Citation, but I don't know if you could convince my wife of that, she liked that Gulfstream so much that she decided to take flying lessons!" The two pilots, smiling a bit and said;

"Yes well Joe affects folks that way; we all love to fly, but that guy really loves to fly. Well Mr. Kelly we didn't know if you had a chance to eat breakfast this morning so we took the opportunity to pick up a few breakfast items at Mc Donald's for you so if you'll board we'll show you around the plane and get you settled in for the one hour flight to Richmond."

As he boarded the plane he realized how they recognized who he was, hanging in the cabin on the bulkhead just behind the cockpit was a framed 81/2 x 11 photograph of him and that explained why they took all those pictures in Richmond last week. Carey noticed Bill noticing the photo and took the opportunity to explain saying;

"I see you've noticed the décor sir, I should explain, we fly a lot of VIP's around and often many lower echelon personnel, salesman etc. so when we have one of our VP's aboard we want to make sure that anyone else that may be flying with us knows who's on board. It also helps the crew to recognize someone we've never flown before as is the case today, so there are no mistakes."

"That's very interesting, hopefully I'll have the opportunity to meet all the crews eventually, but the picture was a surprise."

"Just over here is our small, but very functional galley with a bar, small refrigerator and a microwave these are your breakfast choices and we try to keep your favorite Libations at the bar as well as a selection of soft drinks. you'll find the seating more than comfortable I'm sure and all the way to the rear is the washroom which I'll demonstrate if you'll follow me, after the tour Carey invited Bill to pick a seat as they would be getting underway shortly, which Bill did after thanking Carey for the tour, as he went forward to join Scott in the cockpit.

Bill settled in to make some notes for the trip as the engines were started and soon the small jet started moving toward the runway for the takeoff, the seatbelt sign was on along with the no smoking sign and soon the plane moved onto the runway and started its takeoff roll, quickly we were in the air headed for Richmond as Bill sat back to work on his notes and enjoy an Egg McMuffin as he was a bit hungry.

After reaching their cruising altitude of 35000 feet Scott came back to see if Bill was comfortable or needed anything, Bill assured him he was fine and they needn't be concerned about him. Scott smiled and went back to the flight deck.

Soon the sun was peaking over the horizon they were flying toward daylight and were starting their decent into Richmond where a limo was already waiting for Bill to arrive with Berry waiting patiently to take Bill to the hotel and then to the Bracken building. The plane touched down at 8:45am Richmond time as the 14th floor folks were just starting to arrive at work with Bill soon to follow.

Pulling up to the designated parking area for the aircraft the limo was waiting with Berry standing alongside as the pilots shutdown the engines and Scott and Carey left the flight deck to open the cabin door and help with the luggage as Berry opened the trunk and the door of the car and said;

"Welcome back Mr. Kelly" as he helped with the luggage and garment bag, the pilots said their goodbyes and busied themselves preparing the plane for its next trip as Bill entered the car and Berry drove away.

Bill immediately sent a text to Barb saying he had arrived safely and was on his way to the hotel to check in and then head for work.

After checking in at the hotel they arrived at the Bracken building and this time upon walking into the reception area Bill was immediately recognized and greeted by a young woman named Terry who said "Good Morning Mr. Kelly do you require an escort to your office?"

"No I believe I can find it on my own Terry and if not I'll ask along the way, but thank you."

"Very well sir and welcome home" she said with a smile as Bill walked away. She quickly called Bill's office to let Corrina know that her boss was on his way up.

Bill headed for the elevators briefcase and top coat in hand as he pushed the up button and was joined by two ladies also waiting for the car as he said "Good morning ladies." to which they responded;

"Good morning" as the elevator door opened Bill stepped aside to allow the two woman to enter the car, he followed and as he entered he pushed the button for the 14th floor and asked the ladies which floor they wanted, to which they both replied with a smile fourteen sir, obviously realizing he was somebody when he selected the 14th floor. As the car arrived at the 14th floor the door opened and Bill stepped aside once again to allow the ladies to exit followed by Bill who was now a bit disoriented and called to the ladies as they walked away asking if they could direct him to Bill Kelly's office to which they replied certainly Sir straight down this corridor to the second right and to the end of that hallway.

"Thank you ladies I'm sure I'll remember that from now on, I am new here, I'm Bill Kelly."

"Oh Mr. Kelly welcome I'm Tess and this is Gloria were from data processing."

"My pleasure ladies and I'm sure I'll being seeing you around and thanks once again." as Bill continued down/up the long corridor following the directions the ladies had given him to the second hall on the right and approaching the end of the hall he saw Corrina who was waiting to meet him at the door to the outer office smiling and saying "Good morning boss I see you found us ok, it takes a bit of getting used to with all the twist and turns on this floor."

"Good morning Corrina and thanks for all the arrangements you made it all went perfectly right down to the limo meeting the plane, you don't leave anything for me to worry about do you?"

"Well sir you're not supposed to have to worry about the small details, you have much more important things to concern yourself with and we take care of everything else, by the way I've arranged a pool car for you the limo is not always available for running around in and I thought you'd like the flexibility to come and go as you please and maybe in the evening you'd like to get acquainted with Richmond, there's a list of restaurants and night spots in your computer under the entertainment section."

"Tell me Corrina who do I contact to discuss the sale of my condo back home and the search for a property in Richmond?"

"Your computer also has the contact info for a Mr. Douglas he's handling both the sale and the search. It's in the computer under personal and that area requires a password which you can set at your leisure."

"One more question where's the coffee area I drink a lot of that all day long?"

"I'll be happy to keep your cup full sir, but if I don't happen to be around I'll show you where to go if you'll just follow me and after showing Bill where to get his coffee, at two different places, they took the opportunity to get a couple of cups as Corrina watched closely (for future reference) as Bill fixed his, leaded Boston no sugar, that's easy enough she thought, the same way she took hers. On their way back to the office she pointed out a few points of interest, the Executive w/r and dining room and what was affectionately referred to as the Steam room she would explain that to her new boss when she knew him better. There was a small employee cafeteria on the 14th floor and two other large cafeterias at different floors in the building.

After the short tour and returning to the office Bill was ready to sit down and get to work when he was paid a visit from Wm. Blair the Executive VP and Bill's new boss. Walking in, he was greeted by Corrina saying;

"Good morning Mr. Blair"

"Good morning Corrina I see your new boss is in and hard at it already, I'll just sneak in for a moment, don't announce me I'll surprise him!"

"Certainly Sir" as she just tapped the secrete button to warn Bill that one of the higher ups was on his way in, they never wanted to be announced, she had already explained the secret code to Bill during his office orientation a few minutes ago, he was more than grateful, though he smiled a bit when it was explained to him.

As Blair opened the door to Bill's office, saying with a rather warm smile "Good morning Bill happy to see you here, but you didn't have to rush it you have a lot of good people who will keep things going til you get settled, but I'm glad to see you're anxious to get your feet wet so to speak!"

"Getting my feet wet is exactly what I'm doing Mr. Blair, I thought I'd use this time until the permanent move as kind of an orientation period performing some maintenance or housekeeping functions if you will."

"As I understand it you plan on being in town til the later part of the week so I think we should do lunch one day, Wednesday would be good!"

"I'll mark my calendar Wednesday's good for me also" as he wrote it down.

"Well Bill I'll get out of here and let you get to it, once again good to see you." As Blair turned and walked out, shutting the door behind him.

After Blair left Bill stepped into Corrina's office and said "Thanks do you get many opportunities to use that signal around here?"

"Yes Mr. Kelly and understand, If I may, the only time it is used is if the person coming in is a member of the super staff (one of your bosses) no one else would walk in without being announced so unless you direct otherwise, I'll continue to use the signal, all the VP's have them."

"No that's fine Corrina, but I don't understand why the super staff doesn't know about it as they were once corporate VP's themselves?"

"The truth is they probably do, but they don't let on sir."

"Ok Corrina let's talk for a moment about office etiquette when anyone is around you can call me Sir, Mr. Kelly, boss or whatever you feel comfortable with, but when were alone I have no problem with you calling me Bill and I wouldn't take that the wrong way, I've never been very status conscious, that being said you do what you feel good with."

"Well Sir I appreciate the more relaxed atmosphere you project, but for now I'd like to keep it more formal, so I don't slip at the wrong time, but thank you!"

"I understand Corrina and certainly respect your feelings; we'll leave it there for now."

As Bill went back into his office he wondered how to take Corrina's response to his offer, was it a put down or something else, he would think about it for a long time to come she was a very profound and smart woman he thought, this would not be easy!

Bill buzzed Corrina asking her to set up a meeting with Mr. Douglas to discuss his progress with the properties and how it was to be handled from here on in.

The next thing on Bill's agenda was to set up a meeting with the people reporting directly to him, to introduce himself as he didn't know anyone in the group and in his past assignments at Bracken in Engineering at McCook he had no reason for any interaction with these folks.

Once again he called Corrina into his office asking for her ideas on how to go about arranging this meeting and after explaining what he wanted to do and why, she was quick to suggest the following;

"Well sir, because of the people being located all over the country and you're basically just wanting to introduce yourself, initially I would suggest video conferencing as an expedient and of course she was right."

Bill, not surprised at her intellectual approach to the question and the logic behind it he quickly agreed asking her to set it up for Wednesday morning which she agreed to do. Well Bill had accomplished quite a bit this morning and it wasn't even lunch time yet so he sat back to consider once again Corrina's responses to his probably premature offer of friendship and familiarity and somewhat upset with the way he had approached the issue. He decided to get a fresh cup of coffee and as he got up to go and get it his office door opened and in walked Corrina with the coffee in her hand offering it to him with a smile and saying;

"Boston no sugar sir" Bill was a bit overwhelmed by the instincts this beautiful young woman had, how did she know he thought?

"Thanks Corrina I was just about to go and get this!" holding the cup up in a gesture to emphasize what he was talking about, she understood as she turned and left the office.

Bill stayed in his office thru lunch as he had a lot to think about and the time had escaped him. Midafternoon Corrina came in once again giving him a set of keys to one of the pool cars and indicating it would be parked in spot #225 in the parking garage at street level, once again she left no stone unturned he thought.

A couple of minutes after 5:00pm Corrina came in once again to say she was leaving for the day and asked;

"Will you require anything further sir?"

"No Corrina you've done a good job getting me thru this my first day, enjoy your evening and I'll see you tomorrow."

"Yes sir, I hope to and you do the same, goodnight than."

It was 6:30pm when Bill left with his laptop in hand, ending his first day at the office and missing his lunch he was quite hungry, as he got on the elevator to the parking garage he decided to drive around find a place to have dinner while getting familiar with the city at the same time.

As the elevator car stopped at the garage Bill exited and started looking for #225 and finding it also found a black Cadillac STS, it wasn't a BMW but he was pleased. As he drove out of the underground, not being sure which way to turn, but not really caring he went left and he was off to dinner.

After dinner at a little Ma and Pa restaurant he found, that had great meatloaf, mashed potatoes and a pleasant atmosphere, afterwards finding his way back to the hotel, though it required many tries and while becoming more familiar with the city as he went along, the first thing he did after getting to his room was to call Barb, who was anxiously awaiting his call.

"Hi hon, how did your first day go, well I hope, is everything ok?"

"Ya I missed lunch and just had a little dinner, meatloaf, I think I'm going to relax a little before I go to bed. We accomplished a whole lot today and I have scheduled several meetings this week before returning to Chicago on Thursday."

"Well things are going well than, I'm glad, are you staying at the same hotel we stayed at (a clever way for her to remind Bill of their togetherness and intimacy while they were away from each other) or did the company put you up somewhere else."

"No the same one its nice here don't you think?"

"I do it's our place away from our place!"

"It is that, have you had dinner yet or what are your plans?"

"I'm eating in tonight and Nancy and I are going out tomorrow night, Lisa may join us."

"Sounds nice, tomorrow night I will probably eat at the hotel as you know the restaurant here is nice and the food is good and I don't have to do a lot of running around!"

"What time are you coming in Thursday and are you flying commercial or one of the company planes?"

"Hon I don't know I haven't made those arrangements yet and that reminds me I had better do that tomorrow thanks."

"Well when it comes to getting you home, I'll remind you every day if that's what it takes!"

"Not to worry you'll be here with me soon and that reminds me, did you give your notice yet or are you still procrastinating?"

"No I told the doctor this morning, but it didn't matter as he was already looking for a replacement it seems he knew I'd be leaving, so that's taken care of at last."

"I'm going to hit the sack soon as I have an early day tomorrow and I am glad you took care of that notice, I had pictured me living alone in Richmond because you couldn't give up your job or give notice!" Bill said laughing just a little.

"I couldn't do that hon! I wouldn't have any place to live, your company would have taken our condo away by then and I'd be on the street!" she responded laughing back.

"Ok babe, well goodnight for now and I'll call you again tomorrow."

"Bye Bill and goodnight to you!" as they both hung up Bill decided to make a few notes on what he wanted to do tomorrow and Barb went about heating up a can of Ravioli with buttered French bread and a beer.

Both finally went to sleep but 600 miles apart, Barb thinking of Bill and him thinking of Barb, Brenda, Judy Channing and Corrina but tonight mostly Corrina! Lately his life seemed to evolve around beautiful desirable women and he needed to get that under control!

ANOTHER NEW DAY

The next day, Tuesday 12/20/2011 he was up early shaved, showered, dressed and down to the hotel restaurant for a continental breakfast and off to the office arriving at 8:20am in the reception area where he was once again greeted by an attractive young girl saying;

"Good morning Mr. Kelly."

"Good morning" Bill said, on his way to the elevator, now becoming more familiar with the surroundings and routine, he was quickly becoming just another face around here and that was fine with him, he really didn't enjoy all the notoriety that comes from being the new junior VP.

As he stepped out of the elevator on the 14th floor, this time knowing the way to his office and the coffee, as he noted only a few others in this early, but arriving at his office only to find Corrina already there busying herself on the computer and already sipping a cup of coffee, was this her normal routine he thought or was it to impress him?

As he walked into his office he greeted her saying "Good morning Corrina, getting an early start I see how's the coffee this morning and by the way, who makes the coffee?"

"Good morning sir and this morning I made the coffee usually the first one in takes care of the first pot, its already set up and the rest of the day one of the commissary girls takes care of it and no this is my usual time in the office I avoid the rush hour that way."

"You know, back in Chicago we have rush hours too, but I was always lucky enough to be going in the opposite direction so I avoided it and that reminds me can you arrange transportation back to Chicago for me on Thursday afternoon?"

"I've already done that sir; you had mentioned your intentions when you called to make your initial request so I took the liberty to arrange the return trip subject to change of course, I hope that was ok it's usually better to schedule the corporate jets as far in advance as possible insuring a ride!"

"I see, you not only don't leave much for me to do, you don't even leave anything for me to think about, that's refreshing I must say, I'm not used to the secretarial staff having that much insight I guess, the only one I'm used to having those instincts is my wife."

"Well Sir, if I may, secretary has a demeaning connotation it suggests ignorance and servitude and we both know that's not the case, most people who make that connection have never had a secretary or ever will, that being said, Executive Secretaries are trained differently, whether it's thru education, on the job training or both its much more than handling correspondence, filing, taking dictation, answering the phones and looking attractive, we prefer to think of ourselves as Executive Assistants because that's exactly what we are and now sir I'm going to get off my bandwagon and go to the ladies room and be sick for talking to you that way, you certainly didn't deserve it!"

"No-no Corrina you'll find I also have some quirks and one of those is listening to people who are close to me and an executive assistant certainly falls into that category, I'm glad you vented, giving me the opportunity to do the same, we'll both have a better understanding of each other in the future and I do appreciate what executive assistants do for their bosses as I'm sure the others do also, but let me make this absolutely clear I would never underestimate the worth/value of a secretary or executive assistant, I am reminded every time I walk into the office that I couldn't do this or any other job I've had were it not for the help I've received from folks like yourself!"

"I'll get your coffee sir."

"Yes, thank you, and get a refill for yourself while you're at It." as she left, Bill once again was glad she was here.

When Corrina returned with Bill's coffee she told him the video conference was arranged for 10:00am tomorrow morning and she would show him the conference room when he was ready so he could get acquainted with it. That video conference tomorrow should take him to lunchtime with his boss Wm. Blair at noon.

Bill was in his office checking his computer for his meeting schedule and found a meeting scheduled for 10:30am this morning with Mr. Douglas which he was looking forward to as he wasn't really sure of the status of the move.

It was 10:15am when Mr. Paul Douglas walked into Corrina's office introducing himself and asking to see Mr. Kelly, he was early so Corrina asked him to have a seat as Mr. Kelly was tied up for the moment on a conference call, he thanked her and took a seat while waiting, realizing he was in fact early. At 10:25am Corrina pushed the button on the intercom saying;

"Sir Mr. Douglas is here to see you."

"Please show him in Corrina."

"Yes sir, Mr. Douglas would you follow me please." as she opened the door to Bill's office and introduced the two men, they shook hands and Bill asked;

"Would you like a coffee or something?" as Corrina waited for a response before excusing herself, but Douglas said.

"No thanks I'm just fine." Corrina left closing the door behind her.

"Well Paul it was good of you to take the time to see me, I've been a bit concerned about the timing of this process and you are working between two major cities and I'm not at all sure I understand how this all works?"

"Mr. Kelly I totally understand your concern, but let me put your mind at ease if I may. First of all we work with a colleague in Chicago and you'll be surprised to hear we have already completed our appraisal of your property and I'm prepared to present you with a check today for $177,500.00 for your condo and I also have three properties to show you in a rather affluent suburb of Richmond as he pulled the paperwork out of his briefcase, as you already know Bracken will also pay your moving expenses and are willing to handle the financing of your new property when you decide on one."

"Firstly Paul call me Bill please and I see you seem to have things well in hand as he picked up the pictures of the properties Paul had mentioned saying it would be a waste of time for me to look at these sights without my wife Paul, so well have to do that another time, as for this check I'll be happy to accept it now as I'm sure my wife will agree with this offer, I notice the check is from Bracken is that normal and when do we have to be out now that we've been bought out?"

"You can stay there as long as you need Bill because Bracken's purchasing the condo and your one of their elite so to speak, I can't imagine them kicking you out, I'm sure they'll give you all the time you need to decide on a new property in Richmond and complete the transaction and the check is yours once you sign here."

Bill signed the papers took the check and Paul's business card completing the business for the day as the two men said goodbye and Paul left, leaving Bill happy as a lark he was only expecting about $162,000.00 for the condo, Barb would be elated!

It was almost lunch and Bill thought he'd try the executive dining room today. Leaving the office he told Corrina where he was going and asked if there was anything he should know about the dining room or the food, she was sure he would enjoy it, but was also sure it would be a business lunch.

The lunch was excellent the conversation pleasant and centered around his move to Richmond and the commute he was now going thru and of course they were all interested in possible properties the Kelly's may be looking at. Bill decided not to let Barb know about the check for the condo over the phone he would tell her when he got home the reality of it being sold and her being alone could upset her and he would not be there to get her through the difficulty.

On his way back to the office he noticed a room with a sign on the door reading Video Conferencing with a red light above the door and a sign reading DO NOT ENTER WHEN LIGHT IS ON! It wasn't, so he went in to find a conference room setting with a large TV at either end of the room and remote controls at each seat position with headphones and jacks and what appeared to be a master control at the head end of the table. It was an impressive room and he was anxious to try it out tomorrow morning, Corrina would be there to guide him and a video conferencing tech. in the event there were any problems, as he understood the process previously explained by Corrina.

Once back in his office he told Corrina he had stumbled on the video conf. room and investigated it on his own, though he would like her to take him thru it before the meeting. He then started to make some notes on his laptop for the meeting and asked Corrina to print him a hard copy of his organization chart for the meeting.

Back home Barb and the girls were planning their night out dinner and the lounge for the evenings libations and there would be many hopefully. Their choice was La Flambé as everything they required was right there, good food and a bartender they knew well and who would take good care of them, they were looking forward to the girl's night out!

The closer he looked Bill found one of the properties Paul had shown him caught his interest and he decided to take a drive by on the way back to the hotel this evening. It was a five bedroom Colonial 31/2 bath with a library, formal dining room, office, and a recreation room all on two completely landscaped acres in a gated community and the price was right Bill thought and it was on a hilltop, as close to a 24th floor condo as they would get. He pondered the pictures awhile and finally asked Corrina;

"Corrina, are you familiar with this area?"

"Yes I know exactly where that's at, are you looking there for a house? It's very nice there!"

"How far is it from here do you think?"

"About twenty miles I'd say, but it's a quick drive anytime of the day, no rush hour it's all secondary roads you know country driving."

"Well I guess I'll put it in my GPS and head that way after work to have a look, thanks for the info!"

"I like house hunting myself, it's fun and that's a great area, though I've never looked at homes there, it's a bit out of my price range, maybe someday though."

Bill thought, was this a hint that she'd like to go along, or was it a test to see if I would offer to take her, either way he refused to fall into that trap again, asking and then being turned down, he may be way off base, but he wasn't prepared to fail again this soon, so he just let it pass as he smiled and went back into his office!"

After saying goodnight to Corrina as she left saying.

"Good luck with your house hunting tonight Mr. Kelly I'll be anxious to here all about it tomorrow." as she left for the evening.

After he left the building and following the GPS to his destination he found the area and saw the house on the hill thinking it was just what he and Barb would enjoy, the setting was breathtaking to say the least as he sat a while to enjoy the view, the house and the surrounding area, as he left he decided to get Barb here ASAP to look at this and other properties and get this move over with. Though Bill enjoyed the private jet commute, maybe not quite as much as Barb, but he wanted to get settled in and devote his time to his job, not to travel as had been the case thus far.

The rest of the evening came and went quickly, he had dinner at the hotel dining room which was quite satisfying and convenient, he had a drink at the bar, went up to his room made a few more notes on his laptop and went to bed, before he knew it the morning was upon him once again.

WEDNESDAY ANOTHER BUSY DAY

As Bill woke and got up to what would once again be a busy day, with a video conference scheduled followed by lunch with his boss and then back to work to finish the day going over details from the video conference. Once again he had breakfast at the hotel dining room and afterwards headed for the office.

Arriving and parking the car in its assigned spot in the garage #225 and this time taking the garage elevator to the 14th floor avoiding the reception area totally, he was learning his way around and reaching his office he was no longer a problem with several options available, it had already become routine. Not surprised to see Corrina already hard at work, though he did arrive a little later today and as he walked in he was greeted with a smile and a "Good morning Sir, I'll get the coffee."

"Ah yes thank you Corrina."

"Would you like a sweet roll also?"

"No-no coffee would be just fine Corrina, but thanks for asking."

Returning with his coffee she suggested they visit the video conferencing room to answer any questions he may have for her, Bill agreed and they both headed that way with their coffee as they entered the room she pointed out that Bill would be seated at the head of the table with the master control panel, that seat being reserved for the person who was conducting the meeting, she pointed out the different controls on the panel and explained their use which Bill had no problem understanding as he was an electrical engineer and this was not his first video conference experience, but he enjoyed watching Corrina do her thing.

The morning seemed to fly by the video meeting came and went, taking about an hour and a half, Bill meeting the people reporting to him which was the purpose of the meeting, he was left with mixed impressions of the folks two Plant managers and three Directors of planning and one Director of research it did become obvious that Bill's responsibilities were more diverse then his title would indicate. He was ready for lunch with his boss who had just arrived to collect him saying, "Come on Bill the Limo's waiting and I'm about to starve!"

Bill replied as he got up to follow, "Well let's not keep the Limo or the chef waiting Sir."

After lunch at a local Private Businessman's Club which he was asked to join sponsored by his boss and subject to the approval of the club recruiting committee, he was given a packet containing all the material and info he would need to make a decision about joining, other than that the lunch went well and he thanked his boss for introducing him to the club, that he had no intention of joining, at least right now.

Returning to the office after lunch, he was greeted by the forever smiling Corrina who asked.

"Well sir how was your lunch, enjoyable I hope; your wife called asking that you call her when you return, no emergency!"

"I see, thank you Corrina and the lunch was ok, but they didn't even have burger's on the menu, you know back home you can get the best burgers in the world there's this one place I go for the burgers and they have one they call a sub-burger that you'd die for, well I'm getting carried away, I guess it's time again for a burger!"

"You know we have some real good places right here for burgers I'll have to tell you about them the next time you're in town and have the urge."

"Sounds good I'm a burger guy at heart."

"I'll have a list for you sir!"

"Thanks I guess I'll make that call now." as he walked into his office to call Barb, who, as it turned out, just wanted to pass the time of day and asked for Bill's arrival time tomorrow so she could plan the evening, he told her he expected to be at the condo about 4:30pm.

Realizing he would not make another trip here before the Christmas break as it was already Wednesday 12/21/2011 he thought he might cut the afternoon short and go out and do a little Christmas shopping for a few folks around the office. About 2:30p.m he told Corrina he was leaving for the day as he picked up his laptop and left.

After spending several hours navigating around Richmond and sorting out the many ideas he had for gifts for everyone while learning the whereabouts of all the shopping malls in the area he finally made his gift selections, concluding the shopping spree.

On his way back to the hotel he decided to stop at the little Ma and Pa restaurant he had found so pleasant earlier in the week for dinner and then go back to the hotel to relax.

By the way he ordered a burger and fries for dinner and it was great!

Before going to bed, Bill packed for the trip back to Chicago leaving out only what he needed in the morning and his Dop kit.

Once Bill was done he took a shower and by the time his head hit the pillow he was fast asleep for the night.

THURSDAY 12 22 2011

Bill had left a wakeup call for the morning, but before the phone rang, Bill was already up and getting ready to face yet another busy day and a travel day to boot. Once ready he called for a valet to pick up his luggage and take it to the lobby while he ate breakfast and checked out of the hotel. After breakfast the valet put his luggage into his car and Bill left for work.

Arriving at the office he did want to go over some details from the video conference yesterday and then pass out the gifts he had purchased while saying Merry Christmas and Happy New Year to everyone before leaving that afternoon for Chicago.

As Bill got off the elevator and while walking to his office and organizing his thoughts he noticed Corrina standing in her doorway holding his coffee in her hand and he wondered how she knew he was coming, so as she handed his coffee to him he took the cup and asked, "Corrina how in the world do you do it, is it part of your covert operations? You seem to know exactly when I get off that elevator, by the way what time is my plane scheduled today."

"It's scheduled for 3:00p.m sir, but it can be moved if necessary."

"No-no that will be fine, by the way my luggage is in the pool car in the garage, would it be possible to have Berry put it to the limo for the trip to the airport?"

"I'll take care of it right away sir, will you require anything else for your trip and have you planned your next trip to Richmond yet so I can arrange for transportation?"

"I haven't made those plans yet Corrina; I'll have to let you know. I'm sure my wife will accompany me on the next trip as we have to look at some properties."

"I see, that reminds me how did you like the house you went to see the other night?"

"Oh that was beautiful it was perfect you wouldn't believe it! That's the main reason I want to bring my wife back, as far as I'm concerned that is the one, but I can't make that decision on my own, you know."

"It obviously impressed you sir, I'd like to take a drive by after you leave and have a look myself, maybe over the weekend if that would be ok?"

"Of course it would be ok I'll leave the address for you."

Bill took his coffee and went into his office to do a little work and take care of some last minute details before leaving for home, which seemed an odd thought, where was his home now Chicago or Richmond?

Bill worked on his video conference notes from yesterday and some concerns he had with one of the employees, later he would need some help with this possibly from Jack, but that was for after the holidays, for now he would put it aside.

Bill checked his email and other messages and finding nothing pressing he decided to take a walk around the 14th floor and say happy holidays to the folks and drop off a few of those gifts he had bought. He made a special trip to Jack's office to drop off a little gift for Maxine who had been such a help during his vetting process.

When all was done Bill returned to his office and took the opportunity to give Corrina her gift.

"Corrina, would you steep in here for a moment please."

"Yes sir" as she walked into his office with her pad to take dictation, she was never without it as he asked her to sit down saying;

"I had planned on being back one more time before the Christmas break, but that won't work so I wanted to take this opportunity to say thank you for what you've done for me this year, all kidding aside, you've been a significant help and I wanted to say Merry Christmas and give you a little token of my appreciation." as he handed her the attractively wrapped gift. Her obvious look of surprise said it all as she became a bit emotional saying;

"Sir, I had no idea and certainly didn't expect this or deserve it we've only been together a short time so to speak, but thank you so much!"

"Well you do deserve it and please open it before I have to leave and not get to see your reaction."

She smiled as she opened the gift and when seeing the name Kindle on the box she almost screamed with surprise and joy, it was obvious she did not have one!

"My God, how did you know, I've wanted one of these I love to read, it's beautiful and exactly the one I wanted I can go on the internet with this model also, you have no idea. Oh thank you Mr. Kelly I really don't know what to say, I'm so excited!" as she ran out of the office clutching the Kindle tightly in her hands, but quickly reappearing with a small gift in her hand and saying;

"I didn't know if it was appropriate, but I got you a small gift also!" as she handed him a small gift box wrapped in a Christmassy well-chosen shiny red and white paper with a bow.

"Thank you, but you really didn't have to do this Corrina!" as he gladly reached for the gift as Corrina explained;

"Well sir all the girls give their bosses Christmas gifts and I didn't want you to be left out just because you're new around here your still part of the family!" once again thanking her for the sentiment and opening the gift to find a brown leather monogramed credit card holder with a dedicated section for business cards, it was quite good looking and very VP looking, Bill knew he would carry it everywhere with him.

"Corrina it's stunning I'll carry it always, I think we've both done well and once again Merry Christmas!"

"And to you sir" with that Bill hastened to get ready to leave for the airport as he packed his briefcase while Corrina called Berry to confirm his being on time. Corrina buzzed Bill saying, "Berry is downstairs sir and has your luggage in the limo."

"I'll be right down Corrina thank you." as he picked up his briefcase and left the office stopping at Corrina's desk for a final goodbye, finding her into her Kindle and saying;

"Have a wonderful holiday and enjoy your time off Corrina, I'll see you next year!"

"The same to you sir and thank you again for this wonderful gift, have a safe flight!" as he left headed for the elevator, her smile burned into his memory, to hold him til he returns next year!

Downstairs passing the receptionist and saying goodnight he walked out the doors to find Berry waiting with a greeting of his own saying "Mr. Kelly I'm sure your anxious to get home and we'll, the pilots and I, will see you safely there sir." as he opened the door for Bill who asked once they were both in the car.

"Tell me Berry do you know which plane we'll be flying today?"

"I'm sorry sir I don't, but I could make a call and find out for you."

"No that won't be necessary Berry we'll find out soon I'm sure, it was just a point of interest."

"Yes sir" Berry said as they pulled away from the building and started on the thirty minute trip to the airport.

Arriving at the airport and pulling in the gate designated for the private Jet access, for both passengers and owners, usually transited by limousines Bill noticed three of the four Bracken Jets on the tarmac But only one with the door opened and that was the Gulfstream 5 and sure enough as they pulled up to the planes Joe and Mike stepped out to greet Bill who was more than pleased as he stepped out of the car and extended his hand to meet theirs. After the greetings the luggage was loaded into the belly of plane and Berry said his goodbyes and drove away, but not far as his protocols required him to remain in case, for some reason, they were unable to depart he could take the passenger, in this case Bill back to the hotel.

Bill and the crew boarded the door was closed and soon the engines were started as the gulfstream started to taxi to the runway, Berry would wait though until the takeoff before he would leave, soon he heard the roar of the engines and the gulfstream thundered down the runway on its way to Chicago as Berry left and Bill settled in with a drink and his laptop for the one hour flight home.

The busy week continually ran thru his head like a loop tape on a recorder the highlights jumping out one at a time over and over the flight, his arrival at the office the first day, the young girl greeting him at the reception area and knowing his name, the encounter with the two ladies from data processing on the elevator, his surprise to find Corrina in the office when he arrived early he thought, the Paul Douglas meeting and surprise check, the house on the hill, the video meeting, Corrina's feelings on secretaries and the exchange of gifts with Corrina and then it started all over, quite a week indeed!

With his preoccupation with things Bill failed to notice their decent into the Chicago area and approach to midway and before he knew it they were on the ground and parking on the tarmac, after securing the aircraft Joe and Mike opened the door and helped Bill with the luggage wishing him Happy Holidays and Bill returning the sentiment happily as he got into his car and headed for home.

As he pulled into the parking garage he noticed that Barb's car was still not there, she was not home from work yet and that would give him a chance to get settled before she arrived.

Soon the front door flew open and Barb yelled "Honey, I know you're here I saw your car, welcome home!" As she threw her coat down and ran to the bedroom to find Bill freshly showered and naked on the bed displaying an unmistakable indication of his intentions, Barb, ripping off her clothes to indicate her needs and desires as well. An hour later they both lay alongside each other totally spent.

The rest of the evening was spent bringing Barb up to date on the goings on in Richmond and telling her of the house he had seen and fallen in love with and finally showing her the check for the condo and yes she too was surprised at the amount being in excess of what they were both expecting so she was quite happy, but wanted to clarify the status of the sale of the condo as she didn't quite understand until Bill explained that in fact the condo had been sold and was no longer theirs, they were homeless!

Still she did not understand as she had never signed any papers and only Bill's name was on the check. As they talked Bill did not like the way the conversation was going and instinctively knew there was a problem surfacing and how best to avoid it had become his newest challenge!

The problem was Barb didn't need to sign any papers as she didn't own the condo it was Bill's before they were married and Bill never had the opportunity to add Barb's name to the property since the marriage and it never came up for discussion until now and now it was too late, her name would certainly be on the new house and the condo had become a non-issue! Maybe he was the only one that felt that way though!

Barb thought for a moment finally asking "You mean, God forbid that if anything ever happened to you the house would not be mine, is that right?"

The question caught Bill off guard, he really had never thought about it and certainly he had no intention of causing her any difficulty in the event something happened, to be perfectly honest he had never thought about it and neither had Barb. So his answer was as follows;

"Hon we've been married almost two years and neither of us had ever thought about this issue before, we both knew the condo was mine when we were married and neither of us did anything to change it or even talk about it so I guess it's both our faults, but we never had our wills drawn up either, I think we are both two young to worry about these kinds of issues, but obviously we should and the house issue will soon correct itself when we buy a new one in Richmond."

Bill's answer and the shared responsibility seemed to satisfy Barb for the time being, but you could see that she was visibly upset and needed time to get over the shock of being unprotected financially in the event something happened to Bill. In any case Bill explained that the $177,000.00 check would be deposited into a joint account and in the unlikely event that something happened now she would have access to the cash, in addition he now had a rather generous life insurance policy from Bracken and she was the sole beneficiary, she is protected he explained and she seemed satisfied with that.

He then took time to show Barb the pictures of the properties he had received from Paul to see if any of them caught her eye and sure enough the house on the hill interested her. He explained that he also found the house interesting and took a trip to see it and he was impressed though he had not seen the inside as he wanted to wait for Barb to do that. He then suggested a trip to Richmond for the two of them to have a look, she agreed.

"Hon you call in and take tomorrow off and I'll call the airlines to get a flight for the morning"

"The airlines can't you get a company plane?"

"I don't want to do that for personal use hon, it would be taking advantage and that's not right."

"You're right of course I didn't even think of that, you go ahead and I'll call the office."

The airline tickets were secured, Barb had taken the day off, they packed their overnight bags, ate dinner and retired early to rest up for the upcoming trip and what would certainly be a busy day tomorrow. They were expecting to return tomorrow night, but Bill left the return trip open in case they had to stay over. Bill also arranged for Paul Douglas to meet them at the airport and take them to see the house on the hill as Bill had come to call it.

CHAPTER THIRTY SEVEN
BUYING A HOUSE, PLANNING THE MOVE & MOVING

The next morning Friday 12/23/2011 at the airport while waiting to board their flight Barb commented on the difference flying commercial as compared to flying via private jet, though she had only done it twice the experience will stay with her forever and from now on every time she boards a commercial flight she's sure it'll trigger the memory of sitting in the cockpit of the G5 at 33,000 feet while Joe and Mike explained the instruments to her, it was truly an unforgettable experience. Well at least they had first class tickets for this flight, but it wouldn't replace the G5 cockpit or cabin.

In Richmond they were met by Paul Douglas who helped with their bags and got them into his car and headed for the house on the hill. Paul pointed out the rolling hills and peaceful country roads on the thirty five mile drive from the airport explaining it was only about twenty miles from work, the scenery was beautiful, Barb was impressed as they finally pulled up to the guard gate to access the property. Paul was expected and allowed to pass through as he headed for the house soon pulling into the circular drive and parking in front of the double entry doors at the main entrance to the house.

No one was home, but Paul had the keys and arrangements were made for the tour of the property inside and out. As they entered the large Foyer with the Library to the left and Living room to the right, Paul explained the house was still fully furnished and lived in, but furnished in exquisite taste as the Kelly's would soon realize. Paul thought it a better way to show a house, some would disagree.

After seeing the Library and Living room and the double wide stairway off the Foyer they walked around the stairs thru a hallway to the formal Dining room with a double entrance, one at each end thru French doors with a separate kitchen entrance for serving, entering the Kitchen Barb was over whelmed to find a professional kitchen with all stainless steel appliances an eight burner range along with a second four burner unit a double sink along a granite countertop in the u shaped kitchen with a double subzero refrigerator alongside a subzero freezer, a center island with a stainless steel hood and another double sink with a pot washer and double drawer dishwasher, one of two dishwashers in the kitchen, Barb fell in love and didn't want to leave, off the kitchen was a spacious recreation room with a pool table and an assortment of video games and what appeared to be a six foot flat screen TV with yet another exit onto a huge closed in patio overlooking a distant Gazebo, but alas, Barb noted, no swimming pool!

A trip back to the foyer to check out the upstairs, but it wasn't really necessary they both decided this is where they wanted to live, upstairs they found a master suit that was breathing including a walk in bath tub with a wall hung flat screen TV in the bathroom and another sixty inch TV in the bedroom the suite was huge with a walk on balcony via French doors, the four other bedrooms were quite sizable also, there were many more amenities too numerous to mention at this time.

They asked Paul to wait while they took a walk outside to see the grounds, but they really wanted to discuss the house, Paul was fine with that as the couple went out the kitchen exit and on to the patio.

When they returned inside they asked Paul to prepare the necessary documents to make an offer for the purchase of the house, as he reached into his briefcase pulling out the necessary papers asking;

"I'm always prepared, I was a boy scout and never forgot, all you have to do is put a price on the paper work and you both have to sign below and were off and running."

They did as Paul had instructed and Bill called the airline for a return flight, they had a departing flight to Chicago at 2:00pm as Bill turned to Paul asking if he thought they could make that, Paul indicating he could if they left now which they did and Bill confirmed with the airline.

Of course they had no idea if their offer would be accepted and the owner's had 72 hours to respond. On their way to the airport it's all they could talk about, Barb was already making plans for the furniture in the spacious bedroom, not to mention the kitchen and Paul fell right in with their excitement talking about how they might be able to buy the pool table from the current owners they are difficult to move and his understanding was that the couple was moving into a condo and they may not even have room for it.

Arriving at the airport in plenty of time to make their plane, Paul said goodbye assuring them he would be in touch as soon as he heard anything from the owners or their attorney. They thanked him for his time and playing chuffer for them saying they hoped to see him soon.

They decided to have a little lunch at the airport while they waited to catch their plane, as they had not eaten yet today and they were famished, Barb was tempted to raid the refrigerator at the house, but decided against it. They checked in for their flight selecting their seats and went in search of a place to eat finding a Burger King with a bar right across the way Bill thought that would serve the purpose.

BARBARA HAS A PROBLEM

After lunch and while sitting in the bar discussing the house and enjoying an early afternoon drink Barb suddenly realized she was without a home, they no longer owned the condo and didn't own a home in Richmond either and she was sure the next thing Bill would ask her to do was to start packing and with no place to go, what if they didn't get the house on the hill she thought?

Once again, Bill could suddenly detect concern on Barb's face and so soon after her enthusiasm for the house on the hill only an hour ago, she ran hot and cold and Bill was unable to respond as quickly as she could change her mood/emotions, this was not normal he thought, for a woman to react this way to her husband getting a sizeable promotion, perhaps she needed to talk to a professional!

The flight home was without incident and only a few words passed between them as Bill didn't want to excite her, but by the time they landed in Chicago she was back to her enthusiastic self, wanting to call Nancy and the rest of the girls to tell them about the house. On the way home from the airport she wanted to talk about how the move was to be handled, did Bracken handle it as they were paying the bill or did they (Bill and Barb) make the arrangements and have Bracken billed and did they pick the moving company or was that left up to Bracken Metals also, all these questions and Bill had no answers he'd have to talk to Paul as to how to proceed, he explained this to Barb and her response was somewhat caustic;

"Well you had better get busy with that call so we get some direction and get the ball rolling, **don't you think?**" Bill somewhat taken aback with Barb's aggressiveness and worrying further about her mental state! He never considered the affect it was obviously having on her, and frankly he had no idea what to do!

"Ya hon I'll call Paul as soon as we get home and see what the next move is for us, if any."

"Ok and I'll throw something together for dinner before I start calling the girls."

After arriving home and getting the luggage upstairs Bill sat down in the kitchen to call Paul making sure Barb would hear the conversation and put her mind at ease as he dialed the number he wondered where this thing with Barb was going to end up.

"Hello is that you Bill?"

"Yes Paul it is you obviously have caller ID set up the reason for the call is to find out if I deal with you about the details of the move or if I contact someone at Bracken to arrange things like selecting a mover and do we do the packing or does the mover how does it all work so we have an idea, whether we get this house or not?"

"No-no consider us an Ad Hoc Branch of the Bracken corporation were contracted to handle the entire relocation of the employee in this case you and Barbara, but I think it better to wait til we know whether or not you get the house, we certainly don't want to be premature with the move, but when the time comes you'll most certainly have input in making the arrangements." Barb heard and seemed satisfied with Paul's answers as she continued with the dinner and Bill continued to dwell on her wellbeing, he was concerned!

Barb went out of her way to prepare a quick yet wholesome dinner for Bill, hot dogs and beans served with candlelight and diet coke on a table set for one, Barb wasn't eating! Bill ate cautiously and immediately afterwards went to bed as Barb cleaned up in the kitchen and joined him saying goodnight, turning over and going immediately to sleep, but insuring that Bill would not.

Bill tossed and turned most of the night wondering what the hell had happened to encourage this kind of behavior? There was really no indication except her initial upset with having to move and leave her job and friends, but Bill had thought they had gotten through those difficulties and moved on. Yet another mystery that Bill wasn't prepared to confront at this time!

Waking up the next morning Saturday 12/23/2011 the old Barb had returned once again to the real world from wherever she had gotten too yesterday. (Bill, sure Barb was still traveling back and forth thru time.) Bill still sleeping after not getting to sleep til almost 4:30am after a restless night and not yet realizing that his wife had returned from fantasyland or wherever she was the night before, but he was about to find out as she woke him not realizing he hadn't slept all night, shaking him she said.

"Honey wake up I put the coffee on and I've got time to make a nice breakfast before I leave for work, so get up, Barb seldom worked on Saturdays and this was one of those exceptions, after all she was off yesterday so she really didn't mind!"

Bill came out to the kitchen rubbing his eyes and surprised by the warm reception he received from Barb, smiles, hugs and kisses, but now he was paranoid, waiting for the big letdown which never came.

"I didn't know you had to work today Barb you hadn't mentioned it."

"Well with all the excitement yesterday I guess it slipped my mind you don't mind do you, after all you went off to Richmond for a week leaving me behind to foot for myself and I'm only going for the day!" **Oh-Oh** Bill thought here it comes he wanted to run and hide in the bedroom til she left, but instead he said reluctantly;

"No-no of course I don't mind I'll just do some planning around here and maybe tonight we can get together with George and Nancy for dinner if you'd like?"

"Yes that sounds good sweetie, why don't you call them and see if they have any other plans for this evening."

"I'll do that right after you leave hon, but right now I think I'll enjoy that delicious breakfast you've made."

As Barb left for work, Bill wasted no time getting to the phone to call George, as he dialed Georges number he had no idea how he would approach the problem with his best friend.

"Hi Bill good to see you on the ID what's on your mind your running around the country so much we never get to talk anymore?"

"Hi buddy I've been real busy and now I've got a real problem I think, its Barb something is seriously wrong!"

"Who wait just a moment I can tell you what it is at least I think I know are you ready?"

"No-no you don't understand!"

"Ya-ya, yes I do the girls all went out to dinner earlier this week and Barb had a bit too much to drink and told all the others that she was sure you were having an affair with your new secretary and she is heartbroken about it. I was going to call you, but you beat me to the punch!"

"What? Are you sure? Where on earth did she get that idea, George I can tell you and I would tell you, but nothing is further from the truth, I only just met the women and the company would never permit it they discourage fraternization and I'd never put my new job on the line just to get laid!"

"Never the less that's what's going on with Barb I can tell you that."

"She made me hot dogs and beans for dinner with candlelight and diet coke last night! He couldn't stop George from laughing.

"She what?" he said that's a classic he thought.

"Listen I promised her I'd call you guys to see if you were free for dinner tonight, how about it?"

"Ya let me check with Nancy if we have to cancel anything, but will be there when my best friend needs me I'm there, I'll call you back in ten."

"Thanks Pal"

Bill thought, Barb gets drunk and tells the girls I'm having an affair, she has a few drinks at the Richmond airport and serves me a ridicules dinner for spite, it sounds like he better discourage her drinking before things really get out of hand!

George called back to confirm their dinner appointment and they both decided on La Flambé thinking the chateaubriand would be a treat and both the girls loved it and if Lenny was working he could be convinced to water down Barb's drinks, they had a plan.

Bill called Barb at work and Lisa answered in the usual way and Bill asked for Barb, but Lisa wanted to talk first saying "Hi Bill how's Richmond and the new job treating you?"

Bill knew he was being probed; Lisa was one of the girls with Barb and Nancy that evening and had obviously chosen sides in a game that wasn't even being played yet.

"Well Lisa you know how it is with any new job and especially when the new job is in a new place to boot, new job, new place and new people, you feel totally lost it takes some getting used to the new surroundings, people you don't really know or trust and a job you're not familiar/comfortable with yet and you can't even find a familiar place to eat, no matter where you go you don't know if the food is good or bad and your alone, your wife is six hundred miles away, every night you wish you were going home not to a hotel, does that about explain it Lisa?"

"Yes it does Bill, I hope it gets better for you guys soon I'll get Barb for you." Bill hoped he didn't overdue it, but he knew he threw a curve at Lisa.

"Hi hon are we going out tonight I hope?"

"You bet I talked to George and were going to the La Flambé for a chateau, how does that sound?"

"Great I love that what time are we meeting them?"

"7:00pm should work for everyone so we set it up for then."

"Great hon I'll see you about 5:30pm then ok?"

"See you then and bye for now love you!" as Bill hung up he hoped the evening would go well, he was sure it would if he could keep Barb from overdoing the drinking as he had surmised the drinking was causing the personality change. The truth was Barb never could hold her liquor very well, but she was always fun until she got the idea Bill was fooling around and Bill couldn't figure out who put that idea in her head, but he would soon find out now that he knew what he was dealing with.

Bill called George again at the office, it was Saturday but that's where he was, catching up he said and Brenda wasn't working so Bill thought he'd stop by and BS for a while if George didn't mind, he dialed the number and soon a friendly voice said "Ha its George"

"Ya it's me again I thought I'd stop by and talk for a while as you're alone and we can talk if that's ok?"

"Absolutely I'm not going anywhere come on down!"

"I'm on my way see you in a half hour bye George."

"Bye pal" hanging up Bill headed down to the garage for the quick trip to George's office.

Arriving he had to knock at the door as it was locked being Saturday and the office was closed for business, George came to the front door and opened it for Bill saying "Hi buddy good to see you this will be twice in one day to what do I owe this honor and from a corporate VP to boot!"

"Ah come on to tell you the truth I'm a bit worried about Barb and what's going on, but there's got to be more to it than what you had suggested, I haven't had enough time to start anything with my new secretary and she knows that I'm sure!"

George thought a moment and said "You know I considered that and I thought about something else, about a month ago Barb stopped by to meet Nancy for lunch like she occasionally does and Nancy had not arrived yet so she was sitting in the outer office and talking to Brenda and Brenda had told her how nice her husband was in fact he was so nice to her that she had even thought he was hitting on her and Bill had even told me to allow her to call Bill by his first name and I agreed, I was in the inner office and had no idea this conversation was going on or I would have put a stop to it, but Nancy told me of Barb's upset at lunch over the whole thing that evening at home and the next day I had a talk with Brenda explaining it had better not happen again! I thought that was the end of it."

"That Bitch! said Bill what the hell was she thinking about telling that to someone's wife?"

"Perhaps a fatal attraction Bill, after all you are an attractive and I guess desirable guy, I can't believe I'm saying that to you, don't get the wrong idea! But I know Brenda's attractive, single, sexy and extremely friendly with the guys that come in here and to be honest I didn't really mind it keeps the customer's coming back and every bit helps, but that doesn't apply to my friends."

"Well now that I know what I'm dealing with George I may be able to turn things around at least I hope I can!"

DINNER THAT EVENING

As they arrived at the restaurant that evening to meet George and Nancy Barb was in an exceptionally good mood and ready to dig into that chateau, walking in they were greeted by Linda saying "Good evening folks good to see you again you've been well I hope!"

"Yes very well thank you and yourself?" Bill replied.

"I'm good thanks for asking, your parties been seated if you'll follow me Mr. and Mrs. Kelly I'll show you to your table."

"You go ahead dear I'll join you in a moment" as Bill headed to the lounge to say hi to Lenny who smiled as he saw Bill approach saying;

"Bill good to see you I thought I saw your friends in the dining room I take it you're having dinner with us this evening." as the two men shook hands and Bill said;

"I need a favor Len any drinks Barb orders needs to be light on the booze if you know what I mean were trying to work through a bit of a problem."

"No problem Bill, I'll just let your waitress know to let me know what she's ordering and I'll take care of it from there, leave it to me."

"Thanks Len you're a life saver will talk later."

"Ok Bill" as Bill walked away and into the dining room spotting his party and joining them saying;

"HI you guys." Bill said giving Nancy a hug and a kiss and sitting down to a conversation already in progress about the house on the hill as it turned out that occupied most of the conversation at least between Barb and Nancy that evening, while George and Bill talked about Bill's office and all the amenities that went along with the job both being careful not to dwell on Corrina or the other secretaries, but George did want to talk about the different aircraft the company had.

They ordered dinner and drinks and afterwards adjourned to the bar to greet Lenny and top off the evening with an after dinner drink, Lenny handled it like a pro, but then he was a pro, Bill could always count on Lenny to come through for him, he was a friend and he has proven it time and again. Bill would miss him right along with all his other close friends and family.

They called it an evening after only two drinks at the bar and left the restaurant at about 10:00pm and headed for home after saying goodnight to George and Nancy. On the way Barb told Bill of her plans for the house, but Bill cautioned her not to get too excited til they knew they had it, but she continued with her plans and Bill let her go on, what harm could it do he thought.

Arriving home Barb asked if Bill wanted a nightcap, he declined, so she sat down alongside him on the couch and they turned on the TV looking for a good movie before going to bed.

CHRISTMAS EVE 12 24 2011

The next morning, Sunday, Bill decided to go Christmas shopping for Barb's gift, it would be his last chance before the big day tomorrow and he had not yet decided what he would get her, truthfully he had not even thought about it til now with all that had been going on. He thought he'd browse around in one of the indoor malls taking his time and enjoying the decorations and maybe getting an idea or two.

He decided to tell Barb what he was doing rather than going out in complete secrecy giving her a chance to let her imagination run wild, things had to be handled delicately now considering her state of mind.

"Ha hon I'm going out and do a little shopping I'm running a little late this year with all that's been going on."

"Oh ok, maybe I'll tag along with you and we can stop for lunch." She didn't catch Bill's meaning or his intentions; he'd have to spell it out.

"No-no hon I'm going Christmas shopping, alone, I don't know how to do that if you're along."

"I get it! I guess I won't tag along, you have fun and spend a lot!"

"I'm sure I will" they ate breakfast, Bill got dressed and made his way to the front door to leave on his mission giving Barb a kiss and saying goodbye as he left for the shopping mall.

On his way he thought about an appropriate gift knowing how Barb loved to read he considered, but only for a moment, a Kindle Fire is what he got for Corrina, but a Kindle DX may be the answer he thought that way if they ever got together and it slipped out Barb would know she got the top of the line so to speak and hopefully both would be happy, he'd have to check out the DX, that will be his first stop.

In the meantime back at the house Barb got ready for Christmas as they would be traveling to her parents' house where they would be joined by Bill's mother and maybe even his brother, it would be a festive day for all. Barb's shopping was done, but she busied herself wrapping the gifts while Bill was out and about, his gift this year was indeed very special and she knew it would certainly be a giant surprise, but you to will have to wait to find out what it is he's getting, right along with him!

Bill was just arriving at the mall and intent on finding the Kindle store or at least a store where they were sold, but wait what about that new Nook Tablet he's heard about, what is it he should check it out also.

As he walked around the mall he was passing a Victoria's Secret store and had to stop, thinking a second gift would be nice and it could be used as a warm up to the main gift, it would be like giving himself a gift that's what Barb would say, it would be fun he thought as a young lady walked up to him saying, "May I help you sir?"

"Where do you keep the whips and chains he asked looking around?" thinking he would catch her off guard, but she quickly turned the tide responding by saying.

"Of course, right this way sir if you'll just follow me!"

"No-no I was just kidding I'm looking for something more conventional!"

"As was I sir and I knew you were also, you didn't strike me as the whip type."

"I'm glad of that" as he looked at the attractive young woman thinking oh-oh not again he was gift shopping not woman shopping.

"Are you interested in sleepwear we have some real nice Teddies and Babydolls."

"Yes take me there I'm sure that's what I'm looking for."

"Certainly sir right over here"

After a short time Bill found a couple of items he liked a Teddy and a Babydoll and unable to decide he took both and thanked the young lady for the help and left, promising himself never to return, but knowing he would.

While walking around the mall he decided to buy the kindle DX probably because that's the first store he found and was already getting tired of shopping, he purchased the unit with a leather case and after it was gift wrapped he headed for home. He was done no jewelry this year; Barb really had a lot of it and wore very little, so she wouldn't miss any additional items he didn't buy he thought, how wrong he was; **Women never get enough jewelry!**

Arriving home with his packages carrying them upstairs all wrapped and pretty he walked in and was immediately confronted by Barb with a curious look on her face carefully sizing up the packages and naturally showing more interest in the smaller of the three and smiling as she gave Bill a kiss saying; "Well I see you've been busy." his usual smart ass comment might have been;

"Not really I already had the gifts in my car; I've been out all day cavorting with other women!" But he decided against that type of joke today considering Barb's state of mind instead he replied;

"Not busy really, I had a plan before I left, I knew just what I wanted and found it quickly efficient I guess."

"Oh I see well then I must be more efficient, I didn't even have to go out and I'm all done!"

"By the way Bill are we picking up your mother or is your brother bringing her? I still haven't heard if he is coming or not?"

"Ya, you know my brother he must have been adopted or a foster child or something else because he sure is different, I'll call and find out!" Bill dialed is brothers number and waited, somewhat impatiently, but soon a voice answered saying;

"Hello"

"Bud it's Bill how are you doing we're looking forward to seeing you tomorrow and to be honest that's why I'm calling, Barb and her mother are trying to work out some details for tomorrow, but haven't heard from you as to whether or not you'll be coming?"

"Oh I'm sorry about that, yes I'll be there I'm picking mom up on the way, I guess I thought mom would call and let them know so I didn't follow up, sorry!"

"No apology necessary what you're saying makes sense and I'll clear up the confusion."

"Thanks, how's the big move coming did you guys find a house yet?"

"Ya we put an offer on a great house, but we haven't heard back yet, I'm sure we will next week, our condo is sold though."

"Well that was quick, especially in the present economic atmosphere, I would have expected it to take a bit longer, but you always were the lucky one."

"Ya well listen we can continue this tomorrow I have a few last minute things to do myself so I guess I'll say goodbye for now and see you tomorrow."

"Ok bro we'll see ya" as they hung up, Bill rolling his eyes a bit as he turned to Barb saying;

"He'll be there!"

"Thanks hon I know that was difficult for you, maybe I should have called Bud myself, but it's good for you to talk with him occasionally."

They both relaxed the rest of the afternoon and evening and after a quick dinner; they watched a little TV before going to bed for the night.

They were both anxious to wake up Christmas morning and exchange their gifts to each other before going to Barb's parents to spend the day with their families, exchanging gifts and eating one of Barb's mother's famous dinners, she was a superb cook Bill thought, even better than his mom, but he would never say that. Bill was also sure that seeing all the little kids running around would once again get Barb talking about her biological clock and with all that was going on in their life right now it wasn't something Bill wanted to encourage!

CHRISTMAS 2011

Waking up the next morning and looking out the window it didn't look much like Christmas in Chicago, a bright sunny day mild temperature and not a snowflake anywhere in sight, but it was Christmas as Barb who was up first naturally went to wake Bill, more anxious to give him his present than to receive hers!

"Honey wake up its Christmas and you're going to sleep right thru it, Santa Clause was here and left some things under the little tree for us, **come on get up!**" Bill starting to stir and running his fingers thru his hair said he'd be there in a moment or two and asked if the coffee was on and what was for breakfast and things like that driving Barb absolutely crazy with his indifference to the occasion and he knew it smiling as he got up and headed for the living room to calm her down.

"Hi Merry Christmas hon!" as he gave her a hug and kiss, once again checking on the status of his breakfast and receiving a not so gentle punch in the shoulder for his query!

Barb went to the tree picking up a beautifully wrapped box in the shape of a 6" cube and handed it to Bill saying "This says it's for you from Santa dear."

"Santa dear, I thought it was Santa Clause?"

"You never stop do you, just open it!" but first he went to the tree and pulled her three gifts out handing them too her saying;

"These are from Santa dear and he hopes you enjoy them!"

"She smiled saying thank you as they both went to the couch to sit and open their gifts"

"Which should I open first hon?"

"Open the small one dear, how about me?"

"You are such a smart ass!" as Bill gently (unlike most men) removed the wrapping from his gift soon revealing the word ROLEX on the box saying;

"Oh my God I don't believe you did this honey!" as Barb put her hand on his saying;

"Ok wait a minute your too excited, it's not what you think it was a joke, but I can see your too excited, I had Emily get me the box as a joke and I'm already sorry I did it, but it's nice and I'm sure you'll enjoy playing with it!"

The look on Bill's face changed to one of disappointment though he did his best to hide it while continuing to open the box, the look of joy and surprise returned once again when he found his new Rolex watch in the box while loving and cursing Barb at the same time, she was indeed up to countering his humor with that of her own and he should have known that as he gave her a big hug and a thank you! This was a two tone Rolex and had to cost about $10,000.00 which is why he never bought one, but always wanted this very watch, he was a happy man!

As Barb observed the look on Bill's face she said "Hon it goes with your new job, you deserve it and think of me every time you look at it ok?"

"I will dear, but open yours though it's not a Rolex, maybe next time." as she opened the Kindle she screamed with joy saying;

"Hon you choose perfectly now my books can go everywhere with me and it's a DX I've been looking at them how did you know?"

"I'm glad you like it hon, but I hope that you can put it down when it's time for other activities and things if you know what I mean!"

"Not to worry dear, but you already know that."

"Ha how about those other two packages over there?" as Barb smiled knowingly she started to open the gifts, already suspecting what was inside and soon discovering that she was right and they were nice outfits though she slept in the nude and could never understand putting on something that looked like nothing just to take it off again almost immediately after getting into bed with it on, but the men seemed to like it so she guessed it was worth it though she was sure she could attract men without the use of props!

"Thanking Bill once again and quickly going back to her Kindle, while Bill busied himself trying to figure out how to set his watch and admired it both on and off his wrist."

Barb went to the kitchen to start breakfast as Bill continued to admire his Rolex, it was quite a gift!

After a great breakfast they both showered and got ready to leave for Barb's parents' house and a Christmas celebration. They loaded the gifts into the car and left on the drive which took about an hour and a half to arrive at a farming community northwest of Elgin. They lived in a large and very old, but nicely preserved farm house on about thirty acres with two horses and a pet cow, yes a pet cow is how I would describe Elsie who spent most of her time in the front yard getting hand feed, but still milked twice a day with most of the milk being consumed by the family and the grateful few neighbors close by. One year they decided to raise a couple of Turkeys for this very holiday, but when the time came they went to the local butcher shop to buy a couple of birds, you guessed it they had a couple of new pets.

Well Christmas came and went Bill got along with his brother who immediately noticed his Rolex, but said nothing though you could see the envy in his eyes and not because Bill had it, but because Barb had bought it for him, this bothered Bud, maybe because he didn't have a wife of his own, though Bill didn't know that for sure!

The get together broke up and Bill and Barb got back home about midnight and went right to bed after a long and tiring day, Barb with her Kindle and Bill refusing to take off his new watch, but then deciding to put it on the night stand so he didn't scratch it in his sleep while tossing and turning, they loved their gifts!

The week between Christmas and New Year's went by without much activity though Barb did have to work a couple of those days; Bill spent his time off checking his emails and visiting his friends showing off his Rolex, they all loved it, Jerry was convinced it was a knockoff, but of course Bill knew better.

New Year's Eve 2011

New Year's Eve once again and the Richmond office along with the plants across the country would reopen on Monday January 2, 2012 for business, but tonight we'd be going to a small party with friends at a local club in the neighborhood so close we could almost walk there.

Barb left for work, another working Saturday, but only a half day today, not as lucky as the big industrial workers who've had almost ten days off with pay, helping to keep the price of products up and the competitive edge down.

During the Christmas holiday period Paul Douglas had called saying that the owners wanted to wait til after New Year's before giving their answer on the offer, Bill and Barb agreed so Bill expected to hear by tomorrow at the latest. While sitting in the kitchen he decided to check his email and maybe even answer a few of the more pressing ones, though he had not started to receive many of those yet. Most of what he had gotten were holiday greetings from co-workers in Richmond and a few from the plant in Mc Cook he also noticed in his sent mail that Corrina had sent the folks on the 14th floor greetings from Bill's office, she was already a cherished asset Bill thought, but he wouldn't repeat that, at least not at home.

Barb got home about noon suggesting they have lunch and lay down for a little nap before going out tonight, Bill agreed as they weren't going out til 8:00pm and probably wouldn't be home until 3:00am in the morning or possibly latter if Jerry had his way he always wanted to go out for breakfast and that took another two hours or so.

Well that's about the way things went a nap up at 6:30pm out at 8:00pm Meeting the gang at 8:30pm, hugs and kisses at midnight and headed for the all night restaurant at 2:00am, home at 4:30am and falling into bed til noon on New Year's day.

SUNDAY NEW YEARS DAY 2012

Bill was the first one up this time and made the coffee while thinking about another trip to Richmond, but after hearing from Paul Douglas on the status of the sale. They (Barb and Bill) were thinking about what they might do if the offer was turned down, would they up the offer or look elsewhere, Bill thought his offer was fair, but realized Barb loved the house and would be extremely disappointed if they lost it and to be honest Bill loved it also.

Finally Barb came walking out of the bedroom still rubbing her eyes saying "Good morning hon is the coffee ready?"

"It sure is can I fix you some toast or something to go with it?"

"No thanks hon coffee is all I want, what time did you get up and what are you doing?"

"I'm just trying to figure out when I'm going back to Richmond; I really need to get back to work, I'm trying to learn my job and I've got a lot to learn!"

"Do you want me to go back with you?" Bill knew he had to move cautiously here so he said;

"Certainly you can go were staying at the hotel and you'd be there all day by yourself and Richmond is not Chicago you're not familiar with it and you have no friends there and no car to run around in, we could fix that with a rental I guess, so ya! You could go with, but how about your job?"

"Oh you're right about everything I guess I'll pass, but what about the house?"

"I'm sure the minute Paul hears anything he'll call and I'm not intending to leave til I know something so we can talk it over together as to what's next and I'm expecting to hear no later than tomorrow!"

"Sounds like a plan hon" as she sipped her coffee deciding to have that toast and a poached egg asking if Bill wanted something also?

"Ya thanks, I'll have a poached egg on toast also that sounds good and its light that early morning breakfast is still sitting there like a lump in my stomach!"

Well the day came and went without further incident a totally lazy day Barb never got dressed and soon it was time for bed again and that's how this and every other day ended, in bed, for one reason or the other Barb reading her Kindle and Bill still wearing his new watch to bed something he had never done before the Rolex. Soon they were both asleep.

The next day Monday January 2, 2012 as the couple started to stir in bed to meet the new day and the new year, realizing it was back to work for all, the holidays were gone for another year and the next time they rolled around Barb thought, things would be considerably different they would be living in Virginia, not in Chicago and to get together with the folks would mean someone had to travel, us to them or vice versa, but someone would have to travel or there would be no family reunion at Christmas, Barb was thinking a year ahead and planning next year's activities and Christmas dinner.

Bill looked at his watch deciding it was time to get up and face the world; Barb was already in the bathroom, grooming herself for the new day as Bill came in to use the commode, Barb running out to give him his privacy they had not yet allowed their marriage to sink to that level, observing one and other disposing of human waste, while other married couples thought it dignified to attain that degree of intimacy, **you decide for yourself!!**

While in the kitchen having their coffee and Barb her toast before she left for work, telling Bill to be sure and call her when he heard from Paul, one way or the other she wanted to know, he assured her he would as she left for work after giving him a kiss and a hug.

Bill opened his laptop to find a message from Paul saying their offer had been accepted, Paul had tried to call, but for some reason he could not get through to their home number and Bill's cell number had gotten deleted or something from his cell phone and would he please call! Bill immediately called Paul's number to confirm what he had read and Paul answered quickly saying;

"Hi Bill I don't know what happened to the phones at least you got the email I see I just sent it, well you folks are on a lucky roll I guess, I got a call an hour ago from the Bradley's accepting your offer they believed it was a bit under what they expected, but were willing to reconsider which is why they asked to extend the 72 hour time period giving them time to talk it over with their family as they had already purchased a new condo, so there you have it when would you like to meet the Bradley's their anxious to meet you folks?"

"Well Paul, you bring good news indeed I'll have to arrange financing with Bracken, that's what we decided to do."

"No-no Bill, remember I told you we'll take care of everything for you and that includes financing with Bracken or anyone else you choose, consider it in the works!"

"Thanks Paul, I'll have to call my wife right away and give her the good news so if there is nothing else for right now I'll say goodbye and I'll let you know when we'll be in Richmond to meet the Bradley's ok."

"That's fine Bill I'm glad you're happy, we'll talk soon I'm sure, goodbye!" after hanging up Bill was about to dial Barb's office, but realized she wouldn't be there quite yet, so he waited, instead he dialed Corrina to make tentative travel plans;

"Good morning Mr. Kelly's office Corrina speaking may I help you?"

"Good morning Corrina it's Bill Kelly how did you enjoy your time off?"

"Oh good morning sir I didn't recognize your call in number I'll fix that right now though. The time off was good perhaps a bit long though I almost forgot to come back and how about you and your family?"

"Like you I thought it a bit lengthy, but it was good, getting the best news this morning, we had put a bid in on that house I had told you about that I went to see and the bid was accepted this morning, so were pretty happy!" not wanting to let on that he had told her before telling his wife it wasn't by design it just happened, but Barb didn't need to know that either.

"That's wonderful Mr. Kelly I'm so happy for you folks, I did drive by that house during the shutdown seeing it from the road and from what I saw it was very nice."

"I'll make sure you get a better look at it I think you'll like it on the inside even better, but for now do you know if any of the company planes are available in the next couple of days I was thinking that after the shutdown they would all be busy playing catch-up for a while, but I didn't know."

"To be honest sir I don't know of any of the staff, or super staff traveling, none of the secretaries have said anything over coffee, but I'll check with transportation and get right back to you if that's ok."

"That'll work Corrina I'll wait for your call so I can plan a trip." After hanging up Bill placed a call to Barb's office to tell her the good news about the house, knowing she would be thrilled to hear.

"Triple 'A' dental Lisa may I help you?"

"It's Bill Lisa is Barb busy?"

"No I'll put her on Bill hang on" as she called Barb to the phone telling her it was her husband.

"Hi Bill what's up did you hear from Paul yet?"

"Ya I did and I don't know how to tell you this, so I guess I'll just say it, WE GOT THE HOUSE!"

"Ahhhh she screamed so loud the doctor even came out of his office to find out what had happened, we got the house, we got it! Hon you're not kidding me are you, well are you, please say you're not!"

"No of course not I just hung up on Paul and we have to arrange a meeting with the Bradley's, the present owners, so no I'm not kidding we got the house!"

"Wow I have to hang up and digest this; I'll talk to you later when I get home ok love you?"

"Ok hon bye for now" as they hung up Barb went nuts in the office telling both Lisa and the doctor about the house and jumping around like a ten year old with happiness and joy and calling all her friends to tell them the good news.

In the meantime Bill waited for Corrina to call him and tell him what transportation had said he had a few other calls he wanted to make, but knowing she would call back shortly, as she didn't waste any time, he held off on his other calls. Soon the call he had been waiting for came as the phone rang and the caller ID read Bracken Industries.

"Hello Bill Kelly speaking."

"Mr. Kelly Hi it's Corrina and I just talked with transportation, all the planes are available there's no trips scheduled til Thursday morning so they'd be more than happy to accommodate your needs, I assume your wife will be traveling with you this trip because of the house so I'll have to arrange the hotel suite is that right?"

"Yes I think that's right Corrina could you arrange for us to be picked up on Wednesday morning about 8:00am at midway and could you also call Paul Douglas and tell him we'll be arriving that day he has some arrangements to make while were in town."

"Absolutely sir I'll get right on it and send you a confirming email with details if that's ok and how long did you want to confirm the hotel suit for this trip?"

"I'll be staying thru the weekend and on thru next week, I'm not sure about Barb just yet she'll probably be going back on Sunday or Monday I can't be sure I'll let you know about that later If that's ok."

"That'll be fine sir I'll make the arrangements and let you know."

"Thanks Corrina we'll talk later" as he hung up he dialed George's number at his office not even thinking about Brenda til she answered the phone saying;

"Mr. Richard's phone Brenda speaking may I help you?"

"Good morning Brenda its Bill Kelly is George in yet?"

"I know who you are Bill I recognized your voice immediately, it hasn't been that long since we've talked, how have you been? I guess you're traveling a good deal of the time, I manage to keep track of your travels through George he talks about you all the time, he's very proud of you as many of us are!" Bill was tempted to confront Brenda about what she had told Barb, but the temptation passed quickly as he didn't want to display his anger and possibly start a confutation between the two of them so he just responded to her questions.

"Yes I'm traveling quite a bit Brenda and I appreciate you guys support believe me everything is new and strange to us (Being sure to include Barb) and takes a bit of getting used to, but it's fun also."

"Well I'll buzz George for you Bill and have a wonderful day and you know how to get hold of me if you just want to talk or anything else!"

"Thanks Brenda."

"Hi Bill what's going on pal do you want to buy a bunch of copying machines for Bracken?" Bill laughing a bit said;

"No, but I'll keep you in mind if that ever comes up I'm calling to tell you we bought a house in Richmond at least our bid has been accepted so were on our way I guess."

"Wow I'd like to say I'm happy and I am for you guys, but I have mixed emotions you are my best friend and we're going to miss you guys around here things won't be the same for any of us I'm sure!"

"George we appreciate the sentiment, but we'll expect you and Nancy to come and stay with us we'll have plenty of room and to be honest I may be coming back from time to time on business there's been some talk about additional responsibilities for me though I'm not exactly sure what that means, but I have an idea, in any case gone is not forgotten."

"So the big moving day is approaching I guess ha Bill what about this house we haven't heard that much about it?"

"It's awesome George I'll send some pictures I know that's all Barb talked about New Year's Eve at the party, I'm sure Nancy has all the details though, but the plan now is for Barb and I to leave for Richmond Wednesday morning and I'll be gone about a week and a half Barb will be back sooner and I'm sure with all the details and I know she won't be keeping them a secrete at that time I'm sure the packing will proceed and it won't take long as were having it done."

They ended their call and Bill proceeded to make a few other calls to tell their friends of their plans for the next couple of weeks and when the final move may happen and everyone had mixed emotions the goodbye party had come and gone so nothing of that nature would be planned, but Bill was sure that they would probably have a dinner with each of their close friends on an individual bases before they left for good.

Barb came home that evening with both smiles and tears as she said tomorrow would be her last day at work and the office would be closed from twelve to two as the doctor was taking both her and Lisa out for lunch in celebration of her last day a goodbye lunch if you will.

Bill told Barb of the plans for the rest of the week with everything dependent on when they could meet with the Bradley's after which Barb would return to start packing and making arrangements for the final move.

"Bill will I be flying back on a corporate jet or on a commercial Flight?"

"You know I have to check on that I don't know the policy on flying non-employee passengers on company planes it never came up in my conversations with anyone so I'll have to find out, but that's a good question, though I know sometimes the planes are used to fly customers around!"

WEDNESDAY JANUARY 4, 2012

Well Wednesday morning came around before they knew it as they got up showered had a quick and light breakfast grabbed their luggage and headed to the airport to meet the plane and takeoff for Richmond Va.

As they arrived they saw the now familiar Bracken jet on the corporate hanger tarmac it was the G5 once again and Joe and Mike were waiting to greet them and before they knew it they were onboard and taxing to the runway for the takeoff and quick trip to Richmond, Barb was in her glory with the expectation that she would be invited once again to the cockpit for a visit and soon she was, not to Bill's surprise.

Once again landing in Richmond they found Berry waiting at the Bracken parking area for them to arrive and as the plane pulled up to the parking area, the engines shutdown and Mike opened the door for them to disembark Berry was already in the luggage compartment loading their luggage into the limo for transport to the hotel and after Barb and Bill had thanked the pilots for the comfortable ride and care they had shown them they got into the limo and quickly headed for the hotel were Barb was left, Bill however continued to the office to pick up a pool car and stop in the office to catch up on the goings on after the lengthy shutdown.

Walking into his office he was greeted by Corrina who said with a smile "Oh sir you just missed Mr. Trax he just dropped in to say hi, I hope your trip in was enjoyable and the plane ride smooth."

"It was great as usual Corrina are these the keys to my pool car (picking up a set of keys on her desk) I think I'll take a walk down to Jack's office and say hi to everyone down there."

"Ahhhh yes sir, But those keys are mine these are yours" as she pulled another set of keys out of her desk and held them up for Bill to take.

"Oh I'm sorry! A bit presumptuous of me I guess or maybe a Freudian slip, here you go Corrina the next time I'll wait til you offer."

"That's quite alright sir it happens though I'm sure you'll like the pool car much better."

As Bill left the office to visit Jack and Maxine picking up a cup of coffee on the way and thinking once again about Corrina while his wife sat alone in the hotel, even Bill thought that improper, but still he could not help himself!

On his way to Jack's office his cell phone rang and it was Paul Douglas and he had to take it "Bill Kelly what's up Paul I'm just on my way into a meeting."

"I'll make it quick Bill, are you available this evening to meet the Bradley's at 7:00pm?"

"We are Paul set it up!"

"Ok I'll call you later with details see ya!"

"Bye Paul"

Walking into Jack's office greeted by Maxine saying "Well good morning stranger it's nice to see you Mr. Kelly are you here to stay?"

"Not quite yet Maxine we've just purchased a house and are here to take care of some details, but I will be here through next week, I have a lot of catching up to do and I'm already getting tired of the commute it's a long way to work every day, is Jack in I understand he was just down at my office?"

"Ya I'll buzz him, Mr. Trax Mr. Kelly's here to see you."

"Great send him in Maxine!"

"Go right in Bill he'll be glad to see you" as Bill walked into Jack's office he was greeted by his old friend warmly with a hand shake and a hug saying;

"Bill boy how are you doing I'm sorry I missed you before the holiday break, I was in Seattle longer than expected, but it was a profitable trip there and all are happy back here I guess. Tell me though how are you doing?"

"Pretty well Jack we just bought a house and things are being arranged for the final move here, but honestly, I've got a lot to learn about the new job and the people, which reminds me are you familiar with any of the folks reporting to me?"

"No, not really Bill why is there a problem?"

"I'm not sure, but not to worry I'll figure it out!"

"Ha what are you doing for lunch today, I'm free and always looking for a lunch partner, what do you say?"

"I better not Barb's at the hotel by herself and no transportation I'd feel guilty about leaving her alone thanks though."

"Ha that's an idea we can go over there and have her join us in the dining room right in the hotel they have great food, we go there often."

"Now that'll work I'll call her what time should I say?"

"We'll be there by noon I'll meet you downstairs at 11:30a.m ok Bill?"

"Ok Jack I'll see you later." as he walked out he said goodbye to Maxine and walked back to his office.

The lunch plans went well Barb was happy to see Jack, the food was excellent and Barb was happy she wasn't forgotten about, she spent the entire time talking about the house and Jack showed great interest, he was widowed and lived in a condo, but the truth be known he missed a house, since losing his wife five years ago he didn't have much use for all the responsibility that went along with being a home owner, a condo fit his lifestyle just fine.

On the way back to the office after lunch Bill asked Jack about Barb flying back on a company plane if one was available and Jack said sure just call transportation after all the company was relocating them and it was just part of the move, but for future reference traveling without Bill as a matter of routine would be frowned upon and Bill understood that so he would not make it a habit.

After work that afternoon on the way back to the hotel after talking to Paul again who said he would meet them at the house at 7:00pm. During the drive, Bill thought once again about Corrina not knowing yet how to figure her out, but knowing there was something more to her and the more he thought the more he wanted to get Barb on a plane and on her way back to Chicago. He was determined not to risk his future over a woman, but not sure he could convince his whole being of that!

Once back at the hotel and up in the suite with the unsuspecting Barb talking about their visit and meeting with the Bradley's for the first time, while Bill freshened up and dressed more casually for the evening's activities.

Barb already looking good and anxious to get going as they headed for the parking lot and the car to start the twenty five or thirty mile trip to the house, both engaging in casual conversation deciding if they would make an additional offer for the pool table as the Bradley's may not have room in the condo and other possible furniture interest they may have as the selections in the home were exquisite and most worth considering as they would have to buy a great many things anyway and most of the Bradley's things appeared new.

It was 6:50pm as they pulled up to the guard gate explaining they were visiting the Bradley's as the guard checked their name and said "Of course sir your expected go right ahead do you need directions?"

Bill said "No thanks we've been here before."

"Go right ahead then folks and enjoy your evening."

As they drove to the house about two city blocks from the gate and pulled into the circular cobblestone drive, stopping in front of the double front doors getting out of the car, walking up the three steps to the front landing and ringing the bell which was soon answered by the owners Mr. and Mrs. Bradley with Paul Douglas standing behind them and making the introductions;

"Mr. and Mrs. Bradley I'd like you to meet Mr. and Mrs. Kelly."

"Please Jeff and Cortney and your?"

Bill extended his hand and said "Its Bill and Barbara (Barb)."

"Please come in won't you?" Cortney said as they stepped aside allowing the Kelly's to enter, Jeffery saying;

"Why don't we steep into the living room and get acquainted we understand you've been through the house and grounds and obviously liked what you've seen, but do you have any questions since you've had time to think about things?"

"You have a lot of lawn to cut Jeff." Bill said with a smile.

"Yes, well we have a lawn service, I have a nice tractor in the garage, a cub cadet, but it is seldom used except to entertain the grandkids, the landscaping service does a good job with the lawn and the gardens and the kids love the woods at the back of the property, have you folks any children?" asked Cortney with nothing but good intentions.

"Not yet, but were talking about It." said Barb, smiling and looking at Bill.

"Our children are all out of state, married and raising families and to be honest that is the reason for the move to be closer to the Grandchildren." Cortney said with a smile, but we'll miss this place won't we dear?"

"Yes indeed we will it's been a wonderful place to live and raise kids."

Paul finally chimed in saying "Well Bill, Barb, did you have anything specific to discuss with the Bradley's?"

"Yes Jeff did you want to sell the pool table, it's a beauty?"

"You know we wanted to talk about that and to be honest more of the furniture, most of what we have won't fit the décor of the new condo which is significantly smaller then this place also, so were going to have to make some sacrifices, though we love the furnishings here and most is nearly new, so if you'd like any of it we would make you an excellent deal and that does include the pool table Bill!" Barb suggested they have another walk thru, but this time with the furniture in mind, they all agreed.

After two hours of a detailed walk thru not only looking at furniture, but learning more about the home and the little things you never learn when buying a house they returned to the living room to discuss things and Barb's list. Barb asking if they had a copying machine, which they did, to copy her list and leave it with the Bradley's for their consideration and pricing as it was a big house and Barb would need a good deal of furniture beyond what they owned to furnish it.

After a long and productive meeting with the two couples really liking each other and enjoying the meeting immensely, the Kelly's decided to leave and continue another time giving everyone a chance to digest what they have learned thus far, so Paul and the Kelly's said good night and took their leave.

On the drive back to the hotel Barb said "You know hon there going to want a fortune for their furniture and it's probably worth it, but the house is so big it'll cost a good deal to furnish it anyway."

"Hon let's not second guess them let's just wait and see what they come up with and go from there!"

"Your right of course, but that's a very large and impressive living room and it's furnished just the way I'd like to do it myself, I wouldn't change a thing would you and the same goes for the Library it's perfect and the kitchen is just remodeled it is new, the house is perfect!"

"Well I'm glad you're happy hon, I'm sure we'll both enjoy it." They hadn't had dinner and thought they'd get room service and relax as Bill had to work tomorrow early. Once back in their suite they ordered room service and sat down to eat with Bill asking;

"Hon, when do you want to get back to Chicago to start the packing process, I have to know so I can arrange transportation for you?"

"Want to get rid of me ha?"

"Don't be silly there's a lot to do and I can't be in both places at once, so I'm relying on your help!"

"Of course I'm just kidding, well I'm done at work, so I'm available anytime, do we know who the mover is yet, you know, I can pack if I can get the boxes somewhere, but if they do it I won't have anything to do and I'll go nuts, besides I don't know if I want strangers going thru our personal things, both Karen and Nancy have offered to help!"

"Well I'm sure I can get the moving company to supply the boxes and the wardrobes to use, but are you sure you want to do it the movers offer a turnkey operation."

"What's a turnkey operation?"

"It means they do it all, we don't have to touch a thing!"

"Ya, no you get the boxes and the girls and I will pack them up ok."

"What if they don't show up when you need them it happens you know, you think about it tonight and we'll talk again tomorrow ok?"

"Ok" she said as there was a knock on the door, room service and just in time Bill was starving and all talked out, as he tipped the server and thanked him. It wasn't fancy, but it was plentiful a couple of giant burgers buried in a huge serving of French fries with a generous portion of Cole slaw and a large chocolate malt to boot and the same for Barb, but with a strawberry malt, the burgers had to be three quarters of a pound on a grilled bun and unlike other burgers these were hot!

The next morning as Barb joined Bill in the dining room for breakfast she told Bill that he could arrange transportation for Saturday if that was possible and she would do the packing of the boxes if he could get them. He agreed and said he would call as soon as transportation was taken care of and he'd get Paul to get the moving boxes and wardrobes needed for the move. They finished their breakfast and Bill said goodbye as he headed for the parking lot and his car. He thought his next trip here he'd drive one of their cars rather than trying to bring them both at once.

Barb went back to the room and started in making several list of things to do when she got back home and making a few phone calls to the girls lining up the help she would need. Downstairs off the hotel lobby there was an attractive gift Shoppe she wanted to browse around in, maybe after lunch she thought.

As Bill arrived at work and parked the car taking the garage elevator to the 14th floor, the closest elevator to Bill's office. Getting off the car and walking toward his office past the video conferencing room reminded him of something he wanted to do as he walked into Corrina's office finding her hard at work and saying;

"Good morning Corrina I'll need you in my office in a couple of minutes with your ever present pad and pencil, which reminds me I thought all you girls used a personal assistant now a days?"

"Many of us do, but I find shorthand quicker if you're proficient at it and I don't want to lose the knack if you know what I mean."

"I do, give me a couple of minutes before coming in wont you!"

"Certainly sir" as Bill walked into his office and removed his coat to get comfortable and sat down to go over his notes as Corrina walked in with a cup of coffee for him, her timing was flawless as she sat down ready to take dictation.

"Let's get started shall we first I need you to arrange transportation back to Chicago for Barb on Saturday if our planes aren't available get her on a commercial flight she has to get back and start packing. Secondly get hold of Neil Johnson in Pittsburg and get him here the week after next for a meeting, no subject for the meeting and finally get Paul Douglas on the phone for me if you will."

"That'll be all sir?"

"Yes, that's it for now Corrina thank you." She got up to leave; Bill's eyes followed her out of the office til she made that left turn toward her desk and disappeared out of sight.

Soon across the intercom came Corrina's voice saying "Mr. Kelly I have Mr. Douglas on line 2 as Bill picked up the phone;

"Hi Paul listen can you work on getting the moving company to deliver the necessary moving boxes and wardrobes to the condo we've decided to do the packing ourselves rather than having it done by the movers."

"Let me check Bill that may be a problem I think the movers quote a turnkey operation and they'd have to re-quote the job."

"Paul I'm sure they haven't quoted our job yet they haven't been there and my experience has been that they'll send a representative out to inspect the move site and detail the pieces to be moved, you know were on the 24th floor and that has to be different then a ground floor move to establish a price or am I wrong?"

"Of course you're right Bill, let me do a little checking with the Bracken folks and the movers and I'll get back to you if that's ok?"

"Alright Paul I'll look forward to hearing from you soon, but goodbye for now!"

"Goodbye Bill"

Bill buzzed Corrina "Yes sir"

"Corrina, could you check and see if Mr. Blair is in?"

"Certainly sir"

"Mr. Kelly Mr. Blair is in his office, but he's in a meeting right now."

"Thanks Corrina" Bill thought he'd take a walk down to the Executive Office complex where the big four, as they are referred to live the **CEO, COO & PRESIDENT, CFO AND EXEC. VP** it's quite a place. He wanted to talk to Blair about Neil Johnson, wondering if he had any dealings with him in the past.

Once again Corrina walked in with a fresh cup of coffee saying "Mr. Kelly I have Mrs. Kelly scheduled on one of our jets Saturday morning at 10:00am if that's ok the planes are all available so it wasn't a problem."

"That's perfect Corrina we won't need Berry I'll take her to the airport myself."

"Very good sir, I was sure that would be the case so I didn't schedule Berry, I hope I wasn't too presumptuous."

"Of course not you were right as usual, as long as you planned on confirming your decision after the fact."

"I did sir and I did sir" she said with a slight smile and Bill responded in a like manner afterword's they both returned to the serious side of business as Corrina left the office and once again Bill watched til she was out of sight, but never out of mind!

Soon a buzz on the intercom and Corrina indicated that Wm. Blair was now available as Bill left his office thanking her on his way out and heading for the executive suits and Blair's office and walking in asked his secretary Carman;

"Hi Carmen is he available?"

"Hi Mr. Kelly I'll check" as she buzzed him on the phone so his response couldn't be heard by others around her desk, an idea Bill agreed with, but hadn't been on that end of his intercom so he didn't know how Corrina handled it, but now he would inquire.

"Yes sir, go right in" Bill smiled and walked into William's office saying;

"Good morning Mr. Blair" as he was quickly interrupted by Blair suggesting Bill call him William or Bill he didn't stand on formality and didn't want his people to either.

"Well Bill thank you and that will be an easy name to remember. I'd like to talk for a moment about Neil Johnson if you don't mind, I had a video conference before the holiday break and frankly I was a bit surprised at his attitude it stood out from the rest even a bit combative and I was wondering if it was my imagination or if you had prior complaints?" Quickly Bill found Blair laughing and even enjoying the moment a bit and saying;

"Bill I wouldn't worry, he'll come around, you see he was being strongly considered for your job, one of your competitors and the only one left by the time we decided on you and to make matters worse he had had some difficulties with Jack Trax who was your strongest advocate so he has some healing to do, he's a good man though so be patient won't you?"

"Of course sir I was sure you'd have some input, I'm glad we talked and thank you."

"My door is always open Bill and how is everything else going, I understand your making some progress on finding a home, you've got a lot on your plate right now if we can help please don't hesitate to ask, Bracken can be pretty accommodating if it becomes necessary!"

"As a matter of fact Bill, we bought a house and are just now finalizing the details with the help of Paul Douglas he's been a tremendous asset to both Barb and I and Bracken Industries!"

"That's good to here were happy with him also, well keep plugin away Bill and it's been good talking with you." It sounded like Bill's signal to end the visit which he did without further delay as he said goodbye and took his leave. Now he had something to talk about with Neil next week common ground if you will!

Back in his office he decided to call Barb and let her know about the trip scheduled for her return to Chicago on Saturday, but then he thought he'd wait til he heard back from Paul and could give her more detail so she could start planning her activities back home.

Soon the phone rang; Corrina answered and buzzed Bill saying it was Paul Douglas on the phone as Bill answered saying "Hi Paul I hope you have good news for me I'm anxious to get started on the packing!"

"I do Bill, you can figure on going ahead on your own, they'll deliver the packing supplies you'll need on Monday and while there they'll figure the move for Bracken, one of their sales estimators will come along with the delivery fellas."

"Great Paul I'll let Barb know what to expect, have you heard any more from the Bradley's today?"

"Yes I have a message to call them, but I haven't gotten around to it yet that's my next call though I'll let you know what they have to say."

"Ok bye for now Paul."

"Bye Bill" hanging up Bill called Corrina in to follow up on what he had observed in Carmen's office and the way she used the telephone intercom system which he never thought about."

"Yes sir, you called?"

"Ya just a quick question and don't be offended I observed something at Mr. Blair's office that I had never thought about, but I know that at the Mc Cook plant it was done differently so I wanted to check. When you call me on the intercom can anyone at your desk or anywhere in the immediate area hear my responses to you?"

"Absolutely not sir I never make open line calls to you, unless I'm absolutely sure were alone! I don't think anyone on this floor does, as a matter of fact it's in our procedures manual, it's not allowed, but it can be done the system allows for it for conferencing purposes, but no it's not done."

"Well thanks Corrina, that's a load off my mind I didn't want to be constantly guarded when on the intercom with you!"

"Well sir let me caution you if I may, if someone is close to me or my desk and your talking loudly on your end, these phones are sensitive enough that under those circumstances you may be heard slightly, but under those circumstances I would caution you!"

"I'd be relying on it and I'm sure you would Corrina, thanks!"

Lunch time and Bill headed back to the hotel to meet Barb for lunch deciding to discuss everything there rather than calling her, telling Corrina as he left not to expect him back today as he had moving details to attend to before Saturday and time was running short.

As he drove to the hotel his cell rang it was Paul, he answered saying "Hi Paul I'm on the road headed to the hotel can I call you back when I arrive there?"

"That's fine Bill I'll wait for your call goodbye." Bill continued to drive, the hotel was just on the outskirts of the city and away from the business district and in a rather affluent area of Richmond there were several restaurants and fast food places around the hotel and as he drove he spotted one that looked most appealing and decided to try it for lunch today, it reminded him of the Poseidon back home.

He called Barb and asked her if she was ready for lunch and would she meet him out front in about ten minutes and she said she would. He continued to drive take in the scenery and as he pulled into the hotel Barb was waiting at the front entrance with a smile when she realized it was him and getting in the car saying; "Hi hon where are we going?"

"I saw a place on the way here I thought we'd try it for lunch, it looked good."

"Ok I'm starving!"

"Me too I could eat a three quarter pound burger with all the trimmings!"

"You and your burgers that's all you think about!"

"For lunch I do, not for breakfast and only occasionally for dinner, I like burgers, when we get there remind me to call Paul he has some info for us I guess."

As they pulled into the parking lot and parked the car Barb said "Oh this looks nice don't forget to call Paul."

"Ah yes" he said as he pulled out his cell and dialed Paul's number walking into the restaurant with his phone in his ear.

"Hello Bill can you talk now I have good news I think; first of all the Bradley's have decided to let you have everything you asked for except the pool table for an additional fifteen thousand dollars and if you agree they'll throw in the pool table and the tractor in the garage along with all the tools in the garage to boot, for free! I think that's a great deal if you don't want it I'll take the deal myself that furniture has to be worth a hundred thousand the only thing they want is their bedroom set and the dining room set with the china cabinet."

Bill turned to Barb and told her, she was elated and said take it we couldn't replace those things for five times that for the like quality!

Bill agreed and said "Paul have an agreement drawn up or add it as an addendum to the contract and let's get this thing done and get a closing date set!"

"It's in the works Bill, I'll be talking with you."

"Ok Paul, goodbye for now."

They were seated and enjoyed a great lunch before heading back to the hotel for some afternoon delight, that wasn't on the restaurant menu.

Later Barb was thrilled to here she would be going back on one of the corporate jets making sure she had Bill's car keys so she had something to drive when she arrived at Midway Saturday morning, meaning she would have to pick Bill up when he arrived home a week later, she was also glad to hear she would do the packing and would be able to start on Monday when the boxes arrived she had to call the girls she thought, but that could wait until tomorrow.

Later that afternoon they decided to drive around getting familiar with the area and maybe finding a nice place for dinner possibly a steak house as they were driving taking in the sites Barb was busy looking up the finer eating places on her smart phone, but finding more than she had bargained for and deciding on a place called Montana's Famous Beef Restaurant and Lounge, just the ticket they thought and it was actually on the way to their new house for future reference, but right now they would continue to drive as it was much too early for dinner.

Barb was busy looking up things on her phone shopping near the house and the nearest shopping mall; she found two large malls and asked Bill to drive to one of them as she asked her GPS for directions which it quickly provided.

Arriving at the mall which turned out to be an indoor mall, perfect Barb thought noting that the property was beautifully kept and well maintained the vast parking lots were spotless with no garbage or even paper all over the place as she said;

"Bill, lets park and go inside to look around and see what it's like in there, it's nice out here and it's the closest mall to the new house, its sure big I'd be happy shopping here I'm sure, but let's go in!"

"Ok well have a look around inside" as he looked for a convenient entrance and parking place which he found quickly it sure wasn't Chicago he thought as he parked and they got out quickly finding themselves inside the second level of the three level center with literally hundreds of stores from Art stores to the Zodiac stores and everything in between with a food court containing many of the most popular fast food places as well as specialty stores a steak house and a noted Italian restaurant. The mall was massive the Directory indicating almost two hundred stores including nine Jewelers, eight different candy stores forty plus clothing stores and many-many more stores to choose from, Barb admitted she would enjoy shopping in this mall.

After browsing for an hour or so they were both getting hungry and decided to leave for the restaurant they had decided to try. They soon arrived at Montana's Famous Beef and Lounge once inside they found themselves in a place similar to an Outback Steakhouse, not exactly what they were looking for, but they were here and decided to give it a try and they were not disappointed the steak and the trimmings were very good, but they decided to go back to the hotel lounge for a nightcap.

The next morning Friday Bill was up and dressed early deciding to leave Barb sleep awhile longer as he went down to the hotel restaurant for breakfast finding Paul sitting at a table having breakfast himself, both men surprised to see each other especially when Bill realized this was an accidental meeting, as it turned out Paul explained he lived near here and often ate here he was not here to see Bill, but was happy to have Bill join him for breakfast which Bill did and naturally they discussed the progress on the move to date, both were pleased with the progress thus far, but Bill admitted he was anxious to get it done and over with so he and Barb could settle into their new life, Paul assured him that things would move even faster now and the end was insight.

After the men had concluded their meal and conversation they said their goodbyes Bill picking up the check, it didn't matter though Bracken would get the bill in either case.

Bill left and headed for the office where he had an early morning meeting with his boss and Jack Trax to discuss an upcoming project in which Engineering and Design and Planning had to interact as was often the case between these two departments and this project would have even more common interest between the two VP's as it involved the McCook plant.

Arriving at the office and greeted by the ever smiling Corrina who said good morning and headed for the kitchen to get Bill's coffee returning quickly and asking "Sir Will you need anything special for your meeting this morning, I'm not aware of the subject it's been kept quit?"

"You know I don't think I will other than my laptop, I think Jack and I will be surprised also I'll let you know when I get back if I'm allowed!"

"Alright sir and I've already confirmed your wife's flight for the morning shell be on the G5 again which will continue on to Las Vegas after dropping her off in Chicago."

"Oh my I hope they don't tell her that, she won't get off the plane in Chicago and she will be busy next week with the packing and all the other preparations for the move. We're getting close Corrina my next trip here I'll be driving my car instead of flying so that's progress."

"You sound anxious sir I hope everything stays on schedule for you folks and you get settled in soon!"

"Thanks Corrina I got to go."

A MEETING WITH THE BOSS

"Have a good meeting sir!" as Bill left the office for the executive suite and Blair's office meeting Jack in the hallway along the way and as they walked together, both wondering what the meeting was about as they knew the nature of the new project and figured it was just a kickoff meeting.

Walking into Wm. Blair's office suite Cortney said "Good morning gentleman, go right in Mr. Blair's waiting for you."

"Thanks Cortney." Blair's door was open so they walked in shutting the door behind them and both men said "Good morning Bill." as he invited them to sit starting the meeting by saying;

"Well you two are about to embark on a very ambitious project you already know the basic overview and today I want to give you a bit more detail, but I must caution you both that what I'm about to tell you must remain here for the time being as the product we are about to manufacture only has one customer and of course that's the federal government and to further define the customer it's the military.

Bracken has developed an extremely light weight armor plate that the military has become most interested in and has committed to purchasing several million pounds in several configurations and it has just gotten thru appropriations so were in business. Wm. Looked at Bill saying "Young man you've had a good deal to do with this and didn't even know it!"

"Oh how's that William I don't recall anything like this that I worked on, but then you said I didn't even know it, didn't you?"

"Well let's see, do you remember you were the project manager and electrical design engineer on a new furnace project in McCook, well that furnace was designed primarily for the development of this armor plate and proved a success in the development and acceptance of the armor plate by the military and because you designed the electrical controls and were the project manager thanks to Jack here picking you and the project was so successful, all of which had a great deal to do with you getting the promotion over Neil, so there you have it a bit of history and now for a bit of the future, but first would you fellas care for some coffee or something?"

Jack and Bill both said yes as Wm. Asked Cortney to see if she could find three cups of coffee and shortly she came in with the coffee exactly the way each of them took theirs, but how did she know Bill thought, Jack seemed to know and said to Bill with a smile, "She called Corrina."

"Of course" said Bill.

Wm. Smiled and said to Bill, "These ladies do an amazing job Bill, don't you agree?"

"I do sir, sometimes it's beyond me how they do what they do this (holding up the cup of coffee) is a perfect example they just seem to know."

ADDITIONAL RESPONSIBILITY

"Yes well back to the task at hand it seems we have a problem we never anticipated and that is we're losing one of our VP's Bob Masek who's in charge of the metals group and that includes the McCook plant. Bob has decided to move on to the auto industry, I understand he's had an excellent offer, we wish him well, but it leaves us hanging out there with no group leader!"

"Oh no" Jack said.

"Does Bob know about the government contract it's not like Bob to leave us in the lurch like this I can't believe it!" Jack said, but after a minute of thought, he said;

"I may have a solution William, if you'll bear with me for a moment obviously we need to replace Bob and I assume there are no viable candidates right now and to dump the whole metals group on another VP would be a hell of a burden and significantly reduce his effectiveness, but if we could break the McCook plant away from the metals group even on a temporary bases then you could put the additional responsibility under one of the other VP's"

"Someday Jack you'll have my job, that's the exact solution we've come up with and one of you two will have that additional responsibility, so who's it going to be?" Bill and Jack looked at each other questioningly both with a great deal of experience in the McCook plant and both would have a piece of the new project, who indeed?"

"Well, let me help you guys decide!"

Jack smiled saying "William you've already made that decision why don't you just let us in on it so we can get started doing our job!" Bill wouldn't have taken that attitude with the boss, but Jack had been around longer and had Blair's total respect and could get away with it. Blair turned to Bill and said.

"Pack your bags young man and get back to McCook and reintroduce yourself to those folks they need to meet their new boss!"

"I don't exactly know what to say sir, this is certainly an opportunity, but I'm just starting to get my hands on my new job I hope I can give this project the attention it deserves I guess I hope I'm up to all the changes that are going on in my life, but I can promise you I'll do my very best, I won't make you sorry you put your trust in me!"

Jack chimed in saying "Don't worry Bill I'll be there with you to pick up the slack when needed, together we've never failed."

"As long as you put it that way Jack I'm sure we'll get through this one also (turning toward Blair, Bill added) sir you've made the right choice, I'll pack my bags!"

"Ok guys pick your team and run with it, keep me informed and good luck." as he stood up shaking hands and ending the meeting.

Jack and Bill walked out and back to their offices, on the way Jack said to Bill let's get together later to discuss this, Bill shaking his head affirmatively as he continued to his office.

Walking into his office he asked Corrina to get Jack Richardson in McCook on the phone to which she replied "Yes sir."

Bill sat down at his desk wondering what would be next, he was about to leave Chicago permanently and now he takes over the responsibility of running a plant in Chicago and he hasn't even met the employees in his new area of responsibility with his promotion to VP yet! He didn't need coffee he needed a drink! Soon Corrina announced that Jack Richardson was on the phone.

"Hi Jack how's the weather back home? Pleasant I trust, the reason I'm calling I'd like to set up a meeting with you about noon on Monday if you're going to be there I know this is short notice, but it needs to happen, have you heard from Bob Masek yet?"

"Yes I have Bill an hour ago, I couldn't believe it and was sorry to hear it naturally he was a hell of a boss, I'm going to take a wild guess here and say you're coming to announce that your my new boss, is that about it?"

"You have great insight as always Jack, but we have more pressing matters to discuss also and it's not something we can talk about over the phone. I plan on arriving mid-morning on Monday my secretary will call with the details if you could arrange to have me picked up at the airport it would be appreciated as my car is not available."

"Absolutely we'll take care of everything Bill and you'll be here for lunch what would you like, I know the staff will be anxious to see you again. "The lunch is up to you Jack as I recall your executive chef is quite competent and as for your staff I would enjoy seeing them all again at lunch, but our discussions are for your ears only Jack! I hope you understand!"

"Of course Bill I'll look forward to seeing you on Monday."

"Good Jack bye for now."

"Corrina, could you steep in here please?"

"Yes sir" she said as she walked thru the door to Bill's office pad and pencil in hand as usual.

"I need you to get me on one of the planes on Monday morning to Chicago a priority trip to McCook if we have to bump someone Blair will authorize the bump I need to arrive at midway by 9:00am and could you contact Jack Richardson's secretary with the details and have her arrange to have me picked up at the airport, I'll be returning to Richmond the same day so hold the plane the whole day for me."

"Of course sir I'll get right on it, will there be anything else?"

"No that's it for now Corrina." Corrina noted the fact that something must have happened in Blair's office as this was the very first time Bill had talked to her like a VP, more bossy and business like than friendly and charming as was his usual demeanor thus far, oh well she thought it was inevitable.

Before he left that day all the arrangements for his trip had been made and Corrina had put all the details on his laptop, now all he had to worry about was getting Barb on her flight tomorrow morning.

That evening at the hotel he brought Barb up to date on the day's events, including him taking over the McCook plant as a part of his organization and the loss of one of Bracken's VP's and his plans to come to Chicago on Monday for a meeting with Jack Richardson and a quick return to Richmond later that same day.

Barb detected a sense of urgency in Bill's tone that evening, but let it go leaving it to him to work out without a lot of probing from her; he was obviously under some pressure!

After dinner in the hotel restaurant, which they both liked, it was a good place to eat the food was always great, the selections were numerous and the server's extremely friendly. They both went back to the suite after a short stop in the gift shop, Barb couldn't walk by it without stopping and she did it several times a day as it turns out, but it kept her occupied and that was good with Bill being gone all day though she could now keep busy planning for the new house.

In bed that evening Barb said goodbye in her usual way, Bill never seemed to mind, it made for a good night's sleep for both of them and she was looking forward to her flight in the morning. Soon they were both fast asleep the hours ticking away toward the morning and a new day.

SATURDAY JANUARY 7, 2012

The next morning they were both up early Barb was packed and ready to go; Bill was busy making sure last minute details were taken care of making sure Barb had his car keys her condo keys, money in her purse and so on. Once showered and dressed and ready to go they went down to the restaurant for breakfast before leaving for the airport to meet the plane.

After breakfast they loaded the car with Barb's luggage and got started for the airport about a fifteen mile ride the conversation was casual mostly about the new house, Barb wondering how soon the closing would be as she was now anxious to get in and get started nesting, she was also wondering if Bill intended to stop by the condo Monday when he was in town to which Bill replied;

"Absolutely hon, you don't think I'd come to town and not stop do you, but how long I'll be staying is another story!"

Soon they arrived at the field and driving thru the gate they noticed Joe and Mike at the G5 waiting for them to arrive and opened the door for Barb as Bill stopped alongside the plane. They greeted the Kelly's and Joe said "I understand we'll be taking you to midway on Monday sir and making it an all day trip."

"Oh I didn't realize I was lucky enough to catch you guy's for this trip too, but I'm happy to hear it, ya I'll see you Monday morning in the meantime take good care of my wife on her trip back today I know you guy's will and I understand your headed for Las Vegas after Chicago do you have a layover there?"

"Yes sir a short one."

"What's your game Joe?"

"Black Jack sir Mike here loves Craps!"

"What I want to go!" said Barb, but knowing that would be impossible as she laughed a little, giving Bill a kiss and a hug to say goodbye as she boarded the plane after the luggage was stowed away in the belly of the plane. Bill stood and watched as the air stair was retracted the engines started and the G5 started to taxi as he and Barb waved goodbye to each other. Bill watched as the plane moved into takeoff position on the runway and the engines started to roar on the takeoff roll soon the jet was in the air and Barb was headed for home in Chicago. Bill got in his car and headed for the office for a few hours as long as he was out and about anyway.

Arriving at the office and not expecting to find anyone on the 14th floor on Saturday Bill was surprised to see the lights on in Jack's office as he walked by so he stuck his nose in and greeted Jack saying "Good morning, I didn't expect to find anyone here today, what brings you in on a Saturday?"

"Oh I spend a lot of Saturdays here Bill, I don't have a lot to do with my spare time since Gladys died, so I guess this is not only my job it's my hobby as well, but what brings you in today?"

"Well I just put Barb on a plane back home and I don't have a lot to do either, so I thought I'd do it here."

"I see let's get a cup of coffee shall we, I'll buy"

"In that case I'll have one Jack." as the two men walked to the kitchen where Jack had put a pot of coffee on earlier. Jack taking the opportunity to feel Bill out a bit asking what Bill really thought of this idea of giving him the additional responsibility of the McCook plant and a high profile project to boot? Bill shrugged his shoulders saying.

"I feel a little put upon I guess Jack, after all I'm still trying to get my head around the new job and all, I haven't even met the people that are working for me yet, I was told my title, but the associated responsibilities were never defined, so I'm figuring them out as I go along on my own and then to add the additional responsibility of another plant, from a totally different area of the business and with a major project to take on might be a bit much, until they said you and I were in this together, that gave me the confidence I needed to run with it, we'll be fine I'm sure!"

"Well you've got a good attitude Bill and you're right we'll get through this and move on to the next challenge and the next one beyond that, it's what we get paid for and the benefits and rewards are worth it believe me. Ha it seems were both bachelors today how about dinner tonight?"

"Ya great Jack I'd really enjoy that what time and where?"

"I know a really great steak house Bill as a matter of fact it reminds me a little of the La Flambé you like so much can you handle a really great steak?"

"You bet I can Jack and the place sounds exciting do they have a bar?"

"They have a great bar and lounge, but they don't have a Lenny, the Bartenders are all ladies there, but there are a few entertaining ones if there working."

"Entertaining?" Bill questioned.

"You'll see I don't want to spoil it for you, you'll have to wait til tonight!" they arranged a time and a place to meet and Bill went off to his office to do a little work. Suddenly Bill's cell rang it was Paul he answered quickly;

"Hello Paul what's up on a Saturday morning or I guess its afternoon now?"

"Hi Bill I just thought you'd like to know that Tuesday the 17th is your closing date on the house I've notified the Bradley's also, any problems with that for you guys?"

"Hell no Paul the sooner the better, I don't know if we can be out of the condo by then though, but were working on it."

NEWS ABOUT THE CONDO

"You don't need to be out by then, it's a totally separate issue, remember Bracken is the owner of the condo and I'm certain there not going to put you out on the street although I do have some news about the condo that you may not believe!"

"Oh what's that Paul?"

"Well it seems that Bracken was toying with the idea of furnishing it for an executive stay over in the Chicago area or a place to put up clients, but then they got a rather generous offer for the place from and this is what you won't believe a young couple that you may know a Mr. and Mrs. Richards."

"**What you're kidding!** George and Nancy they never said a word your right that is hard to believe I have to call Barb right away and tell her, thanks Paul and what time is the closing scheduled for?"

"I don't have that yet I'll let you know as quickly as I know Bill."

"Fair enough, but I've got to go right now and give Barb a heads up by the way is Bracken going to accept their bid?"

"That hasn't been decided yet Bill, but I understand their leaning in that direction I guess you could persuade them one way or the other if you had a mind to do so."

"Ya thanks Paul, we'll talk soon and thanks for the heads up I'm sure I'll see or at least talk with you before closing, but I'm sorry I have to cut you short, I have several other calls to make so we'll be talking to you Paul!"

"Of course Bye Bill"

Bill looked at his Rolex to see if Barb had enough time to get to the condo, so he could call her to tell her the news and deciding she would be there he dialed the condo and it was answered almost before it had a chance to ring "Hello" she said Bill could tell she didn't know who was on the line as he said.

"Hi hon it's me I take it the caller ID wasn't much help this time the new corporate phone isn't in there yet I guess. How was your flight? Have I got news for you are you sitting down?"

"The flight was wonderful as always those guys are very entertaining, but extremely professional at the same time and yes I'm sitting down so what's your news?"

"Well as it turns out Bracken was going to keep our condo for entertaining purposes, you know so executives and clients had a place to hang when they were in town a great place with a great view and so on, but then they got an offer to buy it that they had to consider because it was on the market and the profit was more than they had hoped for and guess who made the offer!"

"I have no idea, but because you asked I take it someone we know, Oh No! George and Nancy I bet!"

"Ya how did you guess that?"

"You know engineers aren't the only ones that use logic, I guess it was the way you posed the question, along with the fact that I just hung up with Nancy and she told me everything, I think it's great don't you!"

"You know I'm going to hang up now and ponder my life with you, one who out smarts me at every turn and takes great pride in so doing, but having said that, closing is on the 17th but I suppose you already knew that too, so the only thing left to tell you that you may not know is I'm having dinner with Jack tonight, I caught him working in the office this morning and he invited me, you know he seems lonely since losing his wife so I said yes and that's about it, unless you have news for me?"

"The 17th that's quick isn't it, when do we have to be out of here? I'm going to start separating everything into piles for packing so when the boxes arrive all I have to do is put them in a box and set them aside to be picked up by the movers, I have a plan! The girls will be here bright and early Tuesday to help me. What made you go into the office on a Saturday morning?"

"I don't know a way to while away the hours I suppose, nothing else to do so why not be productive and work no one here to bother me it was dark when I walked in except for Jack's office and I am getting some things done."

"Well hon you know best I thought you'd take some time for yourself and just go shopping or for a drive, you know, relax!"

"I guess, but I like what I'm doing for me it is relaxing and I'll relax tonight with Jack, well I'm sure you just got off a flight and got home so you need to relax a bit yourself, I'll let you go for now and call you tomorrow and see how you're doing ok?"

"Ok hon bye for now and I love you!"

"Love you too bye" hanging up Bill decided to call George to talk about his buying the condo and any help he may need that Bill could possibly help with. He dialed the number and got the answering machine, but left no message, deciding he'd try later.

Sitting at his desk and entering the closing date for the house in his laptop the 17th he noted a conflict Neil Johnson was scheduled in town the same day for a meeting, that would have to be moved out so he sent an email to Corrina to make the necessary changes to his schedule and Neil's, obviously since talking with Blair that meeting would have a different tone then first intended.

A SURPRISE MEETING

Soon Bill left the office for the day and the weekend not expecting to return until Tuesday after his planned trip to Chicago on Monday to meet with Jack Richardson and the staff for lunch a quick stop at home and back to Richmond in the evening. On his way back to the hotel to take a break before dinner with Jack and sitting at a stop light who did he see standing on the corner but Corrina, he reacted as most would and blew his horn, she turned a bit confused and then realized who it was and waved to him, he waved her over and rolled down the window as the light turned green he said jump in we'll pull around the corner which she did without hesitation saying;

"Good morning sir what on earth are you doing in this part of town?"

"I was just leaving the office and headed back to the hotel, but please we couldn't be any more informal then we are right now both in jeans away from work and out and about with no place special to go so please under these circumstances call me Bill ok?"

She thought for a minute finally saying "Ok Bill I guess under these conditions its ok, but this is not the most direct route to the hotel from the office what brings you this way?"

"I go a different way every day just to learn the area I guess there's always a chance I'll find a good place to eat along the way." As he pulled to the curb and parked the car to talk awhile saying;

"I'm sorry Corrina I must be keeping you from something, I didn't mean to, but seeing you I just had to say hi, can I drop you somewhere, you look like you were on a mission, I'm just going to continue looking for a place to have lunch."

"You know Bill if you'd continue the way you're going for two more blocks and then make a left for three more blocks you'll come to a place called Steven's restaurant and I'm sure you'll be very impressed with the food and the service, I eat there often and it's excellent!"

"Great have you had lunch yet because I hate to eat alone?"

"Ahhhh I don't know, no I haven't eaten, but I'm not sure it would be proper, you understand don't you? People might talk I think it better if I just went about my business, but it was nice running into you like this and catching you in jeans and polo with a bomber jacket, I must admit I never pictured you that way!"

"I'll tell you what I'm going to drop you by your car if that makes you more comfortable and then I'm going to that restaurant you suggested and have lunch and I'd love having you join me if you'd like and then we both leave in our own cars and nobody did anything wrong, I'd even tell my wife about it and if you don't show up I'll see you on Tuesday, which way to your car?"

"Straight ahead and two rights at the first street and I'm right there."

Bill followed her directions to the letter and pulled up alongside her car and she got out saying.

"Thanks Bill and it was nice seeing you I'm sure you'll enjoy the restaurant bye for now!"

She got in her car and Bill pulled away toward the restaurant she had suggested not knowing whether she would follow or not and pulling into the parking lot and getting out of his car he saw her car pulling in as she pulled up alongside his car opened her window and said;

"You forgot something Bill, me, I hope you don't mind, I am hungry!"

Smiling he said as he opened her door "Come on you nut let's eat!"

Once in the restaurant they were seated in a booth more intimate than a table and her choice as it turned out. Bill's first words were "Ok tell me what's good here; you know do you have a nick name or something that friends call you?"

"Well ya some call me Rena, I kind of like it and it's simpler than Corrina!"

"Oh do you mind if I call you Rena I don't think it's too personal and your right it's easier and I like it also."

"No Bill you can call me that if you like, I don't mind, but around the office you'll have to decide what you are comfortable with, it is your office and your rules of conduct I wouldn't dare call you Bill around the office or even the building for that matter." Bill laughed admitting that was a little different, but assuring her she could call him Bill in any non-business function or situation.

"I'll accept that as my responsibility Rena and I'll think about it and let you know on Tuesday how I've decide to refer to you while were at work ok, now what's good here?"

"Everything Bill I'm a burger gal myself, but I occasionally have a salad or a hot turkey sandwich and the Monte Cristo here is out of this world!"

"With that kind of a recommendation I could do nothing else, I'll have the Monte Cristo" as he looked at Corrina who ordered the same but with extra fries saying;

"The fries here are superb I hope you don't mind."

"Of course not Rena" as Bill told the waitress to make his order the same way, thru lunch the conversation centered on the office though Bill occasionally drifted to the personal side of things, Corrina's interest, how she spent her off time, did she have any hobbies, was this her home town, were her parents nearby etc. and she was quit forth coming with the information, taking her opportunities to probe Bill a bit, they both got along well.

After lunch Bill walked her to her car saying a polite goodbye, as she thanked him for lunch and the pleasant conversation and drove away saying;

"I'll see you Tuesday Bill." He waved turned, got in his car and drove away, headed to his hotel for the rest of the afternoon, but his thoughts remained on this beautiful young desirable woman, he seemed to have no control over his thoughts!

Back at the hotel and settled in his suite he decided to try to call George once again and dialed the office number and naturally Brenda answered saying, "Sales Brenda may I help you?"

"Hi Brenda its Bill how are you?"

"Hi Bill did you want to talk with George because he's not in til late this afternoon."

"I see well just say I called and I'll get back to him at home tonight."

"I'll let him know you called Bill." detecting some distance in her voice and not wanting to pursue the reasons, he simply said goodbye and hung up.

Bill decided to take a nap before his dinner date with Jack, but found sleep was just not in the cards as his mind once again was totally filled with fantasies involving Corrina, he had to clear his head and return to reality.

Meanwhile back in Chicago Barb was busy tearing the condo apart, making phone calls to friends; even Lisa was coming to help and Nancy not saying, but probably having an ulterior motive, that being to get Bill and Barb out so George and her could move in, but Barb was happy for them and hoped they would get it as they both loved it so much, no matter how many times they came over George could not get over the view. Barb was sure Bill would help them if they needed it as he was in a position to help his friend.

Barb and Bill both had a lot on their plates the 7th was quickly coming to an end and the 17th was closing on the house in Richmond, they could move in any time after that. The shipping materials were scheduled to arrive on Monday and all Barb's help on Tuesday the mover had not been scheduled to make the pick up as yet, but that would probably happen toward the end of the week next week and Barb would leave for Richmond with her car soon after that so she could be there for the closing date on the 17th and then stay at the hotel with Bill til they could move in.

Barb had to be in Chicago for the movers and in Richmond for the closing and this would require close coordination by Paul Douglas and all concerned!

Barb was invited out for dinner that evening with Karen and Emily kind of a farewell get together as time for getting together was growing short, they were good friends and Barb would miss them all!

Back in Richmond Bill was starting to stir after finally falling asleep for a while and looking at his watch he realized Jack was picking him up in an hour and a half for dinner though his Monte Cristo was still hanging in and he wasn't really hungry yet, but he was thirsty as he headed for the shower.

Soon it was time to go down to the lobby to meet Jack who was going to do the driving and was never late for anything, Bill realized he looked more at his watch recently and noted Jack was do in about three minutes, but was sure he was already there and steeping off the elevator and walking toward the main entrance Bill noticed Jack's car in front, he walked out and got in saying;

"Right on time as always Jack, but then I expected nothing less."

"Actually seven minutes early Bill, but who's counting, how are you doing this evening I hope you're hungry and ready for a really great meal, it's about a half hours ride out toward your new house and in the middle of nowhere in the middle of a field actually, you'll see."

While driving Bill thought about his stupidity about his travel plans for Monday he didn't need a return flight he should take advantage and drive his car back Monday as time to do that was getting short and he told Jack he needed to change the pilot's schedule, Jack put his mind at ease saying "When you board Monday morning tell the guys there's been a change in plans its one way they can return immediately and be home for dinner, they'll love it, these things happen all the time, I've seen them get changes in mid-flight and have to turn around and go back to where they just left, that's what private jets do!"

"Great, if you don't think it's a problem Jack."

Finally on a country road in the middle of nowhere Jack said "There Bill on the right about a half mile off the road in the middle of that field, see that structure that's it!"

"You're sure right Jack it's out of the way, I'm going to need my GPS around here I have no idea where we are or how close to our new house we are right now, the only thing I'm sure of is we were headed in that direction."

"I'm just guessing you understand but I believe your about 7 or 8 miles that way from here, close enough to enjoy the place often if you like it."

"Well let's find out shall we." Bill said as Jack pulled into the large parking lot ¾ full probably because it was Saturday night, the building was enormous more like an aircraft hangar with a giant sign reading **THE CHATEAU** that you could see from the road, but they had valet parking which Jack used.

Walking into the main entrance though was a total surprise, had you not been there before and looking from the outside you were led to believe it was a country western dance hall and expecting to see everyone wearing plaid shirts, jeans with huge belt buckles and ten gallon hats, doing the two steep or line dancing on a Gilley's style dance floor, but no, quite the opposite and that was the surprise.

The inside was done in dark woods and subtle lighting, immediately to the left of the entry vestibule was a piano bar seating about twenty five persons with candle lit round tables to the right a coat check and a hostess station and straight ahead the spacious main dining room at the back of the dining room was the entrance to an extremely large lounge and dance floor with a boomerang shaped bar at the back of the lounge against a giant aquarium background with soft blue lighting and as Jack had indicated all lady bartenders. The servers were mostly guys dressed in tuxedos and a couple of women also in tuxedos the house specialty chateaubriand and Lobster with many other steak and seafood selections.

After being seated they meet their waiter Jeff who gave them their menus and asked if they would like the wine steward to which Jack replied "Yes" and Bill said to Jack;

"You were certainly right Jack this has been a surprise so far and on the inside it does resemble the La Flambé though much bigger I'm sure I've never been in a steak house this huge before and decorated so luxuriously, I'm impressed!"

"Well there are still a few surprises in store Bill and the quality of the food is one of them."

Well they selected a wine with the steward and decided to have a chateaubriand for two as they both loved it, they were meat eaters, but Jack never ordered it when he was by himself as it was too much food for him to eat.

After an enjoyable dinner they adjourned to the lounge for the evening's entertainment. If you remember the Tom Cruise movie cocktail you could relive the bar scenes here as the lady bartenders put on the same kind of a show behind the bar and drew quite a crowed, it was fun and Bill swore he would have to bring Barb here.

The evening ended and Jack dropped Bill off at the hotel about midnight with Bill thanking him for the diner and entertainment and saying goodnight as he went in to hit the sack.

Sunday came and went without incident, Bill had the Sunday brunch at the hotel restaurant followed by a drive to continue his familiarization with the city and later ending in the same area where he had run into Corrina yesterday, maybe hoping to find her again, but that was just not in the cards for today. Remembering the way to the Chateau he thought he'd start from there and see if he could find his way to their new house and check the mileage for future reference.

Finally arriving at the Chateau he noted the mileage and started for the house he knew it was northwest so he looked on his map to find the best road to take for the most direct route to the house finally deciding on the route he would take. Twenty five minutes later and 7.2 miles he arrived at the house without getting lost, he was happy with the results of his experiment, but what a useless way to spend the day he thought though he was fast becoming familiar with Richmond and that was a good thing.

Back at the hotel he decided to visit the lounge and with his trusty laptop in hand he ordered a Gin Ricky from the lonesome bartender who was happy to see anyone, early in the afternoon on a Sunday wasn't the busiest time in the lounge so the bartender wanted to talk while Bill wanted to catch up on his emails and send a few to Corrina about his trip in the morning, but it looked like the emails would have to wait!

Back in his room he remembered he had never gotten hold of George so he thought he'd try him at home and dialed the number and waited, but only a couple of rings and George answered saying;

"Hello Father George speaking, May I show you the way into heaven today, its Sunday you know and you have a good chance, but today only!"

"Really George, I'm not sure Heaven is on your itinerary, but stranger things have happened I'm sure, what are you doing home why aren't you over at my place painting the walls in the colors you guys like?"

"You heard! How you found out so fast I don't know we only put an offer in on Friday I can't believe you heard already, I wanted to tell you myself!"

"Well I had two sources for the info, Bracken and even better Nancy, so the reason I called was to offer my help if needed it seems I may have a little pull with Bracken Industries, but on a serious note I can't think of anyone I'd rather see get the condo than my best friend who I know truly loves it, I'm happy you guys decided to make the move that way when we come to visit we won't get lost trying to find your house!"

"Real funny Bill, ya we do love the place and thanks for the offer to help I may take you up on that if Bracken turns us down, but I don't anticipate that, do you?"

"I know Bracken had other plans for the property before you made your offer so I guess we'll have to wait and see, I'm also told that it looks like Bracken is reconsidering their position, but if it doesn't go your way I'll steep in and see what I can do ok?"

"That's all I can ask Bill and thank you again."

"Listen I have to go, but I'm in town tomorrow for a short time why don't you guys stop by the condo and say hi before I leave again, I'm taking my car back this time."

"We'll see you tomorrow night let us know when."

"We will goodbye for now George."

"Bye buddy."

Hanging up Bill decided to call Barb and tell her of the change in plans for tomorrow's trip back to Richmond asking her to pack a few more essentials for Bill's extended stay in Va. Shirts, underwear, socks etc. that he could throw in the back of the car for his trip back. He placed the call to her cell phone and waited a short time when Barb answered saying;

"Hi hon how's your Sunday going, you should see this place you wouldn't know it for all the clutter I've created, you can't believe how many things I've found to throw away or give away that we really don't need or never really did!"

"Well I don't have to ask how you're doing you've already told me, so I'll tell you why I called. I'm going to be driving my car back tomorrow I'm going to cancel my return flight and take advantage of the unexpected trip in to take one of the cars back and you'll be driving on your next trip so that will take care of the cars. I need you to pack a few things for me to take along also or I'll have to go to a laundry as I'm running out of the essentials ok?"

"I'll take care of it dear."

"Oh and I've asked George and Nancy to stop by tomorrow and say hi I don't know how much more we'll get to see them before we move."

"Oh no you have no idea how this place looks, I can't entertain here, no way Bill!"

"Hon were not entertaining it will only be a short visit as I'll have to get on the road anyway and don't forget you have all the girls coming over to help you move they'll surely see the place the way it is and as a matter of fact Nancy is one of those ladies."

"Ya I guess you're right Bill, but somehow it's not the same."

"Ok dear, I guess I'll let you get back to trashing the place and I'll see you tomorrow love you!" Bill said.

"Love you to hon; I hope we get through this move as smoothly as we plan to, I'll see you tomorrow."

Hanging up Bill decided to relax the rest of the day and Barb decided to have a healthy quantity of Bill's Jack in the liquor cabinet for any other surprises that may arise.

MONDAY JANUARY 9, 2012

6:00am when Bill's alarm went off to alert him to the new day and what he had to do today, travel, meetings and more travel, this time the hard way in his car it would be a busy and a long day. After his shower and dressing in his freshly steamed suit he went to the dining room for breakfast and he was off to the airport to meet his plane and Joe and Mike.

Arriving at the airport and driving thru the gate he saw the G5 parked but standing all alone the other planes were gone and as he pulled up to the plane Mike came out to greet him. Getting out of the car as Mike approached he waved Mike off saying "Good morning Mike no luggage today it's a quick trip."

"Mike smiled saying good morning Sir; Joe will join us shortly he's at the hanger taking care of a last minute detail your earlier than expected."

"Yes well I had a quick breakfast I'll just get settled in and take care of a few details myself, by the way there's a change in plans you can drop me off and takeoff again, I guess in this case that's being literal, but you can head back home, I'll be returning by other means and you're going to have a short day I guess."

"Really well I'll just let dispatch know they may have other plans for us as everyone else is flying it's a busy Monday all of a sudden." Mike went into the cockpit to notify his dispatcher of the change in plans while waiting for Joe to return.

It wasn't long before Joe returned and said "Good morning Mr. Kelly sorry to keep you waiting, but we weren't expecting you quite so early we'll get started right away sir."

"Good morning Joe its fine I told Mike about a change in my plans that will impact you guys you'll be returning without me, I'm driving back myself."

"Oh did you want to race sir?"

Bill laughing loudly said "I don't think so, but if you'll give me a head start I might entertain a wager!"

Laughing Joe headed for the cockpit closing the air stair on the way saying "We'll start up and get some sky under us shortly sir."

About a half hour into the flight Bill picked up the phone and called his office and hearing Corrina answer he said "Rena its Bill" she replied;

"**Yes Sir Mr. Kelly** I'm at work now **sir**."

"I see yes you are and that's why I called I'm in the air and there's been a change in the plans, I need you to get the pool car at the airport picked up I won't be needing it again I'll be returning in my own car this evening very late I would imagine and I've told the pilots to return without me that's about it I guess."

"I see I'll have the car picked up and notify transportation of the change though I'm sure the pilots already have, will there be anything else sir?"

"No that's it Corrina I'll see you in the morning."

"Very well sir, be careful driving back it'll be late!"

"Thanks I'll see you in the morning Corrina bye." as he hung up he realized she was concerned for his safety that was nice of her he thought, loyalty to her boss or maybe something more?

Landing in Chicago to meet with Jack Richardson Bill had no idea what was in store for him and Jack Trax in the near future with the project they had undertaken, but the web of intrigue was being spun even now! Taxing to the corporate hanger, now becoming a familiar routine for Bill, he prepared to disembark hoping his ride to the plant was there waiting as the day was filled with scheduled meetings and activities and the timing was tight.

As the plane came to a stop on the tarmac in front of the corporate hanger the engines were shut down and Joe emerged from the flight deck to open the air stair as Bill grabbed his briefcase thanked Joe and left the plane to find the McCook plant chauffer waiting at the limo and walking out to meet Bill and get the luggage introducing himself as Wayne and asking if there was any luggage?

Bill shook his hand and said "No Wayne no luggage just me and my trusty briefcase." as they walked to the waiting limo, Wayne opened the door and as Bill got in he heard the engines on the G5 start a short stop for those guys indeed he thought not even time for coffee, but realizing they had coffee on the plane and as it turned out they didn't go home they were routed to PA. To pick up some salesman who were on their way home.

On the drive to the plant Bill called Barb to let her know he was in town and would see her later. Arriving at the plant this time was quite different he was greeted in the entry foyer by Jack along with Rita and Judy Channing and this time he wasn't stopped by the Guards.

Jack said, "Good morning Bill I trust you had a pleasant flight, did you have a chance for breakfast this morning?"

"Oh yes Jack, but I never get enough coffee and how are you ladies this morning?" (He was still attracted to Judy Channing and he believed she knew it, but never let on)

"Were just fine sir it's good to see you again, but we understand you're on a really tight schedule."

"Yes well I'm driving back tonight, were moving in the next couple of weeks so I'm driving my car back this trip, it'll be a late night for me I'm afraid."

Jack took the lead back saying "Well than let's get started shall we there's plenty of coffee in the office Bill and we may even be able to find a donut or two, these ladies will be joining us for lunch today." Jack said as they adjourned to his office and a private meeting.

As they sat down in Jack's office Bill started out by saying "Jack I'm here today to convey two very important messages to you! The first is the reason were sitting here alone, out of a strict sense of security, it is absolutely essential that this project be kept in house, secret if you will, confidential or any other adjective you want to use to describe your people keeping their mouths shut, if it gets out what we're doing here the McCook plant will become a target for the enemy and for industrial espionage, our competitors will want our product!

Secondly Jack! What you need to figure out is how to build this product, in a way that nobody really knows what their producing! I'm convinced it's possible; after all I designed the electrical controls for the furnace without really knowing what it was destined to be used for, I was also the project manager and was never let in on the real intended use of the furnace and we built it without that knowledge!

Jack I'd like a list of those in the plant that have total knowledge of what we're doing here and they need to sign confidentially agreements immediately, even if they previously signed something prior to this meeting. These documents have been prepared by our legal folks in Richmond (Bill laid out some papers from his briefcase on Jack's desk) I've brought the documents with me. In addition I'll need your plan on how you're going to conceal what we're building from the employees in manufacturing and the union, at least for the time being, for their own protection and the protection of the product while continuing to be productive with all the cloak-and-dagger hanging over your head.

What I've been told Jack, is that when we start delivering product to the end user we can relax the security as the anticipated risk will be almost nonexistent by then, but that's the governments take on things!"

"Well Bill you've tasked me, possibly beyond what I'm capable of I don't know, but there are only four people other than myself that are read in on the project and so far we've managed to keep the details to our small group, but there are questions out there on a limited basis right now because of the low volume we are producing on an experimental level at the experimental station and there's always something going on there so most are not overly interested as it's not a production area. Having said that, I'll put together a plan to maintain that element of security we already have in place at the experimental station for a full production run."

"Alright than why don't we figure on seeing you in Richmond on the 30th with your security plan in hand for further discussion, by than I should be able to give you more details about the project as I'm getting it hand to mouth also?"

"Ok Bill I'll look forward to seeing you on the 30th do you prefer me being there at any special time?"

"You can catch an early flight and I'll expect you for lunch, we have quite a dining room also, it's possible you've already been there and before me I would expect."

"I have Bill and your right it's quite good, but I think ours is better, why don't we go and find out for ourselves?"

"Lead the way Jack I'm looking forward to seeing the folks John Ballock and the others, but it will have to be a short stay today I have a long drive this afternoon and I have to stop and say hi to my wife before I leave town."

"I Understand Bill." as they walked into the dining room and joined the others already there, about a dozen or so including the two ladies who were there by special invitation Rita and Judy Channing. Folks were getting settled down when Bill spotted John Ballock and walked over to say hi and shake his hand as Jack asked for the group's attention;

"Ladies and Gentlemen if I may have your brief attention before getting started with lunch I'd like to make an announcement, most of you know this gentleman Bill Kelly Vice President of Design and Planning and for those of you who don't know him, get to know him as he's our new boss, Bill has taken the McCook plant under his wing so to speak as our previous boss, Bob Masek, has decided to leave the corporation to broaden his horizons, we wish him well and welcome Bill Kelly back, I'm sure we'll all live up to his expectations and even go beyond, but having said that I'll let Bill say a few words and then we'll get on with our lunch!"

"Thank you Jack, I'll be brief I promise we can't let the food get cold, it's good to once again be associated with the McCook facility where I got my start with Bracken this plant has always had a **can do** attitude and I'm sure that will continue, there are challenges ahead, but nothing we can't handle, so that being said let's eat shall we!" they all clapped at Jack and Bill's announcements and the lunch was served. Afterwards Bill took the time to meet everyone he hadn't met before or didn't know and then he was escorted to the waiting limousine that would take him home to their condo for a short visit with Barb and possibly George and Nancy, before driving to Richmond.

A QUICK STOP HOME

Finally arriving at the front entrance to the LSD condo Wayne opened the door for Bill asking if there would be anything else he could do for him to which Bill replied;

"No thank you Wayne I'm good and I'm sure I'll see you on my next trip to Chicago take care!" Bill shook Wayne's hand and walked into the building as Wayne drove away.

On his way up the elevator Bill hoped Barb was home realizing his keys were on his keychain with his car keys which he had given Barb so she could get home from the airport, he called Barb on his phone to announce his arrival so she could open the door, she answered, "Hi hon when are you coming home?"

"Open the door and look down the hall I think you'll be surprised!"

"Oh!" as she ran to the door and opened it seeing her husband approaching from the elevator and ready with hugs and kisses to greet him and welcome him home. After exchanging their mutual affections outside the unit Bill walked into an absolute catastrophe, though he had been forewarned, he didn't know this much disorganization was required to organize a move, he was now further inspired to make the long drive to Richmond tonight.

He came in and sat down to a cup of coffee while Barb explained what she was doing the shipping boxes had arrived along with the estimator to size up the move as he described it. He busied himself making a detailed list of the furniture, taking measurements and estimating the number of boxes that would be needed for packing purposes as well as checking out the freight elevator and talking to the building manager about any other scheduled moves and any rules the moving company needed to be aware of, he would also be sending additional packing materials.

After explaining it all to Bill, she was interested in a quick romp in the hay before he had to leave again and even got a bit aggressive about it, but Bill had to discourage it as they were expecting company and he really needed to get on the road. Barb disappointed, but understanding put the thought out of her mind and turned the conversation to the visit at the McCook plant and that continued until the buzzer rang and The Richards announced their arrival, Barb buzzed them in and smiled saying, "I guess we're lucky we didn't get anything started after all hon." as she went to the door to open it and greet George and Nancy.

The two couples passed the time for about an hour or so talking about both their plans to move Bill and Barb to Richmond and George and Nancy to their condo. George got up from the kitchen table and made his familiar walk to the window to admire the view thinking this is worth the price and asking Nancy to join him saying to Bill and Barb;

"How could you guys leave this? You've been here so long you take it for granite, but it really is breathtaking you know, we'll be happy to take over where you leave off!" putting his arm around Nancy, while Bill did the same with Barb.

After the relatively short visit Bill said he had to get on the road and George volunteered to help him load the things Barb had packed for him to take back in the car and while the guys took the things down to the car the girls were planning tomorrows attack on the project before them. While they were alone George asked; "Ha buddy are there any good looking girls where you work? I always picture those executives being surrounded by highly efficient old ladies approaching retirement and rarely smiling!"

"Not in my case pal there all beautiful even the older ladies and they never stop smiling so your type casting in this case doesn't hold water!"

"Well good luck with that, being surrounded by beautiful women could be a problem, I occasionally have difficulty having Brenda around, but it passes."

They got the car loaded and on their way back up to the condo George said "Well don't push it on the road tonight pal if you get tired get a room or at least pull off the road and take a break, late night driving when you're tired is an accident waiting to happen I know I spend a lot of time on the road in my business and I've had some close calls so be careful!"

Once back in the condo they all decided to walk down to the garage with Bill to see him off on his trip. They all walked hand in hand Bill and Barb and Nancy and George to the elevator and as the car arrived Barb got a little emotional telling Bill she would miss him and would see him soon in Richmond after the movers had finished the move assuring him she would be there in time for the closing at the bank and ready to move in the new house. Once in the garage George and Nancy said goodbye giving the Kelly's time alone before Bill left. Bill and Barb kissed and hugged and Barb said "I love you, but you better get on the road before I decide not to let you go!"

"Ok your right I better get going I love you." as he gave her a last kiss and started the car pulling out of the garage as she stood and watched him drive away. Expecting about a nine hour drive ahead he sat back making his way to the toll road to get him out of the city.

A few hours down the road Bill found himself getting both hungry and a little tired, but wanted to keep pushing on to at least the point of no return, as the pilots would refer to the half way mark or slightly beyond, before stopping to eat. About five hours into the trip stopping only for gas he found himself in the Cincinnati Oh. Area decided to stop eat, gas up and stretch a bit before continuing his trip. Soon he came upon a Cracker Barrel restaurant and stopped he had enjoyed these restaurants in the past while on the road. After eating, calling Barb to report his progress and gassing up next store he started on down the road once again totally re-energized and hoping to continue the trip to its completion which he did rolling into Richmond about midnight and his hotel at 12:40am ready to hit the sac and that's just what he did.

TUESDAY JANUARY 10, 2012

The next morning the first thing Bill did after waking up was to call Barb and let her know he had arrived safely the night before and was thankful to get into the bed after a long and strenuous day and night. She was glad he called and was up early to start her packing project as the girls would be arriving soon to help and the additional packing materials would be arriving today also. They both said goodbye and went about their particular business for the day which included Bill going into work a bit late and bringing Wm. Blair and Jack Trax up to date on his trip.

    Breakfast in the hotel restaurant and off to work this time in his car arriving and parking in his reserved spot in the parking garage and taking the elevator to the 14th floor and finding the ever smiling Corrina at her desk saying, "Good morning boss." and waiting patiently for his response to learn how he would refer to her in the office environment in the future as he had promised;

"Good morning Rena, how are you this morning?" smiling even more now she said;

"I'm just fine sir and how was your trip back last night? Uneventful I hope!"

"It was fine Rena, I have to get used to that name, but I like it." as he walked into his office laptop in hand and leaving almost as quickly, telling Rena he was going down to Blair's office, but expected to return shortly, which he did. Returning he asked Corrina if she had rescheduled Neil Johnson, or did she leave the meeting open ended. She responded saying "I wasn't sure of a date it being so close to the closing sir so I left it open, did you want me to reschedule now?"

"No let's wait a little longer Rena, but please send Jack Richardson an email thanking him for the hospitality yesterday and let him know I got back alright after the long and tedious drive last night."

"Certainly sir I'll attend to it right away, will there be anything else?"

"Yes I need you to redo my organization chart adding Jack Richardson and the Mc Cook plant to it, but hold the distribution, I'll advise you on that."

"Yes sir I'll have it updated by the end of the day."

"Thanks Rena."

The rest of the day was pretty much routine about 2:00pm Corrina buzzed saying "Sir Mr. Douglas is on line one." as Bill picked up;

"Paul, how are you?"

"Just fine Bill thought I'd let you know the Bradley's scheduled their movers for Thursday as it turns out after you guys bought all their things, they don't have that much to move other than boxed items and their having the movers do their packing, so they expect everything to be gone by Saturday."

"Really, isn't that a bit unusual doing all this before closing, what if the sale doesn't go through?"

"Well Bill, you're doing the same thing aren't you?"

"Yes, but that's different Paul, Bracken is buying my condo and I know that sale is going to go through I already have the money!"

"They have a similar advantage Bill as Bracken is doing your financing the sale is guaranteed anyway they asked if it was ok and I told them to go ahead."

"I see and how about my movers are they scheduled to make the move yet or are they waiting for a call?"

"I'm waiting on Barb, the movers only need a days' notice so when I hear she's done packing I'll give them the go ahead!"

"So the Bradley's will be out of the house by Saturday am I hearing that right Paul?"

"Yes Bill and I know your next question and the answers no, you can't get the keys til closing, legally it's not your house until than and we could get in a lot of trouble jumping the gun so to speak."

"I guess your right; we'll just continue to follow your lead til the end it's worked so far, so if there's nothing else I do appreciate the heads up, but I'm off to a meeting, we'll talk later ok?"

"Ok bye Bill" as both men hung up, Bill a bit irritated with Paul and not really knowing why, but realizing not even a VP could always get his way, perhaps that was the origin of the irritation so he just blew it off and charged it up to experience!"

Meanwhile back in Chicago Barb and her friends were busy packing boxes with great care, probably greater care than a mover would use and still Barb was sure they would break something. Lisa was going to join them after work and the plan was to work well into the night, Pizza was the plan for dinner and wine, girl talk would continue as it had all day so far, but they were having fun. Barb's plan was to finish the packing by Wednesday night if she could rely on the help to be there as promised.

The rest of the week went as planned, in Chicago Barb had finished the packing and the mover was notified and scheduled for Friday morning. Barb planning to be on the road to Richmond Saturday morning after making sure the condo was presentable after the move, she didn't want to leave her friend Nancy with a mess to clean up before moving in!

Back in Richmond the Bradley's movers had started there packing on Thursday per the schedule and were moving ahead with greater speed then expected probably finishing late Thursday or early Friday and the closing was still on schedule with a time now set for 10:00am on Tuesday, things were coming together.

Friday January 13, 2012

Bill was already sitting at his desk and sipping his coffee when Corrina came in to work, the first time he had gotten there before her as she said, "Well good morning sir, I see you're at it bright and early this morning, worried about the move I guess, I'm sure everything will be fine its certainly been well planned and all Mr. Kelly."

"Yes well if I were a superstitious man Corrina this would not be a good day, but I'm not however, my wife is and that's what's got me a bit on edge I guess."

About 2:00pm Barb called Bill on his cell to say "Hi hon the movers are finished and had left after several walk through inspections we finally determined there was no more to go, they were done. So I'll do some cleaning now the oven and so on Lisa Is on her way to help as well as Karen and Nancy and I'll be on my way in the morning unless something unforeseen happens!"

"That sounds good hon it didn't take them long to load up I guess what time did they get started this morning?"

"They were here at 8:00am and ready to go to work there were three of them they move fast, I couldn't believe it being on the 24th floor and having to wait for the elevator, but all things went well!"

"Did you call the utility companies to get everything out of our name and the phone shutoff?"

"Yes dear everything is taken care of, by the way do we have to come back for the closing with George and Nancy?"

"No there closing with Bracken not with us we are not the owners remember we already closed with Bracken and have our money?"

"Oh that's right I don't know why I was so confused about that Nancy and I were talking about it last night and it came up."

"When you drive away tomorrow were done with it, drop the keys off with the building manager on your way out."

"Ok dear I'll talk to you later this evening before I lay down to go to sleep on the floor!"

"The floor, why don't you go to a motel or stay with Nancy and George or something, sleeping on the floor isn't necessary."

"I don't mind honest my last night here and all, oh by the way my parents came by for a few hours last night and helped, but I think they just came to say goodbye, mom was a little upset I think."

"I guess that's normal hon, especially for mom's they can come and visit anytime they want to we have plenty of room and that goes for all of our friends also things will be fine you'll see."

"I know, but leaving is kind of sad, there are a lot of memories, the girls being here helped a lot, anyway I'll be on my way tomorrow I don't know if I'll drive straight thru though I might get a room if I get tired and make it a two day trip."

"Absolutely I'd feel better if you did that, you have enough time."

"Alright I'll let you get back to work I guess and we'll talk tonight love you!"

"Ok bye-bye hon say hi to everyone for me!" after hanging up Bill thought he'd check with Paul once again on the progress of the Bradley's move as his things were on the road. He buzzed Corrina asking her to get Paul on the phone, before long she reported having Paul on line two and Bill picked up saying;

"Hi Paul I just thought I'd call to tell you our things are on the truck and on the way."

"Well Bill your half right your things are on the truck, but there not on the way, there scheduled for delivery on Wednesday after you close."

"I see I should have known you were on top of things, thanks Paul how are things going with the Bradley's move?"

"Their move is done also, their staying there tonight as they still have three bedroom sets there and they'll be out in the morning."

"Thanks for the update Paul let me know if things change for any reason, we'll talk soon."

"Ok bye Bill"

SUNDAY JANUARY 15, 2012

Saturday came and went, Barb was on the road and Bill expected her to arrive in Richmond this afternoon sometime and was staying at the hotel to be sure he would be there when she arrived. The Bradley's were gone they would see them on Tuesday at the closing and they too would be off to their new home.

Bill spent a part of the day Saturday getting a bank account set up near their new house luckily their bank back in Chicago had a branch near their house so he didn't have much to do.

Barb had talked about a house warming in the near future so that would give her something else to keep her occupied and that would be good til she got used to not working.

Bill slept late this morning and decided to go down to the Sunday brunch in the hotel dining room again as it was so good the last time he had tried it. The hotel restaurant put on quite a feed and it was delicious eggs cooked to order and just about any breakfast item you could imagine along with prime rib, ham off the bone, three or four kinds of potatoes and all washed down with a decent Champaign, a great way to spend Sunday morning he thought as he left the room to go down and partake of the feast.

After brunch and looking at his watch he saw it was a little after 1:00pm and realizing the bar would be open he decided to continue the Champaign therapy in the bar with something a bit stronger and as he walked in once again finding the bar empty and the bartender anxious for company and someone to talk to said "Yes sir what can I get you today?"

"Well how about a Gin Rickey, there always good, I'm Bill by the way."

"Ok Bill one Gin Rickey coming up and I am Andy."

"Hi Andy"

Placing the drink on the bar in front of Bill he said "I think I remember you from about the same time last week Bill you ordered the same thing and were working on your computer are you here for an extended stay?"

"The truth Andy is were moving here and were waiting for our house to be available, in the meantime I'm staying here."

"I see than I expect you have a job lined up because I know a few jobs that are available in the area."

"I appreciate that Andy, but I'm all set in that department I guess." he said with a smile as he finished his drink pushing the glass at Andy indicating he needed a refill. Andy took the glass and quickly brought it back filled asking;

"Is your new house near here Bill?" Bill wondered if all bartenders were this inquisitive/nosey, but then he realized they were, how else would they keep a conversation going he thought so he said;

"About twenty five miles from here in a little community called Gateway Andy so it's not across the street, but it's not that far either."

"Gateway I know that place you must have a pretty good job to be moving out there did you want to run a tab?" he said with a smile;

"No Andy just put it on here as he pushed his Bracken credit card at the bartender." picking up the card and looking at it Andy said.

"Bracken industries, oh your one of those guys, Bracken folks are here all the time, their customers stay here to, Bracken keeps several rooms here, but I guess you already know all that, ah, I can put the tab on your room if you wish Bill?"

"No that's fine Andy just put it on the card, thank you."

"Wow! I can't believe I was trying to get you a job, pretty silly ha?"

"I don't think that's silly at all you were just trying to be helpful that's all, well one more Andy and I gota go!" as he once again pushed his glass toward the bartender, it seemed he had made another friend, Andy would remember him!

Back in his room the afternoon was passing slowly as he anxiously waited for Barb to arrive, he naturally had plans for this evening and was sure Barb would too after being away from each other for a week or more. As Bill sat on the couch in his suite the alcohol took over and he soon fell fast asleep.

Suddenly Bill woke to the annoying ring of his cell phone and looking at his watch he noted the time 5:10p.m it was Barb, he answered saying "Hi hon, I guess I was dozing off a bit, where are you at now?"

"I'm in Richmond, I must be close the GPS says 14 miles to go so I guess I'll be there in about a half hour, are you ready?"

"You bet I am I've been warming up all day to perform my marital duty! Unloading your luggage and carrying it in."

"You're funny! That's why they have valets and bell boys, your marital duties are a bit more personal and psychically demanding then that, so once again! **Are you ready?**"

"I think you'll find me more than accommodating Barbara, so hurry it's almost dinner time and then we'll face another delay!"

"That's what you think, you'll find your dinner in the bed and you can't leave til I've had enough, if you get the picture!"

"I got it! Your bringing dinner with you, that's good because I'm getting hungry, but I do like room service; see you when you get here."

"The GPS says eight miles to go, see you in a few hon."

As Barb pulled into the hotel and up to the front entrance, Bill was in the lobby waiting, and seeing her pull in went out to meet her at the car, along with the valet, she stopped and seeing Bill jumped out throwing her arms around him and him around her; they hugged and kissed for a long moment and went inside telling the valet they would take care of the luggage later.

They quickly found themselves in the room with the **Do Not Disturb** sign on the door and Barb insisting on a shower first as she had been on the road all day, Bill reluctantly agreeing. After a quick shower and still wet, she jumped into bed with the ever ready and waiting Bill. They ravaged each other for hour's first making love and then having sex then making love again all ending in a call to room service for a hard earned and well deserved dinner followed by a good night's sleep realizing they were in Richmond, and this time to stay.

MONDAY JANUARY 16, 2012

After a long and restful night the sound of Bill's alarm woke both he and Barb who wanted to continue to bask in her slumber. Bill headed for the shower to start getting ready for work and a busy day as he would not be there tomorrow. As he emerged from the shower dried off and went back in the room he found Barb still sprawled on the bed fast asleep her naked left leg out from under the covers more than halfway up her thigh, this picture stimulated Bill to the point of utter distraction, he had to turn away and continue getting dressed or he may not have made it to work til much later in the day!

Once he was ready to leave, Barb was starting to stir so he walked over to the bed, her naked leg now well hidden under the covers and giving her a kiss goodbye said "Hon if you want breakfast in the dining room just have it put on the room bill, call me later when you're up and about ok?"

"Ok love you, I'll see you tonight bye." Bill grabbed his briefcase and headed for the dining room himself for breakfast he had come to like the place. Once he had finished eating he walked to his car in the lot and started the twenty minute drive downtown to his office.

Arriving at the Bracken Building and pulling into the underground he noticed two cable company trucks parked there and several reels of data cable on the ground, but he was not aware of what was going on thinking he'd ask around. Making his way to the elevator he ran into one of the installers and asked, "Good morning I see you have quite a bit of cable there where is it running to?"

"Pretty much throughout the building sir we have a lot more coming!"

"Really and what is it for?"

"We can't say we just run the cable and then a different company comes in to do the installing of the equipment, and hooking it up to whatever, we just run the cable though!"

"I see well thank you." as Bill got on the elevator to the 14th floor wondering if that cable was for a Bracken project or one of the other companies that rented space from Bracken.

As Bill exited the elevator he saw some men walking around wearing hard hats with tool pouches on their belts once again stimulating his curiosity. As he approached his office he noticed Maxine in there talking with Corrina and walking in he said "Good morning ladies there seems to be quite a bit of activity around here this morning, does anyone know what's going on?" to which Corrina replied;

"Do you mean you don't know either sir we were sure you would?"

"Oh what makes you think I'd know?"

Maxine jumped in saying "Well Bill (She took some liberties, which she could get away with) you are the VP of planning and design."

Bill thought for a moment suddenly realizing she was absolutely right he was in charge of planning and design for the entire corporation and this couldn't possibly happen without his or his staff's approval and yet he knew nothing, now he had a mission!"

"You're absolutely right Maxine! I'm the one that should know what's going on, Corrina can you pull up all the projects approved or pending in the last 24 months specifically for this facility the Bracken corporate headquarters?"

"Yes sir I believe I can do that I'll get right on it!" as Maxine said;

"Well Corrina it looks like you have your work cut out for you so I'll leave you to it, we'll talk later."

"Ok Maxine later it is, maybe at lunch." after a bit more thought, Bill walked back into Corrina's office and said;

"Rena if you fail to come up with something, search the engineering projects also though I can't believe Jack Trax would also be unaware if it was his area of responsibility, I'm sure this couldn't have happened without engineering's involvement to some degree!"

"I'll check it all sir" after about an hour of intense investigation she finds what she believes is the answer to the short lived mystery and taking her findings into Bill's office saying;

"Excuse me for a moment sir."

"Of course Rena did you find something?"

"I think so it seems there's a project in the works, but not under engineering or planning and design it's under HRM and Personnel it's a security and surveillance project with a project number 100 which is for this facility."

"Wow I guess I don't understand how any facilities project can get approved without engineering and planning and design being involved, it makes no sense I'll have to look into it and I will! Thanks Rena and good job!"

Bill thought that's a subject for another time, first he wanted to understand the corporate bureaucracy better before making an issue of this incident.

Well on to other things he thought as Corrina walked into his office with a cup of coffee in hand and a smile on her face saying "I thought you might like this sir as it's your first this morning."

"Thanks Corrina by the way where do I find my total budget in the computer it's not under budgets those are all project budgets?"

"Look under annual budget sir and you'll find it I don't know why accounting wrote it that way, but they did."

"Ah there it is Thanks Rena."

"Of course sir, will there be anything else? By the way did your wife get here ok yesterday?"

Oh yes she got in about dinner time were here to stay now."

"That's wonderful sir and you'll be off the next couple of days getting into your new house do I have that right?"

"Exactly Corrina, you have it right I'll return Thursday morning."

"Very well sir and good luck with everything."

The rest of the day went on as usual Paul Douglas had called to reconfirm the time of the closing tomorrow and the title companies address where the closing would be held, and to let Bill know that one of Bracken's attorney's would be there also along with Paul, so all was set to go.

That afternoon as he wrapped up his business for the day and prepared to leave he couldn't help but think about how far he had come in a relatively short time and where it would end, would he stay with Bracken and maybe someday be the CEO or would he leave for a better offer as did Bob Masek, he was very young to hold the position he held, perhaps he had become successful to young, but the way he saw it right now the sky or even beyond was the limit.

As he left for the day he said goodbye to Corrina and holding up his phone in a gesture to indicate if you need me you know how to get me, she smiled and said;

"Goodnight sir and once again good luck tomorrow!"

On his way to the hotel he called Barb to let her know he was on his way, but as it turned out she didn't really care, as she wasn't at the hotel, she was out and about shopping and driving around learning the city much as Bill had done. Bill told her that was fine he'd be at the hotel resting up for dinner.

When Barb returned she found Bill sleeping on the bed still dressed, it was 6:00pm and she was getting hungry so she shook him saying; "Ha sleepyhead wake up and let's eat what do you say?"

"Hi hon, ya about that, how about if we eat downstairs tonight were going to have a long day tomorrow and the next couple of days after that so let's relax and get some rest tonight and turn in early?"

"Ya the restaurant here is fine with me so throw some water on your face and let's go down!"

Once seated in the dining room and looking over the menu Bill said "Earlier I thought you said you were shopping did you buy anything for me?"

"No, for the house, I left it all in the car as were going there tomorrow anyway, were going to stay there tomorrow night aren't we?"

"Ya I don't see why not the house is practically fully furnished after you bought everything they owned, all four bedrooms were fully furnished, I know they took their bedroom set and that's it except for the kitchen items and their personals cloths etc. the only thing is we don't have any bed linins here yet so you'll probably have to go out and get those things tomorrow after closing ok?"

After dinner and the usual quick stop at the gift shop on the way up to the room they decided to pack, shower and go to bed early, but first Bill called the front desk to let them know they would be checking out in the morning and to leave a 6:30am wakeup call as he had packed the alarm clock, soon after all that they were fast asleep.

TUESDAY JANUARY 17, 2012

The next morning rolled around quickly as the phone rang with their 6:30am wakeup call, Barb answered as the phone was on her side of the bed, Bill was still in a deep sleep, Barb had always wanted to wake him with a cold glass of ice water, but had never drummed up enough courage and she still hadn't, but someday she would, of that she was sure! Today though she would wake him with kindness, after all he was buying her a new house today and that deserved a little kindness."

Soon Bill responded to Barb's gentle shaking and woke up saying "Is it that time already?"

"It is hon, today we become homeowners once again aren't you excited? I can hardly wait to get there, sign the papers and get out to the house to go thru it on my own without any pressure to hurry up or move along I can dwell on anything I want for as long as I want it'll be great!"

They showered, dressed and packed their last minute items calling for a Bellhop to pick up the luggage and leave it in the lobby while they had their breakfast and checked out. Soon the Bellhop knocked on the door to pick up the luggage, Bill tipped him and they all left.

At breakfast they decided to take one car to the closing and pick up the other car on the way to the house after the closing, so they wouldn't be playing follow the leader through a city they weren't too familiar with.

After breakfast and on their way out to the car Bill stopped by the front desk to sign the bill that would be forwarded to Bracken for payment, he checked the bill, signed it and thanked the desk clerk for their hospitality and asking if they could pick up the luggage on their way back from their closing, the clerk said that would be fine.

Once in the car Bill programed the GPS with the address of the title company which indicated 11.2 miles to their destination and they were off with plenty of time to get there by 10:30am for their meeting. As they wound their way through the city streets Barb continually pointed out points of mutual interest.

Arriving at the office with time to spare they parked and walked in finding Paul Douglas in the waiting room accompanied by Brian Levin one of the Bracken Attorney's, the Bradley's were not there yet as the attorney explained a few things to the Kelly's after being introduced by Paul. Soon the Bradley's walked in with their attorney Allan Just, everyone was introduced around, the two attorneys stepped aside to talk with each other while the Bradley's and the Kelly's talked about last minute details, Cortney told Barb that she had stripped all the beds, but had bought new linens for one of the rooms bed so they had new linens to sleep on while waiting for their own furniture.

Barb said "Oh Cortney thank you you're so kind, but you really didn't need to do that, as a matter of fact we had talked about stopping and doing that very thing, I can't tell you how very grateful we are, thank you so very much. Do you have your new phone numbers yet?

"Not yet dear, when we get in our new house, I'll call and give it to you in the meantime you have my cell number don't you?"

"Yes we do"

About that time a young woman came out of one of the offices introducing herself as Jennifer Kimble their closing officer and asking everyone to step into the closing conference room where the official closing took place the papers were signed the checks were exchanged and the keys turned over to the new owners and all the business concluded in short order without a hitch.

Everyone said their goodbyes and left the office all heading in different directions as Bill and Barb headed back to the hotel to get their luggage and Barb's car, once that was done they were off to their new home Bill leading with Barb close behind as she really didn't know the way near as well as Bill.

After about a forty minute drive from the hotel, Bill having to drive slower than normal they arrived at the guard shack to the gated community and stopping they introduced themselves as the new owners, giving the guard their address and he took their license plate info realizing they would need to get Virginia plates and got them signed in introducing himself as Matt and welcoming them to the community as he raised the gate allowing them to pass.

Pulling into their driveway they both got out of their cars and Barb ran to the front door asking Bill to hurry as he had the keys, but as he put the key in the door and flung it open he grabbed Barb saying;

"This is a special occasion hon a memorable moment and calls for a special entry!" so he picked her up and carried her over the threshold, once inside they both began to explore, but after about twenty minutes, as Barb was opening the patio sliding door, she screamed! Confronted by a Police officer pointing his gun at her and telling her to stop and remain still! As Bill came running in response to her screams he too was told to stop! as yet another officer came back to the patio with his gun drawn, but pointing it down at the ground, it seems they had tripped a silent alarm and the police responded after being called by the alarm company, this was clearly a mistake as they attempted to explain it to the officers.

The guard told the responders, as they came through the gate to say why they were there and where they were going, that a new couple had just moved into that address and were there now. So this did help the officers to remain cautious when confronting Barb on the patio, but the incident would need some explaining!

The police, after putting their guns away, asked their dispatcher to call the alarm company to sort it out, while Bill called the Bradley's, to tell them what had happened and asked them what they could to do to resolve the problem.

It seems that in all their preparation for the move their calls to the utility companies and everything else they had to do the one thing they forgot was to call the alarm company and cancel the service til the new owners decided whether they would continue it or not and now they would have to call to straighten it out, they apologized profusely and made the necessary call. Soon it was straightened out with the police also and they prepared to leave, but not before apologizing to the Kelly's about the gun scare explaining it was standard procedure, they said they understood and after experiencing the police response decided to keep the alarm system.

After the police left and they composed themselves once again, noting that this indeed would help them remember their move in experience along with Bill carrying Barb over the threshold!

After several more trips in and around the house investigating everything, but still never getting to the basement, that would have to wait til later, they were impressed with how clean the Bradley's had left everything though Barb intended to go over it all again.

They decided they needed to go to the grocery store and get a few basics they would need for the next few days until Barb went out to do a big shopping, today though they would go together, normally it was Barb's job, she liked shopping alone and taking her time with no pressure to hurry up.

They left and asked the guard on the way out where the nearest grocery store was and he directed them to a shopping center about two miles down the road with both a large grocery store and a super Wal-Mart if they choose, after explaining their run in with the police to the inquisitive guard they left for the store.

They decided on the Super Wal-Mart for the groceries and if Barb decided she needed a non-grocery item while they were there she could just pick it up. Bill didn't like to go shopping Barb thought, but if he kept throwing things in the basket she'd have to get another basket furthermore she wouldn't have to do her big shopping he was doing it for her right now.

After concluding their shopping, then considering a meal out, but deciding against it as Barb wanted to muddle around in her new kitchen, though they had no pots and pans to cook in, dishes to eat from or utensils to eat with!, this would have been a perfect time for fast food and absolutely justified, but Barb had a plan, microwave TV dinners and plastic utensils, what could be better Bill thought, but it made her happy!

At home while Barb muddled around in the kitchen, Bill sat down with his laptop to check his email and schedules for the next few days and he sent Corrina an email to let her know they were in the house and would have a phone number by tomorrow as the phone company was scheduled to be there in the morning to install the additional lines and get the service up and operating.

After Barb's creative dinner they decided to tryout the master bedroom shower it was a thing of beauty, a walk in with multiple shower heads and enough room for about six people something you only saw in the movies, but now it became a reality for them it was for lack of a better word, "NEAT"! But the towels they used to dry themselves had the hotel name on them, what the hell everybody did it, the bed they would have to use for the next couple of nights was another story, they were used to a king size bed and the spare bedrooms all had full size beds and Bill didn't want to be crowded, but would have to live with the inconvenience for a couple of days til their furniture arrived.

All in all things were pretty well organized for the first night in a new home at least the house was almost totally furnished and they had comfortable places to sit, Bill was totally enjoying the library and adopting it for his office though Barb had different ideas as there was an office available, but unfurnished as Jeffery used the Library also, there were many things to sort out and that would come with time, but first they had to get totally moved in.

After the shower they got into bed with every intention of making love on their first night in the house, but started talking about the day and soon they had both talked themselves to sleep, the lovemaking would have to wait til another day!

WEDNESDAY JANUARY 18, 2012

The next morning waking up in their new house and a strange neighborhood for the first time, with no coffee pot, toaster, cereal bowl or any of the other morning essentials they had come to rely on and take for granted, and no close by neighbors who's door they could knock on to borrow a cup of sugar so to speak like they had in the condo back home, indeed things had changed, but they both knew with time things would get better, for now though they would get dressed and find a restaurant.

After finding a great little restaurant nearby for breakfast and afterwards returning home as the phone company was expected to get their phones working and they didn't want to miss them. As smoothly as this move went with all the help they had from Paul Douglas and Bracken along with all their friends back in Chicago there were still many disruptions to contend with, but by the weekend they would start to settle in to their new surroundings and get over the initial shock.

CHAPTER THIRTY EIGHT
BACK TO WORK

Today, Thursday January 19, 2012, Bill would settle into his new job after the move to Richmond and all the preparation preceding the move. The new project was taking up a good deal of his time and the inconvenience of running back and forth was taking away from time he should be spending with the project.

They were in their new house Barb getting used to things and already talking about getting a German Shepard puppy for a companion, she loved dogs and Bill had to admit he did also and by the way Barb had not for a single moment forgotten about flying lessons, she was making inquiries as to the best place to start her aviation career, talking to all the Bracken pilots, one of them being a flight instructor himself and willing to take on the challenge of teaching Barb to fly.

Bill decided to stop for breakfast at the little Ma and Pa restaurant they had found yesterday, before continuing his drive into work from their new home for the first time this morning, while taking in the scenery and from his own car rather than a pool car Bill thought how fortunate he was with all of this, a great job, with a beautiful wife at home and a beautiful secretary at work, what more could a man ask for? He smiled to himself knowing the answer and struggling to avoid the inevitable, but aware of the reality of his feelings!

At the office Corrina was waiting with a beautiful welcome home cake, a surprise for Bill, as they (Bill and Barb) were now officially Richmond residents and they were home at last.

Bill pulled into the underground parking area and to his assigned space with his name and all as he exited his car and walked toward the elevator he realized this was his new life, Chicago was in the past he'd come a long way in a relatively short time it seemed like only yesterday he was a time traveler and now he was a corporate executive with all that goes along with it and he was young he wouldn't be stopping here he was only beginning, the executive suits would be his next stop, but where it would end he had no idea.

Exiting the elevator and walking toward his office he noticed some unexpected activity and the one person that stood out was John Pasmore the COO as he got closer he also noticed James Gross the whole executive suite was here what was going on he thought, he checked his watch he didn't want to walk in late with the two heavy hitters waiting, but he was early though executives didn't have start and quit times. As he walked in they all clapped to welcome the new Richmond resident and noticing the cake which read **welcome home Bill and Barb** John Pasmore the COO saying "Well Bill you guys finally made it think of all the money were going to save on jet fuel you should probably get a bigger bonus this quarter for that alone!" as everyone laughed and Bill smiled not knowing what to say, But finally saying;

"Welcome home, that's the sentiment I would have chosen, I wish my wife were here to share this with me though, the cake at least, this is her favorite cake!" Bill said, with a smile and laughing a little, as Gross stopped him saying;

"Well, say no more young man" as James Gross turned toward Bill's office to welcome Barb who came walking out to Bill's surprise, as Gross extended his hand to her and putting his arm around her shoulder said;

"Your husband was just saying he wished you were here to share the moment and here you are, we at Bracken can work wonders when needed!" as he guided her to her husband who smiled and kissed her not believing what he was seeing and asking how long she had known about this, it had all the markings of Corrina on it he thought and to be honest Bill was not completely at ease with Barb and Corrina in the same room knowing Barb's feelings about Corrina, though he still had no idea how those feelings were developed, but they both seemed to be getting along fine right now however Corrina didn't know the history or Barb's feelings for her and Bill intended to keep it that way!

Soon the gathering was winding down though there was plenty of cake and coffee left and it was being taken to the little kitchen area for all to partake, it would all be gone by the end of the day nothing left, but a memory.

Bill was talking to his boss and Jack Trax when he noticed Barb, Corrina and Maxine talking and laughing together almost as if they were good friends, this was indeed odd Bill thought could it be he had been given the wrong information or had misunderstood what he had been told by George, which came to him second hand by Nancy, after the girls drunken night out, whatever the case time has passed and hopefully Barb's suspicions have also, indications were positive Bill thought.

Bill had to get Barb back home as the movers were coming this morning, though Bracken had arranged for Paul Douglas to be at the house in Barb's absence, so she could be at the office for the small celebration arranged for her and Bill, had Bill not stopped for breakfast he didn't know how Barb would have beaten him to the office, but he was sure there would have been an alternative plan!

As things returned to normal and everyone went back to their respective offices Bill approached the three ladies saying "Honey I know you're probably anxious to get back and relieve Paul before the movers arrive and Paul has them put the kitchen items in the master bedroom and set the bed up in the living room!"

"Oh my that couldn't possibly happen could it, I guess I better go ladies, but it's been fun and I know Bill loved it as much as I, we'll talk soon and you both have our phone number call anytime and thank you for everything." As Barb and her husband walked away toward the elevator both Corrina and Maxine said goodbye and returned to work.

As they approached the elevator Barb said "Well that was nice of everyone to put this together for you and it was especially nice of them to include me and arrange for me to be here!"

"Yes it was Barb there a great group of folks, call me when you get home so I know you got there alright."

"I will bye-bye" giving Bill a kiss as she got on the elevator.

Bill walked casually back to his office feeling even more like one of the Bracken family and noticing Corrina's absence as he arrived back at his office he went in and sat down at his desk and opened his laptop as Corrina walked in with a cup of coffee for him saying;

"I thought you might like another cup sir maybe you'll get a chance to finish this one, I could get you another piece of cake if you'd like, I didn't notice if you even got a piece when everyone was here?"

"I did Rena it was delicious, who's idea was this little get together anyway? We sure enjoyed it! I detect your involvement am I right?"

"Maxine and I sir, but everyone helped, getting your wife here was the hardest thing, we had to get a baby sitter for your house, but it all worked out, by the way I really enjoyed talking with your wife, she's really quite lovely and very nice."

"Yes she is and thank you Corrina." Bill said as Corrina smiled, turned and walked away obviously happy with what she and Maxine had pulled off at least as far as the arrangements for the little get together, it went well.

As she left, Bill could not help but watch her til she disappeared into her office once again. Watching her long flowing and wavy hair down to her waist with just the right amount of bounce as she walked, each time landing on her light gray sleeveless low cut silk blouse with a dark gray camisole tucked into her form fitting, but not too tight gray suit skirt ending mid knee and accentuating her proportionately tapered calves to her slightly built ankles and all ending in a pair of dark gray spiked heal pumps. Bill sat back in his chair, closed his eyes and for a moment let his imagination run wild, knowing that someday his curiosity, **HAD TO BE SATISFIED**!

WAKING UP IN A DIFFERENT TIME

THE END

EPILOGUE

The end or maybe just the beginning there are many adventures ahead for this successful young couple.

For Bill the many challenges his new job offers and the many challenges trying to resist the temptations a young, good looking and sexually aggressive guy runs into when constantly surrounded by beautiful women.

Barbara's challenges are somewhat different, but keep in mind she is also attractive and sexually aggressive, but right now getting used to a new house in the suburbs, in a different state, far from her friends and her parents for the first time since she was born and no job for the first time in years, trying to figure out how to spend her many boring and lonely hours, trying to develop new interest and find new friends to share her new life with.

So the adventures of Bill and Barbara are evolving there's much more to come before I move on to other projects, so follow us and enjoy the **FURTHER ADVENTURES OF BILL AND BARB.** Well there you have it one mystery solved and another unfolding

right before your eyes, the adventures will continue with the next book being finished by the end of the year 2013 so look for it.

CPSIA information can be obtained at www.ICGtesting.com
Printed in the USA
LVOW081242180413

329701LV00001B/1/P